ALIEN NEIGHBORS

NANCY GOLDEN

GOLDEN CROSS RANCH LLC

For information or inquiries contact nancy@goldencrossranch.com

Library of Congress Control Number: 2021922789

Published by
Golden Cross Ranch LLC
Carrollton, Texas U.S.A.

Cover Design by Betty Martinez
https://bertamar.wixsite.com/bettymar/

For my husband Phil Golden, first and foremost. If not for his support, encouragement, and sacrifice, the words would not have found themselves on these pages.

In loving memory of Lynn Sherman, Judie Whitaker, and Danny Morse, all of whom touched my life in profound ways. Their kindness and compassion immortalize them beyond mere words.

I often look up at the moon and wave, while saying "Hi, Lanjo!" with a grin. To all those who, like me, are stirred by the possibilities...and to the One who made it all possible.

PROLOGUE

"Can you see okay?" Sefanganjo reached a long slender arm past Lanjo to the control panel, turning a potentiometer with the sixth digit of his right hand. The image in front of them sharpened.

"Yes, but I think we need to increase the contrast. Using video transmissions from Earth to their Moon for the evaluation was a good idea," Lanjo grimaced cheerfully. "And provided an excellent reason to go off-planet. I always wanted to visit this solar system." He pushed a button on the panel and the contrast increased slightly. "There, that's better. I think this will greatly enhance the evidence we need to present to the council. They are an interesting species. I didn't expect that to happen. The human race is full of surprises."

Sefanganjo grimaced in return. "They're not so unlike us, I think. I hope the vote goes in their favor."

"Me, too."

"Prejudice exists, but humans also have the capacity to overcome prejudice. We need to make sure and include this in our report," commented Lanjo.

"I've already written it up," Sefanganjo replied. "It's one of my favorite parts, their ability to change how they think. I wonder, is it a universal trait?"

"Theoretically, yes, but we don't have enough empirical data," Lanjo observed. "When we consolidate our findings, we will be able to determine how prevalent it is."

"The only thing left to be examined is technical aptitude. If we can prove their technology has progressed to an acceptable level, we can present enough evidence to the council to initiate a First Contact."

Lanjo sighed. "For that, we'll have to wait and see if they manage to return to the Moon utilizing their current technology."

"Maybe we'll still be here if they succeed," Sefanganjo replied hopefully. "I'm going to ask to be part of the First Contact, if it's approved."

"You'll have to get in line," Lanjo replied, grimacing. "As the humans would say, *I've already called dibs.*"

Inside Cycle Life Fitness, the stench of sweat and determination filled the air. The song "Danger Zone" blasted from the speakers. Tom put his head down and pedaled harder and faster, images from the movie *Top Gun* flitting through his mind. He envisioned himself flying an F-14 Tomcat fighter jet, his heart pounding in his chest. He glanced at the heart rate monitor on his smartwatch and noticed a text from his boss.

Without more capital, their nuclear fusion research would be shut down in a matter of weeks, leaving him, the chief scientist on the project, jobless. His boss was trying to get a meeting with the Secretary of Energy to request additional funding, but Tom didn't want to think about that right now. He needed to train for his upcoming bike ride. The text could wait. He put his head back down and closed his eyes, zooming through the skies. Cycling helped him forget his work and marital troubles, at least for a little while.

Two songs later, Tom got off his bike and wiped it down. His breathing steadied to a more normal rate. Dabbing the sweat streaming down his forehead with his towel, he lifted a soaking wet wrist and pushed the button on his smartwatch. The text from Darryl read, *Meeting in 2 hours. Be there. Conf. Room 5D.*

"Yes!" Tom jumped up and pumped his fist, then froze, his mind whirling. *Oh, crap.* Conference Room 5D was on the Hill. His boss sent the text fifteen minutes ago. He'd barely have enough time to go by his house and change out of his sweaty T-shirt and shorts. He lifted his damp T-shirt up off his chest and sniffed. Yuck . . . He'd better get moving. Even if he cut it close, he could slip into the back and be there for technical questions.

Tom jogged through the fitness center parking lot. Squinting in the bright sunlight, he could see a bright red car next to his with its hood popped open. A brunette dressed in business casual was circling it. Her pace was short and jerky as she motioned with one hand and held her cell phone to her ear with the other. He glanced at his watch. He could offer to help, if he hurried.

The woman removed the cell phone from her ear, dropping it into the bag on her shoulder as he approached. She took in his sweaty disheveled appearance and her nose crinkled. She met his gaze with an unreadable expression.

He cleared his throat. "Uh, looks like you're having some car trouble."

She bit her lip and nodded. "I can't get it to start."

Salty sweat stung his eyes and pooled under his arms as the sun beat down on the asphalt parking lot. She wasn't sweating at all. He surreptitiously rubbed his hands on his pants. "Would you like me to take a look?"

"Well . . . sure. That'd be great."

He hastily stuck out his hand. "I'm Tom Whitaker."

"Nice to meet you, Tom Whitaker." Instead of grasping his hand, she reached into her bag and pulled out some papers. She offered them to Tom and he instinctively closed his hand around them.

"Tom Whitaker, you've been served." She smiled sweetly. She turned back to her Toyota CR-V, closed the hood, got inside and started it up. She rolled the window down. "Sorry, Tom. It's just the job. I got bills to pay." She rolled the window back up, put the car in drive and pulled around him. He watched as her perfectly running car exited the parking lot.

Leaning against his car door and skimming the divorce papers, Tom's jaw clenched. He was 0—2 in the relationship department. The infamous Hotter'N Hell Hundred endurance bicycle ride he was training for was a metaphor for his life: A long, hard ride that could possibly incapacitate him physically and mentally. *Yeah, perfect metaphor.*

He folded the divorce papers and shoved them into his pocket. Opening his car door, he slid into the driver's seat and turned the key in the ignition. Rarrrr-rarrrr-rarrr. He turned the key again, rarrrr-rarrrr-rarrr. "Uggghhhh!" Tom slammed his fists down on the steering wheel. He tried to crank the engine yet again and this time it didn't even turn over. He would have to call an Uber and leave his car, if he were to have any hope of making it to the meeting on time. The quick shower and change of clothes he had hoped for was out of the question.

No transportation, a two-hour notice for a meeting that could dictate the future of their entire nuclear fusion program, and he just got kicked in the gut. On top of all that, he literally stank. Not exactly how he had thought his day would go when he got out of bed this morning. *Yeah, the Hotter'N Hell . . .*

Tom shook his head in an effort to clear his thoughts and focus on his current problem. He opened the Uber app on his cell phone and requested a ride. He wished he wasn't so far away from the Hill. It was going to be close. He locked his car and leaned against the hood, scanning the parking lot for his ride to approach. "Come on, come on, come on," he repeated under his breath.

No, it couldn't be.

Tom pulled up the app. Red Toyota CR-V. Brunette driver. He checked the time—way too late to request another driver. The CR-V rolled up to the same spot it had exited a scant ten minutes ago. The woman in the driver's seat rolled the window down and gave him another sweet smile. "Did you request an Uber, Tom?"

Tom's legs were lead weights as he stood gaping at her.

"Come on, get in. I'm just a girl trying to make a living." She handed him an old towel. "Do you mind putting that down on the seat first? I'd rather not get your sweat all over my backseat."

Tom numbly spread the towel out, got into the back, and closed the door. She turned and looked at him over the seat. "It looks like you're headed to D.C. Some of the streets have been closed for a visiting VIP. I'll do my best, but no guarantees I can get you there by your requested time."

Without waiting for a response, she sped out of the parking lot and onto the highway ramp. Tom sagged into the seat and wiped the sweat from his forehead with a shaky hand. He stared out the window, willing the car to make it to the meeting on time. Even if he wasn't the one going up front, his boss would be mad at him for being late, especially if Darryl had managed to get a meeting with the Secretary of Energy and not just one of his subordinates. He settled deeper into the seat and closed his eyes, thankful the driver chose not to make any attempts at conversation.

He'd been wrong. *The Hotter'N Hell would be a piece of cake compared to this.*

2

Tom was still breathing hard from his sprint through the hallways of the James Forrestal Building, headquarters of the U.S. Department of Energy on Independence Avenue. The Secret Service man gave him an odd look, but checked his I.D. and let him into the conference room. Tom didn't have time to wonder about the heightened security as he tugged at his shirt and ran his fingers through his unruly hair.

Conversations buzzed around him and the possibility of slipping in unnoticed seemed pretty good. Heading towards the back of the room, he heard his name called out. Darryl caught his eye and waved to the seat next to him. Tom made his way to the front and sat down where his boss indicated. The conversations ground to a halt as everyone took in Tom's sweat-stained T-shirt and shorts. His half-hearted efforts to clean up with the towel he had used as a seat cover had not helped, and the pungent odor of stale sweat permeated the small room. He froze at Darryl's next words.

"Tom, we've been waiting for you. We need you to explain our plans to obtain clean energy to the president."

The President of the United States?! Tom's stomach did a flip. He stared at his boss and his mouth opened, then closed.

"Tom," Darryl repeated impatiently. "Let's go. The president doesn't have all day."

Tom gulped and scanned the room, looking for the president. Or better yet, an escape route. There he was, three chairs to the left and surrounded on either side by men wearing dark suits and coiled earpieces. William B. Ferris, The President of the United States.

Sweat poured down Tom's forehead, blurring his vision. He swiped at his burning eyes frantically. Darryl finally took pity on him and handed him a Kleenex.

Tom dabbed at his eyes and turned towards the president. "Uhhhh . . . helium-3. Yes. Helium-3 is what we need. We can get clean energy from helium-3." His mind whirred as he desperately tried to think of what else to say, while trying to stop his legs from shaking so hard. He licked his lips in a feeble attempt to moisten his mouth.

The Secretary of Energy, Ray Donaldson, snickered. "Helium-3 you say? That sounds like a candy bar. What are you talking about?"

Tom blinked at the secretary, confused. "What? Candy bar?"

Darryl glared at Ray. "Give him a chance, Ray." Darryl leaned into Tom and said under his breath, "Pull it together. We need this." He straightened up. "Explain what helium-3 has to do with clean energy and why we need nuclear fusion," he prompted.

Tom nodded. He took a deep breath and said the first thing that popped into his head. "We have to do something. We have an energy crisis. If we sit back and wait for the problem to go away, it'll be too late and it will be impossible to meet our energy needs."

Tom paused and shifted in his chair. His shirt stuck to his skin and the cool air from the air conditioning vent chilled the wet patches under his arms. He desperately wished he'd been able to change. He took another calming breath. "Helium-3 is what we need, and the Moon has about one million tons of the stuff. If we go—"

"I don't get it," Ray interrupted. "Why helium-3? It's not renewable. Why not solar or wind?" Crossing his arms, he sneered at Tom. "Next, you'll be telling us we need kryptonite."

Someone stifled a laugh. Tom suppressed a very strong urge to run and cleared his throat, trying to gather his thoughts and calm his rebellious stomach.

"We can't guarantee sunshine or wind in many parts of the country. Then there's the storage problem. We're also running out of fossil fuels. Efforts at conservation have failed miserably." Tom fought to still the trembling of his hands and steady his voice. An image of his daughter Stephanie flashed through his mind, triggering his next words. "We can't ignore these facts if we're to leave a legacy for our kids. Solving the energy crisis is essential to future life on Earth. Space exploration is a critical part of that solution."

"And I say you're full of crap," Ray shot back. "You should be concentrating on finding your solutions on good ol' mother Earth."

Darryl stepped in before the conversation could deteriorate further. "Ray, I appreciate your opinion," he said diplomatically, "but that's not why we're here today. The president is a busy man, so I suggest we stick to today's agenda."

Ray glanced at the president, who nodded his agreement. "Darryl's right, Ray. We all know how you feel, but today's conference is not about the Earth's resources, it's about the Moon's."

Tom nodded eagerly. "Helium-3 from the Moon can provide us with virtually all the energy we'd ever need, in the form of fusion —40,000 years' worth!" He scanned the faces in the first three rows. Turned-down mouths. Folded arms. Head shakes. They weren't buying what he was selling.

"Why don't you explain how, Tom?" Darryl suggested.

Tom looked longingly at the exit sign. *If only he could get out of there . . . but they need the funding for the program to survive.* He took a breath. "Remember the components of an atom?" He looked around at the nodding heads and continued. "If we rearrange the nucleus of the atom, we can create a nuclear reaction."

Ray leaned forward, sarcasm dripping from his voice. "I appreciate the chemistry lesson, Tom, but how does this relate to helium-3?"

Tom sighed. He'd much rather be back at the lab, working on their fusion reactor prototype. "If we introduce helium-3 to deuterium, a hydrogen isotope, we can create a reaction that produces clean energy. This is a nuclear fusion reaction in which the deuterium and helium-3 atoms come together to give off a proton and helium-4, another isotope of helium. The end result weighs less than the original components and the missing mass is converted into a tremendous amount of energy."

"Sounds like a fairytale to me," Ray jabbed back.

Tom waved a hand in the air. "It's no fairy tale, Mr. Secretary. Helium-3 has virtually no radioactive by-products, making it inherently safe. In fact," Tom's voice became louder and he smiled for the first time since he'd entered the room. "Some researchers estimate twenty-five tons could provide enough energy to power all of the United States for a full year. Just 2.2 pounds of fusion fuel is the same amount of energy as eleven thousand tons of fossil fuel."

Ray scowled at Tom. "Except none of that matters. We have no space vehicles capable of a lunar landing, let alone lunar mining. We can't get any of your helium-3 fairy dust even if we wanted to."

Tom leaned back, considering his next words carefully. "You're right, Mr. Secretary. We don't. Not yet." He paused. The worst they could do was laugh at him. No, that wasn't exactly true. He could lose his job, but he still had to try. He took a deep breath and exhaled. "Which is why we need to develop a program that takes us back to the Moon."

The president had been leaning back in his chair, eyes half-closed. The regal grandfather clock located by the door chimed the hour, causing him to open his eyes. He leaned forward, his sudden movement commanding everyone's attention. "Helium-3 is a valuable resource we can't afford to ignore. NASA has been pushing for years to get their lunar landing program reinstated. It's time to give them the green light." He turned to one of his aides. "Let's see about getting a media campaign started in that direction."

Tom jumped up and pumped his fist at the president's words, but paused his celebration as a nagging thought crossed his mind. Stinky shirt and all, he couldn't let the opportunity slip away. He lifted his hand hesitantly, uncomfortably aware that the sweat pattern under his arm was even more obvious, but he succeeded in drawing the attention of the president back to him. "There is one other problem that needs to be addressed, sir."

The president raised his eyebrows. "Yes?"

"We don't have a working fusion reactor. Not yet."

"I see." The president sank back against his chair and exhaled. "And how far out are we from creating one?"

"Thirty years," Tom replied with a straight face.

Darryl almost spit out the sip of coffee he'd just taken. A few chuckles were heard across the room.

The Secretary of Energy leaned in towards President Ferris and murmured, "Old joke, sir. They've been saying that for years."

The president smiled, but it didn't reach his eyes. "We better make sure we have one by the time we return from the Moon. You'll have to get it built a lot quicker than that."

"Yes, sir!" Tom replied, sensing now was not the best time to explain why that probably wouldn't happen.

Tom splashed water on his face and remained at the sink of the bathroom outside of the conference room, gazing into the mirror and trying to process what happened. *Did he seriously just pitch going to the Moon for helium-3 to the President of the United States— while wearing a sweaty T-shirt and shorts?* The president had ordered him to get nuclear fusion going. Surely now they would get the funding they desperately needed to move on to the next phase of their research.

He checked his watch. It was a relief to have been kicked out of the rest of the meeting while the powers-that-be sorted out the high-level details. He exited the bathroom, still damp and pungent, but at least somewhat washed up. He poured a cup of coffee and waited for Darryl in the lounge area, dreaming of what he would do when they received the funding they needed.

A few minutes later, Darryl strode into the lounge and took a seat across from Tom. "Great news. You're the Scientist in Charge for the lunar mission."

Tom dropped his cup and it hit the floor, coffee splattering across the tile. He grabbed a paper towel roll and hurriedly sponged up the mess. He threw the cup and soggy paper towels forcefully into a nearby trash receptacle, with a groan of frustration. "The SIC? Why me? I already have enough to do. Can't you pass that off to someone else?" *Why can't I just be left alone to work on my nuclear fusion prototype?*

Darryl snorted. "Believe me, this was not my idea. You're the one that got this whole thing started when you told the president we needed helium-3 to solve our energy problem and sold him on going back to the Moon." He waved his hand towards Tom. "You impressed the president with your lecture, and he suggested we ask you to be the SIC." Darryl's eyes hardened uncharacteristically. "Only it wasn't a suggestion and it's not a request."

Clenching his fists, Tom paused and looked at Darryl more closely. Darryl was being unusually aggressive and Tom realized why. Darryl's daughter had been in and out of the hospital for the past six months. He let his fists relax.

"How's your baby girl, Darryl?"

Darryl's eyes softened. "She's hanging in there. The latest blood-work results weren't that great."

"Can they do anything?"

Darryl dropped his shoulders and shook his head. "No. All we can do is watch and wait." He sighed. "She's doing pretty good for now." His voice cracked. "I just hate having this hanging over her head."

Tom reached over and squeezed Darryl's shoulder. "She'll be okay. She's tough like her Dad." He smiled at his boss. "All right, I'll do it."

Darryl gave Tom a weak smile in return. "Good man. It'll be great —you'll see. This buys you a front row ticket to all of the action."

The last place he wanted to be. "Sure, thanks."

3

15 MONTHS LATER

"Hey Jason, what's that weird software with the different colors?" Thiru asked his roommate. Thiru was an accounting major, and Jason was studying engineering with a minor in astronomy. The strange looking graph on Jason's computer resembled something from a science fiction movie.

Ever since NASA announced their back to the Moon campaign over a year ago, the astronomy program at the University of Texas at Austin tripled their enrollments. Jason grinned at the opportunity to talk about his SETI screensaver. "That's a frequency-time-power graph. It's analytical software, downloading data from SETI. I volunteered my computer's idle time, so its processing power can be used to analyze data from their radio telescopes."

"What's SETI? I've never heard of it."

"It stands for Search for Extraterrestrial Intelligence," Jason explained. "The goal of SETI is to find intelligent life outside of Earth by using radio telescopes to listen for narrow bandwidth radio signals from space. Since those signals don't occur naturally, it could indicate an extraterrestrial presence."

"You mean aliens?" Thiru shook his head. "That's crazy. What would happen if you found one?"

Jason shrugged. "I don't know, but it sounds cool. They don't tell us anything—they just use our computers for processing, then the results are uploaded to their mainframe. I guess if we find anything, their computers will flag it and we'll see it on the news."

He glanced back at his desktop. He really didn't understand how the software processed the data, but he liked how it looked. Maybe he could use it to impress that cute blonde in his planetary science class. The digital clock on the screen reminded him he'd better get going. The spaceship Triumphant had successfully landed on the Moon late yesterday, and they would be discussing the landing today in class. It was going to be awesome!

Jason grabbed his books, and Thiru followed him out of their dorm room, neither one noticing the unusual activity as a narrow bandwidth neon-green spike registered on Jason's desktop. It disappeared minutes later as the system refreshed, and the data was uploaded to SETI, to be replaced by another set of perfectly ordinary-looking signals.

Tom cracked open the door to Mission Control, observing the activity inside through the gap. The atmosphere of organized chaos in the room beyond was intimidating, as NASA employees went about their tasks with quiet intensity. Feeling torn between his desire to leave and his obligation to be present as the Scientist In Charge, he took a deep breath and made himself enter. Tom had visited Johnson Space Center on a school field trip, seeing it through the eyes of a twelve-year-old. As he stood as unobtrusively as possible near the doorway, he felt the same sense of wonder he had back then. Mission Control looked oddly familiar even with the updated equipment, the removal of the large obser-vation windows, and the giant monitoring screens hanging high on the walls.

It was hard to believe NASA could accomplish a return to the Moon just 15 months after that fateful meeting when he'd showed up stinking with sweat, but the R&D had never stopped. The lunar mission was mostly a matter of finally getting to fund and implement existing technology, similar to the ultra-fast develop-ment of the covid-19 vaccine back in 2021.

A communications technician in a white lab coat appeared. Without a word, he peered at Tom's I.D. and pointed him towards a bank of computers in the inner circle. The technician grabbed a headset and offered it to Tom. He accepted it hesitantly, and the technician gestured impatiently. Tom placed it over his head and positioned the mike under his chin. The technician adjusted some dials on the console and spoke briefly out loud: "Testing 1, 2 . . . Testing" and looked at Tom. "Say something."

Tom looked at him in puzzlement.

"Say something, I'm testing your mike."

Tom looked at him in surprise, but obeyed. "Something," he mumbled.

The technician shot him an aggravated look and Tom quickly started reciting the alphabet. "A, B, C, D, E . . ."

The technician finally nodded and said, "You're good to go," and walked off.

Tom didn't feel good to go—except, perhaps, good to go home. He swallowed and continued to look around, wiping his sweaty palms on his pants as he waited for what was next.

"Places everyone," someone shouted, reminding Tom of a movie set. Men and women scrambled to their workstations. The acronym for his new position reflected how he felt—*SIC*.

Capcom Jack Walgreen stood center stage in the inner circle, just a few feet from where Tom was stationed. Jack scanned the room and smiled. "We should see Keith momentarily, folks." He glanced at Tom, who was clenching his hands together to keep them from shaking. "The Triumphant co-pilot's mission for today is to begin construction of the solar panel energy station. We'll have approximately a 1.25 second delay in communications. This is an internal NASA broadcast only."

Tom directed his gaze upward as the video screens flickered, and a sharp image came into view. The contrast between the High-Definition color image in front of them and the blurry images recorded from the original Moon landing startled him. Keith was moving about the rocky gray lunar surface. Tom could hear Jack in his headset, "Keith, come in, Keith. Houston here."

Keith looked towards the rover at the camera mounted on its frame. His headset automatically up-linked to the communications channel, and he responded, "Good to hear from you, Houston, greetings from the Moon!" He gave a little hop, propelling himself upward a few feet, holding his arms out to steady himself. "I'm getting used to traveling in this lighter gravity. Even with our practice simulations back on Earth, it's still tricky." He paused, directing his gaze towards Earth. "We seem so alone. Hard to imagine the Earth has billions of people on it and just the five of us up here."

Tom's eyes remained glued to the video screen as Keith continued to move forward in small hops. "I want all of you to see this." Tom's gaze followed the direction Keith pointed, and he gasped as the American flag came into view, bleached white by the sun on what must be the Sea of Tranquility. *Neil Armstrong and Buzz*

Aldrin took their first steps on the Moon on July 20, 1969 and planted that flag. We're finally back and he was a part of it. His thoughts were interrupted as a gravelly voice came through his radio headset.

"Take me to your leader."

Sharp intakes of breath accentuated the silence as the Mission Control team froze in place. Tom's stomach did a sudden flip-flop. Another figure entered the camera's field of view, approaching Keith. It was wearing some type of spacesuit, less bulky than NASA's standard issue. The helmet was form-fitted to the creature's face, giving the illusion it was not wearing one at all. It towered over Keith.

And it wasn't human.

Keith turned violently. He sailed through the lighter gravity with his arms flailing and his body spinning erratically. He landed twenty feet away, flat on his back. The alien continued its approach until it stood in front of Keith. A long, slender arm reached out to him, as if to assist him to his feet. The arm belonged to a lanky body that would be classified as humanoid on Earth, and terminated into a large hand with six digits. The alien spoke again, its voice coming through their headsets in a lighter, softer tone. "Are you okay?"

Keith gawked at the alien for a long moment, then glanced at the rover camera and managed a nod.

"I wanted to experience a common ground in humor," explained the alien. "I'm sorry, those were not the instructions from my superior. I just couldn't resist. I guess I've been watching too much of your television."

Tom broke into a sweat, watching helplessly as Keith stood up and began to scramble backwards. Jack spoke into his mike. "Stay calm, Keith. It doesn't appear hostile."

Keith came to a stand-still as the alien made its way towards him. Suddenly, Keith fell over, backward into the rocky material of the regolith, a poof of dust barely discernible as his body hit the loose surface. The doctor monitoring Keith's vitals in the control room reported in a loud voice, "Astronaut 372's systolic pressure is 90. He is experiencing a vasovagal syncope due to an unexpected hypotension episode."

Jack snorted impatiently. "English, doc. Tell us in plain English!"

"Keith fainted. He should be okay, but it may last a few minutes." *If the alien doesn't hurt him first* hung unspoken in the air.

Before Jack could respond, movement on the video screen grabbed everyone's attention. The alien broke into a run towards Keith's prone body. The screen went blank.

"What . . . what happened? Get me back that signal!" Jack turned to the comm tech who had helped Tom with his headset.

"Working on it," the tech responded in a crisp voice. Everyone in Mission Control held their breath as the tech worked, adjusting dials and checking signal strength. One of the workers bowed his head and moved his lips in silent prayer.

Tom couldn't take his eyes off the screen. His teeth clenched painfully. His leg muscles tightened, and he jammed his hands into his armpits to stop himself from running.

"What's the problem, Comm? We need that picture back now!" Jack stared at the screen and tapped his foot, as if he could will the connection into being.

"Astronaut 372's health monitor is no longer transmitting," announced the doctor.

"What does that mean?" Tom's voice shook. "Is Keith okay?"

The doctor rubbed his chin. "It's impossible to tell. It could have stopped transmitting for any number of reasons."

An ominous silence filled the air. Seconds turned into minutes.

Tom's eyes darted around the control room. "Why doesn't someone do something?"

Jack reached over and put a hand on his shoulder. "Calm down, son. Everyone in this room wants Keith to be okay, but all we can do is wait." He glanced at the comm tech.

"I think I found the problem," the tech reported. "The frequency drifted, and it won't stabilize. I can get Keith back online for a minute or two, but the real fix is to change the board." He continued to fiddle with the dials, and the image shimmered into view. The visual of the surface of the moon coalesced onto the screen, but Keith was no longer in sight.

Tom started to hyperventilate. *A murderous alien had abducted Keith, and it was his fault. He was the one who suggested they go to the Moon to obtain helium-3. Who knew what the alien was capable of?* He watched the comm tech continue to work the dials on his console. The view on the video screen began to rotate. Keith, still unconscious, lay in the alien's arms. It carried him to the rover and carefully propped him against a bundle of equipment.

"Health readings back online," commented the doctor softly. "Systolic pressure 95 and climbing." He glanced at Jack. "That means he's improving." The alien sat several feet away, observing Keith. It turned to face the camera on the rover and its soft voice filled Tom's headset.

"It is not our intention to harm your astronaut." The alien glanced at Keith, who remained inert. "We have been on the Moon for over a century, but we had a strict policy of non-interference the first time your people landed here. Now that you have returned, we have decided it's time we meet, especially since you are trying so hard to find us."

The alien blinked and an expression resembling a grimace crossed its face. "You have some very observant representatives of your race involved with the search for extraterrestrial intelligence at the SETI Institute. One of your astronomers, Carl Sagan, had the right idea when he said, 'Absence of evidence is not evidence of absence.' We simply did not wish to be found."

Signaling to Jack with a wave of his hand, the doctor wrote on a pad and walked it over to the Capcom. He held it up, and Jack silently read, "Keith has recovered. Vitals have returned to normal. Faking sleep."

Jack nodded. He needed to keep this guy talking while he figured out what to do. "How do you know what frequency we're using to communicate?"

The alien grimaced again. "We have devices capable of isolating communication links being generated in a specific area. They can analyze them to determine the exact modulation protocol and frequency being used. You possess this capability as well. We've just taken the technology further and developed portable scanning devices that can analyze the wavelengths and extract the data."

"That makes sense. Uhhh . . . so where are you from?" Jack asked, deciding to try to get as much information as possible while giving Keith a chance to recover.

"We don't live in your solar system, but we share the same galactic neighborhood. Our planet is located approximately 500 light years away in what you refer to as the Cygnus constellation, or alternately, the Swan constellation."

Tom's mouth fell open. *Five hundred light years. They must have faster than light travel. It was possible!* Before he could absorb the ramifications, the alien continued.

"Some of your species may be disappointed we are not more exotic, especially after watching the diverse assortment of aliens in your Star Wars franchise, but our evolutionary paths are very similar." He held up his arms. "We also have four appendages and are bipedal. We are carbon-based life forms just as you are, and our internal organs are roughly the same. We also have two eyes, a nose, and a mouth."

"You're not wearing some sort of disguise, so we can relate to you?" Keith asked, sitting up. "This is what you really look like?"

The room drew a collective sigh of relief. It seemed Keith was going to be okay. Tom's first day at NASA might not end in disaster after all.

"You are correct," replied the alien, grimace still in place. "I'm glad to see you've recovered. It was not my intention to startle you. I was chosen for your First Contact because of my intensive studies of humans with a focus on American culture. I am what would be comparable to a university professor with a research grant, specializing in the study of human behavior."

First Contact! The words slowly sank in and Tom's heart rate quickened.

"Well, uh, greetings on behalf of Earth," Keith said. "My name is Keith Sanders, United States astronaut for NASA and co-pilot of our spaceship Triumphant. Our mission commander is Theresa McDonnough. We're on the Moon to build a permanent installation to use as a portal to the stars and to conduct scientific experiments."

Good. It was probably best not to mention helium-3 just yet.

"What should I call you?" Keith asked.

"My name is Lanjo Verfabtholar Frastero Kolanpatchibe."

"Lanjo Verfub . . ." Keith made an attempt to repeat the alien's name, but couldn't get past the second word. The creature made the grimacing expression Tom deduced was an alien smile.

"It's okay, Keith, I usually go by Lanjo, and I am an adult male. We record our family names through the female's lineage. Verfabtholar is roughly equivalent to Verfab, son of Tholar, who is my birth mother. Lanjo is what we call a favorite name, for informal use, probably similar to a nickname. The rest comments on my education, profession, and family grouping."

Lanjo stood up slowly and moved closer to the rover camera, allowing everyone to get a better look at him. Although it was difficult to see much detail because of the space suit, the alien's body looked similar to a human's. He was skinnier and taller, with a skin pigment nearly matching Tom's own.

Lanjo turned and gazed directly into the camera. Tom was surprised at the depth of his large brown eyes and star-shaped pupils, his face almost eerily human. His nose was somewhat broad, and his mouth had a different muscular structure, evidenced by the unfamiliar expressions that passed across the alien's face.

"Our mission is to . . ." the video shimmered again, garbling the alien's words. " . . . danger . . . supernovae . . . another planet to move our—" and faded completely out. Video and audio were dead.

All eyes swung to the comm tech, who held up his hands. "I can't get the signal back until the board is replaced."

"How long?" Jack barked.

"Several hours, sir. It's a complex system, and I will have to do a series of diagnostics that depend on satellite positioning."

"Can we contact the mission commander?"

"No, sir. Not until I have the board's frequency multiplexer back online. It handles communication for all five astronauts."

Jack immediately glanced around the room and uttered the phrase he had hoped he would never have to use. "Lock the doors!" He turned his gaze on the video techs. "Make sure that video feed stays secured—no one outside this room is to see it, and nothing we have seen or heard today is to leave this room." He turned his attention back to the comm tech. "Keep working on it. I'm taking this to the President." Looking around, he spotted Tom, who was trying to make himself invisible.

"You, are you the SIC?"

"Yes, sir," Tom admitted.

"Come with me. We need to get a flight to D.C., ASAP."

Tom sighed. *He'd just found out aliens do exist and he just heard one hint at a coming cataclysm. The last thing he wanted to do was be pulled into another bureaucratic meeting.* "Yes, sir."

⚛

The president's weekly briefing with the Secretary of Energy on the fusion project was just winding down. They were in the same conference room where it all started, just over a year ago. Darryl was explaining why they needed additional funding in order for his team to get to the next stage of their research, when Jack and Tom entered the room. With the president's permission, the Capcom explained what happened just a scant four hours ago. Tom tried his best to do what his mother always said to do—keep his mouth shut and his eyes open. Uncertainty gnawed into his stomach as the alien's words played in an endless loop through his mind . . . *danger . . . supernovae . . . danger . . . supernovae.*

After Jack finished his account, Ray commented caustically, "Just what we need, another Roswell."

Tom's blood pressure shot up at the secretary's words. Pounding his fist, he toppled a water glass, spilling its contents across the conference table and soaking Darryl's notes. "No, Mr. Secretary, this is not another Roswell. This is not some government cover up. This is a real First Contact!" He pounded the table again. "We need to understand what they're capable of. We don't know what their real intentions are."

He paused and took a deep breath, disregarding the stares directed at him. Thinking of his daughter, he continued, "Our future, Earth's future, could very well depend on how we proceed."

Tom ignored the shocked expression on Darryl's face as his boss grabbed some napkins and tried to soak up the water. The president held up his hand for attention.

"Tom's right." He looked pointedly at Ray. "We need to keep cool heads and get all the facts." He turned to Jack. "So what do we know about Commander Theresa McDonnough? I know she's competent to lead the lunar mission, but an alien contact was not factored into the equation. I vaguely recall her from some PR stuff we did during our 'Back to the Moon' campaign. She struck me as a very competent, self-assured woman."

"That she is, sir," Tom exclaimed, drawing curious looks from about the room. He could feel his neck flushing red, the color traveling upward as he fought for composure. The president raised his eyebrows in silent question.

"We dated in college," Tom admitted. "But that was fifteen years ago."

"Any insight into her abilities in this type of situation would be invaluable, Tom. We'll pull her file of course."

"It's on its way, sir," an aide interjected.

Tom took a calming breath. "I understand, sir. We couldn't have a better person to handle things. Theresa is absolutely unflappable." He remembered that quality well, since it contributed to their breakup. Tom had immaturely interpreted her ability to take things in stride as a lack of passion. He would have done a lot better marrying Theresa, but at least his marriage to Patricia had given him Stephanie, even if it did end in divorce. His mind continued to drift and he forcibly turned his attention back to the matter at hand and took a sip of water. He needed to stay focused.

The president nodded and looked at Jack. "When will you have communications back up? Our first priority is to see to the safety of our astronauts."

"Two more hours, sir."

"As I recall, NASA has a contingency plan for every possible scenario, including alien contact. Is that correct?"

Jack nodded.

"Okay. After you confirm the status of the lunar mission team, we need to know what the alien meant by ' . . . danger . . . supernovae . . . another planet to move our.' Let's hope and pray we don't have a hostile takeover attempt on our hands. Jack, keep me in the loop as things develop. Everyone, a First Contact is historic, but we don't yet know how this will end. Nothing said here leaves this room. Let's get back to work."

At only twenty-three years old, Marco Esposito was lucky enough to know what he wanted to do with his life. Currently working towards his doctoral dissertation at the Center for SETI Research, he had always been preoccupied with space and the possibility of life beyond Earth. Whenever he looked up at the Moon, he'd wonder what Buzz Aldrin and Neil Armstrong felt, walking on its surface over 240,000 miles away. Today he wondered the same about Keith Sanders and Theresa McDonnough. He envied yesterday's Moon landing. It was just a matter of time until the private sector's push would establish safe and affordable space travel for everyone. Marco only hoped it would be within his lifetime.

His dreams of journeying through space were abruptly forgotten as the large flashing red LED registered on his consciousness. *What the heck?*

The spectrum analyzer reported a 1420.4 MHz signal, duplicating the strongest candidate for alien radio transmission ever detected. The same 21-centimeter hydrogen line dubbed the WOW! signal when it was intercepted by SETI in 1977, was being received from the direction of the constellation Cygnus. At about 500 light years away, it was at the very edge for two-way communication to be possible. *The swan was up to something!*

4

The First Contact had changed everything. Tom recalled the relief everyone felt when communications were re-established with Keith, and the astronaut had remained unharmed. The president's invitation to Lanjo to come to Earth and visit Camp David was classified. Only the highest-level government officials knew about the alien's existence. Tom never dreamed he would be invited to Camp David for the top-secret Cygnan-U.S. summit. Maybe invited wasn't the right word. He had the distinct impression refusing wasn't an option, at least if he wanted his career to remain intact.

"Stephanie!" Tom looked around the living room, taking in the peanut butter cracker wrappers scattered on the carpet and a new stain in its worn fibers. A glass, which with 100% certainty held Dr. Pepper and melted ice, was on the coffee table. He took a deep breath and let it out slowly. "Stephanie, where are you?"

"Mmmmm . . ." came the groggy reply. Tom turned towards the sound. Taking a closer look at the pile of blankets on the couch, he realized his daughter was buried between them.

"Come on, Steph, get up. I have to work overtime. You're gonna have to go back to your Mom a little early." It was four o'clock in the afternoon, and his twelve-year-old daughter wasn't glued to her phone or playing with Lela, the Lhasa Apso puppy she talked him into getting a few months ago. "Where's Lela?"

Stephanie sighed dramatically and pushed the top layer of blankets partially off the couch. Lela's furry muzzle came into view. "Right here, Dad. We were bored and decided to build a fort. After I got all the blankets out, I ran out of energy and decided to take a nap instead."

How can a twelve-year-old run out of energy? was the first thought that popped into Tom's head, but he held it back. He didn't get to see Stephanie very often, and the last thing he wanted to do was alienate her, especially now when he had to cut their visit short.

"Okay kiddo, maybe next time I can help you build it." He cringed inwardly at the disappointed expression flashing across his daughter's face. He wasn't imagining it, even if it was there for only a few milliseconds.

Stephanie forced a smile. "Sure Dad, next time would be great." She got up and walked over to the chair where she'd dumped her backpack that morning. Tom didn't know whether to feel relieved or hurt when she didn't ask why he had to go back to work. His ex-wife hadn't asked either, when he called to tell her he needed to bring Stephanie back early. His instructions were to tell no one about the First Contact or Lanjo's visit to Earth, but he didn't need the story he'd made up, after all.

The exchange was as awkward as usual. Tom could feel his ex-wife's accusing eyes behind the fake smile. He didn't want to consider what Patricia must really be thinking. He turned his attention to Stephanie, who was waiting, as she always did, with those big hazel eyes looking up at him wistfully. He reached out his arms for a hug, and she wrapped her arms around his neck. She whispered in his ear, "Don't worry Daddy, it'll be okay."

Startled, Tom wondered when his baby girl had grown up so fast. But he would definitely take it. "Thanks, kiddo. Love you."

"Love you too, Daddy!"

With those words to sustain him, Tom got into his car and headed to the airport.

Lanjo looked around the Laurel Lodge conference room with his customary grimace in place. He elected to wear his space suit without his helmet to this historic meeting, since that was the way his new friends were used to seeing him. He took a deep, calming breath, reminding himself that Earth air was eminently breathable for his race. A bit thinner than he was accustomed to, perhaps, but definitely breathable. He doubted he would need his emergency puffer, but it was good to know he had one, just in case.

Learning all about the 1978 Camp David Accords had been required reading in his doctoral studies. Lanjo was so excited to be at Camp David, he had to forcibly keep his eyebrows from quivering so as not to alarm his hosts. He wasn't as prepared for snow as he thought he would be. It was one thing to study it in a textbook or on film, quite another to hold the cold substance in his hands and feel it smoosh between his fingers as it dribbled down his skin. Temperatures below 45 Fahrenheit was an anomaly on his home planet and he wasn't sure how he felt about the lower temperatures. The dingy regolith of the Moon had not prepared him for the assault on his sensitive retinas caused by the sun reflecting off of the snow. It was almost a relief to go inside.

The room was devoid of press with the exception of two journalists specifically selected for their reputation for circumspection. That quality earned them a front row seat in a meeting that could very well change the course of humanity. Tom and Darryl were seated behind them and sat talking quietly. Lanjo noticed Tom staring at him and wondered at the intense expression on the human's face. Grimacing in return, he felt his eyebrows begin to quiver again, but this time out of trepidation. He suppressed his emotions, hoping the humans in the room understood his peaceful intentions.

Keith Sanders and Theresa McDonnough entered the room, representing NASA. Their familiar faces comforted Lanjo, as he unexpectedly found himself fighting to keep his composure. As much as he thought he had the intercultural interaction between humans and aliens down, being in the midst of this many humans proved to be more challenging than he had imagined. He felt confident in his ability to communicate with the humans, but he found himself wishing there were also other Cygnans in the room. It somehow felt lonely. He grimaced gratefully when Keith guided him to some seats at the large conference table and sat down next to him. "How're you holding up, Lanjo?" Keith whispered.

"Holding up . . ." Another English idiom he searched his memory to define. He wasn't robbing anybody. No wait, that was "hold up." Keith inquired as to how he was holding up . . . he scanned the *Human English Idioms Dictionary* that had been part of his doctoral dissertation. It was loaded onto a microchip embedded in his body that his neural network could access at will. It also served as a transceiver and tracking device with a very narrow communications band, among other things. He knew most Americans would consider such a mechanism an intolerable invasion of privacy, but from his more mature technological perspective, it made perfect sense.

To continue to function without losing force or effectiveness; cope.

"I'm holding up fine, thanks," Lanjo whispered back. He leaned forward in his chair and reached for the glass of ice water that a uniformed server offered him. Glancing at Keith, who gave him an encouraging nod, Lanjo lifted the glass to his lips and sipped. This small act caused all activity in the room to freeze. An alien sipping a glass of water in a conference room at Camp David must have seemed so surreal, it impinged on the collective human consciousness as a moment to be observed. Lanjo, taking note of his audience, took a longer drink and grimaced dramatically. "Tastes great, less filling!"

A beat of utter silence followed this pronouncement, broken by Tom's outburst of laughter. An alien quoting a beer slogan from the late 20th century was just too much. Soon the entire room was laughing and the tension generated by the uncertainty of Lanjo's presence began to dissipate.

⚛

The president, dressed in a polo shirt and khakis, entered unannounced, followed by several staff members. He made his way over to where Keith and Lanjo were sitting. Following Keith's lead, Lanjo sprang to his feet, towering about six inches over the President. Having been briefed by Keith and Theresa the day before, the president smiled and offered Lanjo his hand. "It's good to finally get to meet you, Lanjo. Welcome to Camp David."

Lanjo returned the president's handshake with a firm grip. The president was distracted for a split second by the extra digit, but Keith had prepared him to expect it.

"Thank you, Mr. President," Lanjo responded with his character-istic "smiling" grimace Keith had explained in their meeting yesterday.

The president briefly wondered what emotion corresponded to a human smile for a Cygnan, as he had come to think of them. That sounded more dignified than, "the swan guy" and warmer than, "the alien." Regardless, Lanjo was obviously conversant with human social conventions and seemed like a nice guy. He just hoped his first impression of the alien held up.

"I hear you're very interested in learning about culture here on Earth. Later today I can introduce you to bowling, one of our more popular hobbies. We happen to have a bowling alley at Camp David at our disposal."

Lanjo accessed his microchip again, this time looking up the term bowling in the *Human English Encyclopedia*. The president was rewarded with a huge grimace, then another expression that he couldn't quite interpret. Lanjo held up one of his hands, displaying his six fingers.

"Ahhhh . . . that won't be a problem." The president smiled in an effort to reassure the Cygnan. "You don't need to have a hole in the ball for every finger. I'm sure you'll do fine."

The president glanced around the room and noted all of the key participants he had requested were present. He nodded his head and continued, "Why don't we begin. Lots of folks are very inter-ested in learning more about you and your race, myself included." He patted Lanjo's arm in a friendly gesture and moved to the seat in the middle of the table reserved for POTUS.

Everyone took that as a signal to get seated and quiet. The presi-dent took a few moments to make eye contact with the attendees and smile or nod. He cleared his throat. "So let's get started. This is a momentous occasion in human, er . . . in interplanetary history. I know we are all eager to hear from our Cygnan guest, Lanjo." All eyes swiveled to the alien seated among them, and Lanjo took another calming breath, then stood, enabling everyone to see him.

"Greetings from the planet you refer to as Kepler 186f," Lanjo began. Before he could continue, an enthusiastic murmur went through the crowd. "I knew it," Tom whispered to Darryl. "SETI was right!" Puzzled looks were mixed with smiles of comprehension among the participants.

The president looked around, and his eyes landed on Tom, who squirmed uncomfortably in his seat. "How about it, Tom. Can you give us a little detail?"

Tom gulped and nodded, trying to still the cartwheels in his stomach. He'd hoped he could just be an observer, but unfortunately the president had taken a liking to him. At least he'd used plenty of antiperspirant this morning. He glanced at Lanjo who grimaced back at him. He reluctantly stood up. His heart rate increased, but this time he managed to keep his voice from trembling.

"Uhhh . . . yeah. Okay. Kepler 186f was first detected in 2014 by NASA's Kepler space telescope." Tom could recall the excitement it had caused. He was studying for an exam at MIT when the news announced the discovery. "It was the first Earth-sized planet found orbiting the habitable zone of a star other than our own sun. There was a lot of speculation about the possibility of life existing on Kepler 186f. Unfortunately, the 500 light years distance from Earth has been too big an obstacle to discovering the truth about life existing there." Tom glanced at Lanjo again. "Until now."

Tom sat back down and all eyes turned to the alien.

Lanjo paused for dramatic effect. "I am happy to say, life does indeed exist."

The room burst into a jubilant uproar. While everyone present had been briefed they would be attending a meeting with a "First Contact," only a select few had known Kepler-186f was the alien's home planet. It was a moment to be soaked in, as the scientific community could see the fruition of their efforts, government officials could see tangible results for their funding, and to everyone else, the universe had just became a much smaller place.

"People, people, I know this is exciting, but let's allow our guest to talk." Joe Ricinski, special aide to the president, took the news in stride. "Please, be quiet and let Lanjo finish." Tom tried to calm his heart, which had not quit racing.

The room finally became silent, and all eyes were again on Lanjo, who had sat back waiting for the commotion to subside. "So, as I was saying, life does indeed exist on Kepler-186f. Since it's 'home sweet home' for me, I naturally know it by a different name instead of the scientific naming convention used here on Earth. My people call our planet Lanzeron. We think it has a nice ring to it." Lanjo paused, grimacing.

His audience was also coming to understand his grimace as the alien equivalent of a smile. A few chuckles were heard as Lanjo continued, "You might notice that the beginning syllable is the same as my name. Now I would like to tell you that implies I am planetary royalty, but sadly that is not the case." More chuckles. "'Lan' is a naming convention of my people. All of us have several names, and the first one always begins with 'Lan,' which is why we have to have more names, so we can be uniquely identified." Lanjo's grimace grew wider. "I am a bit of a rebel at times. I have chosen to go by my first name of Lanjo, although that is not typical for my culture.

"My very first conversation on the Moon with Keith included a brief discussion on my full name, Lanjo Verfabtholar Frastero Kolanpatchibe. It can be a bit intimidating when you first hear it, but then, what's in a name? A rose by any other name would smell as sweet."

Surprised looks at Lanjo's reference to Shakespeare's Romeo and Juliet prompted Keith to stand up. "Lanjo is a serious student of humanity and often facilitates cultural interaction through literature and historical references. I'll be happy to share what I've learned about Lanzeron naming conventions after the meeting." Keith sat back down and winked at Lanjo.

"Ah yes, I've been told by my superiors I sometimes get carried away," admitted Lanjo. "But I think they say that when they don't get the reference." He took a sip of water and continued.

"Lanzeron is about ten percent bigger in diameter than Earth. Your scientists have postulated it is one of five planets in orbit around the M-dwarf star you have designated Kepler-186. It is actually the sixth planet out of seven. The other planets vary in size and are not habitable." Lanjo paused and tapped his chin before continuing. "You are correct about the star—it is a red dwarf. However, it's part of a binary star system also containing a white dwarf. Lanzeron has a stable orbit around the red dwarf, our 'sun' if you will, despite the proximity of the white dwarf."

The scientists and NASA personnel in the room could no longer contain themselves, and the room erupted in conversation. Lanjo's revelation of a binary star system seemed significant. Tom racked his brain, trying to remember why it would be, from his long ago undergrad astronomy classes. The two reporters were diligently taking notes, aware Lanjo had said something momentous, but not exactly sure what it was. Joe Ricinski took charge again. "Quiet, everybody, please," he said firmly. "Quiet, let the president speak!"

The room settled back into silence, the sense of anticipation palpable. The president was twirling a pen between his fingers, but he stopped and placed it on his notepad. He searched the room with smiling eyes. "It seems we are at an incredible juncture. Nothing will ever be the same after today. We are learning more about the universe we live in, than we ever thought possible. That's a good thing. You've been invited to this meeting because of your areas of expertise. I know I can trust each of you to respond rationally when presented with the unknown. It doesn't get any more unknown than this." The president turned and smiled apologetically at Lanjo before continuing.

"We can't wait any longer. We need to make an announcement to the American public and to the world, that a 'First Contact' has been made. I'll be making that announcement this evening. I'm counting on each of you to be the voice of reason in your various areas, so the alien hysteria we've seen in Hollywood movies such as *Independence Day*"—a few in the crowd snickered—"does not become a reality."

The president's eyes hardened as he made eye contact among the participants, and the room became quiet again. "I am confident I can count on each of you." His expression softened. "Since Lanjo comes from the Cygnus constellation, with his permission we will be referring to his race as Cygnans."

Lanjo nodded and grimaced at the president's words. "Lanjo has consented to stay with us for the next few days at Camp David. We'll be having a series of meetings on different topics. For now, we are opening the floor to questions."

"Lanjo," one of the reporters pounced, beating everyone else to the punch. "How does it feel to be part of the First Contact with Earth, and why did your race choose to initiate contact?"

Lanjo glanced at President Ferris, who nodded. "It is both an honor and the culmination of my life's work. I have studied Earth for years. To be able to be here with you today has been my greatest dream. I was selected to represent my race because of my extensive studies of Earth culture, both in the broad sense and with a specialization in American culture and history. The Return to the Moon campaign implemented by the United States was the perfect opportunity to initiate contact."

"But why?" pressed the reporter. "We've been to the Moon before, and with your advanced technology, surely you could have reached out sooner?"

Joe made a mental note to personally brief Lanjo before any future press conferences. This line of questioning might present more information to the public than he wanted to reveal at this time. He sighed. It was too late to do anything about it now.

Lanjo gave the Cygnan equivalent of a chuckle, which sounded strangely like a hiccup. "Yes, you are correct. Some of us wanted to. But like you, we have a structured government with different factions and an entrepreneurial private sector. Before now, many of us thought it was too soon. Just like in *Star Trek*, we were following the ethical principle known as the Prime Directive: noninterference with other cultures and civilizations."

Lanjo paused and took another sip of water. "We finally got the majority to agree that an exception was appropriate in the case of making contact with Earth. Self-preservation is a strong motivator."

Lanjo's last sentence caused the room to momentarily fall into a shocked silence before breaking into an uproar again, as the scientists began to postulate the possibilities. Joe cringed. His opportunity to keep that information confidential until he had a chance to examine all of the ramifications had just slipped away.

"Self-preservation? Can you explain?"

"Certainly. Our sun is part of a binary star system. One of the stars is a carbon-oxygen white dwarf, and it has steadily been stealing matter from our sun, a red dwarf. We are fortunate to be in the red dwarf's habitable zone. However, due to the white dwarf's activity, we're starting to feel the effects of our sun's shift in mass. To make matters worse, when the white dwarf accumulates too much matter, it will explode. This will result in a supernova, which our planet will not be able to survive. Our decision to initiate contact is a result of our desire to exchange valuable technology with you. In return, we want your help in transporting the inhabitants of our planet to a new home. We have three teams evaluating three possible planets at this time."

That's it! Tom thought. *A binary star system could produce a supernova explosion. No wonder the Cygnans wanted to make a First Contact —they need help relocating to prevent the annihilation of their species.*

"What valuable technology are you talking about?" called out one of the scientists.

Lanjo grimaced. "Working nuclear fusion. Unlike you, we are not 30 years away. In fact, we use nuclear fusion to power our spaceships."

Tom's heart pounded even harder at the alien's words, but this time from excitement. *Working nuclear fusion!*

The room was quiet as the implications of Lanjo's words settled in. Before Tom could ask Lanjo to elaborate, one of the NASA scientists called out, "Rumor has it a 21-centimeter hydrogen line duplicating the WOW! signal was received by SETI from the vicinity of your planet a few weeks ago. Was that you, and if not, do you know who transmitted it?"

Lanjo made a noise that was obviously a Cygnan sigh. "It turns out there is another faction of Cygnans, from the private sector. They are more interested in a business deal than in the exchange of technology our governments envision. Capitalism and free enterprise are common denominators we share. That signal was their attempt to contact Earth, so they can begin business negotiations.

"We haven't been able to locate a planet to colonize containing a suitable atmosphere AND helium-3. They probably want to partner with an entrepreneur on Earth in the operation of a fusion reactor to process the helium-3 on the Moon. They see it as a business opportunity to capitalize on our future energy needs and are jumping on it.

"This, of course, would be in direct competition with the collaborative efforts of our mutual governments. While our entire planet is aware of the threat from the white dwarf, they are unaware of what has transpired on the Moon and my coming here, except at the highest levels. There must have been a leak somewhere for this faction to attempt to contact you at this time.

"Regarding the interaction between my government and the private sector, let's see, I believe you would say . . . 'It's complicated.' I can't predict how their efforts will affect the negotiations between our governments."

Tom's head spun at the possibilities. His anxiety over Lanjo's presence and the Cygnan businessman as an unknown quantity warred with his desire to ask about their fusion process. As he was formulating the words to ask Lanjo about fusion, the scientist spoke up again.

"Lanjo, can you guarantee there won't be any hostile action towards Earth from the Cygnan private sector?"

"It's highly unlikely," responded Lanjo, "but what is that phrase you humans are so fond of saying? 'The only certainties in life are death and taxes.' I believe Benjamin Franklin originated the expression, but my favorite author, Mark Twain, was also known to quote it."

Tom's stomach rolled again. He struggled to maintain his composure. The room broke out in excited conversation, and this time Joe made no attempt to stop it.

5

Sheila Palazzo entered her apartment, automatically scanning for the presence of a lithe furry creature, which in all likelihood was stealthily approaching her to pounce. The one good thing about having a cat for a roommate was its self-sufficient nature. That and an automatic feeder and litter box in the bathroom made for no worries when she had to work overtime. She put the bag containing a Tasty Turkey sandwich from Einstein's Bagels on the coffee table.

Sheila continued to look around, wondering when Jessup would show up. If he thought food was involved, he'd take his time to retain the element of surprise. If he didn't make an appearance soon, the smell of turkey would draw him out.

She sighed. It had been a very long day, and she was looking forward to watching a couple of Shark Tank reruns. She kicked off her flats and propped her feet up on the coffee table. Grabbing the remote, she flicked the channel to 102. It was good to be home.

Sheila leaned over and grabbed the paper bag containing her dinner, reaching inside for the sandwich. Mark Cuban was about to make an offer when a special news bulletin interrupted the show. The President of the United States was going to address the nation. She sat up a little straighter and took her first bite just as President Ferris' familiar face came onscreen.

Jessup chose that particular moment to launch his attack. His goal of a covert operation involving the turkey sandwich was thwarted by Sheila's frustrated scream.

"Jessup, get out of the way!"

She swatted at him and missed, knocking over her iced tea instead. The lid was fairly secure and as Jessup made his turkey-less getaway, Sheila righted the tea and turned her attention back to the T.V.

The president was relaxed and smiling. ". . . a historic day indeed. We have new friends, and they don't live on Earth. As a matter of fact, they don't originate from our solar system, although they are inhabitants of the Milky Way galaxy. I want to personally reassure you, they only have peaceful intentions. They opened a dialogue with us during our last trip to the Moon."

Sheila choked on the bite of turkey she had taken a moment earlier and barely managed to swallow it, dropping her sandwich unnoticed onto the floor.

"We felt it to be of paramount importance to understand their reason for contact before bringing this news to the public, as a matter of national security, thus the delay. We are not only satisfied that our new friends mean no harm, we will be embarking on a mutually beneficial relationship for both humans and aliens. I am meeting with their chief diplomat over the next week and will keep you updated on further developments. In the meantime, let's celebrate together a new era for humanity and extraterrestrial relations. Thank you."

The camera cut away, replacing the president with the CPN news anchor, Juan Gonzalez. "Now that was an unexpected revelation," he commented. "We have no further information at this time except to offer an 800 number which can be seen at the bottom of your screen. If you feel a need to talk about the president's announcement, please dial that number and someone will be happy to speak with you. We now return you to our regularly scheduled programming."

Sheila sat frozen in place. Her role as civilian mission psychologist on the Triumphant crew had been very stressful. A First Contact had never been mentioned as a possibility, and her xenophobia had been very difficult to keep under wraps during the lunar mission. She had no idea when she was debriefed and sworn to secrecy about the events on the Moon, that Lanjo would be making an appearance on Earth. But it must be him. With trembling hands, she picked up her cell phone and searched her contacts.

Jonathan Howe had seen the advantage of pursuing communications over other fields early on. By cornering the comm market, he didn't need to carve out a marketing niche—his products were a necessity for any organization to be able to operate effectively. Like Ma Bell, his company HoweTek Communications controlled almost all U.S. telecommunications. He prudently avoided the same fate of the Bell System monopoly, broken up in 1984, by paying careful attention to funding innovation and keeping consumer costs low.

Jonathan was a respected and well-liked member of the business community, with his corporate offices based in Maryland. He was also Keith Sanders's future father-in-law. His daughter Brittany was madly in love with the amiable astronaut, and Jonathan was okay with that. Keith was impossible not to like. He wished Keith's job didn't take him away from home so much, but Brittany knew what she was getting into when she said yes.

Jonathan leaned forward in his leather chair, clutching the arm rests so hard it made his hands hurt, as the president delivered his speech. Processing the president's words, he made a mental note to ask Keith about the First Contact next time he saw him. He pulled his cell phone out of his shirt pocket and called his assistant.

"Dan, did you see the president's address?"

"Sure did, Jon. Now that was unexpected!" Dan replied cheerfully. "I never thought I would see the day aliens came to town."

"Neither did I. We need to think about this. There should be some way to capitalize on it, and I want to be ready as events unfold. Put our best people on it."

"Will do, Jon. I'll keep you posted."

"Thanks. Oh, and Dan . . ."

"Yes?"

"Let's keep a low profile on this one."

"Will do, boss."

⚛

"What? Me? I'd rather not," Tom shifted uneasily under the presidential aide's direct gaze. Joe Ricinski made him uncomfortable. When he'd called to request a meeting, Tom reluctantly agreed. The guy was always watching everybody, and Tom wondered just exactly what Joe knew about him. Not that he had anything to hide, but a person liked to have some measure of privacy.

With the background check required for double top-secret clearances, Tom wouldn't have anything private anymore, including his feelings about Theresa, something he wasn't ready to examine too closely yet. Besides, what effect would this have on Stephanie? She was the only good thing that came out of his failed marriage. The last thing he wanted to do was anything that would have a negative impact on their relationship. Her mother would go ballistic if she knew he was working with an alien. She was particularly closed-minded when it came to interracial relationships. He could only imagine her response to extraterrestrials. How did he fall in love with Patricia in the first place? He certainly had a lot of empirical evidence to prove that love is blind.

"I was hoping our team would be asked to head up the effort for developing fusion technology with the Cygnans. I really want to be a part of this, but I'd much rather be just a worker. Darryl is already our team leader, and he's much better suited for that stuff."

"Darryl's a great asset and will remain team leader," Joe agreed. "We need his administrative talent to successfully facilitate what we anticipate to be a greatly accelerated timeline. Logistics will be crucial, and Darryl will be handling that. Your designation would be Cygnan liaison." He paused, weighing his next words. "We also want to be sensitive to the fact that Darryl may have to devote his attention to his daughter at any moment. We need our Cygnan liaison to be available if needed."

Joe took a sip of coffee and nodded sympathetically. "I understand your desire to focus on your research, Tom. I really do. We're fortunate to have you on the science team and we deeply value your expertise. But this is a matter that goes beyond all of us, and we need someone that not only has your core competencies, but your experience and enthusiasm. It takes a special personality to be able to deal with the unknown."

Ahhh, apparently working with aliens is not a highly sought-after position. He looked directly at Joe. "So you need a scientist/alien babysitter?"

"I wouldn't put it quite that way, but yes. We need an expert in fusion science who is also comfortable with extraterrestrial interaction. You're probably only one of ten people on the entire planet with the advanced key competencies in nuclear physics and mechanical engineering necessary for the task. You would work with the Cygnans on developing a fusion reactor for powering interstellar spaceships and processing helium-3. Modifications must be designed and implemented to make the Cygnan technology compatible with our own. You've done a good job as the SIC and your psych profile checks out okay."

That's because there were no "How do you feel about aliens" questions on the test, he thought glumly. Where did Joe get the idea he was okay with aliens anyway? He should have never agreed to be the SIC. Just because he was there during the First Contact and laughed at one of Lanjo's jokes at Camp David didn't mean he was comfortable with him. A thought popped into his head, and before he could stop himself, he blurted, "But what if they intend to harm us? How do we know they aren't hiding something?"

Joe gazed calmly back at Tom. "Like what?"

"I don't know. Some kind of powers."

Joe sighed. "All of our data indicates it'll be okay, but I have no guarantees. You're a scientist. You know that better than I do. Isn't that what you guys signed up for? Exploring the unknown?"

Tom rubbed his forehead tiredly. A lot had happened these past few days. They had kicked into high gear at the lab, anticipating the necessity for an even more focused effort on fusion technology. He looked at Joe. "It seems I don't have much choice, do I?"

"Oh, you always have a choice," Joe replied. "You just need to make the right one. Your country needs you." He got up and straightened his jacket. Reaching into the breast pocket, he pulled out a card and handed it to Tom. "Let me know what you decide. But I need to know by close of business today. We have work to do." He held out his hand, and Tom shook it.

Tom was surprised at the firm handshake and warmth in Joe's eyes. Maybe the guy wasn't so bad after all. "Will do, sir."

Joe smiled. "Call me Joe."

For the third time that morning, Tom looked down at the business card Joe had given him. It had the seal of the United States embossed on it along with Joe Ricinski, Presidential Advisor, with his direct line and his cell number. He flipped it over and reread the quote Joe had on the back:

A citizen is a political and moral agent who in fact has a shared sense of hope and responsibility to others and not just to him or herself.

–Henry Giroux

Wondering why Joe chose that particular quote, Tom reached for his cell phone. He scrolled through his contacts and tapped on Theresa. Despite their breakup, they had remained friends, although they didn't talk much since he'd married Patricia. Theresa knew Lanjo. Maybe she could help him think this one through.

Theresa picked up on the fourth ring. "Hi Tom, how's it going?"

He loved hearing her voice. Trying to keep his own from shaking and his hands steady, he replied, "It's going good, Theresa, just wanted to get your opinion on something."

"Sure, what's up?"

"Got a visit from Joe Ricinski today. He uhhh . . . he asked me to be the Cygnan liaison. He wants me to spend time with Lanjo while we work with the science team."

"That's great, Tom. Lanjo is a really nice guy. You'll like him."

"But, I'm not sure about this . . ."

"What are you not sure of?"

"I don't know. How do we know we can trust Lanjo? We don't know anything about him besides what he's told us. What if . . . what if he has powers we don't know about?"

"Powers? What kind of powers?" Tom could hear the confusion in her voice.

"I don't know. Weird stuff, I guess. Like *Guardians of the Galaxy.* Who knows?"

"Tom." Her voice changed, a familiar bare hint of exasperation entering her tone. "You are seriously comparing Lanjo to a comic character? Come on, you have to have a little bit of trust and faith." He heard the unspoken words. *Like you should have had with me.*

Tom sighed, making sure Theresa couldn't hear it through the phone. He had trusted his now ex-wife Patricia and most recently the Uber driver when he tried to help her. It hadn't worked out for him in either case. He had a feeling Theresa wouldn't understand.

"You're right, Theresa. Okay, thanks." The cell connection filled with awkward silence, and Tom finally cleared his throat. He knew Theresa was patiently waiting for him to continue, something she was very good at.

"Uh, Theresa . . ."

"Yes?"

"Uh, I just wanted to say I'm sorry about," Tom hesitated. "You know . . ."

"Yeah, I know you are. Don't worry about it." Theresa's tone softened. "Let's get a bite sometime, okay?"

Tom silently exhaled in relief. "Sure, that'd be great."

After he hung up the phone, he stared at it, knowing Joe was waiting for an answer. It was hard to have trust and faith. He had failed miserably twice with human relationships. Women from Earth were hard enough to understand—how could he even begin to understand someone from another planet?

6

The large windows in the break room allowed Tom to observe the nature trails winding away from their facility. He found it energizing to have a cup of coffee and watch rabbits, squirrels, and the occasional deer that chose to visit. Working on the George Washington University's Ashburn, Virginia campus made the drive to D.C. for meetings inconvenient, but for him it was well worth it. When the joint Cygnan-human science team was formed and he was named Cygnan liaison, it was decided to move fusion research from the Washington D.C. Institute for Nuclear Studies to here. The facility was located at the far end of the campus and out of the public eye, making it easy to put restricted access protocols in place.

"Cream and sugar?" he asked Lanjo, grabbing two mugs and pouring them both a cup of coffee.

"No thanks," Lanjo replied. "Black is fine. Coffee is one of the many accomplishments of the human race I deeply appreciate."

"Most people would agree with you. Many humans require coffee in the morning to function well."

Tom handed Lanjo the mug he had poured. Lanjo rotated it around in his hand and a puzzled expression crossed his face. He held up the coffee mug, showing Tom what was imprinted on the side: *Instant human, just add coffee.* Lanjo hiccuped, and Tom chuckled. "My daughter knows how dependent I am on coffee. That was my Father's Day gift last year."

"Yes, Father's Day." Lanjo nodded knowingly. "I studied your cultural phenomenon of specific days defined as days of celebration for different occasions: Mother's Day, Grandparent's Day, and others. I found it puzzling that special days had to be assigned for people deserving of recognition to receive gratitude. Cygnans think expressing gratitude is a daily opportunity. It was the conclusion of my professor in my cultural traditions class that these special days were a stroke of marketing genius driven by the greeting card companies, as a way to increase profits."

"It's a sound theory," Tom concurred. "While it is nice to be recognized, I agree it doesn't require a special day to do it. However, some humans get very upset if you forget them on their day. I speak from experience." He laughed.

"Interesting," Lanjo replied, peering closely at Tom's expression. Tom's smile did not reach his eyes and Lanjo changed the subject. "I noticed you were riding a bicycle yesterday. It looks like a very enjoyable mode of transportation. We don't have bicycles on Lanzeron. I always wanted to learn how to ride one."

Tom's smile deepened. "Yeah, I love bicycling and try to go riding every chance I get, which hasn't been much lately. I was supposed to ride in the Hotter'N Hell last year, but work got in the way."

They were sitting at the table with the best view of the outside, while sipping their coffee. Lanjo started to ask what a Hotter'N Hell was, but some birds distracted Tom. "Look. Those birds by the bushes are a pair of Eastern Bluebirds. We don't see them around here very often." They watched the two smallish blue-colored birds flitting around, looking for insects. "The female has the duller colors."

The female was having a hard time. While her companion could fly about easily, she had a feather sticking up at an odd angle on her left wing, hindering her ability to take off.

"It looks like the female is having trouble," Lanjo commented, his expression unreadable.

"Yes, her feather looks like it's been mangled somehow." Tom frowned. "I wish we could help her. If she can't gain altitude, she'll be cat food before the day is over."

"But we can." Lanjo moved his chair closer to the window, peering intently at the bird as she attempted to lift herself into the air. She was unsuccessful, barely managing to maintain a straight enough trajectory to avoid running into a tree trunk. Lanjo made a soft *shhhhh* sound as he continued to stare at the bird, his eyebrows furrowed with intense concentration.

Tom followed Lanjo's gaze and froze, unable to believe what he was seeing. The mangled feather was no longer mangled. The female lifted her wing and extended it, showing the previously damaged feather lying smoothly amidst the other wing feathers in the correct position. She lifted it up and down cautiously at first, then took a running leap and extended both wings in the air, becoming fully airborne.

Lanjo turned back to Tom and grimaced, but Tom was no longer smiling. He was grimacing in return, his face twisted with the human emotion of strong disapproval. Lanjo reached out to touch Tom to reassure him, but the human quickly backed away.

"What's wrong, Tom? The bird is okay now."

"What did you do?"

Lanjo could hear Tom's heart racing and the human had turned pale. From Lanjo's studies, he knew his current physical appearance indicated Tom's condition had become distressed. "I just helped the bird, Tom. That's all. I straightened her feather and moved it to its proper place. I caused her no discomfort."

"But how—"

"Telekinesis. I thought your species were familiar with psychic abilities." Lanjo paused, thinking hard. "I'm not sure why you're so upset, unless you're relating my ability to the horror novel *Carrie* by Stephen King. Please Tom, let me assure you, Stephen King's imaginary character is just that—imaginary. I would never harm anyone."

"Stay away from me. I've gotta get outta here," Tom stuttered and ran out the break room door and into the lab. He brushed by Darryl, who gave him a puzzled look, but Tom kept going. Darryl paused, noticing Lanjo in the break room. He walked over to where the alien was sitting, his shoulders slumped and an unfamiliar expression on his face.

"Hey, Lanjo, are you okay?" Darryl pulled up a chair at the table.

"I'm fine, Darryl, but I'm afraid I frightened Tom." Lanjo looked down, unsure of how to explain what had just transpired. Both bluebirds were flitting back and forth, feasting on the evening bugs as dusk approached.

"What happened? It's not like Tom to lose it like that."

"Well, it seems my attempt to help our feathered friends out there resulted in that reaction. I used my limited ability to move matter to disengage a twisted feather from the female bird's wing. I smoothed it out so it would lay properly and enable her to fly again."

Darryl's eyes widened. "Telekinesis?" His voice rose an octave.

"You used telekinesis? Do you have any other powers we don't know about?"

Lanjo hesitated, his eyebrows quivering. He had not predicted this type of reaction from his human acquaintances. After all, Earth literature and entertainment were full of stories that included psychic abilities. It seems he had underestimated the fearful response that it provoked. Something to file away and consider later, since it might relate to other areas he may have misunderstood. It seems reality and the expression of reality through entertainment media may be further apart than what he first thought. His paper, "Does Culture Dictate Entertainment on Earth or Does Entertainment on Earth Influence Culture," may have some holes. He'd better wait before submitting it to the *Journal of Xenosociology.*

"No, and my ability to move objects is very limited."

Darryl shifted in his chair and frowned. "So, how does it work?"

Lanjo grimaced slightly. "I'm not sure. I am a xenosociologist, not a physicist. What I do know is that about ten percent of our population is born with this ability. It has something to do with our genetic heritage and a slight variation in the way our brains are structured. I can tell you the ability is very limited. We can only exercise it in our line of sight and the farther away, the less certain the results. Whatever mechanism allows us to amplify our control to the cellular level and beyond is unknown, but we can't separate things that are already joined, only move them."

"Okay, I got it," Darryl replied, nodding. "So here is what I think happened to Tom. The fact that you could do telekinesis was probably disturbing to him, but it wasn't what triggered his running away response. It was the thought you might have other powers."

It was Lanjo's turn to look puzzled. "What other powers?"

Darryl shrugged. "I don't know." He met Lanjo's eyes and wondered how to fully comprehend them. The brown depths were warm and non-threatening, but definitely not human. "What powers do you have that we don't know about? Can you read minds?"

"Can I what?" Lanjo asked, confused.

"Read minds?" Darryl shot back.

"No, of course not. No Cygnan has that ability. No other psychic power either. Only the ten percent of us who are able to do limited telekinesis."

"Okay." Darryl relaxed. "That's a good thing, given Tom's reaction to your telekinesis. We don't want mass hysteria because humans think you can invade their minds."

"Yes, I see your point." Even for an alien, Lanjo looked utterly dejected. "So how can I fix things with Tom? Not only is it imperative for us to work together for the success of our mission, I really like him."

Darryl found Lanjo's feelings of friendship towards a person not of his own species refreshingly touching. He rubbed the back of his neck. "Don't worry, Lanjo. Just give him a little space. I'll talk to him." He patted the alien's shoulder. "It'll be all right."

Good thing Lanjo can't read minds, Darryl thought. He had no idea if it would be all right or not. He looked out the window to where the bluebirds had been searching for their dinner. Neither one of them could be seen.

7

"It shouldn't be too hard," Stephanie said out loud in an attempt to reassure herself. It'd been three whole weeks since her dad brought her back home. It wasn't fair of her mom to keep her from seeing him. Stephanie missed him terribly, and not only that, he was on the greatest adventure of all time. She took a deep breath and put her foot on the ledge outside her bedroom window. Carefully placing one foot after the other, she maintained her grip on the white lattice for balance and started making her way down the wooden railing.

Once she cleared the gardenia bushes, she would be able to jump into the flower garden, and its softer surface would help break her fall. She would have to make sure to miss the azaleas, or her mom would kill her. She got to the end of the ledge, took a moment to gauge the distance, and made a small leap, landing right in the middle of her mom's beloved flowers. So much for not getting killed. She had a feeling once her mom found out she'd run away, the azaleas would be the least of her problems.

Brushing the dirt off her shins, she headed to the shed where she'd left her bike instead of bringing it into the garage. Her dad always said, "Planning ahead is the first rule of a good manager." Not that he was a manager, but he said it was good advice for anybody.

Thinking about that made her miss him even more. It was hard to believe her dad was the Cygnan liaison. It was all over the news that he'd been chosen to work with the alien named Lanjo and their science team to develop a fusion reactor. She knew it was more than just the overtime that prevented her from seeing him. She used to get to visit her dad at his work all the time. Her mom didn't know she saw their texts. She could still see them in her mind:

Can Steph come up to the lab for a visit?

No!

But it's the opportunity of a lifetime.

NO. Absolutely not!

Please reconsider. I haven't seen her in weeks.

If you allow our daughter near that alien, I promise you will lose ALL of your visitation rights. You know I can do that.

I don't think you are being reasonable. I guess I have no choice. Alright.

It was so unfair!

She opened the door to the shed slowly so it wouldn't creak. Her eyes took a moment to adjust to the darkened interior, and she looked in the corner where she had propped up her bike. It had taken her a while to get used to no kickstand on the Trek 7.3 FX her dad had bought her for her birthday. Serious bikers, he had informed her, don't use kickstands. Seemed weird, but whatever. She grasped the handlebars and turned it towards the door. A sliver of moonlight cast a dim line on the ground for her to follow, and she wheeled the bike out of the shed. As she cleared the doorway, a furry blur streaked across the lawn towards her. She didn't need any additional light to know it was Lela.

"Oh no, Lela. How did you get out?" The puppy jumped around her legs, licking her ankles as she wheeled the bike towards the back gate. "You need to stay here, Lela," Stephanie told the puppy in a firm voice. Lela barked in response, causing Stephanie to drop the bike and scoop her up. "Shush, Lela. You'll wake Mom and that'll mess up everything. You gotta be quiet!" She looked around, trying to decide what to do about her puppy. If she left her behind in the yard, she was sure to start yipping and barking, and Stephanie needed time to make her escape. She sighed. "Okay, Lela. You win. Just be quiet."

Stephanie went back into the shed and rooted around until she found what she was looking for—an old backpack she took on family camping trips. It was roomy enough for a Lhasa Apso pup. Lela was used to Stephanie taking her places in an oversized purse. If Stephanie put her in the backpack with the top part open, that should work. She was sort of glad she was taking Lela along, since she didn't know how long she would be gone. It would be nice to have some company on her adventure.

"Come on Lela, hop in." Lela jumped in like an old pro. Fortunately for Stephanie, a purse and a backpack were apparently the same thing to a canine. She lifted the backpack and carefully slid it over her shoulders, slowly closed the shed door, and getting her bike from where she'd left it laying on the ground, she was finally on her way.

Should she ride her bike to her dad's house or to the lab at George Washington University? He probably wouldn't be home. She knew from past experience he kept a cot at the lab to sleep on when he was working on a hot project or was nearing a deadline. She'd seen on the news that his new lab even had a dorm for the science team. From her calculations, it would be twenty-two miles to get there. It was a good thing he had moved to the Virginia campus. She wouldn't have been able to bike ride to the lab in D.C.

Before the divorce, she and her dad rode their bikes all of the time. Last year they'd even went on a thirty-mile ride together. She'd never ridden more than a few blocks alone before, but she knew she could do the twenty-two miles. It was late at night, so overheating wasn't a threat. She had two water bottles to stay hydrated like her dad taught her. It was strange riding at night alone, and she found Lela's presence comforting as she pedaled away the miles. Thankfully the roads were quiet. While she was out past curfew, luck was with her and she was able to travel unobserved.

Two hours later, she pedaled through the gates of George Washington University. Like many college campuses, it was a 24-hour facility, and a bicyclist traversing its streets at an odd hour didn't attract any attention. The university was a giant maze of buildings, but she had a campus map and knew where to go. She rode down George Washington Boulevard past the student services building. She pedaled by the Colonial Cafe, a reminder of how hungry she was. It wouldn't be open for a few more hours, so she opened a granola bar she had stashed in her jacket pocket. She took a bite, chewing but not really tasting it, as she thought about what to do next.

Her dad worked in a restricted area. First, she would have to figure out how to get in, so she could see him. She continued down George Washington Boulevard and made a right on Bridgefield Way. It changed names to Research Place where the guard station would be. It would probably be smarter to detour to the woods by the Potomac River, hide her bike there, and sneak through the fence somehow. Just as she began to veer off towards the woods, Lela gave a little yip. On second thought, she'd have to forget this stealth stuff. Lela was sure to give her away, especially when she spotted the security guard. Stephanie would just have to bite the bullet and take the straightforward approach. After all, she had the right to ask for her dad, didn't she? Never mind it was about 2:00 in the morning.

Stephanie slowly pedaled down the street to the entrance of the guard station, shielding her eyes when the security guard shined his flashlight towards her. Just as she predicted, Lela started barking. "Lela, shush!" Stephanie hissed. Lela whined, but quieted down. Stephanie got off her bike and walked it up to the barricaded entrance.

"Can I help you, miss?" the security guard asked. He wasn't alarmed. The scientists kept all kinds of late hours. He peered more closely at her. "Aren't you awfully young to be out this late at night? Stay right there." He stepped out of the guard shack, reaching out to take a handle of the bicycle to help Stephanie steady it.

Lela was not happy about his proximity and resumed barking from her place in the backpack. "Lela, I said be quiet!" Stephanie gritted her teeth in frustration. "You'll wake the whole place up."

The security guard waited patiently for Stephanie to collect herself. "So what business do you have here?" he inquired. Stephanie noticed the badge on the front of his shirt pocket, the polished metal shining in the moonlight.

"I'm here to see my dad, Tom Whitaker," Stephanie replied. There, she'd said it. She knew this was a top-secret clearance facility and her request might be denied. It all depended upon the security guard's judgment. She gave him her best innocent, big, hazel-eyed smile.

"Tom's your dad?" The security guard smiled back. "He's a nice guy. He's up here practically 24/7. I'll see if I can find him. You gotta stay right here though. This is a secured area. No one without proper clearance can enter."

Stephanie breathed a sigh of relief. "Yes, sir."

Wishing she had a kickstand, she laid her bike on its side and slid the backpack off, dumping Lela unceremoniously to the ground.

"Her mother's going to kill me," Tom muttered, unable to control a smile at the sight of his daughter. Lanjo was a few feet behind him, having followed him outside when Vic informed them of Stephanie's arrival. Tom rubbed his eyes and thanked the security guard, then focused his attention on Stephanie.

Lanjo interrupted. "I hope that is an idiom, Tom. I would hate to see your early demise."

"I hope so, too," Tom replied. He raised his eyebrows at his daughter. "So? What on Earth were you thinking?"

Lanjo turned his head and grimaced, trying to hide his amusement. Humans were awfully fond of that phrase. You would think they went off-planet frequently, considering how often they stipulated "on Earth" in their questioning.

"Dad, I missed you! I haven't gotten to see you in almost a month and it's just not fair!"

Lela sat pressed against Stephanie's ankles. She yipped in agreement, then looked towards Lanjo, took a few steps in his direction, and whined. She sat and wagged her tail slowly like a pendulum.

Apparently meeting an alien did not disturb her in the least. Lanjo didn't seem to bother Stephanie either, but then, his face would be familiar from all of the television news bulletins.

Tom hugged Stephanie then stood back, putting his hands on her shoulders. He gazed at his daughter affectionately. "I understand, kiddo. I really do. I've missed you, too. Unfortunately, I have to respect your mother's wishes, and she has expressly stated she does not want you to be with me during this project. She feels that is in your best interest, and while I don't agree, she gets to call the shots."

"But what about what I want?" Stephanie replied, fighting back tears.

"I'm sorry, Steph. It's just the way it's gotta be, for now. You know I'm always here for you, no matter what." He took his thumb and wiped away a tear that had escaped and was rolling down her cheek. "I tell you what. You're here now, so let's make the most of it. I'm not about to call your mom at three in the morning, and she hasn't texted me yet, so she doesn't know you're gone. We can hang out for a few hours. Did you sleep in again this morning?"

Stephanie looked down and grinned sheepishly. "Yeah."

"All right then, you should be able to stay up for a while." Tom turned to the security guard standing off to the side. "I know it's against regs, Vic, but I haven't gotten to see my daughter in weeks. I can leave with her and go home, but it would be a lot nicer if we could hang out here. We'll just go for a walk along the Potomac. If anyone has a problem with that, I'll take full responsibility. What d'ya say?"

Vic scratched his head and thought a moment. "Since you're outside, it shouldn't be a big deal. Go for it. Just don't go into any indoor areas with restricted access."

Tom nodded. "Thanks, Vic. I owe you one."

Tom was still mentally processing what he'd felt when Lanjo healed the bird yesterday afternoon. While he was still deeply disturbed by it, he deliberately put it aside. He wasn't sure how he was going to respond moving forward, but for now he wanted to make every second of this unexpected visit with his daughter count. The morning with all of its problems would come way too soon. He might as well enjoy his time with Stephanie, while he could. He noted Stephanie's Trek bicycle on the ground. "So you rode here, huh?"

"Yup," Stephanie replied proudly.

"Impressive," Tom replied. "Not very smart, considering, but impressive." He turned to Lanjo, who was waiting patiently. "You can go on back to bed now, Lanjo. Stephanie is fine."

Lanjo grimaced. "If it's okay with you, Tom, I would like to stay awhile and visit. Your daughter is the first human young I have met. This is a wonderful experience for me."

Tom sighed. Apparently Lanjo didn't get his hint, or chose not to. Lanjo was a xenosociologist after all. Studying a human family group would be high on his wish list, and with the work at hand, he had not been given the opportunity.

"Okay Lanjo. I guess that'll be all right. Vic, we're going to take a walk down by the Potomac. It's a beautiful night, so let's not waste it." With that, he turned towards the woods and started walking. He'd give Lanjo a few minutes to get to know Stephanie. He headed for a picnic table where they would be able to talk. Staying outside would also limit the number of people aware of Stephanie's unauthorized visit.

Lanjo and Stephanie looked at each other, then hurried to catch up, Lela trotting alongside.

"So what's it like on your planet?" Stephanie asked Lanjo.

"You would be surprised, Stephanie. It is not as different from Earth as you might think. The atmosphere is a little thinner here, but certainly within our tolerance. We have family units similar to Earth, although probably closer to Middle Eastern culture with a more extended family structure." Lanjo sighed. "It's such a huge topic, I don't really know where to begin."

Stephanie nodded, thinking. "How about pets? Do you have pets, like Lela?"

"While we have deep feelings for all of the life forms that inhabit our planet, pets are a uniquely human phenomenon. We would not think to live in such close proximity with them." He looked down at Lela and grimaced. "However, if I had a life form like your Lela come live with me, I could see how that would enhance my life experience."

She had heard commentators explaining Lanjo's "smile" and smiled in return. Wow, her friends weren't going to believe this. She thought she would only get to see her dad. Meeting Lanjo was completely unexpected. And, she thought wryly, exactly what her mom was trying to prevent. She didn't care though. He seemed nice, and he liked Lela, so he was okay with her. She had seen weirder characters at Comic-Con.

They stayed on the wooded path, which was easy to discern in the moonlight. As they approached the river, Tom called over his shoulder, "Be careful, the banks are rather steep at this spot." He barely finished his warning when Lela took off, speeding by him after some prey that only she could see. They had probably startled a rabbit or squirrel, and Lela thought she was much bigger than she really was.

Before Tom could stop her, Stephanie was in full pursuit of her wayward pup. Tom yelled, "Nooooooo," clenching his fists. Moments later, both Stephanie and Lela tumbled down the steep bank of the river. Somehow, Stephanie managed to grab Lela with one hand while holding precariously onto a branch sticking out of the bank with the other. The branch didn't look too sturdy, and a mild landslide caused the ground around her to become a slippery precipice.

Tom's face reddened, sweat dripping down his forehead. How could he save his baby girl? She was hanging precariously onto the branch, the river crashing below. "Hang on, Steph!" he called out, trying to keep his voice calm. The bank wouldn't bear his weight and there wasn't much time. He didn't bother to tell Stephanie to let go of Lela because he knew she would refuse. Acid rose in his throat as he desperately scanned the bank, searching for a way to reach her. Tom moved forward hesitantly, his foot slipping on the shale. A rock dislodged and ricocheted down the slope, disappearing into the rapids.

"*Shhhhhh.*"

Lanjo squatted on the ground next to him.

"*Shhhhhh.*"

Lanjo stared intently at Stephanie, fluid—sweat?—beading on his forehead.

Tom looked back at Stephanie holding onto the branch, then back at Lanjo. He could barely breathe. *How could he save Stephanie? Should he jump in and risk them both drowning? Trust this alien who'd said earlier his ability to move objects with his mind was limited? How limited was it?* His throat hurt. Torn by indecision, he began to pray. *Please God, save my little girl.*

8

Lanjo lay unconscious on the riverbank, his clothes soaked with sweat. Stephanie and Lela stood a few feet to the side of him. Stephanie was trembling, but seemed otherwise unaffected. Panting, Lela walked over and nosed Lanjo's still body. Tom grabbed Stephanie and hugged her fiercely, then gently pushed her back. He dropped to the ground next to the alien who had just saved his daughter from certain injury, maybe even death. Tom could see his chest rising and falling, but couldn't tell if he was injured. Lanjo had assured him that Cygnans were not that different from humans biologically, but Tom had no idea what to do to help him.

Stephanie put her hand on her dad's shoulder. "I'm sorry, Dad. When Lela took off, all I could think of was saving her before she fell into the river. I didn't mean to hurt Lanjo. He saved me, Dad." This time Stephanie made no attempt to stop the tears. "I hope he's okay. He saved me!"

"Yes, he did. I don't know how he did it, but the important thing is he did."

Tom tried to recall his first aid training from so many years ago.

He cautiously shook Lanjo's shoulder and uttered the opening salvo from his long-ago CPR class, "Are you okay?" He got no response. At least Lanjo was breathing. Tom barely remembered how to do CPR on a human, let alone an alien.

He took a breath to calm himself. Lanjo wouldn't have any broken bones since he had not fallen far when he passed out. He gently extended Lanjo's body and carefully scooped him up. The guard station wasn't far.

"Stephanie, grab my cell phone and dial the guard station. It's in my contacts. Vic should answer. Ask him to call Darryl. Tell him there's been an accident and Lanjo needs medical attention. Hurry!"

Stephanie scrambled to make the call as they walked rapidly back towards the lab entrance, Tom doing his best not to jar Lanjo as they marched along the wooded path. Lanjo's body was strangely cool considering the amount of energy he had just exerted, and thankfully much lighter than Tom expected. It didn't take long for them to enter the clearing that bordered the lab. Vic was waiting alertly and hurried to help Tom carry Lanjo to the guard shack. It wasn't equipped to accommodate a prone body, so he grabbed a couple of blankets and spread them on the soft grass behind the shack. They carefully placed Lanjo on the blankets, hoping to see some movement. The alien's eyes remained closed, and he didn't react to being laid down.

Vic disappeared inside the guard shack and came back with a bottle of water and a roll of paper towels. Tom tore off a towel, poured some water on it, and knelt next to Lanjo. Not knowing what else to do, he began to gently bathe Lanjo's face and forehead and prayed he would be okay. Lanjo's skin felt cool to the touch, and his breathing was slow and steady. Relief flooded over Tom when he saw the flashing lights in the distance headed their way.

"Yes, Dan, what is it?" the CEO of HoweTek Communications had just started to doze and allowed irritation towards his assistant color his voice.

"Turn on the news, Jonathan. You'll want to see this."

Jonathan punched speakerphone and picked up the remote sitting on the nightstand. He clicked it to CPN. A news crew was streaming live in front of Inova Loudoun Hospital in Leesburg, Virginia.

"The word is, Lanjo has entered a state of hibernation," Dan said. "They expect him to come out of it, but it could take days. Seems he rescued some kid that almost fell into the Potomac. This just might buy us the time we need to make contact with the private sector aliens transmitting the WOW! signal that SETI managed to isolate."

"So where are we with contacting them?" Jonathan asked.

"Interstellar communication is just as tough as we thought. I don't know how they amped their transmission to reach us so quickly, but our guys have ruled out quantum entanglement as a possibility. Tachyons would be a violation of the Lorentz invariance and create problems of causality paradoxes, so they are a no go. We think it may have been a wormhole, since it has to be faster than light to get to us soon enough to do any good. If they already have one in place and we can get the coordinates, our communication problem may be solved. You may even want to change the company's name to Galactic Communications," Dan joked.

"Hmmmm . . . it looks like your call was on target, Dan. I really thought funding SETI was a long shot. Having access ahead of the government was a good move."

"Yeah, it just might pay off. Speaking of the government, Joe Ricinski called. He wants a meeting."

Jonathan sighed. When Joe Ricinski says he wants a meeting, it's not a request. "Okay, put him on the schedule."

Sheila waved as the Secretary of Energy entered the coffee shop and headed for her booth near the back. "Thanks for meeting me so quickly," she said. "How's Mary Beth and the kids?"

"Everyone's fine, Sheila," Ray responded brusquely. "But I don't think you asked me to meet you just to talk about family."

Sheila sighed. "Of course not, but I can still ask about my cousin, can't I?"

"Sorry, it's been a stressful week and I'm short on time. What's up?"

"What's up is that I had no idea Lanjo was going to be permitted to come to Earth after our meeting on the Moon. When I was the botanist and team psychologist for the Moon landing, we all returned in the Triumphant, and he wasn't on board. How did he get here?" She tugged at her scarf. "And why is he here? I thought you were pushing for no involvement with aliens. When CPN interviewed you, you said, and I quote, 'We have to find our own solutions to Earth's energy problems, not some extraterrestrial agenda that could affect the future of our planet in a negative way.'"

Ray held up a hand to stop her verbal barrage. "Regarding your first question, Sheila, it's classified. Yes, yes, I know you have top secret clearance, but that information has been branded 'need to know' only. And it really doesn't change anything. Lanjo is here, and we have to deal with it."

"Exactly. That's why I called. What are you going to do?"

"Well, last I checked, the United States Secretary of Energy still has some say in how we solve our energy problems. I'm not convinced Lanjo and his buddies have our best interests in mind. Why would they? I'm not buying their story about needing our help either. Ronald Reagan was right when he said how quickly our differences would vanish if we were facing an alien threat from outside our world. We need to band together in order to guard against any threats that may surface. I think the best thing for all concerned is to send Lanjo on his way, but it will take a while to bring the president around."

Sheila's face went pale and her hands clammy. An image of E.T. flitted through her mind. That alien creature was so creepy, it freaked her out just thinking about it. She remembered having nightmares when she watched the movie as a little girl. Lanjo was more humanoid, but he still freaked her out. "You don't think Lanjo is really a threat, do you?"

"At this point, I don't know anything. But why take the chance?" He stood up. "Sorry I can't stay. I have a meeting on the Hill in an hour. Just sit tight, Sheila. I assure you we won't allow aliens to dictate our energy policy. Not if I have any say in the matter, and my office can bring a lot of pressure to bear."

"Okay, Ray. Thanks for making the time. Give my love to Mary Beth and the kids."

"Will do."

Sheila sat mindlessly stirring her coffee with her spoon as she considered Ray's words. Her anxiety escalated and she reached for the Valium she had tucked into her purse before leaving her apartment. An idea began to form, and she tried to squash it. She never dreamed she would ever consider rebelling against the government, but somebody had to do something.

9

"Actually, it's quite simple." Lanjo sat up in his hospital bed. "It's the same technique I used to help the bird."

Tom insisted on a visit as soon as Lanjo regained consciousness. "I didn't know telekinesis works that way." He rubbed his chin thoughtfully. "I thought it was for manipulation of matter with much less mass."

"You're correct, Tom. It usually is. Do you remember that story all over the news last month, about the woman who was able to lift a Toyota Camry up in the air to save her child? Everyone said it was a miracle. Acts of superhuman strength that seemingly violate the laws of physics have happened many times. The essential ingredient is always motivation, such as an intensely strong desire to save a life. The only problem with releasing that much mental energy for a Cygnan is we can exhaust ourselves physically and, worst case scenario, strain our brain's neurotransmissions past their breaking point. If that happens, normal brain function would not be recoverable. Fortunately for me, the latter did not occur."

Tom looked steadily at Lanjo's warm brown eyes, and he returned the gaze without wavering. Tom finally looked down. "I was afraid you would read my mind, you know," he mumbled. "Not that I have any deep dark secrets, but just the thought freaked me out."

"I know, and I'm sorry. Darryl explained to me about the human anxiety that often surrounds psychic abilities. I made the unfortunate mistake of assuming that it wouldn't bother you." He waited until Tom looked back up and continued. "But you also need to know, Tom, no Cygnan has that power. Telekinesis is the limit of our abilities. Even if I did have more—which I don't," he rushed to add—"I would never impose myself on you or anyone else without your permission."

"I know that now. I'm sorry about the misunderstanding when you healed the bird. Actually, that was a very cool thing you did. And I can't thank you enough for saving Stephanie's life. My daughter means everything to me." Tom leaned forward and held out his hand. Lanjo gripped it in his own slender hand firmly. This time the extra digit didn't even bother Tom. A thought crossed his mind as they shook, and he made a quick decision. Now was as good a time as any to extend a little trust and faith.

"Hey Lanjo, ever read the American classic, *The Adventures of Huckleberry Finn?*"

"By Mark Twain? It was required reading for my undergraduate degree in Literature of Earth. One of the more entertaining selections, I might add. I found *The Grapes of Wrath*, another required text, a much more difficult read, particularly regarding the historical context and thematic undertones."

"Yeah." Tom nodded. "That book is very complex. I can see why you prefer Huck Finn. Mark Twain is definitely more my speed, too. Do you remember how Tom and Huck became blood brothers?"

"Sure, I found that . . . fascinating. It was to mark that their relationship had become one that was committed in the same fashion family members are committed to each other—correct?"

"Yes, and it's a custom that still remains today, although we don't have to cut ourselves and mix our blood. Which, considering the circumstances, probably wouldn't be a great idea. We don't know if our microbes are compatible, and I would probably get fired if anyone found out. But the principle is the same. Adoption is taking a person into your family."

Tom paused and gathered his thoughts. "You saved my daughter, and I can't begin to express how grateful I am. I've been thinking about how to thank you. We got off to a shaky start because of my unwarranted fears. I'd like to change that. I want to invite you into our family." He looked intently at the now-familiar eyes of the alien who saved his daughter's life at the risk of his own. "Would you agree to become my brother and Uncle Lanjo to my daughter Stephanie?"

For once, Lanjo was silent. When he had first discovered his passion for xenosociology, he never imagined he would actually be able to visit the cultures he dreamed about. Being invited to be a part of a family was beyond his wildest expectations. His eyebrows began to quiver vigorously and he hastily stilled them. He gazed back at Tom and slowly replied, "I would be honored."

Tom broke into a smile and reached into his pocket. He pulled out a colorful bracelet made of thread and offered it to Lanjo.

Lanjo accepted it and examined it curiously. "This is very beautiful, but what is it for?"

"It's a friendship bracelet. It's a tradition, especially among humans Stephanie's age, to give a bracelet to another person as a symbol of their friendship. Stephanie made it for you."

He didn't think he had ever seen Lanjo grimace so big. "When can I see her?" he asked eagerly.

"Well, that's a bit complicated. Her mother isn't thrilled at the thought of her interacting with alien cultures. However, I think you may have scored major brownie points by saving her life."

"Brownie points?" Lanjo asked, eyebrows raised.

"Uh, yeah, another idiom." Tom chuckled.

Lanjo did a quick scan of his *Human English Idioms Dictionary*. "A hypothetical currency earned for doing a good deed," he quoted. "Its origins are found in the achievements of a group called Brownies, the youngest members of the Girl Scout organization." He paused. "So how does one cash in on their currency?"

"Well, that's hypothetical too, especially with my ex-wife. It's hard to explain. Let's just say we might have a better chance at Steph visiting the lab since you rescued her, but her mother doesn't always respond logically. She thinks she is acting in Stephanie's best interests. We'll have to wait and see. I have a feeling Stephanie will be able to convince her. She can't wait to see you again. She's been very worried about you." He laughed. "Raising kids and knowing the right thing to do is much harder than designing a working fusion reactor!"

Lanjo hiccupped in return. "We think so, too."

"Oh, by the way, the official story is that you saved Stephanie by grabbing her in time before the bank crumbled, but in doing so you slid and hit a tree trunk. The injury, although minor, triggered a healing mechanism in your species, sending you into a semi-hibernative state while your body healed."

Puzzled, Lanjo asked, "Why the fabrication?"

"Remember my reaction to your telekinesis demonstration with the bird? I had already met you, and while I had some misgivings, at least I had started to like you. Just think of the effect that knowledge of your psychic ability would have on the parts of our population that are xenophobic and haven't had the opportunity to get to know you."

"You're right of course," Lanjo agreed sadly.

"It's all right. People will come around once they see you really don't mean any harm and this is a mutually beneficial relationship. And . . . I have exciting news. While you were asleep, we received the go-head for the Cygnan scientists to join us at the Institute for Nuclear Studies. We're still waiting for final approval from Congress, but it looks like you and I will be leading the Cygnan-human initiative. Darryl will be the official chief administrator on the project, and we'll lead the team building the fusion reactor. A separate team will start working on the spaceship design once the fusion reactor specs are nailed down. I know you aren't a fusion scientist, but everyone agrees we need you to be the intercultural contact, if our teams are going to be able to work together successfully. Like *Remember the Titans*. You are going to be our Coach Boone."

Tom had a gut feeling Lanjo would know what he was talking about. He and Stephanie had watched that movie many times together.

Lanjo's eyebrows quivered in acknowledgment and the two friends grinned at each other. After a moment, Tom's smile began to fade as a thought struck him. "Now we just need to figure out a way to get Vic off the hook. They want to charge him with dereliction of duty. He shouldn't of allowed Stephanie on site, and it's my fault."

"That's easy, Tom. I'll make it a stipulation of our continued work for all charges to be dropped and he be reinstated to his former post. Discreetly of course."

"Thanks, Lanjo."

"No problem, Tom."

"Oh, one other thing. Rumor has it Jonathan Howe, the CEO for HoweTek Communications, is attempting to use SETI to establish a communications link with someone on Lanzeron. Do you know anything about that?"

Lanjo's expression shifted into a Cygnan frown. "No, but that's not good news. It looks like someone on Lanzeron is trying to," he paused and scanned his *Human English Idioms Dictionary*, 'beat us to the punch.' I was afraid this would happen after SETI received the WOW! signal."

"Do you think they can?"

"I don't know. It depends on who it is and what resources they have access to."

Tom nodded. "Okay, I'll let Darryl know your take on that. Try to get some rest. We need you back at the lab."

Lanjo grimaced. "I'll do my best."

For the first time in quite a while, Tom felt lighthearted. A burden he had not fully acknowledged lifted from his shoulders during his visit with Lanjo. He whistled as he walked. Maybe he would go for a bike ride when he got home, if he had enough daylight.

When he caught sight of a person coming alongside of him out of the corner of his eye, he didn't think much of it. Several people were striding through the crowded hospital parking lot. Then a stack of papers were slapped into his chest. The voice in his ear telling him, "You've been served," slammed down on his shoulders, as a feeling of dread crawled through his stomach. He flashed back to when he'd received his divorce papers, and acid rose in his throat. By the time he turned around, all he could see was the back of a man clad in business casual clothes walking quickly away. He looked down at the top sheet.

Order of Protection

Articles 4, 5,6,8, 10 of the Family Court Act

Petitioner: Patricia Whitaker

Respondent: Lanjo Verfabtholar Frastero Kolanpatchibe

Contact: Thomas Whitaker

The respondent is hereby notified that any intentional violation of this order is a criminal violation and can result in your immediate arrest or issuance of an arrest warrant.

A petition under Articles 4, 5, 6, 8, 10 of the Family Court Act has been filed. The respondent having not been present during Court and this Court after hearing determined good cause has been shown for the issuance of this Order.

Now therefore, it is hereby ordered that Lanjo Verfabtholar Frastero Kolanpatchibe will observe the following conditions of behavior: Stay at least 100 yards away from Stephanie Whitaker, Stephanie Whitaker's residence, and Stephanie Whitaker's school. Abstain from any form of communication with Stephanie Whitaker.

Tom's chest tightened and his back stiffened. He scrubbed his hand over his face. He had hoped Lanjo saving Stephanie's life would have softened Patricia's attitude towards aliens, but instead she was more xenophobic than ever, obviously blaming him for what had happened. *After everything Lanjo had been through, how could he tell him that he couldn't see Stephanie?*

10

Now that Lanjo was released from the hospital, he couldn't wait to go see Stephanie and thank her for the friendship bracelet. He looked down at his wrist at the now-familiar multi-colored threads and grimaced. He was back at GWU, but had not started back to work. The doctors thought he needed a few more days to rest, so he spent his time walking around and enjoying the abundant nature surrounding their facilities. At Lanjo's request, Vic had been reinstated as the night guard. He'd called Vic a little while ago and asked if he could come to the dorm and give him a ride.

Lanjo was glad the round-the-clock guard detail at the hospital had been dismissed. Since GWU was a secure facility, the government deemed they were no longer needed. Vic's familiar jeep rounded the bend, and Lanjo eagerly stepped forward to meet one of his favorite humans. He'd always enjoyed the guard's easy-going demeanor, and he was grateful Vic helped care for him on the night he'd rescued Stephanie. The two had become friends, and from Lanjo's study of human behavior, it wasn't unusual to ask a friend for a ride.

Vic jumped out of the jeep with a huge smile and reached out to shake Lanjo's hand. Grimacing, Lanjo returned Vic's handshake enthusiastically.

"Lanjo, it's so good to see you. You had us all scared for a while."

"I was a little scared, too," Lanjo admitted. "That was the first time I'd expended that much energy. It really isn't known how much we can push the limits of our brain without causing irreversible damage, so I'm very fortunate."

"We all are, Lanj," Vic replied, slapping Lanjo on the back. Lanjo never quite understood why a gesture of affection included mispronouncing someone's name or a physical action such as hitting the other person, but he knew those were often done and grimaced wider in response.

"Thanks so much for getting my job back. I really appreciate it!"

"You didn't deserve to lose it. You were trying to be kind to Tom and Stephanie, and it certainly seemed like a no risk situation. I'm grateful you helped care for me and called an ambulance. Your quick thinking reduced my recovery time."

"That's great, Lanjo." Vic smiled. "So, where do you need a ride to?"

Lanjo's face took on an odd expression. He didn't quite know how to articulate his feelings for Stephanie. He was incredibly touched when Tom invited him into his family. Cygnans took family relations very seriously. Being Stephanie's uncle not only recognized an affectionate relationship between family members, it came with solemn responsibilities. Lanjo wanted to go see Stephanie, and as her uncle he felt an urgency to do so before any more time passed by. He needed to see for himself she was okay and unhurt from her tumble at the edge of the Potomac.

"I just need a ride to Stephanie's house."

"Stephanie? Tom's daughter, Stephanie? Are you sure?" Vic looked closely at his friend. "You do know that Patricia isn't too thrilled with Cygnans. She's made it clear to Tom that she doesn't like aliens and doesn't want Stephanie around them. I overheard Tom tell Darryl she's grateful you saved Stephanie, but Stephanie would've never been in danger in the first place, if she hadn't snuck off to be with him."

Lanjo sighed. Apparently any brownie points he had earned had already been cashed in. But he had an obligation to Stephanie, and nothing would keep him from it, even her xenophobic mom.

"It's okay, Vic. I'm just going to visit with her for a little while. I need to make sure she's okay. It's a Cygnan custom. As her uncle, I share in the responsibility of her welfare." He glanced back down at the friendship bracelet. "I have to go. Please take me."

"Okay, Lanj, sure."

"Thanks, Vic." Lanjo punched him lightly on the arm. "You're the best."

Vic's smile widened, and Lanjo grimaced in return. He really was getting these human interactions down.

Stephanie peered through the peephole, gave a happy scream, and yanked the front door wide open. "Uncle Lanjo! It's you!" She threw herself through the opening and gave Lanjo a fierce hug, then peeked around him. "And Vic!" She disentangled herself and gave the guard a hug too. "Come on in. Mom won't be home for a couple more hours."

Lanjo turned to Vic, who smiled and nodded. "Go on ahead, Lanjo. I can hang around for a while. Why don't you two visit for a little bit and I'll just watch some television." He looked at Stephanie. "If that's okay?"

"Sure, Vic. That would be great."

Vic and Lanjo followed Stephanie into the living room. Lanjo's head swiveled around, his range of motion about 25% more than the average human, taking in the furnishings and wall decorations. It was much different from the dorm. He hesitated, but Stephanie grabbed his hand and pulled. "Come on. Let's go in the backyard. We can sit at the picnic table and play ball with Lela."

At the sound of her name, Lela started whining, and Lanjo found himself being propelled out the back door. "Watch out for Mom's flowers," Stephanie cautioned Lanjo as they walked along a narrow path, Lela running ahead with her ball in her mouth. Stephanie stopped at the picnic table and pulled the ball out of Lela's mouth, then threw it across the yard. Lela ran as fast as her short legs would carry her and grabbed the ball. Instead of bringing it back, she dropped to the ground and released the ball into the grass in front of her.

"Is she going to bring it back?" Lanjo asked, watching Lela curiously.

Stephanie sighed. "No, probably not. I really wish she would, but usually all she does is chase it."

Lanjo laughed. "Maybe I can help." He looked intently at the ball in front of Lela, and Stephanie heard a *shhhhhhh* sound. She followed his gaze and looked in amazement as the ball popped up in the air, and on its own volition, flew back towards her. She picked it up with a big smile and turning to thank Lanjo, she spotted their neighbor's fifteen-year old son, Jimmy, looking over the fence. To make matters worse, he had his cell phone out and was filming everything. When Jimmy saw he'd been spotted, he ducked back onto his side of the fence and ran away.

"Who was that?" Lanjo asked. He never intended anyone else to see him use telekinesis; he had intended it as a special moment between just them.

"That was Jimmy, Uncle Lanjo. I have a bad feeling about this. I think he was filming us."

"I better not stay much longer. I don't want to get you in trouble."

The two looked at each other in silence until Lela ran up to Stephanie, whining for the ball. Stephanie gave it back to Lela instead of throwing it. "We'd better go back inside."

"Sure, Stephanie." He patted her on the back. "My main reason for coming today was to make sure you're okay." He held up his wrist with the friendship bracelet. "Now that I'm your uncle, I am responsible for your welfare. On Lanzeron, uncles and aunts have a responsibility to all of their siblings' children."

"You already saved my life, Uncle Lanjo."

"That's just the beginning. We have a saying on Lanzeron: *Nahlilito ahsunjango fovato tilapatao.* 'Family are the friends you choose.' We'll always be family."

Stephanie's eyes sparkled and she bounced lightly in place. "Thanks, Uncle Lanjo. It's nice not to hear arguing when I'm with you. Mom and Dad . . ." Before she could say anything else, their conversation was interrupted by the chop chop sound of whirring blades. They looked up to see a police helicopter circling overhead. "Uhhhh, Uncle Lanjo . . . I think we better go inside right now." She grabbed his hand and pulled him along the path, trampling some of her mom's precious flowers in her hurry to get him inside.

Vic met them as they burst through the door, and sirens began to shriek in the distance, approaching rapidly. "What's going on?"

Stephanie's voice shook. "Jimmy must have posted the video he took of us in the backyard on Facebook and tagged me. My Mom is going to totally freak out."

The young policeman that arrested them kept blinking. He'd been almost apologetic. Perhaps the human was worried about creating an interstellar incident. Lanjo was glad he didn't put him or Vic in handcuffs. The ride to the police station passed in silence, just taking a few minutes. They entered a well-kept building that was part of the city government complex. Another policeman steered Vic to a desk across the room, and the one that had arrested them escorted Lanjo to his desk to be processed.

"Take a seat please."

Lanjo looked at the officer in puzzlement. "Where shall I take it to?"

"I'm not kidding."

"I'm not either . . . oh, you are not being literal. Sorry about that."

Lanjo sat in the chair next to the desk, forcing the officer's gaze upward.

"Full name?"

"Lanjo Verfabtholar Frastero Kolanpatchibe."

The officer exhaled loudly. "Can you spell that?"

"Certainly. L-a-n-j-o V-e-r-f-a-b-t-h-o-l-a-r F-r-a-s-t-e-r-o K-o-l-a-n-p-a-t-c-h-i-b-e"

"Home Address?"

"Planet Lanzeron, L-a-n-z-e-r-o-n."

"Do you have a local address?"

"I'm currently staying in a dorm at George Washington University, on the Virginia campus."

Lanjo watched as the officer typed on his keyboard. He leaned forward and cleared his throat, like he had seen humans do when they wanted to get someone's attention.

"Yes?"

"I really don't understand why I am here. I am Stephanie's uncle. I went to her home to check on her. I am sure this is a misunderstanding. I need to call Tom Whitaker, Stephanie's father. He'll be able to explain everything."

"Don't worry about that," the officer glanced up from his keyboard. "Mr. Whitaker has been notified and is on his way."

"But why am I here?"

"You really don't know?" Lanjo could hear the doubt in the young man's voice. "You violated the restraining order filed against you by Stephanie's Mother, Patricia Whitaker. You aren't supposed to communicate with her or get within 100 yards of her."

Lanjo made a choking noise, his skin tone darkening and his cheeks sinking inward in a physiological reaction to the distress he was feeling. *How could that be? And why didn't anyone tell him?*

The holding cell was stuffy, with only a few hardbacked chairs and a toilet area in the corner with no privacy. The absence of clocks made the passage of time impossible to track with any sort of accuracy. He was grateful that it was only him and Vic in the holding cell. Lanjo held up his hands and examined each set of six fingers for traces of ink. When he'd offered his hand to the officer assigned to fingerprint him, the man had flinched and had to ask his captain where on the card the sixth print should go.

"I'm so sorry, Vic. I had no idea this would happen. I'm sorry I got you into this."

"It's alright. I know you didn't get us arrested intentionally."

Vic started pacing the cell, leaving Lanjo to his own thoughts. He sat in one of the chairs. His money and cell phone had been taken from him. The only time he'd become uncooperative was when the officer asked him to remove Stephanie's friendship bracelet. When he informed the officer that the only way it would come off his wrist would be to incapacitate him, the officer took him at his word and didn't ask again. Lanjo glanced at the information sheet he'd been given and sincerely hoped he wouldn't be there long enough to need to learn the regulations listed on it.

"How could you be so stupid?" Tom paced back and forth. Lanjo opened his mouth to point out he didn't know he wasn't supposed to see Stephanie, since Tom had not informed him, but he closed his mouth instead. It had been a long process getting him and Vic released, and it was obvious even to Lanjo's alien perspective that Tom was in no mood for excuses. Lanjo looked up at the television playing in the break room back at the lab, which had not stopped coverage of the story: ALIENS HAVE PARANORMAL POWERS. The whole country was riveted by the revelation that Lanjo was able to move objects with his mind. Jimmy's video of Lanjo and Stephanie in the backyard with Lela, and the ball flying through the air back to Stephanie, was playing over and over. The video was interspersed with interviews of self-proclaimed alien experts speculating on what other powers Lanjo might possess and if he intended to use his powers to harm humanity.

Lanjo sat quietly, realizing there was nothing he could say to make it better. On top of the film disclosing his telekinetic ability, sending the country into an anti-alien frenzy that threatened their mission, his impetuousness had caused Tom to lose his custody rights to Stephanie until a court date was set to consider his fitness as a father. Patricia had responded exactly as Stephanie predicted, and Lanjo had a much greater understanding of the expression "freak out" then he'd ever expected to have. If Tom couldn't convince the judge that Lanjo wasn't a threat, he might not get to see Stephanie again until she was of legal age.

Tom's gaze dug into the Cygnan. "I can't bear the thought of not being able to see Stephanie and all of this is your fault. I invited you into our family and this is how you repay me—by jeopardizing my relationship with Stephanie and betraying my trust." He took a deep breath and let it out. "This is how it's going to be. We are not brothers. We are not friends. We are not anything. We work together, and I only want to see you if it's absolutely necessary. That's all."

"Yes, Tom," Lanjo replied. There was nothing else he could say.

Jonathan looked across his desk in his Baltimore office at Joe Ricinski and waited patiently. Joe had a reputation for being able to read people, and Jonathan had no intention of giving him more information than he had to. He liked Joe. The president's top aide was a staunch protector of national interests, but Jonathan, as CEO of HoweTek Communications, was an entrepreneur who firmly believed in the role of capitalism in a free nation. Unfortunately, the government had a different perspective regarding his right to pursue mining helium-3 on the Moon.

"Come on, Jonathan. We know you have SETI in your back pocket. That wasn't hard to figure out." Joe leaned forward slightly in his chair. "What we need to know is, where are you going with it? Contact with extraterrestrials is considered a matter of national security."

"Now Joe, I'm a businessman. I would never do anything to compromise our nation's security, but I do have the right to pursue space travel as a private enterprise. It's no secret I believe helium-3 is the future of our country. Without a clean source of energy, we'll revert to the Stone Age. I'm not a big fan of aliens either, but the Secretary of Energy is fooling himself if he believes Earth can provide all of her own solutions, and we both know it. This is just smart business."

Joe sat back and exhaled impatiently. "Jonathan, no one denies the right of the private sector to pursue space, but we would much rather collaborate than compete. We're not here to stifle your efforts to reach the Moon and mine helium-3, but we need to make sure you don't jeopardize our relationship with the Cygnans. They're too much of an unknown quantity for us to encourage private communication with nongovernmental factions."

Jonathan's gaze became steely. The government man had touched a nerve. Jonathan was loyal to the United States, but he held very strongly to his constitutional rights, especially when they had a bearing on his business interests. "I hear you, Joe. I'll take your words under consideration."

"I hope you do. I respect you and your reputation for integrity. Please don't make me have to revisit this topic with you in the future."

Jonathan stood up and held out his hand. "Thanks for coming by."

Joe's eyes narrowed, but he returned the firm grip across the desk.

"Thanks for your time."

Jonathan watched Joe exit, then reached down and pushed a button on his desk phone. "Dan, are you available?"

"Sure thing, boss. I'll be right there."

Dan entered Jonathan's office. "Good morning boss. What's up?"

"More to the point, what's up with you?" Jonathan asked. "I can't remember the last time I saw you wearing jeans."

"I'm driving to the airport, to catch a midmorning flight to the SETI Institute. This afternoon we're going out to the radio telescopes. Marco suggested old clothes—apparently we'll be hiking through some brush. I don't think my Armani suit would care for burrs sticking to it."

"So what's going on at SETI today?"

"Marco is field testing a new algorithm he developed specifically for any Cygnan attempts at contact. With the time zone difference, I should get there in time to see it for myself. It's obvious someone is trying to contact us, but we still need to figure out how to communicate. We're moving forward with our idea about a possible wormhole. If our theory is correct, we need to somehow receive its coordinates from the Cygnans."

Jonathan nodded his approval. "Let's make this happen. We need a solid contact with the Cygnan private sector soon. I want that helium-3 and partnering with them will be the fastest way to process it."

"I'll impress upon Marco the urgency of the situation," Dan promised. He picked up the Rubik's cube on Jonathan's desk and started to fiddle with it. "By the way, how'd it go with Joe?"

"Let's just say we better get busy," Jonathan replied, his eyes following Dan's hands as they rapidly brought all the colors of the cube into alignment on each side. "He sees a conflict of interest in our attempting to communicate with a Cygnan businessman. I don't agree with him. I prefer to think of it as healthy competition. If he's concerned enough to make it a national security issue, we may have problems, but for now we're okay. The important thing is not to advertise our efforts. Please make sure Marco fully understands."

Dan put the Rubik's cube back in its place. "Don't worry boss, I got it." Dan smiled jauntily. "I'm looking forward to this field trip. I can talk about tachyons and superluminal communications with Marco, and his eyes won't glaze over."

Jonathan raised his eyebrows. "Now Dan, I didn't get a physics degree for nothing." He lifted the stainless steel ball on one end of the Newton's cradle on his desk and released it, setting it in motion.

Dan was momentarily mesmerized by the balls' movement and forced his gaze back to Jonathan. "I know boss, but I also know you have a lot on your mind. You know where you're at, but you don't know how fast you're going."

Jonathan laughed at Dan's reference to Heisenberg's Uncertainty Principle. "Go on, get out of here."

As Dan was about to close the office door behind him, Jonathan called out, "Oh, and Dan, is your speedometer working?"

He paused. "Yeah, why?"

"Don't get lost," Jonathan grinned.

Dan shook his head. "Touché."

Ray straightened his tie and smoothed his jacket. He wasn't looking forward to going before the Joint Committee on Energy and Alien Relations today, but he knew if he was going to stop this craziness about working with aliens, he had to leverage his position as Secretary of Energy. If he could get an emergency bill drafted, he could present it to Congress and stop this nonsense. It was bad enough having to deal with foreign oil, but at least they shared the planet and had a common interest in protecting their home. Extraterrestrials wouldn't have any innate desire to preserve the Earth.

Standing before the committee, Ray found himself repeating what had become his mantra. "We have to find our own solutions to Earth's energy problems, not some extraterrestrial agenda that could affect the future of our planet in a negative way."

"But Ray, do you have any proof of that?" Senator Wayne McCree from Wyoming asked. "It seems to me utilizing helium-3 is a great solution, and if these alien fellers have the technology to process it and are willing to share . . . well . . . I don't see why you got your panties in a knot."

Ray took a moment to calm himself. It was so unfathomable to him that these people could not see the inherent danger of dealing with aliens. When push came to shove and Earth needed help, why would the Cygnans care? Ray didn't know what would happen if Washington's Alien-Human Energy Pact moved forward, but he had a bad feeling about it . . . a very bad feeling. "Wayne, I understand what you're saying about helium-3. But we're working on other solutions that won't require space travel. We have a lot of promising research on modifying what we've already learned about green energy—including ways to increase efficiency, which has always been our biggest problem for widespread adaptation of renewable technology. It doesn't make sense to look outside of our planet, when the solutions are already in our own backyard."

"That's all well and good, but we've been hearing that for years. Our energy problem will become critical in less than 50 years. I had relatives in Texas when ERCOT started the rolling blackouts in February of 2021 and the temperatures were in single digits. People froze to death, homes were flooded, and the water supply was compromised in some areas. It's not just about gas prices—a sustained energy crisis has the potential to become a humanitarian crisis. I personally want to leave this Earth as good, if not better than when I arrived."

"Believe me, I do, too. I just don't believe pursuing a solution with aliens is in our best interests. Lanjo comes across as a nice guy, but think about it. All we really know about these Cygnans is what he's told us. How do we know it's true? Heck, how do we even know Lanjo is who he says he is?"

"How do we know he's not?" Wayne returned. "Washington ain't stupid. I don't reckon folks like Joe Ricinski are about to follow someone they think would hurt our interests, and Joe is a pretty sharp fella."

"You want a solution? I have a solution. Lots of them. Are you even aware of wave power? We can harness Earth's oceans for an endless supply of renewable energy. One company has a prototype that can generate about 250 kilowatts off a single buoy. Those types of efforts are where we should be pouring our research dollars—not traipsing across the universe in search of something we don't even know exists."

Wayne exhaled forcefully, dropping his easy-going country manner. "You guys are always touting some pie-in-the-sky renewable energy solution as the way to go and that you're close to a breakthrough that'll save the planet, but nothing ever materializes. Frankly, I'm tired of hearing it. Alien or not, at least Lanjo is offering a real solution."

"And I could offer one, too. These technologies are real and have the capacity to supply the energy we need. I could prove it, if I could get the funding NASA keeps siphoning off on useless space projects."

"That's enough." Bahram Mirzaie, the committee chair, broke in. He turned to Ray. "I get what you're saying. But this is different from when we served together during the 2008 energy crisis. It's a new world now. A First Contact changes everything."

"The only thing it changes is the potential for Earth to be destroyed from outer space," Ray shot back.

Bahram started shaking his head, but Ray held up his hand. "Just hear me out. It makes no sense to make a deal with aliens. They have superior technology, and the only reason they are willing to share it is in exchange for our help. How do we know they're not actually planning an invasion, and this is their method of reconnaissance?"

"Because it just makes sense, Ray. Why do they need to reconnoiter when by their own admission they have been observing us for decades? What part of exchanging something of value for another item of value do you not understand? Our whole economic system is based on that premise. Washington is treading carefully, but we would be foolish to miss the chance to gain working fusion reactors AND space travel because we were too paranoid to recognize the tremendous opportunity in front of us."

Bahram looked around at the other members of the committee. "I move to continue going forward in creating an amicable agreement between the U.S. government and the Cygnan government facilitating the introduction of Cygnan technology to meet the needs of both parties."

Wayne jumped up. "I second the motion."

"Call for vote."

Ray's face reddened as a chorus of "Ayes" went around the room. Not a single dissenting vote.

"Motion passed. Let's break for lunch and I'll see everyone back at one o'clock."

Ray was barely able to contain his anger and he struggled to maintain a fake smile. He would have to stay on board if he hoped to have any type of limiting effect on the outcome. "All right then," he said. "If you insist on going down this path, you'll need my department's expertise."

Bahram slapped him on the back. "I was hoping you would make that offer. Don't worry, Ray. We have safeguards in place. It'll be okay."

"I hope you're right, Bahram. I really do."

"I was right about speculation significantly impacting oil prices in 2008 when everyone else was saying it was insufficient production not keeping pace with the demand, wasn't I? Have a little faith. Now let's grab some lunch at Amoo's. When's the last time you had some really good kabob?"

Thank God for NASA's legendary insistence on redundancy. Minimal preparation had been needed for another trip. When the president had extended his invitation for the alien to visit Camp David in secret, Theresa and Keith had returned to the Moon under the guise of a "test launch" and brought Lanjo back to Earth for an extended visit. Cygnans did not leave their spacecraft idle on the Moon, and the Cygnan scientist transport returned home to be given its next assignment, as transportation for one of their planet exploratory teams.

When Washington approved the joint Cygnan-human venture, Theresa and Keith returned yet again and ferried the Cygnan fusion scientists from their permanent installation on the Moon, to Earth.

"You idiot—haven't you ever heard of Ohm's law?"

"As a matter of fact, I haven't. For your information, it's called Cherabero's law."

"Hey guys, settle down." Tom peered at the Cygnan's government I.D. hanging around his neck. "All right Feraganjo, take it easy. Brett, calm down."

It was almost comical to see the two scientists, one human, and the other Cygnan, ready to start throwing punches. Tom sighed. It was only the second day since Congress had passed the joint resolution that enabled them to move forward, and already Cygnans and humans weren't getting along. If they couldn't learn to work together, everybody would lose. Tom avoided Lanjo, but still spoke to him when necessary for the success of the project.

"What's the problem here?"

"All I did was ask this guy to wire a circuit." Brett pointed at a schematic that was spread out on the worktable. "He says the resistance values are incorrect. Obviously, they are correct. I don't know how current flows on Cygnus, but here on Earth, current equals voltage divided by resistance. It's basic Ohm's law."

Lanjo walked up to see what the commotion was about and overheard Brett's last sentence. "Hang on, Brett." Lanjo turned to the Cygnan scientist. "Feraganjo, I'm not an engineer, but I've studied Cherabero's law. The humans have the same principle, they call it Ohm's law. So what's going on with those resistors?"

"The human isn't taking into consideration this circuit will be working inside a highly magnetized field. He has not accounted for the magnetic flux variance in his calculations."

"What's flux got to do with it?" Brett sputtered. "Reluctance will change, but that shouldn't affect the base resistance."

"Not normally," Lanjo said. "The law of physics doesn't change, but from my understanding, the way we implement the magnetic field to contain plasma at the smaller size we need to power an interstellar spaceship is considerably different from your current technology. Properties at the subatomic level are affected."

"Yes," Feraganjo added. "Materials have a tendency to change their resistance at the flux density required for our magnetic field. Brett has not accounted for this nonlinear change in his calculations."

"How could I?" Brett shot back. "It makes no sense."

Tom put a hand on both scientists. "Come on, guys, we need to work together. Both our worlds are watching. We don't have the luxury of not getting along." He turned to Feraganjo. "Brett graduated from MIT with honors. He'll be an excellent student of your fusion technology, if you'll give him a chance."

Lanjo turned to the human. "Brett, you have to trust us. We've solved the problems you've been struggling with for the last hundred years and we're ready to share the solution with you, but you have to be willing to listen. Feraganjo volunteered for this effort and learned English so he could work with you, so please, try to work with him."

"He learned English specifically for this project?" Brett was taken aback.

"Yes, I did." Feraganjo held out his hands to emphasize his words. "I wanted to be a part of this. It's my intention to help you as much as you help us."

"Well . . . thanks, Feraganjo." Brett's tone mellowed considerably. "I didn't know that. Uhhh . . . can you show me at what flux density the nonlinearity kicks in . . ."

"I'd be glad to. Keep in mind that the way we are creating our electromagnetic field is much different from the tokamak you're familiar with. It's by implementing . . ." the two scientists ignored Tom and Lanjo as they walked away, deep in conversation.

Lanjo grimaced and looked hopefully in Tom's direction. Tom returned Lanjo's gaze with no expression, his earlier conciliatory manner completely gone. He turned sharply on his heel and strode away. Lanjo's grimace faded, and he ambled back to the lab, intent on getting another cup of coffee. It was going to be a long day.

"We've got to figure out a way to get our people to work better with the Cygnans." Darryl took another sip of coffee and gazed out the picture window.

Tom noticed the bluebirds were back, looking for their evening meal. "It's not easy," he mumbled defensively.

"Lanjo reported three separate incidents he had to smooth over today. Rachel was upset at Keranganjo using her oscilloscope without asking. She wanted to check out a prototype circuit she was working on and couldn't find it. Lanjo explained to him not all lab equipment is considered communal and if a person's name is on it, it's better to ask first." Darryl directed his gaze at Tom and his voice hardened. "And you're not helping matters. What you don't know is that Lanjo enabled you to keep your job. After your meltdown in the breakroom with the birds, I was almost ready to call it quits with you. Your attitude towards Lanjo is jeopardizing the mission. But when I talked to Lanjo about it, he refused to give up on you. He told me he wanted you to be the liaison and wouldn't work with anyone else."

Tom stared at him with a stony expression. "You don't understand. He cost me my daughter."

"What a short memory you have," returned Darryl. "He gave you your daughter. He saved her life. I could lose my daughter any day. That's the harsh reality I live with as the father of a daughter with a blood disease. You need to get over yourself and be grateful for what you have. Lanjo made a mistake, but he was operating under the best of intentions. You made him Stephanie's uncle. There are consequences to that, including taking responsibility, which is all Lanjo was trying to do. Now you need to take your own responsibility and quit blaming Lanjo for everything."

"But he cost me Stephanie," Tom repeated stubbornly.

"Okay, here it is. I talked to Joe about how the synergy on our team has been destroyed because of your refusal to offer Lanjo any grace after you lost custody of Stephanie. Joe agreed we needed to replace you in order to save the project, despite how valuable you are as a member of the science team. We've had enough trouble containing the anti-alien sentiment the video of Lanjo and Stephanie stirred up with the rest of the country. We don't need to have the same fight internally because of your inability to get along.

"When Joe brought Lanjo in to tell him of our decision, Lanjo informed Joe that if we fired you, he would not only not work with another liaison, he would withdraw the entire Cygnan team from the project. The only reason you still have a job is because Lanjo continues to fight for you. Lanjo asked me not to say anything, but you've forced me into a corner. If our leadership is unable to get along, we can't expect the team members to be able to, and we have a long road ahead. Something has to give, and I suggest it's your lousy attitude."

Tom stared at Darryl, trying to process everything Darryl just told him. Losing Stephanie was the hardest thing that had ever happened to him. To lose his job on top of that would have been the final straw. He didn't know what he would do if that happened. The realization hit him like a brick. *Lanjo had saved Stephanie, he had saved him his job twice, and he was here to help save two worlds.* Tom had been monumentally selfish. He needed to do something to make it up to Lanjo. His chin quivered and his eyes got moist. "You're right, Darryl," he said quietly. "I need to fix it."

Darryl studied Tom for a moment, then nodded his head. "Yes, you do. We're on a tight schedule, and we can't go on like this."

Tom rubbed his face with his hands, trying to think of what he could do to make it right. That's when he realized a solution was readily available. "Can I have the afternoon off?"

"Sure, Tom. Go do what you need to, just make sure and get here early tomorrow." His words followed Tom as he got up and raced out the door.

Darryl headed back into his office and buried himself in paperwork. Mounds of forms were inevitable on government-funded projects and theirs was no exception. Three hours later the sound of laughter impinged on his consciousness. He needed a break anyway, so he decided to investigate. Following the sound of loud cheers, he went through the break room door and down the path that curved around the edge of the building to the parking lot. He could see both human and Cygnan members of the science team and, even better, smiles and grimaces on their faces. Looking past them and into the parking lot, he saw something he never expected to see: Lanjo riding a mountain bike and Tom jogging alongside, shouting instructions. By the size of Lanjo's grimace and the laughter floating in the air, Darryl could tell that Tom had managed to fix it.

The following morning Tom was at the lab bright and early and met Darryl in the break room to plan the day. Darryl cleared his throat, as he always did when he wanted to get down to business. Tom peered attentively at him over his coffee mug.

"I got a call today from Joe Ricinski. Washington is expressing some concern over our timeline. It seems Jonathan Howe has somehow found a way to communicate with a private faction on Lanzeron, who is also interested in trading technology."

"That's not good." Tom rubbed his eyes. "How did he get in contact with them?"

"The word is he's been funding SETI and has access to their resources. They must have figured out something. Dan Ross is on Jonathan's team and that dude is one sharp guy."

"Yeah," Tom agreed. "I've heard that, too." He put down his coffee cup and reached for one of the granola bars left on the table for snacks. "Do they know any details about what Jonathan is planning? I know he's after the helium-3 on the Moon, but he can't have any deals in place for a working fusion reactor. No one has one yet. The Cygnan technology will put us well ahead of everyone else, but if Jonathan manages to make a deal with a Cygnan entrepreneur, we could be in trouble."

"Which is exactly what has Washington concerned. In their words, we need to make sure Jonathan doesn't beat us to it. But no one knows how much time that gives us."

"Okay, I'll tell Lanjo, and we'll come up with a new timeline."

"Tell me what?" Lanjo pulled up a chair and grabbed a granola bar. He looked at the label and grimaced—chocolate chip was his favorite.

"It looks like someone on Lanzeron is communicating with one of the leading entrepreneurs on Earth, Jonathan Howe."

"Jonathan Howe?" Lanjo got the look on his face Tom had come to associate with Lanjo making a cultural connection. "Isn't he on *Shark Tank?*"

"That's right," Tom said. "He took Mark Cuban's place when Mark left the show."

"Seems like a nice guy," Lanjo said. "But if he's trying to do an end run around our project, that could cause a lot of trouble. We're quite similar, Tom. We have sharks on Lanzeron, too."

"Do you know what they want?" Tom asked. "Why can't they just wait and let our governments work things out?"

"We have the same problem you do. Entrepreneurs by their very nature aren't used to waiting around or taking orders. They set a goal and they go after it. I'm pretty sure Jonathan Howe is communicating with Paranganjo, a leading entrepreneur on Lanzeron who has a bent towards reaping the financial benefits of cutting-edge technology. We've had fusion for quite a while. He would have access to the same science we are developing here."

"So what's he after?" Darryl asked. "It seems to me he's just as much in need of interstellar transportation as the rest of your planet. Letting our governments work together solves all of his problems."

"That's what we have to figure out," Lanjo replied. "Paranganjo has something up his sleeve. I wouldn't be surprised if he has an interest in the helium-3 on the Moon, and sees Jonathan as a way to get a piece of it. Like I mentioned at Camp David, we haven't been able to locate a planet to colonize containing a suitable atmosphere that also has helium-3. I think Paranganjo sees connecting with Jonathan as a business opportunity to capitalize on our future energy needs, and he is aggressively pursuing it.

"I'm guessing he managed to get Jonathan the coordinates to the wormhole we discovered, which will enable them to have faster-than-light communications. We definitely need to keep an eye on those two."

Darryl groaned. "I'll let Joe know your assessment. We have enough trouble without those two stirring the pot." He noticed a puzzled look on Lanjo's face. "You know, creating trouble."

"The number of idioms used by your species is truly amazing."

"I guess it is." Darryl smiled. "I never really thought about it before." He cleared his throat, and his expression turned serious. "Let's pull out the Gantt chart. We'll need to drastically revise our timeline to make Washington happy, and it'll be tough to figure out how to accomplish that."

Darryl opened his laptop and displayed the projected timeline onto the screen. "The first milestone is critical: to have a working design that both humans and Cygnans can interpret. It's due in two weeks. Because the fusion reactor will be used to power spaceships built here on Earth, the schematics and technology need to be translated to a human format. We need to focus all of our energy towards implementing the Cygnan design into a workable product that can be built by human engineers."

"No way we can speed that milestone up," Tom said, frowning.

"Agreed." Darryl paused and glanced at Lanjo. "It gets worse. In order to transport the Cygnans from their home planet to their new destination, they'll need a minimum fleet of two hundred ships from Earth, in addition to the six hundred the Cygnans themselves are supplying. The rescue effort will be staggered, but our proof of concept needs to be working in six months and the first ship commissioned in one year, if their plan is going to work. Once we have a working ship, we can go into mass production for the rest, using government contractors to expedite the process."

"I understand the pressure of third-party competition in regards to fusion, but why such an aggressive timeline for the ships?" Tom asked.

Lanjo waved his hand. No one even noticed the extra digit anymore. "While we still have years before the white dwarf goes supernova, it's critical we start the move as soon as possible. It'll take years to move all the inhabitants of our planet. We need to do it in stages, so our new home will have an adequate infrastructure in place to support us."

Tom groaned. He could see it was going to be a long night. "I'll be right back, guys." He walked outside and sat on the bench by the silver maple tree that had become the bluebirds' favorite meal hangout. He pulled his cell phone out of his pocket and went through his texts. Sure enough, there was one from Theresa, checking to see if they were still on for dinner. Another text from Patricia informed him Stephanie had gotten into trouble at school again. She may have denied him custody, but she was still intent on letting him know how he failed as a dad. Funny how the future survival of the human and Cygnan species were at stake, yet what was really bothering him at this moment was the fact he would have to cancel with Theresa when he very much wanted to work on rekindling their relationship, and being an absentee father was obviously having a negative effect on Stephanie. Everything felt out of his control.

13

"I thought it'd be fun to be a celebrity—with all the perks that go along with it. Getting to go to the head of the line, everyone knowing who I am. But this is really inconvenient." Jerry Nguyen, NASA scientist, waved his hands in frustration. "I can't go anywhere without someone trying to stop me for an autograph or asking me about the aliens. I can't even go into the grocery store I've shopped at for the past five years without being mobbed. Forget having a cup of coffee at the local diner. I don't know how movie stars deal with it."

This particular conference room at NASA had become the mission crew's weekly meeting place ever since their return from the Moon. The only missing member was Sheila Palazzo, the mission's botanist and psychologist. Sheila's increasingly unfriendly behavior towards the aliens had bordered on xenophobic and when they returned to Earth, she'd been relieved to return to civilian life.

"So what's next on the agenda?" asked Matt Sherwood, the mission geologist.

Keith cleared his throat. "I had dinner with Britanny and her dad last night."

"I still can't believe you're engaged to Jonathan Howe's daughter," Matt ribbed his friend.

"Neither can I. She's the best." He drummed his fingers on the table. "Jonathan connected with someone on Lanzeron and is pursuing fusion technology by obtaining it through his contact, with the goal of mining helium-3 on the Moon."

"That's no surprise. We knew he would try something," Theresa said. "Word of Jonathan's activities has been on the grapevine for a couple of weeks now."

"Yeah." Keith tugged at the front of his T-shirt. "But what you don't know is he's wanting to recruit us for his project."

"What?" chorused Matt and Jerry. Theresa straightened up in her seat and gazed intently at Keith.

"Their plan is to use the Moon as a central depot and conduct their fusion activities from there," Keith said. "They'll need people to work in that environment. He's offering us big money to go to work for him."

"Why would he do that?" Matt asked.

"I'm not sure. He did mention that Dan thought it would be a good idea."

"Well, I know why," Jerry interjected. "He doesn't want to risk his own people, so he wants us to do it and take the fall if necessary."

Matt stepped in. "You know I hardly ever agree with Jerry, but I think he's right on this one. Why would he want us, when the Cygnans already have their own resources?"

Keith tugged at his T-shirt again. "Jonathan is willing to do business with them, but he doesn't trust them. He needs experienced space personnel on board to make sure the Cygnans hold up their side of the bargain. That's where we'd come in."

"And what's the compensation he's offering?" Jerry asked.

"He wouldn't say. Not unless we sign up for his venture."

Theresa leaned back and tapped her finger on her chin. "You know we can't do that, even if we wanted to. We're still active NASA. We would be branded as traitors. Jonathan must know that, too. I wonder what he's up to." She looked around at her crew. "Tell me none of you are even considering it?"

"Of course not," Matt said, and everyone nodded their agreement. "But we better let Washington know."

Theresa turned to Keith. "Sorry, but Matt's right. This is too important to national security to not inform the president of Jonathan's intentions."

Keith sighed. "I know. Sometimes I wish I could've fallen in love with a simple girl from Muskogee, instead of the daughter of one of the richest businessmen on the planet."

"They didn't go for it," Dan picked up the Rubik's cube on Jonathan's desk and began tossing it up in the air. "Theresa met with Joe Ricinski and informed him of your offer. I had a feeling they wouldn't leave NASA for a private business venture, but thanks for trying my idea. Looks like we'll just have to trust the Cygnans, if we're going to run with it."

Dan's report was not surprising. Jonathan's expectation for success had been low. "So how'd it go at the SETI Institute?"

Dan's eyes lit up. "It was amazing. Marco showed me their radio astronomy laboratory in Mountain View, then we took a helicopter from the institute to see the Clarke Telescope Array at the Hat Creek Observatory. It has forty-two antennas in service. Their signal processing hardware and software are brilliant."

"Helicopter, huh. How'd you manage that?"

"Geoffrey Clarke happened to be visiting. It was his idea. That's one energetic guy. Now that his Astrolaunch aircraft is successfully launching satellites into low Earth orbit, he's ready to expand his operations to deep space."

Jonathan got a faraway look in his eyes. He turned to Dan and opened his mouth, but Dan beat him to it. "Don't worry, boss. I'm already on it. Mr. Clarke will be in town next month and will drop by for a meeting."

Jonathan smiled. "And that's why I pay you the big bucks."

"Yes, you do. Speaking of which—how about a raise?" Dan grinned.

"We land this deal with the Cygnans, Dan, and I don't think you or I will be worrying about money ever again."

"Dr. Palazzo, you've personally met with the aliens during your trip to the Moon as part of the lunar mission Triumphant. You were the botanist and team psychologist, is that correct?" The news anchor for a small local station just northwest of the Capitol smiled encouragingly at her unexpected guest. The camera man had not left yet, and they were able to set up where they conducted in-station interviews.

"Yes, it is, Cheryl. I was part of the original crew that landed on the Moon and made first contact with Lanjo and his associates."

"And what was your impression of these aliens? Do you think they really are our friends?"

"I don't think any one of us can answer that question for sure. They are alien, which means we don't really understand their thought processes. I mean, I went to school for eight years to become a competent observer of human behavior. How can any of us hope to understand alien behavior in just a few weeks?"

"Someone needs to contain her, and I mean now!" President Ferris slammed his briefcase down on the conference table. He seldom lost his cool, but this was ridiculous. The last thing they needed was to have an ex-NASA astronaut incite fear among the population.

"We're on it, sir. She's at the local news office and our people are en route. But we can't just shut her down or we'll give her interview credibility. The White House Communications Director is making a call. If they want to continue being welcome at White House press conferences, they'll cut it short on their own." Joe's calming presence defused the tension from the president's outburst.

"What do you suggest, Joe? We can't let her spread rumors of vindictive aliens planning a hostile invasion. I thought she was instructed to keep quiet at her briefing."

"She was, sir. Part of her contract included an NDA with a clause that specifically addresses this type of situation, which is why we'll be able to bring her in for questioning. Participating in interviews without prior authorization and spreading unfounded conspiracy theories is in direct violation of her contract. Something has happened that made her cross over the line. We don't know yet if it's a personal issue, or if someone gave her a reason to do it."

"So, in your estimation, should we be worried? After all, these aliens are supposed to solve our energy problems by sharing their technology."

"Should we be worried? Good question, Cheryl. All I know is, I'm worried. These aliens are an unknown quantity and they're just . . ." she paused to try to formulate what she wanted to convey, "they're just different." Her voice took on an edge. "And to be perfectly honest with you, I don't believe we know if that is a good different or a bad different. We don't know how they think." Her voice went up an octave. "How can we be sure they aren't planning to take over Earth? Even now, they could be infiltrating our brains with their telepathic powers!"

Cheryl glanced over at her producer, who was desperately crossing his hand across his throat. She nodded and turned back to her guest. "It seems we're out of time, Dr. Palazzo. Thank you so much for coming onto our show today."

"Thank you for having me, Cheryl. I felt it important for the public to be warned."

Cheryl turned to the camera. "We are fortunate to have Dr. Sheila Palazzo, formerly of NASA, as our guest. Now for a commercial break."

As soon as the cameras were off, the producer came forward. "Dr. Palazzo, there are some gentlemen in the foyer to see you. They are requesting your presence immediately."

She had been expecting that response and had mentally prepared herself for it. A text to Ray, right before she went on, didn't hurt either. "No problem. Thank you for this opportunity." She strode towards the door. She had travelled to the Moon and back. She could handle this.

$$\diamond$$

"Mr. President, this just came in. There's a protest in front of the steps of the Lincoln Memorial. Best guess is about six hundred protesters, but that's increasing. Social media is going crazy over the Palazzo interview." The White House Deputy Communications Director looked to Joe for direction. Joe held up his hand in a calming gesture, but the president deliberately stepped between them.

"That's all right, let them protest. It was going to happen sooner or later anyway—better to get this over with now. We need to focus on damage control. This is an opportunity, people. Let's make the most of it, instead of crying about it."

Joe looked at the president and nodded. Days like this made him remember why he had voted for President Ferris and came to work for him when he was elected. The man loved his country and worked hard to better the lives of the American people every day. He wasn't afraid to take on a challenge, but who could have predicted the challenge would come from outer space?

A staff member interrupted his musing. "Sir, the 800 number is overloaded We're also getting calls from local law enforcement. Some people are panicking. There's reports of rioting and looting."

The staffer's announcement reminded Joe of a scene right out of 20th century history—the panic caused by Orson Welles' broadcast of *The War of the Worlds* radio drama. The radio announcer's opening line had referenced an alien presence watching the Earth, much the same way the Cygnans had. The similarity was unsettling. While it turned out the reports of panic were greatly exaggerated due to the small radio audience, with the internet at everyone's disposal and the ability for news to be disseminated in minutes, he knew that might not be the case today. He glanced over at the president. "Sir, I think we need a presidential address to get control of this situation, before fear mongers make their case and it goes viral."

"You're right as usual, Joe." The president turned to his press secretary. "I'll meet you in the briefing room in fifteen minutes." He looked at the White House Communications Director.

"Sir, I think we need to . . ."

"Sorry, Katherine. There's no time. I'm just going to have to wing it."

14

"We interrupt our regularly scheduled programming for a message from the President of the United States." *Camera fades in to President Ferris seated at his desk in the Oval Office.*

"Good afternoon, fellow Americans. It has come to my attention that a member of the original crew of the lunar mission Triumphant has expressed concern regarding our friends from the planet Kepler 186f. As an American citizen, it is Dr. Sheila Palazzo's inalienable right to express her opinion, and it is a right I hold dearly. However, when the expression of an opinion can lead fellow citizens to draw false conclusions, possibly resulting in enormous damage, it's my responsibility as leader of our country to come forth and address her concerns publicly.

"Dr. Palazzo's comments are without merit. As you are aware, Congress has passed a Cygnan-human joint resolution moving forward the coming together of Cygnan and human scientists in order to share technology, to the mutual benefit of both parties. The Cygnan scientists are under the supervision of the United States government. There is no reason to fear their presence. In fact, from my latest briefing on the project, our scientists are working well together, and we will have a working nuclear fusion reactor in a matter of weeks, rather than the years it would take without the Cygnan technology.

"For those of you who are uncomfortable with our extraterrestrial friends, may I remind you it wasn't so long ago that the United States struggled with interracial strife. This is not so different, and it would behoove us all to take the words of Martin Luther King to heart now, when he said, 'Nothing in all the world is more dangerous than sincere ignorance and conscientious stupidity.' That applied to justifying mistreatment of a specific race and it also applies to vilifying the Cygnans. I won't stand for prejudice in any form or fashion, be it racial or alien. We have no reason to fear that our trust has been misplaced, and misguided efforts to prove otherwise will only hurt our opportunity to solve our energy problems. I am asking you to come together in support of this unprecedented moment in our history.

"Fossil fuels will not last forever. In fact, our scientists estimate we have less than fifty years before we fall into an unrecoverable energy crisis, unless we find a solution. The benefit the United States of America, and the world, will reap is that solution: a clean, sustainable source of energy for the future of our children and our grandchildren.

"I am asking you to stand by me as we move forward to accomplish this crucial goal. In return, I will keep you informed as we make progress, until the day when we can celebrate together, human and Cygnan, working nuclear fusion reactors and interstellar spaceships powered by the same technology. Once we help the Cygnans relocate to their new planet, we will have a fleet of spaceships that were beyond our wildest imaginings just six months ago. The possibilities are endless, but in order for that future to occur, we need to move forward together in solidarity. I am fully confident the American people will support these endeavors that solve our energy problem while opening up for us a new era in space exploration. Thank you."

"We now return you to our regularly scheduled programming."

The President glanced around at his staff, who had remained seated out of sight of the cameras. "Let's see if that mollifies the naysayers, at least for a little while."

"Good job, Mr. President," Joe murmured. He looked down at his phone at the text from Ray Donaldson:

On my way. Information on Palazzo. Wife's cousin.

"Mr. President, Dr. Palazzo is being brought in for questioning. She violated her mission debriefing instructions by consenting to an unauthorized interview."

"Thanks, Joe. Please keep me informed."

"Yes, sir."

The holding cell at FBI headquarters was not nearly as intimidating as the look on Ray Donaldson's face as he stared at his wife's cousin. Joe leaned forward in the hard-backed chair. His eyes narrowed as he studied Ray and Sheila. Given their relationship and Ray's present mood, it seemed like a good idea to let Ray take the lead.

"What were you thinking? You may have just single-handedly thrown our country into an anti-alien hysteria. I'm not a fan of working with the Cygnans, but what you've done is not only damaging, it's unpatriotic."

"Just wait one minute, Ray. You said you were going to fix this. You said you would be able to block the Cygnan-human energy resolution. But here we are. The aliens are among us, and nobody can see the danger."

"What danger, Sheila? All I can see is that a team of scientists are working towards a solution to the Earth's energy crisis. I never wanted to go off-planet for our answers, and everyone knows that. I don't like aliens. I have made no secret of that. But I would never do anything to jeopardize this country. Your little interview was way over the line. We have to operate within the laws of our nation or we're no better than criminals. What you did with your 'warning' was feed the irrational fears of the segment of the population who were already worried and made those who were not worried start to question the Cygnan presence. You have no evidence to back up your allegation that they may be a 'bad' different or that they are infiltrating our brains."

"And you have no evidence that they're not."

Ray snorted impatiently. "Sheila, listen to yourself. You met Lanjo. You haven't experienced any harm from the Cygnans after having personal contact with them. Now you've created a situation. There's a protest against the Cygnans at the Lincoln Memorial as we speak. #HumanLivesMatter is viral on social media. This is ridiculous and completely uncalled-for, yet it's happening because you decided to betray your oath and do that interview."

Sheila's eyes widened. "Protests? I didn't mean for that to happen. I just wanted to warn people we need to be careful about trusting aliens."

"Well, I wish you'd thought it through. You're making everyone's job harder, including the president's."

Joe cleared his throat, and Ray and Sheila turned their attention to him. "Ray's right. You've created a situation." He met Sheila's gaze firmly. "I need your word that you won't do anything like this again."

"And if I don't?" Sheila asked, looking at Ray, who remained expressionless, and then back to Joe.

"Under Section 401, you will be held indefinitely until it's determined you're no longer a threat to national security. You will also face possible suspension of your psychology licensing credentials for inappropriate behavior."

Sheila turned to Ray, eyes pleading. "But I didn't do anything wrong. You agreed with me. You said yourself, 'We have to find our own solutions to Earth's energy problems, not some extraterrestrial agenda that could affect the future of our planet in a negative way.'"

"There's a big difference. You took an oath when you accepted the position with NASA, to obey the authority of the United States government. You were told not to do any interviews as part of your debriefing. You chose to deliberately disobey that authority. I brought my concerns to Congress and, while free to express my concerns, I was overruled. So while I am certainly free to hold my opinions, it is my duty and obligation to obey the government authority that has been established by our Constitution."

"But—"

Ray slammed his fist on the desk. "It doesn't matter how much we agree on the topic of the alien presence. You broke your oath!"

Sheila looked down, her shoulders slumping. "Okay, Ray. I think it's a huge mistake to welcome the aliens, but it won't happen again." She gazed back up at her cousin's husband. "I'm not sorry for what I did, but I'm sorry it affected you. Tell Mary Beth I'm sorry too, okay?" She turned to Joe, who had patiently watched their exchange. "You have my word."

Joe stood up. "Good. I didn't want to have to move forward with the alternative." He glanced meaningfully towards the door leading deeper into the building.

"You don't have to worry, Mr. Ricinski. It won't happen again."

"Thank you, Dr. Palazzo. You're free to go."

⚛

Ray escorted Sheila to the street and flagged a taxi for her. She pressed her hand to her forehead, closing her eyes momentarily and his voice took on a slightly more sympathetic tone. "It'll be all right, Sheila. Just make sure and do the right thing."

Sheila nodded, fighting back tears. *That's what I've been trying to do.*

"Why don't you come over for Sunday dinner?"

Sheila attempted a smile as she got into the cab. "I'd like that." As soon as the cab started driving off, she reached into her purse for the familiar pill bottle.

She may not be able to talk about the aliens publicly, but nothing Ray had said alleviated her fears. She had to find a way to get rid of them, or she'd never feel peaceful again.

⚛

Dan picked up the end ball of the Newton's cradle on Jonathan's desk and released it. The balls began dancing as their energy transferred. "I'm headed to Switzerland to visit CERN on Tuesday. It's the largest particle physics laboratory in the world. Our Cygnan business partner has a significant interest in antimatter as a possible energy source for our fusion reactor. The Antiproton Decelerator at CERN is attractive to the Cygnans, since it has produced those particles."

"What's the appeal?" Jonathan asked. "I know the existence of antimatter has generated a lot of attention, but there's no way to contain it. How does that help an alien civilization about to be kicked out of their home because of an impending supernova?"

Dan shrugged. "I'm just doing what I'm told, boss. In our last conversation, Paranganjo wanted to know if I could procure some time on the Antiproton Decelerator. CERN has always been open to partnerships and industry participation. I'm just glad they didn't ask for time on the Large Hadron Collider. It's scheduled so far out, that would take years, if at all. I'm going to check into the possibilities for the Antiproton Decelerator."

Jonathan peered at Dan. Something didn't feel quite right, but he was used to letting his subordinates run with their ideas unless they proved to him that his trust was misplaced. "All right Dan, let me know if you need anything. Have a good trip."

"Thanks, boss."

"What? You've got to be kidding!" Tom sank into his chair. It was bad enough they had to weather the short-lived panic Dr. Palazzo's interview created. He briefly gazed heavenward and let out a huge breath. The Cygnan scientists were too fascinated with working on the fusion project to be insulted, and their human counterparts had gotten to know them sufficiently to dismiss Dr. Palazzo's statements as ignorance. He lifted his chin. Their first milestone had been reached three days ahead of schedule. The scenario Brett had just explained was both unexpected and unwelcome. He glanced at Lanjo, who was sitting in one of his office chairs, listening to Brett's update.

"I wish I was, Tom," Brett responded. "But Feraganjo and I have been looking at every possible solution and we just don't see one, given our resources. We're missing the key elements we need to make the magnetic field the size required for a spaceship. The substance they inject the magnetic material with, to heighten the gauss level needed for the flux density required, is not indigenous to Earth. We didn't realize that when we started. It's only available on the Cygnan home planet, but by the time they are able to mine and transport the quantities we need, it'll be too late."

"How could this have been overlooked?" Tom asked the room in general. Every project he had ever worked on had its share of screw-ups. But this was a critical one, and may prove irreparable.

Tom leaned back and crossed his arms, trying to remain calm. "We're running out of time. Our current fusion design is too bulky. Now it feels like we're starting from scratch again. I wish we could use what we already have to further this along."

Lanjo had not said a word. Tom turned to see him staring into space, focusing on some unknown spot. Suddenly he gave a hiccup, turned to Tom and Darryl, and grimaced. "Use what we already have . . . why not . . ." He jumped up, his eyebrows quivering. "I need to talk to Feraganjo." He called over his shoulder as he headed through the door, "I'll be back."

15

Tom put his beer down and took another bite of his wood-fired Neapolitan pizza. He relaxed in his chair with a satisfied sigh. One thing he should have appreciated more about Theresa when they were dating was her lack of pretension. Sitting on the patio of the local pizzeria, sipping on a beer and watching the traffic go by, was comfortable. He was glad they'd finally found time for that bite to eat.

"Seems like old times, doesn't it?" He smiled. The expression that flashed across Theresa's face told him maybe that wasn't the best thing to say. Reflecting on his immature attitude back then, he couldn't blame her. At least she'd been willing to keep in touch all of these years. "I mean, it just feels nice, being together again."

Theresa shoulders relaxed. She returned his smile. "Yes, it does. We had some good times."

"Theresa." Tom reached across the table and took her hand. "I know I was a jerk back in college. I didn't appreciate you the way I should've. I'm really sorry for that."

Theresa met Tom's eyes and licked her lips. "Thanks, but it's just as well. Being commander of a deep space mission has taken up a lot of my time and our breakup allowed me to focus on school and my NASA career. I'm sorry things didn't work out for you in the relationship department. Must be tough to get a divorce after twelve years."

Tom let her hand drop and looked down. "Yeah, it is. But I got Stephanie out of the deal, and I wouldn't trade her for the world. I just wish I could see her. Patricia isn't giving an inch."

"I saw Stephanie's interview on the *Great Day* in the USA show after Lanjo rescued her. She's beautiful, Tom. Smart, too."

Tom puffed out his chest. "Thanks, Theresa. Yeah, she's pretty special." He beamed. "Hardheaded like me though. She doesn't give up on anything once it enters her head." He paused and his expression softened. "I was hoping you might consider a date. I don't want to give up on us either."

Theresa stiffened. "I'm sorry, Tom. You know I care about you and I'm glad we're friends, but I'm at a good place personally and professionally right now and I'm not sure if I want anything complicating it." Her gaze hardened a fraction. "And I just don't think I'm ready to trust you with my feelings yet. They took quite a battering last time."

A look of disappointment crossed his face and he hung his head. "I know they did, and I'm so sorry. I'm a different man now. I was too immature to appreciate you back then."

"So are you able to ride in the Hotter 'N Hell this year?" Theresa asked brightly with a forced smile.

Tom took a calming breath. He needed to back off and give Theresa some room. She couldn't be coerced. She was a NASA mission commander and her own person. He shook his head. "Nope. I had to miss it last year, too. I still ride around the

Potomac by the lab when I really need a break, but training has been impossible with everything going on. We were on a tight schedule to begin with and now Washington has asked us to move it up." He paused to see if anyone was within earshot and lowered his voice. "It looks like Jonathan Howe is making a move with a businessman on Lanzeron. It's really making waves."

"Yeah, I know. Keith told us Jonathan Howe was wanting to hire the lunar mission crew to work on the Moon mining helium-3 and operating fusion reactors on the lunar surface. Of course we said no. Poor Keith, he feels caught in the middle. It's got to be tough having Jonathan Howe as your father-in-law to be."

"I agree. Keith's a standup guy. I got to spend some time with him when we moved the lab to the Ashburn campus—he hung around to help Lanjo get settled in."

Theresa nodded. "As mission commander, I couldn't have asked for a better person to handle the First Contact." She turned and glanced meaningfully at the approaching waitress. "So, is Stephanie in any sports?"

"Actually, she bike rides."

"No surprise there."

"But she's also very devoted to music. She plays the violin." The waitress refilled their water glasses. "Would you like anything else?"

Tom glanced at Theresa. She said, "I'll have another Bud Lite, please."

"Make that two." At least she wasn't in a hurry to end the evening. Perhaps there was hope after all.

This is so cool! Marco could barely contain his excitement. Ever since he set up communications with the Cygnans through the wormhole coordinates they'd transmitted, he'd been able to communicate with them with SETI's radio transmitters/receivers at superluminal transmission speeds. The Cygnans had found a way to harness the Casimir energy at its center so that the wormhole wouldn't collapse. *How 'bout them apples, NASA!*

Paranganjo could only transmit during certain windows, which Marco hadn't figured out yet, so he liked to keep an ear open for the incoming signal audio alarm he had programmed just for a Cygnan space call. *WootWootWoot* . . . .the swan was checking in. He walked over to the transmission decoding equipment he'd set up. The aliens' modulation choice of QAM with its high spectral efficiencies required some upgrading at his end, but Jonathan Howe was happy to fund the new equipment. The Cygnan signal was encrypted when demodulated, but Marco's software quickly decoded the message. Marco read the message on the screen and stepped back, giving a low whistle. Jonathan Howe would be really interested in this. Paranganjo was finally making a business proposition, but it wasn't at all what he was expecting.

⚛

"The bottom line is, we can't let a small xenophobic segment of the population disrupt progress." Bahram sipped on a cup of tea, sucking it through a sugar cube he held clenched between his teeth, a habit from childhood he reverted to under stress.

"I agree," Ray said. "I want us to solve our own energy problems, but I'd never deliberately work to interfere with our democratic process. I'm committed to the resolutions that were passed. Sheila acted on her own."

"I never doubted that. You've always been a straight shooter. But the damage has been done, and it's causing problems from a national security standpoint. We're having to devote a lot more resources to managing alien hysteria, resources that would've been better directed elsewhere."

"I'm sorry for that. I talked to Sheila, and it won't happen again."

"It better not. The word from The Hill is that we're on a very tight timeline. Apparently, there are other factions on Lanzeron that are not disposed to working through official channels. If we're going to keep a handle on this, we need to avoid situations that cause work to be delayed, or it could get messy."

Ray let out an exasperated breath. "Dealing with the official Cygnan government is one thing, but we need to avoid rogue operations we can't keep track of." The words hung unspoken in his mind: *Sheila may be right after all.* "Thanks for the update. Don't worry about Sheila."

Bahram put his teacup down. "The Joint Committee on Energy and Alien Relations is concerned. Senator McCree is starting to stir things up and I don't know how long I can hold him off."

"But I had nothing to do with . . ."

"I'm just telling you as a friend," Bahram interrupted. "A Secretary of Energy was dismissed in 1975. It could happen again. I know you're a presidential appointee, but I also know the president plans on running for a second term. I wouldn't make too many waves, if I were you."

"Sure, thanks Bahram. Please give Rosanna my best."

"And mine to Mary Beth."

16

Darryl took off his glasses and rubbed his eyes. He glanced at Tom, who was staring intently at Lanjo. They had gathered in a small conference room located down the hallway from their lab at the alien's request. "Lanjo, please try again, with more details. You've lost me."

Lanjo took a deep breath and made a conscious effort to speak more slowly. "Project Daedalus. Instead of using a magnetic field to contain and compress plasma, we need to use inertial confinement fusion. You've already done this with Project Daedalus."

"Are you kidding?" Brett interrupted. "Have you seen the size of that thing? Inertial confinement fusion is completely impractical for interstellar travel. That's why we're developing magnetic confinement."

Tom held up a hand. "Hang on a minute, Brett. Let Feraganjo explain."

All eyes turned towards the alien scientist. "You're correct, Brett. Magnetic confinement is a good approach to the problem of fusion-powered space ships. But we've found a way to generate the power needed for inertial confinement that is 1/100 the size of your current technology.

"Your Project Daedalus was on the right track and is well-documented. All we need to do is contribute our energy source to the design and we'll have our spaceship. Instead of the electron beams used in Project Daedalus, we're going to use antiproton beams. You already have a source for the antimatter we need, the Antiproton Decelerator at CERN."

Tom's jaw dropped. Ever since the First Contact, he felt as if he was in a dream and would wake up at any moment. Was he actually in a conversation where his team was going to utilize inertial confinement with antimatter in order to conquer nuclear fusion for space travel? He shook his head. Even a science fiction novel would be stretched to come up with this one. "Let me get this straight. We'll be able to build an antiproton-driven fusion spaceship in the necessary time frame, if we're able to utilize the Daedalus design and antimatter we obtain from CERN." He paused, cocking his head. "Which by the way, they have only been able to generate in very small amounts and have only been able to store for seventeen minutes."

"Yes." Lanjo blinked rapidly. "That's why we need permission to make some modifications. Feraganjo assures me it really isn't all that complicated. Like the old saying, 'If you don't know, it's simply awful. If you do know, it's awfully simple.'"

"Really?" Brett still looked skeptical.

Feraganjo nodded. "It's true. We didn't take the inertial confinement approach initially, because it's more complicated due to constructing the power source. But it is an excellent approach and is our only option, now that we know we can't create the magnetic field we need for our current design."

Brett opened his mouth to comment further, but Darryl interrupted. "Okay, so we have a viable solution. Time is critical. How do we implement it? What do you need to move forward?"

"Access to the Project Daedalus plans would be tremendously useful," Lanjo began.

"I can do better than that," Tom interjected. "I met Alan Bond when he was a guest speaker for my mechanical engineering classes at MIT. He led the research for Project Daedalus. I'll see if I can get him to come out here."

"That would be wonderful." Lanjo turned to Darryl. "We also need to get time on the CERN Antiproton Decelerator and," he paused and coughed, "permission to make some modifications."

"Great," Darryl replied. "The first part of your request is possible, but the second part will go over like a lead balloon."

Feraganjo cocked his head. "Lead balloon? Why would someone inject lead into an object meant to be inflated with a gas?"

Brett chuckled. "It's an idiom, Feraganjo."

"I need to make some calls, and all of you have work to do." Darryl stood up. "Tom, give Alan Bond a call. Let's see what we can get done—we need all of this in place yesterday. Brett, Feraganjo, keep moving on the nuclear fusion reactor. Implement what you know of inertial confinement instead of trying to contain plasma in a magnetic field. Let's get going, everyone."

"English is very confusing. I still don't understand why you would want to inject a balloon with lead. And I will never get your verb tenses straight," Feraganjo said in a low voice to Brett. Brett patted the alien's shoulder. "It's okay. I'll explain later. At least we have them. You've met Chiv, the human in charge of calibrating our test equipment? He's from Cambodia, and Cambodians don't use verb tenses at all."

"I also find it very strange you have so many different languages on one planet. Everyone on Lanzeron speaks one language."

"I don't understand it myself," Brett laughed. "It's hard enough dealing with the metric system at work and switching to standard at home."

"Yes," Feraganjo agreed. "My first night here, I froze the coils of the air conditioner in my dorm room. I had entered a set point of 20 degrees, thinking it was Celsius, but it kept running all night. I should have entered 68 degrees for Fahrenheit." He grimaced. "'If you don't know, it's simply awful. If you do know, it's awfully simple.'"

"It's good to see Brett and Feraganjo getting along so well," Tom observed to Lanjo, watching them walk towards the lab, deep in conversation. "Come to think of it, everyone seems to have worked out their differences. 'A friend in need is a friend indeed.'"

Lanjo cocked his head at Tom. "Another idiom I'm unfamiliar with. Could you explain?"

"Sure." Tom grinned. "It means a friend who is there when you really need help, is a true friend. Like you were for Stephanie on the Potomac."

Lanjo grimaced back and nodded, repeating the phrase to himself. "That's a good one. I'll try to remember it."

Jonathan Howe slowly sat down at his desk as he read the secure email from Marco on his computer:

Paranganjo is ready to make the deal, but he has one condition. He still sees helium-3 as the energy source for both Earth and the Cygnans' new planet. He wants to partner with HoweTek Communications, but you'll have to agree to help stop the government effort.

He wished Dan wasn't 5000 miles away trying to broker a deal with CERN, in Switzerland. Jonathan's entrepreneurial instincts served him well in a world where not everything was always clear. He was accustomed to doing business with strange bedfellows, but perhaps this time he was in danger of going over the line. His words to Joe Ricinski came back to him, "I would never do anything to compromise our nation's security."

Supplying transportation and resources were one thing, but what exactly was Paranganjo implying? And when would Dan be back? It hadn't been Jonathan's idea to ask Keith to work on the Moon, but he'd gone along with it. Dan had argued it would give them an edge over the government effort, but it didn't accomplish anything significant since the NASA astronauts had refused to cooperate. If anything, it had tipped the government off to what they were trying to do. Jonathan sighed. He needed to fully understand Paranganjo's position before his meeting with Geoffrey Clarke in a couple of days. Something was not quite right, but he couldn't put his finger on it.

17

The president smiled warmly as he shook hands with Lanjo. "It's good to see you again, even if you did beat me in bowling. Next time we're at Camp David, I insist on a rematch."

"Certainly, Mr. President," Lanjo grimaced in return. Unable to move about freely due to security concerns, he'd been watching television in his free time. He recently became addicted to watching reruns of *The West Wing* and had a new appreciation for what the president's day must be like.

The president turned to Darryl. "Thank you for coming on such short notice."

"Of course, sir."

"So how's your daughter Sandra doing?"

Darryl's face lit up. "She's fine, sir. Her blood count is normal. It seems the new medication is working."

"Wonderful, Darryl. Wonderful news." President Ferris placed his hands on Darryl's and Lanjo's shoulders and guided them towards the doors to the Oval Office. "Why don't we go on in? Would you like some coffee?"

"Yes, sir, that'd be very nice," Darryl said. Lanjo nodded agreement. Darryl and Lanjo rocked in excitement, their eyes sparkling. Neither had been in the Oval Office before. All of the briefings Darryl attended at the White House had been held in the Roosevelt Room.

Both human and alien gaped in awe as they hesitantly stepped into the oval-shaped room, being careful to avoid the giant Seal of the President of the United States in the center of the light blue and gold carpeting. The office looked just like it did in the movies, except for the president's personal touches. Like most of the presidents before him, President William B. Ferris had chosen to keep the Resolute desk, made from the timbers of the *H.M.S. Resolute*. An engraved wooden paperweight sat prominently on it, the quote looking a bit worn but still legible:

There comes a time when one must take a position that is neither safe, nor politic, nor popular, but he must take it because conscience tells him it is right.

–Martin Luther King Jr.

A curved bookcase lined one side of the room and a fireplace was on the wall across from the desk. Beautifully upholstered occasional chairs were placed strategically around the room and heavy gold drapes added presidential dignity. Lanjo looked around, surprised at how comfortable and warm the room felt, considering he was standing in the working office of the President of the United States. Government offices on Lanzeron tended to exude a more formal atmosphere, that did not encourage one to linger. He wondered briefly if other governments on Earth followed a similar model as the United States president. It would be fun to investigate. He did like the Martin Luther King quote. He had written a paper on the civil rights movement in the United States as an undergraduate student. Martin Luther King was a true visionary.

"Sit down, please. Make yourself comfortable." The president waved them to the chairs located around a coffee table by the fireplace. The president's secretary placed a tray that held a silver pitcher, cups, and a plate of cookies on the coffee table.

"Joe will be here in a few minutes. He's on a call." The president smiled at his secretary. "Thank you, Mrs. Crippen. You can go home now."

"Thank you, sir." She exited through one of the doors. The Secret Service detail stood alertly just on the other side as she closed the door behind her.

Darryl and Lanjo looked at each other. Who could the president's top aide be on a call with? Some head of state that needed him to confirm U.S. forces were in place to prevent an international disaster? Perhaps it was the leader of the AFL-CIO in an attempt to prevent a strike?

President Ferris took the seat facing them, and poured three cups of coffee. "His wife called. He had to run home earlier. Their refrigerator started to go out, and it's fifteen years old. He cleaned the coils, but that doesn't seem to be working. They're trying to decide whether to repair it or buy a new one."

It had never occurred to Lanjo that high government officials had many of the same problems as regular citizens. "Why doesn't he just buy a new one?" the alien asked with a puzzled expression.

"That's what I said," the president responded. "But they don't make them like they used to and if Joe can get this one repaired, he thinks it still has plenty of life in it." He laughed. "Our chief economic advisor would probably advise him to buy a new one to help boost the economy." He glanced at his watch. "We had better get started. He might be awhile."

"Yes, sir, Mr. President." Darryl leaned forward in his chair.

"The situation has gotten rather complicated. A businessman on Lanzeron named Paranganjo has made contact with Jonathan Howe, an entrepreneur who is very interested in helium-3. Paranganjo has the same interest for the future home of the Cygnans and is trying to put a plan in motion allowing him to be at the front of the line. He is in negotiations with Jonathan Howe to form a partnership in mining helium-3 for fusion reactors that his associates will be building on the Moon."

"But if Paranganjo is on Lanzeron, how are they communicating? That's five hundred light years away," Darryl asked.

Lanjo made a whistling noise. "Wormhole."

Darryl turned to the alien in confusion. "What?"

The president jumped in. "The Cygnans have also made advances in communication. They're able to keep a wormhole open in order to use it as a communications hub across the galaxy."

A door to the Oval Office opened, and Joe strode in. "Mr. President." He nodded. "Hello Darryl, Lanjo." He reached over to shake their hands and took a seat.

"I was just telling Darryl and Lanjo about Paranganjo and Jonathan. They've been making plans for a while now. Jonathan's subordinate has developed a working relationship with the Cygnan business faction."

"That's correct," Joe said. "Dan Ross has been very active in building a joint venture between HoweTek Communications and

Paranganjo. He's at CERN right now, trying to negotiate time on the Antiproton Decelerator."

"That's not surprising," Lanjo cleared his throat. "If Paranganjo was human, his job description would be that of venture capitalist."

"What is surprising," Joe added, "is Jonathan's reaction. Commander McDonnough informed NASA that Jonathan made an offer to her crew to go to work for him. He's willing to do business with the Cygnans but doesn't trust them completely. The crew, of course, refused."

The president's brow furrowed. "It concerns me Jonathan is willing to get involved with a rogue faction, especially when he understands what the U.S. government is trying to put in place. His attempt to lure the NASA crew to his operation is not quite treasonous, but close."

"What's even more confusing," Lanjo said, "is that Paranganjo is willing to work with Jonathan. Paranganjo is known to be untrustworthy and self-serving and does not play well with others. He has to be bluffing." Lanjo gazed into the distance, his expression shifting into a blank stare. Darryl stage-whispered to the president, "Don't worry, that's what he looks like when he's thinking."

Lanjo suddenly jerked upright in his chair. "I think it's a diversion. Paranganjo wants to use the imminent demise of our planet as an opportunity to be exploited. He must have something else planned, if he's leading Jonathan Howe on with a possible business deal. In all probability, he is deceiving Jonathan to obtain access to CERN, access that only someone of Jonathan's stature would be granted. What do you know about Dan Ross? Is he completely loyal to Jonathan?"

"I don't know much about him," Joe admitted. "But I'll find out."

"Yes, please do that." The president clenched his fists. "We need to figure out how far Jonathan is willing to go to get helium-3 ahead of us. Dupe or not, it's incumbent upon Jonathan or any of his employees not to cause harm to the interests of the United States. Joe, brief me on Dan Ross as soon as possible."

The president turned back to Darryl and Lanjo and his expression softened. "It's good to see you, as always, Darryl. And Lanjo, the United States appreciates your friendship."

"The Cygnan government appreciates yours, Mr. President." Lanjo grimaced and continued, "'A friend in need is a friend indeed.'"

"Truer words never spoken. Thank you both. Please be sure to give Joe regular updates on your progress."

Darryl and Lanjo nodded and replied in unison, "Yes, sir."

Joe cleared his throat. "There is one more thing, sir."

President Ferris raised his eyebrows at his aide. "What's that, Joe?"

"It seems Dan is on the right track. We need some time on the Antiproton Decelerator at CERN. By we, I mean Lanjo and the science team at Ashburn. Some modifications will be required for their antimatter trap."

The president sighed. "Let me get this straight. I need to ask world-renowned physicists at the premier world laboratory for particle physics to disrupt their current experiments so the aliens can modify their instruments?"

"I wouldn't put it quite that way, but yes, sir," Joe replied.

"And may I ask why?"

"So we can generate enough anti-protons for our fusion spaceships."

"The antimatter?"

"Yes, sir."

"You aren't kidding?"

"No, sir."

The president sighed again. "I'll see what I can do."

"Thank you, sir."

18

"What are you doing here?" Tom's mouth fell open in surprise. "I thought you needed to stay with Sandra."

"I can go after all. Sandra is doing great on her new medication. The nine-hour flight isn't too long, now that she's feeling so much better. Her doctors assured me it was okay for me to leave. I can always hop on a plane if she needs me." Darryl playfully jabbed at Tom. "Guess who's flying us to CERN?"

"Uhhhhh . . . a pilot?" The scientific community was small, and news travelled fast. Apparently, Tom's desire to get back together with Theresa had become common knowledge. He blithely changed the subject. "I never got to ask, how did you get CERN to agree?"

"Since our alien friends have developed a way to store antiprotons, I focused on CERN's need to do the same. The ALPHA collaboration has made only small strides in that area. Lanjo explained to them that Cygnans are able to capture antiprotons in a portable trap, enabling the antimatter to be used as a power source. After a chat with President Ferris, The ALPHA collaboration decided it was in CERN's best interest to allow us time on the Antiproton Decelerator. Provided we share the technology, of course."

Before Tom could formulate a reply, Theresa, wearing her NASA flightsuit, walked up the concourse. "Excuse me," he brushed by his boss and headed to meet her.

"Hey there," he said, wishing he was more eloquent. Just the sight of her made those butterflies in his stomach come back to life. He'd not been able to find time to see her since their pizza dinner.

"Hi Tom." Theresa returned his smile. "The president called NASA and requested me to pilot because of my alien transport experience. I was glad to oblige."

Tom silently thanked the president in his head. "I'm glad, it's good to see you."

"Good to see you, too." Theresa looked around, and Tom immediately sensed a change in her demeanor. In the old days Tom would've misinterpreted her serious attitude as a lack of interest in him, but he'd grown wiser in the years since their breakup. Theresa was a professional with a job to do, and on her shoulders was the responsibility for the lives that would be entering that airplane. It had never occurred to him before what a burden that must be.

"I'd better let you get to work. Dinner in Switzerland?"

Theresa looked startled and gave Tom a second, more penetrating look. "Sure, Tom. I'd like that."

"Great! See you later." Tom turned and walked back to where Darryl stood. The Gulfstream III already contained their luggage, and they were waiting for Alan Bond to join them. Not only had he offered to share his documentation of Project Daedalus when

Tom contacted him, Bond had insisted on accompanying them to CERN.

The jet's airstairs were already deployed. A taxi passed Tom and pulled up next to Darryl. As the taxi driver got out and opened the trunk to remove his passenger's luggage, a man emerged from the taxi and held out his hand to Darryl. "Hello, I'm Alan Bond. I believe I'm riding with you."

Tom jogged up as they were shaking hands. "Mr. Bond! Thank you so much for agreeing to help us."

"My pleasure," he replied, peering over his glasses with steely blue eyes. Tom felt like a wayward student again. "Tom Whitaker? You're the one I spoke with? You're the mechanical engineering student from MIT?"

"Yes, sir!" Tom grinned. "Although I have graduated since then."

"I should certainly hope so," Alan commented dryly. He paid the taxi driver, and one of the ground crew working nearby picked up his two suitcases.

"I'll stow these away for you, sir."

"Why, thank you," Alan responded to the worker's offer. The young man quickly headed to the other side of the plane and disappeared.

The wind picked up, and the three men turned their backs to it so they could hear each other speak. "So how do Cygnans store antiprotons?" Alan asked. "ALPHA has managed to capture atoms of antihydrogen, but the quantities required to use them as a power source are several magnitudes more than anything CERN has been able to store. The little boogers are instantly annihilated when they touch ordinary matter. Even though the ALPHA team can generate thousands of antihydrogen atoms in a single second, they're too energetic to trap. Catching even one is considered a success at this point."

Darryl raised his voice to be heard over the wind. "Lanjo's lead scientist anticipated a possible issue with their original plan and had the foresight to bring their antimatter trap along. From what I understand, their device also uses magnetism to keep the antimatter away from the walls of the trap. It's able to capture the antimatter despite its energy. While rather large, it's still portable. The trap can store the antimatter indefinitely and will be incorporated into our interstellar spaceship design, providing the energy we need for our fusion reactor."

"That's amazing," Alan's eyes widened. "And a bit hard to believe."

"Oh, it gets better," Tom bounced from foot to foot. "Nuclear fusion reactions sparked by beams of antimatter will be the propulsion system for our interstellar spaceships. The fuel for a fusion-driven spaceship will consist of helium-3 mined from the Moon and deuterium, an isotope of hydrogen readily available on Earth. That's where Project Daedalus comes in. Even though Daedalus' fusion reactions would've been sparked by electron beams instead of antiproton beams, we can use the Daedalus plans with a modified energy source, since the Cygnans have the necessary technology to make it work."

Lanjo walked up and held out his hand to Alan, grimacing. "That's my story and I'm sticking to it. Thank you for joining us, Mr. Bond."

Tom and Darryl exchanged an amused glance at Alan's raised eyebrow. "Please, call me Alan." They shook hands, Alan firmly returning Lanjo's grip with a twinkle in his eye. "I'm looking forward to sharing our technology."

"Feraganjo and Brett are already on board along with Keraganjo and Rachel, our two junior engineers," Lanjo said. "They're pretty thrilled to get to go to CERN." He grimaced again. "It seems being a nerd crosses all cultural boundaries."

Before anyone else could comment, an airport official approached. "Time to board, gentlemen. Your flight plan has you in the air in fifteen minutes."

"Yes, sir," Darryl said. "Let's go folks. We have some antimatter to catch."

19

In a plane that could hold nineteen passengers, the science team had plenty of room to spread out for the nine-hour flight. NASA supplied the jet and crew. A stocky Air Force sergeant served as an aide in the passenger cabin, remaining unobtrusive but ready to offer assistance if needed. Theresa's co-pilot was running late. As they sat waiting and chatting among themselves, a sandy-haired head appeared coming up the stairs. "Keith! It's great to see you!" Lanjo sprang up to hug his first human friend.

Keith smiled. "When Theresa invited me along to co-pilot, I jumped at the chance to see you again. How are you?"

"I'm doing great. Working with Darryl and Tom and our science team has been an amazing experience. Going to CERN is a dream come true. I wrote a paper titled, 'Human Advances in Particle Physics,' for my doctorate. I'm very excited to see in person the physics laboratory I wrote about."

"I'm glad to hear that, but I better get to work." Keith winked at the Cygnan. "You know how grumpy Theresa can get when we go off schedule."

"Yes, I do." Lanjo grimaced.

The squeal of the engines drowned out the possibility of conversation as the jet began to roll forward, gaining the momentum she needed to leap skyward. This was Tom's first flight with Theresa as the pilot. The engines roared, and his respect for her increased. She was not the same girl he dated back in college. The plane leapt into the air, diverting his thoughts as he leaned back and closed his eyes, feeling the acceleration go through his body.

The plane leveled off. He opened his eyes and looked out the window. He could see Dulles airport below. The private jet terminal they had taken off from was a tiny square, and the rest of the airport was rapidly receding. The plane headed towards the Atlantic Ocean, and everyone unbuckled their seat belts, anticipating a long, uneventful flight.

Brett and Feraganjo were together as usual. They'd brought a chess set and were already intent on their game. Keraganjo and Rachel were also sitting together. Their role on the science team was to modify the fusion reactor to the design specs of Project Daedalus under Brett and Feraganjo's supervision and to run the tests designed to verify subsystem functionality. The junior engineers were inseparable, living and breathing their work.

Darryl, Tom, Lanjo, and Alan sat scattered around a table. Darryl opened his briefcase and passed out a sheet of paper with contact names and a tentative schedule for their stay. He cleared his throat. "One thing I've found is that I now take for granted working with someone from another planet. When we get to Switzerland, there'll be a lot of curious people. We've managed to keep this visit out of the news, but the officials of CERN have been briefed and are eagerly waiting to make Lanjo's acquaintance.

"Please be patient. I know as members of the scientific community you have little use for 'dog and pony shows,' but we'll need to give them one when we arrive. We're scheduled to meet with members of the CERN Council. They're the highest authority of the organization. Members of the ALPHA team will also be present since antimatter is their bailiwick."

Lanjo looked at Darryl in puzzlement. "My idiom dictionary defines a dog and pony show as a colloquial term meaning a highly promoted, often over-staged performance, presentation, or event designed to sway or convince opinion for political or, less often, commercial ends. But where will we get the dogs and ponies?"

Tom laughed. "We're the dogs and ponies, Lanjo." He got up. "Coffee anyone?"

"Yes, please," Alan replied.

Darryl shook his head. "I've already had too much today."

Tom poured a cup and handed it to Alan. He picked up another coffee mug and began to pour himself some coffee, when the plane lurched. "Owwww." He jumped back as the hot liquid splattered across his hand and down his pant leg. The plane righted and then lurched again. Tom moved to the closest window and watched the right wing drop two feet before coming back up. The sergeant raced to the pilot's compartment.

"What's going on?" Darryl loosened his collar, his eyes darting around the plane.

"It's okay," Tom said. "Whatever's going on, we couldn't have a better pilot to fix it." Just as he finished his sentence, the plane dropped yet again.

Tom looked around at his fellow passengers, all with varying degrees of concern in their expressions. Rachel was sitting with her hands clasped tightly together. Keraganjo sat next to her, awkwardly patting her knee in an effort to reassure her.

"I'll go talk to Theresa and find out what's going on," Tom said. "It's probably just turbulence."

Lanjo jumped up as the chessboard flew off its table and the pieces scattered across the floor of the plane. "I'll go with you. Perhaps I can be of assistance."

The two made their way up the aisle, grabbing the tops of the seats to keep their balance as the plane pitched and swayed. Tom opened the cockpit door, revealing the Air Force sergeant holding his gun to the back of Theresa's chair. He couldn't see the expression on her face, but she was intently working the airplane controls. Keith was sitting straight up in his seat, looking forward, his shoulders tense. No one was talking.

The airplane lurched again and the door handle flew out of Tom's hand. The door banged against its frame and slammed shut, alerting the sergeant he'd been seen.

Tom and Lanjo looked at each other. Tom had attributed the military aide to Lanjo's presence on board, since he usually had a security detail when he went off campus. The sergeant was obviously an imposter. The plane kept lurching, and Tom and Lanjo grabbed each other by the arms to maintain their balance.

"What should we do?" Lanjo asked in a calm, low voice. "The plane has a malfunction, and I'm guessing it wasn't part of the sergeant's plan."

"I think you're right. He probably planned on hijacking the plane, not sabotaging it. I don't know why, but it could have been to prevent us from getting to CERN or to kidnap you and the other Cygnans." The plane lurched yet again, this time harder. "Do you know why the plane keeps doing that?"

"I don't, but I bet Keraganjo does. His hobby is avionics." Lanjo turned and called down the aisle, "Keraganjo, can you join us?"

"Sure, Lanjo." The young Cygnan jumped to his feet and trotted up the aisle. "How can I help?"

"Do you know what's wrong with the plane?" Tom asked.

"Yes, sir. The right aileron is no long responding to its control cable. The pilot is unable to move it."

"What's an aileron?" Lanjo asked.

"It's a hinged flight control surface. It's a part of the airplane wing and is moved up or down to cause the airplane to turn. The ailerons on the two wings are designed to work in opposition so the airplane can bank, causing the plane's flight path to curve. Here, look out the window—see, the aileron is located on the trailing edge of the wing."

"So what does that mean?" Tom asked.

"All kinds of bad things could happen," Keraganjo said as the plane heaved again. "Ailerons control the wing's lift and drag character-istics. If we can't control the aileron and we go into a large bank angle at too slow a speed, we could stall and go into a spin. If the ailerons are not working together the way they're designed, they can cause the plane to go off-balance, which is why we keep lurching. It can cause the pilot to lose complete control of the plane."

By now Alan, Brett, Feraganjo, and Rachel had made their way forward and stood listening. The humans were white-faced and the Cygnans' skin took on a darker cast as Keraganjo explained what was happening.

"So what can we do?" Lanjo asked.

"Well, from here, we can't access the cable—it runs under the flooring and through the cargo department. We need to find some way to stabilize that aileron." Keraganjo paused. "But this is an issue that should be supervised by the captain."

Tom and Lanjo exchanged a troubled glance. Tom met everyone's eyes and put his finger against his lips. He spoke in a low voice. "Normally yes, Keraganjo, but we've been hijacked. We just observed the sergeant that accompanied us. He's in the cockpit, holding Theresa and Keith at gunpoint."

The science team exchanged stunned looks. Alan steadied himself and sat down. Keraganjo swallowed hard. "We'll have to do something very soon. The plane could crash."

"How about that telekinesis thing, like Lanjo did when he saved Stephanie?" Tom asked. "Can you do that with the aileron and keep it in the correct position?"

The young Cygnan shook his head. "I'm sorry, but I can't. I don't possess that ability." He turned to Lanjo. "But I could guide you, if you're willing." His mouth pursed into a pucker, which Tom had come to learn was the equivalent of a human frown—something Cygnans rarely did. "But we'll need feedback from the crew, to know in what position we need the aileron." The plane lurched again, the hardest yet. "We won't be successful unless we can regain control of the plane."

20

Tom's mind was spinning. Part of him was terrified for Theresa, but panicking wouldn't help the situation. The sergeant was aware they knew he was threatening the flight crew. Was he suicidal, or did he expect to survive this flight? If he was going to crash the plane, he could've done so already. Was he out to kill them, or was he diverting the plane? Why didn't he respond to the failed aileron? Was he planning to get off safely on his own? There were too many possibilities. Tom took a deep breath, forcing himself to focus on the immediate problem: how to neutralize the armed man in the cockpit.

"Lanjo?" Tom turned to the friend who had saved his daughter, hoping for a similar solution. "Are you able to use your ability to move the gun away from Theresa and Keith and point it in another direction?"

Lanjo shook his head. "If only I could, but I wouldn't be fast enough. He would still have time to shoot before I could get a good grip. I don't think it would end well. I'm sorry."

"That's okay. We just need to figure something out." The plane dropped again, and Tom struggled to keep his balance. "And fast."

Darryl spoke up. "The only way into the cockpit is through the door. Since this is a military plane, the door won't have a lock. We can have Lanjo and Keraganjo move the aileron to cause the plane to swerve and drop, causing a diversion. While the sergeant is distracted trying to keep his balance, we can rush in and subdue him."

Tom looked at Lanjo. "Are you sure you can't read minds or communicate telepathically?" he asked wistfully. "It would be nice to give Theresa and Keith a heads up."

"Sorry, Tom. I really can't. Telekinesis only."

"Okay, we don't have much time." Tom began issuing orders. "Keraganjo, Lanjo, position yourselves where Lanjo can start controlling the aileron. As soon as I give you the signal, drop the plane. Alan, stay with them in case they need something. Darryl, Brett, Feraganjo, stay with me." He gazed at Rachel, looking very vulnerable and reminding him of Stephanie in a few years. "Rachel, I'll need you to help . . ." He hesitated. "To be ready if someone is injured during our attempt to subdue the sergeant. Go get the first-aid kit out of the rear locker and stand by." Rachel nodded and headed to the back of the plane.

Standing by the window that gave Lanjo the best view of the right wing aileron, Keraganjo and Lanjo switched to their native language. There could be no gap in communication as Keraganjo gave Lanjo the positional instructions for the aileron to cause the plane to swerve, then bring it back to safety. Alan stationed himself nearby, out of the way. Both Cygnans turned to Tom and nodded their readiness. Tom took a steadying breath, said a quick silent prayer, and waved his hand sharply forward to indicate *Go!*

As Lanjo responded by focusing intently on the aileron through the window, Tom was taken back in time to a few months ago. He was once again sitting in the break room with Lanjo, the alien's eyebrows furrowed as he concentrated on the bluebird with the mangled wing. The picture in his mind changed, and Lanjo was sweating profusely, focusing on Stephanie hanging onto the branch over the river. Tom shook his head to get rid of the image. He needed to focus.

He heard *"Shhhhh . . . shhhhh"* and charged forward. Just as he started to push open the cockpit door, the plane dropped several feet in altitude and jerked savagely to the left. Tom crashed through the door and flung himself on top of the gunman. Keith grabbed his arm and wrenched the gun free. It slid out of his hand, hit the floor, and went off. The bullet ricocheted and hit Theresa in the thigh. She screamed and stared down at the bleeding hole in her leg.

Tom roared, pummeling the gunman as the plane lurched violently, slamming their bodies into the instrumentation. Tom wrapped the sergeant in a bear hug, jerked him back, and pushed him through the cockpit door and into the passenger compartment. Brett and Feraganjo dove on top of him. Keith had recovered the gun and trained it on the sergeant.

"Bring the first aid kit, Theresa's been hit," Tom yelled, but Rachel was already responding.

Tom grabbed some duct tape and with Brett and Feraganjo assisting, began to tape the sergeant's wrists and ankles. A hand touched his shoulder as he started to pull the tape tight. "Whoa, Tom," Brett said. "Give him a little room."

Tom looked through the cockpit door and could see Rachel holding a compress against Theresa's thigh where the fabric had been cut away. The bleeding had stopped and Theresa was still flying the plane. *She's alive. She's able to function.* He eased up on the tape. "Yeah, okay Brett."

He scanned the passenger compartment. Alan teetered against the back of an aisle seat, face pale and brow studded with sweat. "Feraganjo, go help Alan to a seat and get him some water," Tom directed, just as the plane took another violent swerve to the left and dropped again. It continued to descend at the same angle it had dropped. Keith shouted from the cockpit, "Move the aileron up as high as you can or we'll go into a spin!"

Lanjo was soaking with sweat as he stared at the aileron. He was starting to weaken from the effort. Keraganjo was keeping up a steady patter of encouragement and direction in their native tongue. "Darryl, help Feraganjo with Alan," Tom ordered. He looked down at the sergeant, who was glaring up at him. Tom had taken great pleasure in taping his mouth shut along with binding his wrists and ankles. He lifted him roughly and shoved him onto one of the seats. "Brett, help me support Lanjo."

The two men joined the Cygnans at the window, standing on either side of Lanjo. "*Shhhhhh . . .*" They placed their hands under his arms and held him up. Tom peered out the window. The aileron was in an upright position. Keith yelled, "Slowly begin a downward angle." Lanjo complied, and the aileron moved downward. The plane leveled off.

"Thank God," Tom said. Brett nodded.

Keraganjo switched to English. "Theresa has managed to level the plane. We'll be fine as long as we're going straight and Lanjo can hold the aileron steady. But it'll get difficult when we need to turn."

"How is Lanjo holding up?" Tom asked Keraganjo, afraid to interrupt Lanjo's concentration.

"He's okay for now, but it's an enormous drain. Please continue to hold him up, so he can conserve his energy. Turning will take a lot of effort."

"Okay," Tom said. He wanted to check on Theresa, but Keith and Rachel would take care of her until they got through this crisis. He turned and looked at Feraganjo. He was tending to Alan, who was sitting back with his head against his seat and his eyes closed. "Is he okay?"

"As much as I can tell from your species, I believe so," Ferganjo said. "It seems he has high blood pressure, which increased under the stress of our situation, causing him to become short of breath. I feared he was approaching a hypertensive crisis, but he seems to have recovered and his breathing is approaching normal."

"Alan, are you okay?" Tom asked.

Alan opened his eyes and smiled weakly. "Yes. Go ahead and hold Moses' arms up. Just a bit more than I bargained for. I'll be all right."

"Yes, sir."

Brett eyed him curiously. "Moses? What does he mean by that?"

"It's a fairly well-known event that occurred in the Old Testament," Lanjo began to explain in a quavering voice.

Tom gazed at his friend with affection mixed with admiration and a touch of exasperation. "Go back to *shhhhhh*, Lanjo, I got this."

"I can't believe he could do that," Keraganjo said. "He actually maintained control while talking to you."

"I can believe it," Tom chuckled. "Lanjo can't resist divulging Earth trivia. Alan was referencing the story in Exodus in the Bible, when Amalek attacked Israel. As long as Moses kept his hands raised, Israel prevailed. But when he let his arms drop from tiredness, Amalek began to win. So Aaron, and I forget the other guy's name, they stood on either side of him much like we are now and supported his arms, so that Israel could defeat Amalek. I learned about it in Sunday School. I thought it was a cool story, but I haven't thought about it in years." Tom grinned. "Leave it to Lanjo to get the reference."

Tom's grin faded when he saw the look on Keith's face, as he exited the cockpit and approached them.

21

"How's Theresa doing?" Tom asked Keith.

"The bullet didn't hit anything vital. It's lodged in her thigh and hurts like hell, but it doesn't require immediate attention beyond what Rachel is already doing."

Tom frowned. He was about to speak when Keith stopped him. "Honestly, Tom. She'll be fine. NASA insists everyone cross trains. I have advanced first aid training, including military first aid. She's okay. You could ask her yourself, but she's insisting on flying the plane and probably needs every spare bit of concentration. Right now, we need to stay focused."

"Okay, so what's the problem?"

Keith took a deep breath. "The problem is getting us safely home. We're currently over the Atlantic Ocean and we need to turn the plane and head to the closest airport, Logan in Boston. NASA's been advised, and they're scrambling an escort, but—"

The plane lurched another three feet, and everyone grabbed their seats. Tom and Brett barely managed to maintain their hold on

Lanjo. His gaze remained fixed on the aileron as he whispered a faint, steady, *"Shhhhh."*

"We need to turn the plane," Keith continued, "which is the ailerons' job. Lanjo has kept the damaged aileron from moving out of position. Because of that, the plane has maintained stable flight. But now, we're going to ask him to maneuver the aileron correctly, so we can execute a 180 degree turn and head back home."

"How hard is that?" Tom asked, his stomach churning and a sour taste in his mouth.

"Normally, it's not a problem because the pilot has a yoke where they can control both ailerons from the cockpit. Theresa will still be controlling the left one to execute the turn, but we'll need to coordinate it with the right aileron under Lanjo's control." He handed Keraganjo a headset. "I'll be giving instructions from the cockpit to Keraganjo, who can relay them to Lanjo. After we make the turn, Lanjo will still need to keep the aileron stable until we get back to Boston—about thirty minutes."

Keith, Brett, and Tom all looked at Lanjo. The alien was sweating profusely, and Tom feared he would dehydrate. "Okay, but before we get started, we better get Lanjo some water. Keraganjo, do you think he'll be okay?"

"I don't know, Tom. Sweating during telekinesis is normal. He's exerting just enough force to keep the aileron in position. However, from what I've heard, telekinesis is very tiring and not normally done for the amount of time Lanjo is doing it. I don't have a good answer for you."

Keraganjo went to the small refrigerator in the back of the plane and pulled out a bottle of water. He quickly returned and held the bottle to Lanjo's lips. Lanjo gulped several swallows while the plane bounced up and down, then he returned to whispering, "*Shhhhhh*" and the plane leveled out.

"Okay, Lanjo. I'm heading to the cockpit. Keraganjo, be ready to help Lanjo with the aileron. We'll be executing our turn momentarily."

"Yes, sir." Keraganjo placed the headset on his head.

Keith reentered the cockpit and settled into his seat. Rachel had stopped the bleeding from Theresa's bullet wound and cleaned the area with the antiseptic from the first aid kit. "Rachel, can you go check on Alan? He was short of breath, probably from all of the excitement."

"Sure. Come get me if she starts bleeding again." Rachel left the cockpit and took a seat next to Feraganjo, where she could easily observe Alan resting with his eyes closed. Feraganjo gave her a silent thumbs up. Darryl sat across from the sergeant, who had ceased fighting the duct tape and lay with his eyes closed.

Theresa glanced over at Keith and forced a smile. "Not exactly what you expected when I invited you to join us, huh?"

"One thing's for sure, Theresa. Serving under you is NEVER boring." Keith's tone turned serious. He moved his mic to his lips and asked, "Keraganjo, can you hear me?"

"Affirmative," Keraganjo's voice confirmed through the speaker. "We are ready to proceed."

"Thank you. Please stand by." Keith turned to Theresa. "We better get this done. Lanjo's getting tired."

"10-4," Theresa responded. "Please ask Lanjo to deflect his aileron downward 30 degrees on my mark."

"Yes, ma'am." Keith thumbed his mic. "Keraganjo, please inform

Lanjo we will need a 30-degree downward deflection on . . ." He looked at Theresa, and she nodded. "Three, two, one, go."

Theresa rotated the yoke left, and the plane shuddered.

The passenger compartment was completely silent except for the "*Shhhhhh*" Lanjo emitted as he focused on the right aileron, and Keraganjo repeating Keith's instructions in Cygnan. The plane began a gradual curve to the right. Keraganjo's words came to Tom's mind. *If we can't control the aileron and we go into a large bank angle at too slow a speed, we could stall and go into a spin.*

Sweat poured from Lanjo's arms, making it difficult for Brett and Tom to maintain their grip. Lanjo began to slip backwards, but his eyes never left the aileron as Brett and Tom fought to keep him upright. The plane shuddered again, but it continued to turn. Tom prayed they weren't going too slow.

Seconds dragged by, and time hung suspended. Finally, Keith's voice came over the intercom. "Well done, Lanjo and everybody. Course correction is complete. We'll now be able to proceed with only minor adjustments and should be at Boston International airport in about forty minutes."

The sergeant opened his eyes and glared at Darryl, amidst the collective sighs of relief. Keith entered the passenger compartment, smiling. "Theresa has us on a straight shot to Logan Airport. We have clear skies, so turbulence won't be a problem. Look out the window and you can see we have an escort to see us home." Everyone turned to see a military jet flying on either side of the Gulfstream.

Keraganjo again hurried to the refrigerator, grabbed another water bottle, and held it for Lanjo. Tom's joy at making the turn successfully turned into concern, as he continued to hold Lanjo's arm. He'd managed to tune out the aching in his own arms while they were turning the plane, but it was becoming more incessant now. He could only imagine what Lanjo must be going through. "Hold on buddy," he whispered. "You can do this. We're here with you." Lanjo nodded almost imperceptibly at Tom's words, never taking his eyes off the aileron.

"Brett, it looks like Rachel can take care of Alan. Why don't you trade places with Feraganjo and rest your arms? We might need you for the landing." Feraganjo, overhearing Tom's words, left his seat and came forward to relieve Brett. The two traded places, and Brett moved into the aisle.

"What about you, Tom?" Brett stopped in midstride. "Why don't we get Darryl—"

"No, I'm fine," Tom said. "I'm not going anywhere."

"Okay, I'll go check on the others."

Tom leaned into Lanjo to make sure he had a good grip and closed his eyes. The steady drone of the plane's systems lulled him, and he almost dozed off. Feraganjo remained on the other side of Lanjo and seemed to have no problem holding him up. The rest of the team sat in varying poses of rest, now that the stress of the previous events was dissipating. In thirty more minutes, they would be preparing to land. If only Lanjo could hold on until then and still have enough strength for the landing.

22

Keith gently shook Tom's shoulder and he opened his eyes, a burst of adrenaline slamming back his drowsiness as he realized what must be next. "We'll be attempting to land in five minutes," Keith said.

Tom nodded and turned to Feraganjo. "Should I get Brett?"

The alien shook his head. "No, I'll be fine."

"Okay, good." Tom turned to Keraganjo, who was putting on his headset so he could hear Keith's instructions. "Are you ready?"

"Yes." He turned and said something in Cygnan to Lanjo, who nodded. "Lanjo's also ready."

"Good." Tom turned his head and raised his voice. "Attention everyone. Please take your seats. We have just one task left, to land safely. May God bless our efforts." He turned back and concentrated on holding Lanjo in as comfortable a position as possible. Sweat puddled at their feet as Lanjo continued whispering "*Shhhhh*" and Keraganjo started repeating Keith's instructions from the cockpit in Cygnan. Lanjo's job was to control the right aileron, stopping any drifting. Alan, Rachel, and Darryl sat in their seats, gripping their armrests. The sergeant lay with his eyes squeezed shut. Brett moved closer to where Feraganjo and Tom were supporting Lanjo, ready to help if needed.

The plane began a gradual descent. An unexpected crosswind caused a flurry of instructions from the cockpit. Lanjo, sagging into the arms of Feraganjo and Tom, deflected the right aileron upward, the plane rocking in response. Coordinating with Theresa's adjustments to the rudder and left aileron, Lanjo's corrections kept the plane lined up with the centerline of the runway. Theresa brought the plane down dead center, but it started to veer to one side. She and Lanjo continued their corrections, Lanjo's sweat-soaked body a much darker shade than usual. The plane finally rolled at a slow taxi speed to the hangar and came to a halt. Airport employees ran out and placed chocks on the wheels.

Theresa's voice came over the intercom. "We've arrived at Boston Logan International Airport. Thank you everyone, and especially Lanjo, for your help in getting us here safely." Hearing Theresa's words, Lanjo finally released control of the aileron and collapsed into Tom's arms.

Tom yelled frantically, "Get a doctor! Someone get help! Hurry!" as he carried his friend towards the exit door. Keith lowered the stairs of the Gulfstream and as Tom made his way through the door, government agents swarmed past him and into the airplane. Tom carried Lanjo to a waiting ambulance and two medics gently lifted Lanjo onto a stretcher and into the back of the vehicle. Before Tom could join them, the doors slammed shut and the ambulance raced away.

The adrenaline that had sustained Tom as he sought help for Lanjo deserted him and he staggered. An FBI agent standing nearby steadied him. "I need to be with Lanjo," Tom desperately gestured at the disappearing ambulance.

"Don't worry about Lanjo. He'll receive the best of care. Right now, let's get you and your team to a hotel where you can rest."

"But I need to be with Lanjo, he needs to have someone with him."

"Right now sir, we need to take care of you and the rest of your team. Lanjo is in good hands." The agent lowered his voice. "The team of doctors that cared for him during his previous hospital stay are en route. They'll implement the correct procedures for your friend."

Tom sighed with relief. "Okay. Thanks." Looking towards the direction the ambulance had gone, Tom recalled Lanjo's words. *The only problem with releasing that much mental energy is that you can both exhaust yourself physically and, worst case scenario, risk straining your brain's neurotransmissions past their breaking point, in which case normal brain function would not be recoverable.* He shoved aside any further thought along those lines. Lanjo just had to be okay. "Where are they taking him?"

"Massachusetts General, one of the top three hospitals in the nation."

Tom wearily rubbed the back of his neck. A yell and the sounds of a scuffle drew his attention. Several FBI agents swarmed around the sergeant freed of the duct tape. He was making his way down the stairs of the plane, struggling vigorously despite the hand cuffs that replaced the silver-colored adhesive strips. When he reached the bottom, one of the agents shoved the sergeant's head down, pushing him into a waiting black sedan. Agents got in on either side. Tom turned to the agent still standing next to him. "Do you know who that sergeant was working for?"

"Not yet," the agent replied, in a voice that left no room for doubt that they soon would. He put his hand on Tom's shoulder and started to guide him to a waiting van. "Let's go, Mr. Whitaker. Your team is waiting for you."

"Don't worry about your luggage," the agent reassured the science team as they got in the van. "We'll bring everything to your hotel. You'll be debriefed later today. Arrangements are being made for your trip to continue in the morning."

Theresa nodded almost imperceptibly. Tom trusted her judgment and kept his mouth shut. He'd have to go along with the agent's instructions and hope Lanjo would be okay. An image of Lanjo, exhausted and unconscious, welled up in his mind, causing the same feeling of helplessness he'd felt when Stephanie was holding onto the branch with the river swirling below her.

"This is completely unacceptable." President Ferris strode back and forth in agitation, wearing a path in the Oval Office rug. "Call up Air Force One. I want to see Lanjo."

Joe moved out of the president's way. "It wouldn't do any good, sir. He's in a deep state of hibernation. I'm told it is equivalent to a coma in humans. The doctors don't know how long it will last."

The president stopped his pacing and ran his hand over his eyes. "I really like the guy. For an alien, he's got more class than a lot of humans I know."

"I agree, Mr. President. We're doing everything we can. We don't know a lot about Cygnan biology, but they aren't all that different from humans. The main concern right now is his brain function. Jonathan Howe has agreed to let us use his wormhole communications system. We're still waiting on his Cygnan contact to provide a doctor that our doctors can talk to."

"I want a full report on how that sergeant got on board and who he's working for. Do we know who was responsible for the clipped cable yet?"

"No, sir. Our preliminary investigation has identified a Richard Thompson as the technician in charge of PM for that particular Gulfstream. Thompson had to pass a background check and Level 2 security clearance to work on a NASA aircraft. He denies any involvement."

"Keep me posted on any new information as it comes in. We need to get to the bottom of this."

They exchanged a knowing look. The need to guard against future attempts weighed on both men's minds. The future success of their joint endeavor with the aliens depended on it. "Yes, sir," Joe agreed. "I'm flying to Boston to interview the science team this afternoon. They're in a secured hotel. Whoever sabotaged the Gulfstream might make another attempt on their lives. We have Secret Service agents in place. We have a press briefing scheduled for this evening. I'll have something for you by then."

"Thanks. You'd better get going."

"Yes sir, Mr. President."

"Who could that be?" Keith asked. The staccato-knock on the hotel door intermingled with Tom's loud voice. Keith opened it and stepped aside. Joe walked into the room just in time to observe Tom glaring at Darryl, his legs planted and his face flushed.

"I'm just exploring options," Darryl was saying in a conciliatory tone. "I didn't say we were giving up. I just suggested we regroup. Whether you want to admit it or not, this has shaken all of us up."

"We can't quit now." Tom pounded his fist against the wall. "Lanjo wouldn't want us to. Feraganjo and Brett know what we need to do at CERN." His voice trembled. He wasn't going to allow

Lanjo's effort to be in vain. "Theresa and Keith have agreed to continue, and NASA is bringing in another plane."

"May I say something?" All eyes turned to Alan. His breathing was completely normal now, and he was no longer pale. He cleared his throat and looked at each of them, his eyes unexpectedly bright. "What we can accomplish here will impact mankind forever. Project Daedalus was the dream, but you have a chance to make it reality. Not often will you find the funding, the personnel, and the science converging at the same time. It is unfortunate," and he glanced at Tom, "that your friend Lanjo is incapacitated, but," and he turned his gaze to Darryl, "now is not the time to back down. At any moment, a critical component to our success could be lost. We must keep going."

Joe stepped forward. "Alan is right. If you lose momentum, you may never get it back. Other factions are obviously at work, and we need to stay ahead of them."

Darryl sat down in the plush hotel chair with a heavy sigh. "Okay. I still think we should take some time to recoup, but obviously I'm outnumbered. We'll leave first thing in the morning."

"It's a good decision, Darryl." Tom smiled.

"Prove me right."

The others released the collective breath they had been holding. Darryl turned to Joe. "I presume you have some questions for us?"

"Yes, I do. The president is quite concerned about your welfare and the success of the program. We have a press briefing in the West Wing this evening, so we don't have much time." He pulled out a notepad from the briefcase he'd been carrying and sat at the hotel room desk. "Let's start at the beginning. Who was on the apron before you took off? I need to know every person that you had contact with before you boarded."

"Just everyone you see here," Tom said, looking around.

"Wait a minute," Alan interrupted. "What about the young man that took my bags?" He turned to Joe. "I arrived at the last minute. Someone I assumed was from the ground crew stepped up and offered to take my bags. I didn't think anything of it."

"Did he board the plane?" Joe asked.

"I'm not sure," Alan replied. "I'm sorry, I wasn't paying attention."

"He wouldn't have had to, in order to access the cargo bay," Theresa said. She was sitting with her leg on a pillow elevated on a chair. She looked tired but alert.

Joe looked at her in surprise. "You're back from the hospital already? How's your leg?"

"Not great, but it should heal fine."

"Shouldn't you be...?"

"No, sir, I am released for duty," she said in a tone that brooked no argument.

Joe hesitated, then conceded. "We are grateful for your service." He returned to his original line of questioning. "Do the aileron cables go through the cargo compartment?"

Keith looked grim. "Yes, as a matter of fact, they do."

23

"It's hard to believe we're in the world's largest particle physics laboratory." Tom shook his head with wonder as the rest of the team gazed at their surroundings in awe. The flight to Geneva had been long but uneventful. They had taken a day to recover from the sabotaged plane flight and jet lag and were eager to get started. A physicist friend of Darryl's, Dr. Nathan Auer, was on a scheduled visit for antimatter research and had agreed to show them around. Later that day they would be meeting with CERN officials to outline the modifications they had come to request. They would also need time on the Antiproton Decelerator to get enough antimatter for their fusion reactor design modeled after Project Daedalus.

The science team was ushered into a conference room and Dr. Auer began to give them a brief overview of CERN. "Part of CERN's mission includes collaboration with nations from all over the world, and we are excited to extend that effort to include our Cygnan friends. You are joining over ten thousand scientists from more than a hundred nationalities that are working to push back the frontiers of technology." He paused, noting the excitement in the faces of human and alien alike, and smiled. "It never gets old, being in this amazing place and working with others who feel the same way.

"Accelerators are designed to create particle collisions. The Large Hadron Collider is the most powerful particle accelerator in the world," Dr. Auer explained. "It works in conjunction with four particle detectors, which allows us to investigate specific areas of interest. For example, I'm sure you've all heard of the Higgs boson." Heads nodded. "ATLAS is a general-purpose detector used to search for it. You'll want to take a tour of the LHC while you're here, but the Antiproton Decelerator is what we use for our anti-matter experiments. It is what you're interested in, if I understand correctly what you're trying to attempt."

Brett stepped forward, barely able to contain his enthusiasm. "Yes, that's right." He pulled Feraganjo next to him. "Feraganjo has an antimatter trap that is able to store antimatter indefinitely. We'll be using it in our interstellar spaceship to provide the energy required for its fusion reactor."

Dr. Auer stared at him for a moment, then shook his head in disbelief. "I guess you've built a better mousetrap then."

"Not mice, antimatter," Feraganjo said. His teammates hid smiles. "And not just me, Dr. Auer." Feraganjo leaned forward, pumping his arms up and down. "We've had this technology for a thousand years."

"I can't wait to see it," Dr. Auer said.

"It came with us on the flight. It's being delivered now."

Dr. Auer regarded the alien and let out a low whistle. "Call me Nate. Heck, anyone who can do what you claim can call me anything they want."

"We received a similar request from Dan Ross representing HoweTek Communications just a few days ago. Fortunately for you, your president has more clout than Jonathan Howe, and we refused Dan's request." Sabitha Radhakrishnan, Director-General of CERN, stood behind a podium back in the conference room, the science team having returned after Dr. Auer's tour and a quick lunch in CERN's Restaurant 1. Sabitha's jet-black hair and colorful scarf was a charming contrast to her stark white lab coat.

Keith sighed with relief at the Director-General's words. He knew his future father-in-law was trying something, but he wasn't sure what. After his offer to hire the lunar mission crew, he'd felt uneasy about what Jonathan might be up to.

Sabitha continued, directing her gaze towards Brett and Feraganjo. "We reviewed the drawings you sent us last week. The modifications are doable. The understanding we have is that you're going to give CERN ownership of the modifications, so we can continue to trap antimatter after you are done."

"That's correct," Darryl said. "Feraganjo has provided the complete specs for the antimatter trap, so a duplicate can replace ours when we leave. The modifications to the accelerator needed to accommodate the trap are reversible and are also well-documented."

"Are there any objections to members of the ALPHA experiment observing? They're the ones who have had success, although limited, in trapping antimatter, and they'll be utilizing your equipment design after you leave."

Darryl nudged Tom with his foot under the conference table and raised a questioning eyebrow. Tom gave an almost imperceptible nod. Just like every other science team, they wanted to be careful as to who they brought in and, with the aliens involved, even more so. But it was obvious they would need to agree in order to be given the access they needed to achieve their goal. Darryl returned his attention to the front of the room and the Director-General. "Sure," Darryl said. "No problem."

"Well, then. At the recommendation of our Scientific Policy Committee and in recognition of the momentous scientific contribution this will make to all mankind, we have secured both permission for the modifications and time on the Antiproton Decelerator. Dr. Auer has agreed to be your guide through the process." The Director-General held out her hand, and Darryl shook it, while the rest of the team cheered.

Tom leaned forward, placing his palms on the conference table. "So, when do we get started?"

"You're in luck," Dr. Auer said. "The current experiment is scheduled to finish this evening. You can begin any time after that."

Tom and Theresa stood on the catwalk of ATLAS, one of the general-purpose detectors for the LHC. They'd taken the short ride to the village of Meyrin and entered the cavern, where they were now a hundred meters below ground at the forty-six-meter long, twenty-five-meter high, and twenty-five-meter wide, seven-thousand-ton ATLAS detector—the largest particle detector in existence. Tom edged closer to Theresa as they looked over the railing and smiled when she leaned into him. He could smell her fresh, clean hair, with no perfume scent, something he always loved about her. His ex-wife's perfume was always very heavy and made him sneeze.

He took her hand. "How's your leg doing? I was worried about you when you insisted on flying us."

"The doctor at Massachusetts General is very confident leaving the bullet in is the best course of action. He said it would cause more damage if they dug it out. Since it isn't near anything vital, I'll be just fine. It's a bit sore but beyond that, it really isn't bothering me."

"Do you think you'll get a purple heart?"

Theresa chuckled softly. "That honor is reserved for members of the armed forces. NASA is a civilian government agency."

"Oh, well, I just thought . . ." Tom stumbled on his words. "Well, you were . . ." Theresa pulled his head close and kissed him briefly on the lips. Tom's eyes widened, his heart thumping in his chest as he reached his hand up and cupping her chin, kissed her back. They separated a few inches and searched the depths of each other's eyes. "I've been wanting to do that for a long time."

Theresa smiled. "Me, too."

"So let me get this straight." One of the members of the ALPHA team, Dr. Johan Mikaelsson of Stockholm University, looked skeptical. Members of both science teams were standing in the room that housed the Antiproton Decelerator. "We're going to trap antimatter into a portable container, and we'll be able to store it indefinitely?"

"Yes," Darryl said.

"And you are going to use this antimatter you have trapped in an interstellar spaceship you are building modeled after the study by the British Interplanetary Society in the nineteen seventies. Project Daedalus I believe it was called."

"You are correct."

"And you are going to use nuclear fusion reactions sparked by beams of the antimatter you have collected for the propulsion system of the spaceship."

"Yes."

"The fuel for the fusion-driven spaceship will consist of helium-3 mined from the Moon and deuterium from Earth."

"Yes, that is all correct."

Dr. Mikaelsson shook his head. "Well, we've been accused of worse madness at CERN, I suppose, but it would be hard to find. If what you claim is true—it will change everything."

"Yes." Darryl smiled. "It will indeed. So let's get to work. Dr. Mikaelsson, our chief scientists are Tom Whitaker and Brett Bailey, both of MIT and more recently of George Washington University, Feraganjo of the planet Kepler 186f, and Alan Bond, who headed Project Daedalus which you have already referenced. The remaining members of our team are associate engineers Rachel Hanover and Keranganjo. Theresa McDonnough and Keith Sanders are representing NASA, and I'm Darryl Henderson, in charge of this motley crew. Of course you already know Dr. Auer, who has graciously agreed to be our CERN liaison."

Everyone made the rounds of shaking hands with Dr. Mikaelsson and his team. Feraganjo spread some plans on a nearby table, so the members of ALPHA could see the modifications that needed to be made. The Cygnan antimatter trap had arrived in a large crate and was sitting on the floor, waiting to be unpacked. Soon the floor was swarming with activity, alien and human engineers and scientists working together.

Tom glanced up at the clock. It was nearly midnight, but it was obvious no one was interested in stopping for the night. He hoped

Feraganjo was correct and the modifications and collection of enough antimatter would take only two weeks. Installing new equipment of this complexity often took months, and they didn't have that kind of time. Being at CERN was a dream come true, but he also wanted to get back to Lanjo.

24

"So what happened, Dan? I thought you said this was a done deal —you knew people at CERN and it wouldn't be a problem to get time on the Antiproton Decelerator." Jonathan made no attempt to mask his frustration.

"I'm sorry, boss." Dan sat in the chair across from Jonathan and picked up the Rubik's cube off of Jonathan's desk, absently rotating the colored sides. "Lanjo had the same idea and got the president to bump us off and give the time to the government team."

Jonathan paused and took a sip of coffee, looking hard at his assistant. "You're a pretty smart guy, Dan. Why did you think you could beat them?"

"I didn't know that would happen," Dan replied smoothly. "I thought we were moving quickly enough to beat any competitors. Who knows who else the Cygnans might have contacted? If Paranganjo is talking to us, who's to say some other Cygnan businessman isn't trying an angle too?"

Jonathan nodded, mentally filing away the seed of suspicion he felt at Dan's glib response. "So what do you have next?"

Dan smiled. "I'm heading to SETI this afternoon for a call with Paranganjo. I'm going to find out what Plan B is."

Jonathan didn't smile back. Joe Ricinski's warning and now the fiasco at CERN . . . something didn't feel right, but he couldn't put his finger on it. He sighed. Unable to define a concrete reason to discontinue their efforts, he decided to keep going and see what Dan came up with. "Okay, keep me posted."

"Will do, boss." Dan placed the Rubik's cube back onto the desk and headed out the door. Jonathan's eyes followed him until he closed it. He picked up his cell phone and thumbed through his contacts until he found Joe's number. He stared at it for almost a minute, then slowly put the phone back down.

Ray got into his car and pulled out of his parking space at the DOE headquarters in Washington D.C. He turned the music to his favorite classic rock station. He had several meetings the next day, including one with Bahram to work on the funding allocations for the fusion reactor being redesigned by Tom Whitaker and his science team. It really grated on him to have to pull funding from his renewable energy projects, but it had to come from somewhere. "Dream On" by Aerosmith came on, and he cranked it up, losing himself in the music. Before he knew it, he was on the old country road that led to his property in Calvert County.

Ray didn't see the dark blue SUV edging into his lane until it was almost too late. He yanked his steering wheel to the right and hit the gravel shoulder at over fifty miles per hour, sending rocks and dust flying. He slammed the brakes and skidded to a stop. The SUV parked in front of him, and its driver, a twenty-something man in black slacks and suit jacket walked up the shoulder towards his car. Ray rolled his window down, his face red and nostrils flaring.

"What were you thinking? Were you texting instead of watching where you're going?"

The young man reached Ray's car door and spoke calmly. "No, sir, I wasn't texting. I swerved into your lane so we could have a talk."

"A talk?" Ray sputtered, "What do you mean, 'a talk'? Who are you?"

"Let's just say I work for a friend who has an interest in stopping the joint effort between the Cygnans and the United States in building a fusion reactor. He asked me to have a chat with you. He felt you would be sympathetic to his interests."

Ray shook his head vehemently. "You've got the wrong guy. I will do everything in my power to forward U.S. policy, even those I personally disagree with. Who are you anyway?" He started to open the door, but the young man shoved it closed.

"That doesn't matter. What matters is that you prevent further funding of the Cygnan-human science team's efforts."

"You don't understand," Ray responded with an edge in his voice. "I already tried. I was outvoted. Funny how democracy works that way. Now get out of my way."

The young man pulled his jacket aside so Ray could see the gun tucked into the waistband of his pants. "Calm down, sir. I'm just here to deliver a message."

Ray took a deep breath and sat back, resting his hands on the steering wheel. He could feel a headache beginning to stab right behind his eyes and resisted the urge to rub his forehead. "What's going on?"

"Nothing yet, but the National Petroleum Consortium is very concerned."

"So that's what this is about. Oil and gas lobbyists worried that clean energy will affect their business. I should've seen this coming. So what do you want from me?"

"My boss mentioned you were in a position to influence the committee."

"He's wrong. They've bought into the program hook, line, and sinker."

"That's too bad. My boss was hoping not to have to do things the hard way."

If the NPC was going rogue, things could get ugly, and fast. Ray looked sharply at the young man. "Who's your boss?"

"You'll find out soon enough." The man backed away, jogged the couple of yards to his car, jumped in, and drove off.

Ray sighed. The gun hadn't bothered him much. He carried a gun himself and the kid didn't draw it—he would've probably gotten a bucket load of grief from his boss if he didn't deliver the message. Politics drew a mixed bag of people, and attempts at strong-arming were inevitable when emotions ran high. Ray preferred to avoid dealing with special interest groups, but his role as Secretary of Energy made that wishful thinking.

He thought about reporting the incident, but quickly dismissed it. He was still mentally recovering from the thrashing he'd received about Sheila and didn't want to expose himself to more aggravation. He turned up the music—Steely Dan this time—and continued on his way. Hopefully, given some time, this problem would resolve itself.

"We did some digging on Dan Ross, sir. Turns out he's the grandson of Daniel Graham." Joe extended a folder marked with the F.B.I.'s insignia and the name Daniel Arthur Ross penned at the bottom.

President Ferris, standing behind the Resolute desk in the Oval Office, leaned forward and accepted the folder. "Daniel Graham, the astronaut? The commander of Apollo 19, our last Apollo mission to the Moon?"

"Yes, sir. They're one and the same."

"Now that's interesting." He thumbed through the pages in the folder, then glanced at Joe. "What else seems to be of interest regarding Mr. Ross?"

"Well, sir, you aren't going to believe this—"

"Really?" he interrupted drily. "After everything that has happened, you actually found something I won't believe?"

"That was just an expression, sir," Joe replied evenly. He took the folder from the president and held up a specific page. The president, about to make a retort, read the page and sat down instead. "You're right, this is even beyond my capacity for belief. Except that it's true—right? I mean, all of this has been verified by NASA?"

"Yes, sir, it has."

"So if I understand this report correctly, Daniel Graham and Martin Lawson had an alien encounter while out in their lunar rover during the Apollo 19 Moon mission back in 1974?"

"Yes, sir. Graham reported it to NASA, but they didn't believe him. They decided it was a shared psychological hallucination occurring on the lunar surface. The contact occurred while they were on an EVA."

The president shook his head in wonderment. Joe continued, "You may have heard of the alien music reported during the Apollo 10 mission. It occurred during the time the astronauts were out of radio contact on the far side of the Moon. That gained quite a bit of publicity and the transcripts of that flight were declassified in 2008. Basically, the crew heard what they described as outer-space type music, but NASA attributed it to radio interference between the radios in the Lunar Module and the Command Module."

"Are you saying the Cygnans were generating the music that the Apollo 10 astronauts reported?"

"NASA and the astronauts don't think so, but I think it's very possible, and I think we might have had a prior First Contact during the Apollo 19 Moon mission. Graham and Lawson spent hours on EVA and, according to Lanjo's timeline, the Cygnans were observing us at that time."

"But what does this have to do with Dan Ross besides being a fabulous yarn to impress the grandkids on a cold winter night?"

"We believe the Cygnans contacted Daniel Graham during an EVA and established a relationship with him that possibly extends to his grandson. We're not sure how, but it's possible his grandson may be a Cygnan plant." Joe blew through his nose. "I know it sounds crazy, but all of the pieces are there. By Dan Ross directing Jonathan Howe's involvement with the Cygnan business faction, both the funding and the influence of HoweTek Communications are available to Ross.

"Incidentally, I ran a full background check on Jonathan. Not only is there nothing to indicate he would engage in treason, he is actually slightly xenophobic, which would account for his placing Dan in charge of their communications with Paranganjo. Lanjo's assertion that he may be a dupe is a credible one from our intel."

"Do you think Dan Ross might have had anything to do with the sabotage of the Gulfstream?"

"No, sir. We believe Dan Ross is an opportunist, but he and who he is working for understand that terrorist acts will completely shut down American-Cygnan relations, governmental and otherwise. No, we're thinking there is another faction involved."

The President's eyebrows crinkled. "Okay. Do we have a list of who may be responsible?"

"A very long one, sir. It seems the Cygnan-American cooperative effort is not popular with a number of groups, for varying reasons."

The president exhaled. "Good work, Joe. Please keep me posted on the investigation. I don't like what Mr. Ross is doing, but at the moment I can't see that he's doing anything illegal. At least we got the jump on him at CERN. Let's keep a close eye on his activities. We need to keep this quiet for now. Jonathan doesn't have clearance and it's still speculative anyway."

"Yes sir, Mr. President. Thank you, sir."

Joe turned to go. He would be meeting with Jonathan tomorrow afternoon. He needed to figure out what to say that didn't violate the president's admonition but still slowed down the progress HoweTek Communications was making with Paranganjo.

25

"Tom, Stephanie's gone!" Tom's ex-wife's agitated voice pierced his sleep-fogged brain and he almost dropped the phone.

He looked around groggily, trying to orient himself. Having worked thirty-six hours straight, he'd fallen into bed in exhaustion just a few hours ago. It sounded like Patricia had said Stephanie was gone. "Gone, what do you mean, gone?"

"I mean, our daughter has disappeared. But she didn't take her bike this time. She left a note."

Tom sat up, his heart racing and nausea crawling up his stomach and into his throat, making him feel woozy. "Okay, calm down a minute. What did the note say?"

"It said, 'Don't worry, Mom. I need to take a trip. I'll be fine, I know how to take care of myself. It's important. I'll be back when I am done.'"

He could think of only one thing important enough to cause Stephanie to run away. The story of the sabotage of the Gulfstream and Lanjo's incapacitation had hit the news last night. He knew where his daughter was headed.

Tom glanced at the clock—2:47am. 8:47pm in Virginia.

"Tom, can you hear me? What are you going to do?"

"Listen to me. Stephanie is very smart and resourceful. She'll be okay," he said with a confidence he didn't all together feel. "I'll call Joe Ricinski. He'll get his men right on it."

Tom hung up the phone and bowed his head, taking a moment to pray for the safe return of his wayward daughter. Feeling his heart rate lower slightly, he scrolled through his contacts to call Joe. He had to admire his daughter's spunk and loyalty, but he wished she wasn't so impetuous. He glanced at the clock again and sighed. They would be testing the antimatter trap in a scant six hours. Perhaps after his conversation with Joe, he could get some rest, but he had a feeling sleep would elude him.

"It's a pleasure to finally meet you, Geoffrey." Jonathan smiled at the CEO of AstroTechStar as he poured him some scotch. "I've been fascinated by the progress of your Astrolaunch aircraft. A great idea, creating an air-launch platform to transport satellite payloads to orbit."

"I'm excited about the progress we're making. We already have private and government contracts with a wide range of missions and payloads scheduled through 2040. We can't keep up with the demand. But I don't think that's why you invited me here." Geoffrey leaned forward in his chair, gazing at Jonathan expectantly.

Jonathan handed him the drink and poured himself one. Taking a seat, he twirled the glass between his fingers. "I know you have an interest in aliens from your contributions to SETI, and I know you're interested in space because of your LEO research and development with AstroTechStar." He paused and rubbed his chin. "I just don't know how you feel about the Cygnans in general, and that makes me nervous."

"Nervous? What does my opinion have to do with making you nervous?" The two powerful business magnates took long moments eyeing each other, then Geoffrey broke into a laugh. "Obviously, I'm not a financial threat to you. Both our expertise is technology, but in vastly different areas. What's really going on here?"

Jonathan decided to take the plunge. "Are you familiar with Stephen Hawking's position on aliens?"

"Of course, anyone interested in SETI for any amount of time would have heard his theory that aliens may be nomadic, seeking to conquer and colonize the planets they visit."

"Yeah, well, I feel the same way."

Geoffrey's mouth gaped open. "But it's well known you're working out a deal with that alien, what's his name? Paranganjo? Dan hasn't been shy about filling me in. He's quite excited at the direction your partnership is going."

"Dan does a good job. To be perfectly frank, I asked him to take the position of intermediary because in the interests of entrepreneurship, it is the chance of a lifetime, and Dan is well-qualified. But personally, I would rather that we never had a First Contact."

Geoffrey raised his eyebrows, tipping his head to the side as he sat back in his chair, taking a slow sip of his drink.

Jonathan downed his drink and continued. "I talked to my soon-to-be son-in-law. You probably know of him, Keith Sanders."

"Of course. He was part of the First Contact. I didn't realize he was engaged to your daughter. Dan didn't mention that. Congratulations."

"Yeah, thanks. The kids are trying really hard to stay out of the public eye." Jonathan got up and paced across his office, then turned to Geoffrey.

"Keith told me that according to Lanjo, Paranganjo is known to be unscrupulous in some of his undertakings. Paranganjo stated in his last message that we need to stop the government in order to beat them to the punch. Dan doesn't think that's a problem. I do." He stopped pacing and looked squarely at Geoffrey. "And I think you should, too."

With a blank expression on his face, Geoffrey shrugged. "I don't know what exactly I was expecting for our meeting today, but it certainly wasn't this. Are you saying we shouldn't work with the Cygnans?"

"I'm saying we shouldn't work with certain Cygnans. Perhaps we should be supporting the government effort instead of trying to compete with it. Something isn't right. I'm not quite sure what, but I can feel it. And there's something about Dan and his enthusiasm to work with Paranganjo that bothers me."

He chose his next words carefully. "I realize you came here thinking I was going to offer you a deal—perhaps cut you in on my partnership with Paranganjo in order to reduce my investment and mitigate the risk to my company, or something of that nature. Your interest in SETI and your space companies make us a natural fit. The problem is, I don't think it's a good idea for any of us to work with Paranganjo. The farther down this road we go, the more I realize we may be hurting American interests. I'm not okay with that, and I have a feeling neither are you."

Geoffrey leaned back and took another sip of his drink. "Agreed. I have great hopes for a cooperative effort with the

Cygnans, but not at the expense of the United States. So what do we do?"

"I'm not sure. Joe Ricinski wants to see me at his office this afternoon. He knows about our meeting today and requested for you to come, too."

Geoffrey nodded. "I'll be there."

The ALPHA team gathered at the Antiproton Decelerator along with the Cygnan-human science team. The atmosphere radiated excitement. Their intense efforts over the last week and a half were about to be tested. Keraganjo and Rachel were making some last-minute adjustments under the hawk eyes of Feraganjo and Brett. With carefully constructed modifications, The Cygnan anti-matter collector had been integrated into the CERN Antiproton Decelerator, replacing the superconducting magnetic trap that existed before. The Cygnan design would allow the scientists to trap antimatter and hold it indefinitely, if the alien technology worked properly.

There wasn't much room for the small crowd that had gathered to witness the historic moment, but Keith and Theresa managed to squeeze in. Darryl and Tom came forward along the catwalk to address the scientists waiting expectantly. Tom searched until he found Theresa's warm, steady gaze.

Taking in all of the eager faces, Darryl turned to Tom and whispered, "Did you ever imagine this would happen?"

Tom punched Darryl lightly on the shoulder. "Nope, but I'm glad we get to be a part of it."

Tom had managed three hours more sleep and felt pretty decent. Joe assured him he would find Stephanie and even agreed to call his ex-wife, so Tom wouldn't have to. He could feel the adrenalin pumping through his body. *The ability to trap and store antimatter was on par with Niel Bohr's work on developing quantum theory. Maybe their Cygnan-human science team would win the first Nobel Prize in Physics to include aliens as recipients. A man could dream, couldn't he?* Tom looked at Feraganjo and Brett and nodded when Feraganjo gave him the thumbs up. "Looks like we're ready, Darryl."

Darryl waved his hands from his place on the catwalk, and the room quieted except for the hum of equipment in the background. Darryl smiled and addressed the crowd. "Thank you all for coming to witness the integration of the CERN Antiproton Decelerator and the Cygnan antimatter trap. Many of you worked long hours to get us to this milestone in scientific history. Not only will we be utilizing the antimatter we trap as a power source for a nuclear fusion reactor, CERN will possess an identical trap that allows scientists to study antimatter in much greater depth than what was previously possible. It is the collaboration of Earth and Lanzeron that has made this attainable. Today we take one small step for man, and one giant leap for human and Cygnan kind." Whistles and clapping drowned out any further speech, and Darryl turned to Brett and nodded.

Tom and Darryl waited on the catwalk. Darryl shifted his weight and whispered, "So what exactly is happening?" Tom didn't take his eyes off of the Antiproton Decelerator and whispered back, "Antiprotons have already been created and subjected to several cycles of cooling and deceleration. They're slowing to one-tenth the speed of light. Soon they'll be ejected into the Cygnan-modified system, where they'll be slowed even more and they'll enter the chamber that'll enable them to be stored indefinitely."

Tom waved his hand. "Cygnan technology created a trap that cools the antiprotons and combines them with positrons to create antihydrogen, keeping the antimatter confined and preventing their annihilation." He bounced on his heels. "It's similar to the electromagnetic traps that were previously employed, but with significant advances stabilizing the antiprotons into a useful state and, if all goes well, we'll be able to use it as a power source." Noting the glazed look in Darryl's eyes, Tom gave a low chuckle and punched him on the shoulder again. "Don't worry about understanding it all, Darryl—that's what our team is for. The important thing is for it to work."

Everyone's attention remained glued to the computer monitoring the antimatter trap. The first antiprotons entered the trap, and the room remained silent as all of the observers held their breath in anticipation. Feraganjo and Brett studied the data as it scrolled across the screen. After several minutes, Feraganjo turned to Darryl with a huge grimace, the smile on Brett's face matching it. Brett called out in a loud voice, "So far, we have collected one gram with no annihilation."

The room froze for a silent moment, then a piercing whoop split the air, followed by wild clapping and cheering. Darryl and Tom hugged. Brett and Feraganjo were pounding each other on the back in glee and Keraganjo and Rachel just stared in awe.

The world had just changed forever.

Tom raced to find Theresa. He wrapped her in his arms, kissing her jubilantly, when a deafening clap resounded through the room. Everything seemed to move in slow motion. The shocked confusion on Darryl's face was mirrored throughout the crowd. Smoke billowed out of the back of the Antiproton Decelerator and the acrid smell of burnt wiring rent the air. The crowd burst into frenzied motion, running towards the exit.

Tom released Theresa. Grabbing a fire extinguisher on the wall next to her, he pushed through the crowd towards the smoke. Keith found another fire extinguisher and he and Brett ran full tilt towards the smokey plumes from different directions. The three men converged on the stochastic cooling system of the Antiproton Decelerator.

"Aim there—at the kickers," Brett yelled.

Tom pulled the pin and squeezed the handle. Keith did the same. White foam splattered the banks of melting fiber optic cable. The acrid smell of burning plastic seared Tom's nostrils, burning his lungs. The kickers generated the electric fields needed to correct the particle angles and were critical components. Tom lowered the nozzle by ten degrees and fired another stream.

The fire sputtered to just a few errant embers when Feraganjo's voice impinged on Tom's awareness. He glanced around, locating the Cygnan scientist calmly directing the last of the crowd out of the exit. Darryl stood dazed, his eyes wide, with his hand on his chest. He had not moved from his position on the catwalk. Rachel crouched by the catwalk, tears trailing down both cheeks, while Keraganjo held his hand out to her. Theresa was . . . gone. *Where was she?*

Satisfied they had dowsed all of the flames, Tom stepped back to survey the destruction of the cooling system. His throat tightened and his stomach dropped like an anvil as he mentally tabulated the damage. The caustic smell was still in the air, although the smoke had dissipated. Keith and Brett came and stood beside him, their expended fire extinguishers held limply in their hands, and the three gazed despairingly at the burnt mess.

Why was someone trying to destroy everything they had been working for? First the Gulfstream, and now . . . Someone could have been hurt or killed in the explosion. An angry incoherent yell ripped from his throat as Tom flung his fire extinguisher against the wall. *Lanjo had not risked his life for this.*

26

Jonathan had been to the Capitol building before, but never to 1600 Pennsylvania Avenue. As a special advisor to President Ferris, Joe Ricinski's office was located in the West Wing. Geoffrey Clarke was already in the foyer, waiting for him. Passing through the security checks, both men were admitted to the office waiting area. Joe's door was closed. They were invited to sit and wait by a tall woman dressed in a conservative pantsuit. The atmosphere was electric as men and women dressed in business formal moved back and forth through the hallways, intent on their tasks. The two men sat in silence, taking it all in.

The door abruptly opened, and Joe motioned them in. "Geoffrey, Jonathan, good to see you. I appreciate you coming over." He shook their hands and gestured towards the chairs scattered around a small round conference table. "Have a seat."

Jonathan sat and leaned forward in his chair, twisting the ring on his finger. Geoffrey leaned back in his, alert but relaxed.

Joe looked at both men with an unreadable expression. "Gentlemen, our meeting is unexpectedly timely. I just got off the phone with Tom Whitaker. The CERN project to trap antimatter was sabotaged. They're still assessing the damage."

Jonathan blew out a breath. "Is everyone okay? My future son-in-law is on that project."

"There were no human or Cygnan casualties. The damage looks pretty extensive and was deliberately pinpointed to the cooling system. That's all I have at the moment."

Geoffrey nodded. "That's a real shame. I've been to CERN. The science being done there will propel us into the future. To sabotage it is a crime against humanity."

"Not just humanity, at this point," Joe interjected. "The Cygnans are deeply affected as well. Their hope for help with moving to their new planet is directly tied to our efforts."

"Yes, of course." Geoffrey looked around. "So, why are we here? I have a feeling it's not about Astrolaunch."

"You're correct, it's not about your aircraft, Geoffrey. The president has asked me to speak to both of you about joining forces with the government effort. This recent disaster at CERN is not the first attempt at sabotage, and we don't think it'll be the last." He looked pointedly at Jonathan. "We're not convinced Paranganjo is operating ethically." His statement hung between them.

Jonathan shifted uncomfortably in his chair. "I've had some doubts about Paranganjo recently myself. To be totally honest, I'm not thrilled to be working with aliens. It's just a business deal. I wouldn't intentionally do anything to hurt U.S. interests."

"Do you really know anything about Paranganjo's character?" Joe asked in a hard voice.

"Only what my assistant, Dan Ross, has told me. Dan's my Cygnan liaison. Geoffrey knows Dan, too. They met at SETI."

Geoffrey cleared his throat and spoke up. "I know Dan. He's quite the Cygnan promoter. He and Marco, the main scientist at the SETI astronomy telescope array, seem to be pretty good buddies." He pursed his lips. "Do you think Dan may be acting against U.S. interests? He is very friendly with Paranganjo."

"We know about his attempts to lure astronauts from NASA and to book time at CERN ahead of the government initiative. I think it might be a possibility." Joe picked up a glass of water and took a sip, allowing the two business magnates time to process what he'd said.

Jonathan looked at Geoffrey and back at Joe. "So do you want me to shut Dan down?"

"No, not at this point. We still need to understand what Paranganjo's ultimate goal is. If we shut Dan down, Paranganjo might go underground, and we won't be able to trace him any longer. Lanjo mentioned that Paranganjo was not known for his scruples on Lanzeron. As the old saying goes, 'Keep your friends close, and your enemies closer.'"

"Okay, so what do you want from me?" Jonathan asked.

"Pretty simple. Just keep an eye on your boy, and if he gets involved in something questionable, let me know."

"Sure, I can do that."

Joe smiled with more warmth. "That's what I was hoping to hear, thanks. And you have the thanks of the president as well." He turned to Geoffrey. "As for you, I have a special request. We need to shake Paranganjo up a bit. We also need to create time for the government effort to bounce back from this latest debacle. This is what I have in mind . . ."

After Tom verified there'd been no injuries from the explosion, he found Theresa walking the perimeter of the lab, doing a security check.

"I haven't found anything suspicious," she reported. "Darryl's gone to his room. He said he needed some time to think." She looked Tom over. "Let's get you out of that mess."

They returned to his room so he could change out of his foam-splattered shirt. Once he cleaned up, he began to pace incessantly.

"Let's go out onto the patio," Theresa suggested. "You're going to wear the carpet out if you keep that up."

Sitting at a table in the shade, Theresa massaged Tom's shoulders. He looked down at the text he'd just received,

Stephanie not found yet. Will update when I know something.

He slowly exhaled, clenching his fists. "I can't believe all of this is happening. First, the aileron cable was cut and we almost crashed, and now an explosion has ruined our progress. You'd think trapping antimatter and creating fusion would be hard enough, without someone finding it necessary to sabotage our efforts. And where's Stephanie?! She should've gotten to Boston General by now. I'm starting to go out of my mind with worry."

Theresa continued rubbing Tom's shoulders. "I'm sorry. If Joe's people don't find her soon, I'm sure she'll show up at Lanjo's hospital room. She's a very resourceful young lady." Her voice softened. "What happened to Lanjo is bothering you, too, isn't it?"

Tom leaned forward and put his head in his hands. "Yeah," came his muffled reply. "I'm afraid he might not regain normal brain function. And today's explosion didn't help. Someone could've been seriously hurt. We're lucky it just destroyed the cooling system, although I have no idea how we're going to be able to fix it. We'll be way behind schedule, no matter what we do." He jumped up and started pacing again.

Theresa sighed and sat down. Her thigh was aching, a subtle reminder of what lengths the opposition was capable of. She touched Tom's hand as he passed, and he stopped. "All right, big guy. Let's not spend too much time feeling sorry for ourselves. We have work to do."

Tom cocked his head, studying her momentarily. He understood her better now. She wasn't being callous, just practical. She preferred action to emotion. He returned her expectant gaze and nodded. "You're right." He paused, thinking about their next step. "Let's meet with the science team this afternoon and see what we can do to repair the cooling system."

Theresa allowed herself a smile. She got up and gave him a quick peck on the cheek. "Sounds good."

27

The hotel in Dubai wasn't their regular meeting place and lacked the opulence of a typical gathering of the International Petroleum Exporting Federation. Only handpicked members from among the member countries of the oil cartel were present, holding in common a shared desire for aggressive action to protect their interests.

Choosing to rebel against IPEF leadership, they were unwilling to move through diplomatic channels to construct a deal with the United States to ensure oil exports would be unaffected by the Cygnan initiative. The room had been swept for bugs before they entered and the rogue IPEF members sat around a conference table with only a samovar, four glass cups, and a bowl of sugar.

"So you're saying the mission was a success?" Ahmad asked, as he poured tea in each of the cups. Everyone waited while he handed each person a cup of tea.

"It had limited success, certainly," Fakhir said. "Our sources have confirmed the operation was carried out successfully on the ground, but due to unusual circumstances in the air, the outcome did not turn out as planned. It was still beneficial in that it inca-pacitated the leader of the alien contingent."

Jorge drummed his fingers on the table, not touching his tea. "You're sure there's no traceability?"

"Yes. The F.B.I. investigated the mechanic in charge of their preventative maintenance. He's been cleared, and they don't have any other names. Our man blended in with the ground crew and was in and out of the cargo compartment in a matter of minutes. We don't think—"

"So what's next?" Jorge interrupted.

Fakhir's expression turned smug. "Maybe nothing. Someone else is doing our work for us. There's been an explosion at CERN. No one's claimed responsibility yet, but it's obviously an effort by another interested party to sabotage the U.S. government's venture with the aliens." He spooned out some sugar and drop-ping it into his tea, he took a sip. "Let's just wait and see. If the Americans and aliens start making progress, we can move again. They're on a tight timeline, so delaying tactics are most effective."

Hamid leaned back, cupping his tea in his hands. "I don't like it. Black ops have never been a part of our business. We're crossing a line."

Fakhir scowled at his colleague. "The line was already crossed when the aileron was clipped. If the U.S.-Cygnan initiative succeeds, clean energy will eventually replace our petroleum exports and we'll be doomed."

⚛

Stephanie peered around the corner of the corridor outside Lanjo's hospital room. The hospital gown she'd stolen from a pile on a cart was way too big for her. She had her clothes on underneath and managed to tuck the excess into her waistband. She took a deep breath, then marched purposefully forward and rounded the corner. The Secret Service agent assigned to Lanjo immediately stood up from his chair and held his hand out.

"Hold it right there, young lady. You can't come any further."

"But I'm looking for my uncle," Stephanie said in her best high-pitched anxious whine. "He was going to meet me here, so we could take a walk together." She looked at the guard with big hazel eyes. "It might be our last time." She paused dramatically. "I don't think I have much longer to live."

The guard smiled. "Oh, you have plenty of time . . . Stephanie." Stephanie's eyes widened at the mention of her name. "We've been told to be on the lookout for you. However, I wasn't expecting you to show up in a hospital gown."

Stephanie pulled off the gown, gathered herself for a fight, then let out her breath and sighed. The element of surprise was gone. She was not sure what to do next. The guard decided for her.

"Your parents are very worried about you. But you're in luck. My instructions are to notify my boss of your safe arrival, and he'll notify your parents. I'm also instructed to allow you to visit Lanjo. Just wait here for his nurse to arrive. She can accompany you and explain his condition."

Ecstatic, Stephanie jumped up and down. "Awesome! Thanks!" She plopped down on the floor and leaned against the wall across from the guard. The Secret Service agent spoke into his mic. "Stephanie has arrived safely and appears unharmed by her travels." He turned back to Stephanie and thumbed the mic off. "A nurse comes each hour—you won't have long to wait." He shook his head and grinned. "You have a lot of gumption."

"Yeah," she replied, grinning back. "I get it from my Dad."

Tom read the text from Joe and whooped out loud. Darryl and Theresa were in the office Darryl had been given for the duration of their stay. Tom yelled across the lab so they could hear him, "She's safe! Stephanie's safe!"

Darryl ran over and squeezed his shoulder. "Thank God! That's great news!" The steel ball of tension weighing Tom's shoulders down evaporated.

Theresa jogged over, her face bright and eyes sparkling. "Wonderful news, Tom! Where is she?"

Tom chuckled. "Lanjo's hospital room of course."

"The apple doesn't fall far from the tree," Theresa teased.

"No, it doesn't," Tom laughed. "Let's go celebrate!"

"You two, go on ahead," Darryl waved his hand. "My wife will be calling soon. I want to talk to Sandra before her bedtime."

"No problem, I understand," Tom replied. He turned to Theresa. "How about dinner?"

"Sure. Meet you at Restaurant 2 in an hour?"

"I have something else in mind," Tom replied, his eyes twinkling. "Let's meet back here. Make sure and wear walking shoes."

An hour later, a short walk brought Tom and Theresa to the Restaurant Le Chase, situated on the Swiss-French border. The sun had dropped below the horizon and they were seated outside on a patio overlooking a garden and pool. The dim lighting of wall sconces broken only by the dancing flames of candles on their table wasn't enough to hide the look of apprehension on Theresa's face. She scanned her menu, and her lips tightened.

Tom put his menu down and looked intently at Theresa. He was still feeling a mixture of joy and relief at the knowledge that Stephanie was safe. He had imagined an intimate, romantic dinner with Theresa to celebrate, but her demeanor said otherwise.

Theresa briefly returned his stare, then uncharacteristically dropped her eyes. Tom reached over and covered her hand with his, grateful when she didn't pull it away.

"What is it? I mean, besides the setbacks with the sabotage. What's bothering you?"

Theresa let out a long sigh, but kept her hand in place. "I'm just tired. So much has happened, and you've had a lot to deal with. Even though Stephanie is safe, you still do. I want to get more serious about our relationship, but you didn't do too well during college when you were under stress. Too be honest, I'm scared."

Tom squeezed her hand. "Look at me."

She did, tipping her head to the side. The waiter started to approach their table, hesitated and looked from Tom to Theresa, then turned on his heel to serve another guest.

Tom took a deep breath. "I know I hurt you. When you applied to test pilot school, I was jealous of your career choice. My ego couldn't handle your dedication." He watched the candlelight flicker across her face, softening her taut features. He licked his lips nervously. "I wanted your attention and didn't understand the sacrifices you were making to pursue a career with NASA. I made some unfair assumptions. When the test pilot program got so tough for you, I didn't believe in us enough to see it through. That's why I left."

A light breeze blew through the patio making the candle flames dance, breaking through the darkness that threatened to engulf their relationship. The silence expanded between them like a fission reaction. Theresa drew in a deep breath, then released it. "You're right. And the problem is, I've been making some assumptions of my own." She scrubbed her hand over her face. "I've been pretty happy as a pilot and NASA mission commander. I'm not sure I want to break out of my status quo. Flying airplanes and rocket ships is easy—caring about people is when things get complicated." She lifted her chin towards Tom. "And you don't have the best track record. We've both matured from those college kids back then, but I can't help but worry this whole thing might be a mistake."

A lump rose in Tom's throat. "Guilty as charged." He paused and took her hand more completely in his, squeezing it gently. "But I really have changed. And I do care for you. I don't think I ever stopped, even after our breakup. A few weeks ago, I asked you if I should even take this job. You told me to have a little trust and faith. Well, that's what I'm asking you to have now."

Theresa met his gaze evenly as the flames danced between them. Finally, she squeezed his hand in return. "Okay. I'm not sure where this is going, but I'm willing to take it one step at a time."

"Thank you. That's all I ask." He picked up her other hand and brought both to his lips, gently kissing them. Theresa's hands jerked as something wet landed on them, dribbling down her fingers.

She withdrew one of her hands from his grasp and reaching forward with her napkin, dabbed gently at the tears rolling down his cheeks. "Perhaps it's time for both of us to have a little trust and faith."

"Would you like a cup of coffee?" Joe Ricinski's administrative assistant smiled down at Ray sitting in the waiting area outside Joe's office. He tapped his fingers against the end table and shifted in his chair, wishing—for the third time since sitting down—that he hadn't requested this meeting. He managed a smile.

"No thanks."

"I'm sorry for the delay," she continued. "Mr. Ricinski shouldn't be too much longer."

"That's all right," Ray managed to mutter somewhat politely. "I'm sure he's attending to an urgent matter."

She merely smiled and walked away. "Let me know if you need anything," she called over her shoulder as she made her way back to her desk.

"I need my head examined for coming here," Ray grumbled under his breath. After hearing about the explosion at CERN, he'd decided to let Joe know about his encounter with the rogue lobbyist. While he'd chalked it up to an isolated threat without any enforcement, it took money to reach as far as CERN, which could indicate NPC involvement. Companies paying lobbyists often had deep pockets and weren't afraid to throw money at problems to make them go away.

Joe strode into the waiting area, smiling, and extended his hand to Ray. Ray rose, and they exchanged a handshake.

"Sorry to keep you waiting," Joe said. "The president called a last-minute meeting in the Oval Office about some diplomatic quandary with China. It seems there's always something going on with State nowadays."

"No problem. We all serve at the pleasure of the president."

"Yes, we do." Joe guided Ray into his office and pointed at a comfortably upholstered chair at the small round table by his desk. Joe sat, leaned back, and stretched. "So, how can I help you?"

"I'm hoping I can help you. I may have some information relevant to the sabotage at CERN."

Joe leaned forward, his good humor vanishing. "What do you have?"

"Well, there was an incident that occurred a few weeks ago. I didn't think much of it at the time, but with the sabotage of the plane and now CERN, I thought I'd better report it."

Joe gazed piercingly at Ray, and for the fourth time that day, Ray wished he'd kept his mouth shut. He opened his mouth to speak but instead pointed at a water pitcher on a table to the left of Joe's desk. Joe poured Ray a glass, handed it to him, then sat back down and waited expectantly.

Ray took a sip. "So I was on Highway 263, driving to my property in Calvert County, when a dark blue SUV ran me off the road. I pulled over onto the shoulder, and this young punk in a suit comes to my window and tries to intimidate me." Ray took another sip and brushed his hair back as the scene replayed in his mind. "At first I thought he was texting, but turns out it was deliberate. He told me he did it to 'have a talk.' He said he works for a guy who was interested in stopping the Cygnans and the U.S. from building a fusion reactor. They thought I felt the same, so they wanted my help. When I told him I would never go against U.S. policy, things got a little more heated. He showed me his piece tucked in his waistband."

"He threatened you?" Joe leaned forward. "And you didn't tell us?"

Ray raised his hands. "Take it easy, Joe. It wasn't much of a threat. He didn't pull the gun, and I have a CCL myself. He was just talking typical lobbyist crap. He was delivering a message."

"What else did he say?"

"He mentioned the National Petroleum Consortium is very concerned, but any political hack could have seen that one coming, which is why I didn't mention it. He did say his boss was hoping not to have to do things the hard way, then he took off."

"Obviously oil and gas lobbyists aren't fans of clean energy, so I can understand your lack of concern, but, 'to do things the hard way?' Any idea what he meant by that?"

Ray shook his head. "No, I don't. But in light of the sabotage at CERN, I thought you might want to know about it. Since no one's claimed responsibility, and the perpetrators have yet to be identified, this information may be worth investigating."

"It is, thanks." Joe's look softened. "You caught a lot of flak because of Sheila, so you're understandably a little gun shy. We know that wasn't your fault. You can relax, no one questions your loyalty."

Ray closed his eyes briefly and exhaled. "Thanks. You can't pick your relatives."

"Believe me, we get it." He paused, then added, "How's Sheila doing?"

Ray shrugged. "She came to Sunday dinner last week. We didn't bring up the Cygnans. She seemed okay."

Joe stood and held out his hand. "Good to hear. Please keep in touch and let me know if anything else happens you find concerning."

"I will. Thanks for seeing me." He glanced at his watch. "I'm off to The Hill. I have a meeting with Bahram. We're going to discuss a resolution coming before the Joint Committee on Energy and Alien Relations in response to the sabotage."

"Thanks for your work on this, Ray. Do me a favor though, don't mention the incident you reported to anyone else. It might throw a wrench in our investigation."

"Sure, I understand," Ray replied, even though he really didn't. He wondered who on the committee Joe didn't trust. Not his business. "Thanks, Joe."

⚛

"You should come to a meeting. You could exercise a lot of influence." Sheila sipped her glass of wine. Jessup was surely plotting his feline revenge for another evening alone. Jonathan had agreed to meet at High-Lawn and she'd come straight from the clinic. The view of D.C. from the turf-lined rooftop never failed to take her breath away. Jonathan had selected a picnic table isolated from the others at the far side of the entrance.

Jonathan sighed. "For the tenth time, someone in my position can't be seen connected with CAET publicly. It wouldn't make sense, given my association with Paranganjo. It would also have negative ramifications for HoweTek Communications. You know that."

Sheila nodded. "I understand. But if Citizens Against Extra Terrestrials is going to have any real influence, we need to have people who can leverage our position."

"Well, I've certainly thrown enough money CAET's way." He took a sip of Johnnie Walker Black. "It would be nice to see a more tangible return on investment."

"We're making progress. We've been working at the grassroots level." Sheila held up her wine glass, waving it around as she spoke, the liquid precariously close to spilling over the top. "More and more people are questioning the wisdom of the Cygnan-human effort. Lanjo and the ball going viral on social media definitely helped. An alien exercising paranormal powers makes most people very uncomfortable."

Sheila's eyes lit up. "We're also working on having one of CAET's members going on the *Great Day in the USA* show. They have a segment coming up on the Cygnan presence with a guest panel. Rumor has it, world-renowned astrophysicist Timothy Cantrell will be weighing in. He's already stated publicly he doesn't trust the Cygnans." Smiling at Jonathan, she took another sip of wine. "It's looking very promising."

"That's good news." Jonathan stared into his glass. "No rational person can expect aliens to be altruistic towards species other than their own. Survival of the fittest and all that."

"That's exactly my point. I have to be honest with you. Some of our CAET folks are wondering why you're doing business with Paranganjo if you're against Cygnan-human relations. They wanted me to ask you why you're persisting with that relationship."

Jonathan sighed again and rolled his ice around in his glass. "It's complicated. Obviously, it's better for HoweTek Communications instead of someone else unsympathetic to CAET to be doing business with the Cygnans. Now that we've established contact with Paranganjo, we'll be more effective by allowing things to run their course. If CAET can convince the government to withdraw their association with the Cygnans, we'll have control over their business interests in the private sector and can shut them down as well. To break off our relationship prematurely will merely drive Paranganjo to seek another business partner that we have no control over."

"I get it, but I had to ask. There's a lot of concern over the sabotage attempt on the airplane and at CERN. We don't advocate violence and want to avoid CAET being connected to any of that, but we do want to be taken seriously. If you made your allegiance to CAET public, that would have a lot of influence."

"And be able to continue my relationship with Paranganjo? Can't do it, Sheila. You'll just have to be content with my monetary contributions for now." He reached into his jacket and slid an envelope across the table. "Here, this should get you some more grassroots support. Our politicians will eventually have to listen to the voice of the people. Focus on that and just make sure you have someone educated and well-spoken for the *Great Day* show."

"We're trying for Michael Arrington, the astrophysicist from Yale. You know, the guy who wrote that New York Times Best Seller: *Extraterrestrials and the End of Time*. He hasn't returned my calls yet, but he'd be a good one to appear alongside Dr. Cantrell."

"Sounds promising." Jonathan smiled. "He's a big name. It looks like you have everything under control." His smile turned downward. "Just make sure and keep a low profile. And for heaven's sake, don't go too far. The president wasn't thrilled with your television interview. If you step out of line, they'll shut you down permanently. We'd be foolish to think they don't know about your connection with CAET after that stunt."

"Don't worry, I won't rock the boat." Nor would she mention that the NPC had contacted her. Jonathan wouldn't be too pleased to learn the people who may have been responsible for the sabotage at CERN wanted to work with CAET.

"Good. Take care, and I'll be in touch." Jonathan got up, tossed some crumpled bills on the table, and headed for the entrance.

Sheila finished her wine, scooped up the bills, and paid their tab. It would be good to go home, put her feet up, and relax with Jessup.

29

"Woo hoo!" Tom leaned back and wiped the sweat from his brow. Feraganjo and Brett stopped what they were doing and gazed in his direction.

"Time for a Snoopy happy dance?" Brett grinned knowingly.

Even the most seasoned scientist couldn't help but feel a small measure of jubilation when they finally overcame a perplexing obstacle, and Tom was no exception. It felt especially good, considering the setbacks they'd experienced and the timeline they were on.

"You bet!" Tom jumped up and started to dance a jig. Feraganjo looked at Brett with a puzzled expression. "Is Tom okay? It seems he's having some sort of seizure."

Brett burst out laughing, and Feraganjo relaxed. He'd become fairly familiar with the human range of emotions and realized what Tom was doing was a good thing.

"We'll watch some Peanuts tonight. I'll introduce you to Snoopy and the gang. Wait until I tell Theresa you thought Tom was having a seizure. He's dancing because he's happy."

Feraganjo nodded and walked over to where Tom was standing by the damaged cooling system. "May I inquire to the cause of your sudden display of happiness, Tom?"

"Sure." He pointed at the new box he'd attached containing several Programmable Logic Controllers. "I think I've mitigated the damage to the control portion by upgrading the system with PLCs. I ran a quick test, and the valves are operating just as I programmed them to."

Feragango slapped Tom on the back. Tom's happy grin confirmed he'd used the gesture correctly. "That's great. Brett and I better get busy with the new connectors. It looks like we'll have the cooling system running very soon."

"Yes, it does, doesn't it?" Tom scanned the room to see if anyone else was present and caught a glimpse of Theresa looking in his direction. She was wearing a pair of coveralls and had been running cables to replace the ones that had melted. He tried to meet her eyes, but she glanced away and directed her gaze downward, focusing on her task. Tom sighed. She'd agreed to give their relationship another try, but it was obvious she still had doubts. He was debating whether or not to go talk to her when Darryl burst through the side door and ran over to Tom and Feraganjo, short of breath and eyes wide.

"What is it?" Tom asked. "Is Sandra okay?"

"Sandra's fine. Her new medication is still working well. It's about the project." Darryl took out a handkerchief and dabbed at his forehead. It was obvious that whatever it was, it wasn't good news.

Tom held both hands out. "I thought the new timeline was okay.

Joe wasn't very happy, but he approved it. We just now got the new control system working—"

"It's not that. The team is doing great. The problem is this." He held up his iPad so Tom and Feraganjo could see a video on the screen. Brett, sensing something was wrong, left what he was doing and joined them. "This played on CNN back in the U.S. about thirty minutes ago."

Tom scrutinized the small screen. "Is that Geoffrey Clarke?"

"Yes," Darryl replied, tapping the screen to get the video to start.

The video started to play, and Darryl hastily unmuted the speaker.

". . . the beginning of a new era in energy. Fusion Origins is leading the way. Our fusion reactor, based on a field-reversed configuration, has reached a major milestone. I am thrilled to report we now have attainable fusion. We have successfully converted a helium-3 sample from the Moon and deuterium into viable energy. Our process is robust and repeatable. We have proved the fusion of 1 kilogram of helium-3 and .67 kilograms of deuterium yields about 19 megawatt years of energy." He grinned. "Thirty years has arrived. We are finally able to get more energy out of a reaction than we put in."

In the video, reporters started clamoring for Geoffrey Clarke's attention. A senior reporter from *The Times* shouted out, "Mr. Clarke, is your process economically feasible?"

Geoffrey nodded. "Let's just say I fully expect to get a return on my investment in the next six months."

A petite blonde from *The Post* asked, "Mr. Clarke, are you going to compete with the government effort to mine helium-3 from the Moon to fuel your fusion reactor?"

Geoffrey's grin grew even wider. "At this point, I think you should be asking the government whether or not they will be competing with us, not the other way around. Getting to the Moon is easy. Viable fusion is hard."

Tom reached over Darryl's shoulder and tapped the pause button. He felt disoriented as he tried to process Geoffrey Clarke's words. He'd been aware of Fusion Origin's proprietary field-reversed configuration to create a superheated plasma environment and their progress in sustaining plasma, but he had no idea they'd been so close to usable compact fusion technology. He began walking off in a daze, and Feraganjo grabbed his arm. "Please wait, Tom."

"Let him go," Brett said quietly. "He needs a few minutes."

Feraganjo dropped his arm and turned to Brett with a puzzled expression. "What just happened? He was so happy a few minutes ago."

Darryl stepped in. "It looks like Geoffrey Clarke and his team of private science and technology investors have solved the problem of fusion. That was Tom's life's work, and Clarke beat him to the punch. That's going to be tough for him to swallow. He's going to need some time to get over it."

Feraganjo turned to Brett. "What does 'beat him to the punch,' and 'tough for him to swallow,' mean?"

"Not now, buddy," Brett replied.

"But how will this affect our effort?"

Darryl just shook his head. Brett patted Feraganjo's arm. "I don't think we know yet, pal. Let's take a break and go grab a bite. We need to let the big shots figure it out." He turned to Darryl. "Do you want to go with us?"

Darryl let out a long breath. "Sure. There isn't anything I can do until I hear from Joe. Last I heard, he's heading our way in the morning." He looked towards the direction Tom had walked, but he was already gone. "I guess he'll be all right," Darryl muttered to himself. He glanced at Brett and Feraganjo and summoned a brief smile. "Let's go."

30

"Joe's flying in this afternoon. Believe it or not, Geoffrey Clarke will be with him."

"Geoffrey Clarke?" Tom looked at Darryl, flabbergasted. He'd spent the morning working on the cooling system. Until he was told to stop, he planned on continuing his efforts towards making their design work.

"Yup. I need you to gather the team for a meeting in the main auditorium." Darryl seemed a little more relaxed, making Tom wonder if he knew something he hadn't shared yet.

"Do you know what it's going to be about?"

Darryl shook his head. "My imagination is running wild, but I don't have a clue."

Tom peered at him more closely. He could tell something was up. "Come on, Darryl. Spill the beans."

"Another idiom you'll have to explain to Feraganjo." Darryl smiled. "Sorry, I really don't know. I just have a good feeling about this."

"Well, that's something, anyway." Tom hesitantly smiled back. "Okay, boss, what time do you want everyone?"

Darryl glanced at his watch. "Let's say four o'clock." He looked sideways at Tom. "That should give you time to have lunch with Theresa."

Tom looked down. "Yeah, maybe," he mumbled.

"Trouble in paradise?"

"Let's just say Theresa seems to have had a change of heart. I'm not exactly sure where we stand."

Darryl punched Tom in the arm. "If you want her, son, you have to pursue her. Don't drift apart because you didn't try. I know you have a lot on your mind right now, but it's the perfect time to show Theresa she's a priority in your life. That is, if she actually is."

Tom gazed at his boss. He thought about the tough times Darryl and his wife had been through, yet their love for each other was apparent to everyone. Perhaps Darryl was right and he needed to be more assertive. He glanced at his watch. He was hoping to have his program tweaks completed today and the meeting just shortened his day. He looked back at the mass of wires and the PLC he'd been working on and shook his head. "I don't know, Darryl. I'll see."

"Sure. It was just a thought."

The entire team that had worked on the antimatter trap began to gather in the auditorium at 3:45 that afternoon. No one knew why they'd been called to meet, and speculation was rampant. Theresa and Keith had spent the morning at the Swiss Space

Center in a collaborative effort with NASA to encourage global partnerships with Switzerland. They hurried back in time to join the others milling around the auditorium.

Dr. Auer was there with the other scientists and CERN personnel. The science team's mood had been fluctuating wildly since Geoffrey Clarke's announcement, from excitement that a fusion reactor solution had been reached, to thinly-veiled disappointment that it wasn't their team proclaiming they had conquered fusion.

Tom entered the auditorium and walked onto the stage. He was as much in the dark as everyone else and eager to hear what Joe had to say. He stepped behind the podium and spoke into the microphone, getting everyone's attention.

"Thanks for coming, everyone. Each of you are here because you're stakeholders in our effort to use the Antiproton Decelerator to trap antimatter for our fusion reactor design. Darryl will explain further."

Darryl took the podium and Tom walked over to stand by Theresa and Keith. Darryl looked over the crowd and smiled.

"It's been quite a ride so far, with the sabotage of our plane, our initial success in trapping antimatter, and the explosion damaging the cooling system. Now it seems our efforts have been in vain, with Geoffrey Clarke's announcement about his working fusion reactor. However, there is more to the story than meets the eye. Joe Ricinski, aide to President Ferris, has flown in to elaborate on what's happened and how we'll be moving forward. But first, I must caution you. The information you're about to receive is classified. There must be NO security leaks. If a leak occurs, the person responsible will be found and prosecuted to the full extent of the law."

A low buzz broke out at Darryl's words, as the audience absorbed the implications. A few moments later, Joe Ricinski stepped out onto the stage, and the room fell silent. He shook Darryl's hand, then scanned the crowd. "Darryl's right, it's been quite a ride. And I'm here to assure you the ride has not ended, despite Geoffrey Clarke's announcement. In fact, we need you more than ever."

Every eye was glued to Joe in anticipation. His next words caught every single person by surprise. "Geoffrey Clarke made his announcement at the request of the President."

Joe paused to let his words sink in, then continued. "There's multiple efforts towards perfecting fusion, and not all of the players have the best interests of Earth or the Cygnans in mind. Some of our competitors are motivated only by their desire for profit. We've identified those who are set on using fusion at the expense of both our worlds.

"Many of you know Geoffrey Clarke has long been an investor in technology. In fact, his company has been working on fusion long before our First Contact. Geoffrey, come on out here." Joe looked towards the side of the stage where the business magnate had been observing the proceedings. Geoffrey walked up the stairs to the stage and stood by Joe. Joe squeezed his shoulder. "Go ahead, Geoffrey. I'll let you explain what happened."

Geoffrey leaned slightly into the podium towards the microphone and nodded to the crowd. "First of all, I want to thank all of you for your work on fusion. I admire your dedication, and I share your enthusiasm." The audience stared back, wondering where Geoffrey was going. "So, unfortunately, I have some disappointing news for you." He paused and took a breath, then made eye contact with the audience. "We do not, I repeat, we do not, have a working fusion reactor."

The room exploded with conversation at Geoffrey's words. Tom turned to Theresa. "I don't know whether to laugh or cry."

Theresa shook her head. "Me neither. I wonder why the deception."

"Hopefully, we're about to find out."

Geoffrey stood patiently, waiting for the audience to get over their initial surprise. He leaned back into the microphone. "So, your next logical question would be, why did I say we have a working fusion reactor?"

All around the room, heads nodded. Geoffrey bounced on his heels, shook his head, and smiled. "Well, it wasn't my idea, I can tell you that." Low laughter rippled through the room at his words. He gripped the podium with his hands and looked around at his audience. "Many of you are familiar with my work and my enthusiasm for technology. It's a passion I share with each one in this room. But right now, we have to look at something greater than ourselves."

Geoffrey released his grip on the podium, extending his palms upward in supplication. "We need to focus on our common desire to propagate each of our species in healthy and happy worlds that have enough clean energy to sustain our children and future generations. As sentient beings, we have all been working towards this goal, but there are some factions that are doing so with the sole motivation of making a profit." Geoffrey rubbed his cheek. "The President of the United States asked me to announce that we have fusion in order to shake up the competition and give the government more time to actually build a working fusion reactor."

Puzzled looks filled the room as the scientists digested Geoffrey's words. Brett blurted out the obvious from where he was sitting. "Mr. Clarke, how does pretending to have fusion mitigate the efforts of our competition? That would make them work harder to beat us. Even when we conquer fusion, there's much work to be done to build the spaceships."

"And that's the point," Geoffrey agreed. "We're trying to push the competition into making mistakes. If they don't think they have much time, they're more likely to expose themselves in their efforts to catch up. We need to get a handle on their ultimate goals, so we can protect both Cygnan and human interests."

Joe returned to the podium. "We don't yet fully understand the motives of the Cygnan business sector, but our intel suggests their intentions are less than honorable. By forcing them to tip their hand, we'll be able to respond to their tactics and hopefully delay their progress, so we can finish building our own fusion reactor. We're currently monitoring their efforts, and in the meantime, we need to continue working as fast as possible. This program is still a go and is a very high priority. As such, funding has been approved as needed for this effort."

At Joe's words, the room broke into cheers. Tom grabbed Theresa's hand, and his face stretched into a huge smile. "It looks like we're on again."

Theresa smiled back. "Yes, it does." Tom, startled at her reply, looked at her more closely. Could she mean . . . ? But before he could think any further, the Cygnan-human science team enveloped them. Brett slapped Tom's back and picked up Theresa and swung her around. Aliens and humans exchanged joyful hugs and handshakes in celebration.

⚛

Still elated from the previous day's revelation and their orders to continue, Tom was once again at his workstation at the Antiproton Decelerator. His PLC control program was working flawlessly, but he'd run into yet another obstacle. The stochastic cooling system was responsible for cooling down the antiprotons, which was critical to their ability to trap them. The kicker was responsible for applying an electric field to the particles in order to correct the deviation measured by the detector, so it was essential they were calibrated properly. The problem was the electric field wasn't providing an accurate correction, and Tom needed to determine the cause. He wasn't sure if the problem was in the detector or the kicker, but he had to figure it out before they could proceed.

His previous elation began to wane as he tried to make adjustments to no avail. He shook his head in frustration. This was only the first step to a working fusion reactor. Once they had the antimatter collected for a power source, they still had to get back to their lab at GWU and make it work with their new inertial confinement design. He didn't know how to make it all come together. Darryl might be the project manager, but ultimately it was up to Tom to get it working. Right now, he couldn't even get the already-existing cooling system to behave. He sighed. Perhaps their CERN guide, Dr. Auer, could shed some light on the issue.

As if reading his thoughts, Dr. Auer opened the door to the lab and strode towards him. He glanced down at Tom and at the bank of sensors Tom had pulled out. "Hmmm, I'm a theoretical physicist, not an engineer, but it seems to me you have a problem."

"Yeah," Tom replied glumly. "The electric field is not making corrections accurately in response to the detector's data. Not sure where to go with this. Any CERN experts I can talk to?"

"I'll check around for you. The original engineering team on the stochastic cooling system is back in the U.S. for a conference, but perhaps I can set up a call. I'll shoot off an email. We'll have to wait until tonight—it's the middle of the night over there."

"Thanks, I appreciate it. Did you need anything?"

"No, I was just in the neighborhood and thought I would say hello. I'll let you know when I hear something from the engineering team." Dr. Auer slapped Tom on the back encouragingly, then strode away.

Tom returned his attention to the cooling system, fighting the headache that had begun when his adjustments failed to work and was now threatening to become a full-fledged migraine. *If he couldn't get it working, nothing else would matter.*

31

The sun was streaming through the gaps in the blinds. It was Wednesday morning Boston time. Bright spears of light played annoyingly across Stephanie's face as she lay on the foldout couch the hospital staff had brought for her to sleep on. She cracked open her eyes and looked blearily at the hospital bed, hoping to see movement, only to be disappointed yet again. Lanjo had not moved one inch since she saw him the day before. The nurse had warned her he wouldn't be responsive, but she didn't want to believe it. Somewhere inside, she held onto the hope her presence would stir him out of his coma. But it hadn't happened yet. She sat up, pulled the blanket under her chin, and sighed. It just wasn't fair. Lanjo saved everybody on the plane, just like he saved her that day on the Potomac. He just had to be okay.

Yawning, she was in the midst of stretching her arms in an effort to wake up when the door burst open. A Cygnan doctor entered, flanked by two human doctors, causing her to fall back startled onto the mattress. She ducked under the blanket and feigned sleep, cracking one eye open and hoping they wouldn't shoo her out of the room.

The Cygnan doctor stepped over to Lanjo's bed and examined him with an unfamiliar instrument. He picked up Lanjo's limp wrist and gazed a moment in puzzlement at the friendship bracelet around it. He shrugged in a very human gesture and continued his exam. The two doctors accompanying him remained quiet as the Cygnan doctor ran the strange device across Lanjo's forehead. He motioned to the two humans, and they gently lifted Lanjo's head so the Cygnan could complete a 360 degree scan of his brain. Lanjo didn't move the entire time.

The doctor finally completed his scan, pushed some buttons on the instrument, and stepped back. He examined the data scrolling across the screen, his face drawing into a Cygnan scowl. Turning to the human doctors, he shook his head. "His brain waves are erratic and degrading. His alpha rhythm is severely attenuated. If we can't stimulate his neurons soon, we're in danger of losing him completely. As it is, his brain function will be questionable, even if we succeed in restoring the brain's correct electrical activity, which is doubtful."

"What can be done?" asked the older of the two humans. "We don't have a good grasp on how to help a comatose human to regain consciousness, let alone a Cygnan."

"If we were on Lanzeron, there are some therapies I could try that have had some success in these instances. As things stand, there is not a whole lot I can do."

"What about transporting him back to Lanzeron in the ship you arrived in?" suggested the other human doctor. "Can't we send him through the wormhole to get him the help he needs?"

"I wish we could, but his condition is too unstable. That particular ship must travel at speeds which would elevate the G force past what Lanjo can tolerate. It would be very dangerous for him to attempt the trip in his current state." He paused and turned his gaze towards Stephanie, who had ducked back under the blanket and was now peering through the thin fabric at him. "I'm truly sorry."

A lump rose in Stephanie's throat. She balled more tightly into the blanket and let the tears come. She didn't notice the doctors leaving as she sobbed quietly into her pillow.

"I never get tired of the three-cheese pizza." Keith grinned, pouring a beer from the pitcher on their table. CERN Restaurant 1 wasn't very busy on Thursday evenings. Tom and Keith took advantage of the available ping pong tables and started a game while waiting for their pizza to cook.

"So what's going on with you and Theresa?" Keith asked as they volleyed to see who would serve first. "I don't want to stick my nose in your business, but she's my commander and more importantly, she's a good friend. You get pretty close to a person when you're training for a lunar mission. I know she has feelings for you and I don't want to see her get hurt." Keith stopped his sentence abruptly as the ping pong ball sailed past him without bouncing on the table. Both men knew he'd been about to say "again."

Tom sighed. He took the few steps to their table and took a swig of his beer. Wiping his mouth with the back of his hand, he picked up his ping pong paddle and looked at Keith. "Ready?"

Keith nodded. "Yeah."

Tom served the ball, putting a fast spin on it. Keith barely managed to return it, and the ball flew back and forth between the two men. "I wish I knew," Tom replied as he focused on Keith's fast, low return. His paddle caught it as it bounced off the edge of the table, and he managed to put it right at Keith's weak spot. Keith usually missed his backhand shot when it went far enough to the side and this time was no exception. "She seems, well . . . preoccupied I guess is as good a word as any. I asked her out a couple of times, but she just makes some excuse. It doesn't take a fusion scientist to figure out she's not interested."

Keith scooped up the ball from the floor and tossed it back to Tom. "1—0. Yeah, I noticed that, too." He deftly returned Tom's serve with backspin and smiled when Tom's return went wild. "I know she cares about you, bud. But I think she's worried about getting involved with anyone. She's dedicated to her career, and it's pretty scary for her to contemplate a personal life that includes considering someone else in her decisions. I felt that way about Brittany. 1-1."

Keith smiled as he slammed the ball off Tom's side of the table. He waited for Tom to retrieve it and serve again. "Being a NASA pilot takes a lot of time and emotional energy, as well as physical training. Don't take this the wrong way, but if you're a career astronaut, being in a relationship can be a distraction. When a relationship starts getting serious, a person has to decide if they're willing to devote time and energy to that distraction. The other person also has to be willing to accept what the job takes. Both parties have to be willing to sacrifice to make it work." He missed Tom's next hit and looked at his paddle as if there were a hole in it, laughing. "Good one. 2-1."

"So how does Brittany feel about you being gone so much?"

"I won't lie to you, Tom. It's not easy. Brittany knew of my dream to be an astronaut going in. For my part, I try to limit my long-term assignments, and I encourage her to get involved in her own work. Did you know she's an architect?"

"No, that's great. Does she work for a firm in the Houston area?"

"Yeah. She's working on a huge project right now. They're designing a shopping mall and she's the lead on the project. She's been with this firm for three years now and her taking lead is a big deal." Keith paused and chased the ball Tom had just skillfully hit off the corner edge, making it an impossible return. He grabbed it from under a nearby table. "2-Up. Good one." He tossed the ball back to Tom. "My point is that you can make it work. The key is to be supportive of each other's careers, and being understanding when things come up. Brit has had some long nights at the office too, and the occasional business trip. We don't like being away from each other, but we do what we need to do to support each other."

"Maybe Theresa needs to know I'm willing to support her career," Tom mused, as Keith's well-aimed ball flew by him. "Hey, I wasn't ready!"

"That's okay, looks like our pizza is." Keith grinned. "Let's eat!"

The two men put down their paddles and headed back to the table where their pizza was waiting. Keith had given Tom a lot to think about. He knew Theresa was attracted to him. He had no doubt about that from their kiss on the catwalk of ATLAS. If Theresa was interested in a relationship but worried about how it would affect her career, he'd have to figure out a way to calm her fears. But how? He took a bite of the pizza, oozing with cheese, and washed it down with a swig of beer. He'd think of something. It was too important not to.

He was lifting his piece of pizza for another bite when he saw Darryl enter the cafeteria. Tom watched him scanning the tables, and he put the slice of pizza down and waved his hand to catch Darryl's eye. Darryl hurried over, slightly out of breath.

"Sorry to bother you, Tom, but it's Sandra. She's not doing well."

Tom jumped up, grabbing his friend by the shoulder. "What is it, Darryl? What's wrong?"

"Her red blood cells are decreasing, and she's becoming anemic. They aren't sure why, but they're going to have to do a transfusion. I need to get back immediately. My flight leaves in two hours."

"Of course, don't worry about things here—I got it covered."

Darryl looked Tom in the eyes and gripped his shoulder back. "I'm really sorry, Tom."

"Don't be. Go take care of Sandra. She needs her daddy. We'll be fine."

Keith walked around to stand by Tom. "I can step up and help out too. Don't worry about us. We'll be praying for your little girl."

Darryl nodded. "Thanks, we'd appreciate that. I better go. I still need to finish packing."

Tom gave Darryl's shoulder another reassuring squeeze then stepped back. "Godspeed."

Darryl turned on his heel and practically ran out of the cafeteria in his haste. Tom and Keith looked at each other and slowly sank back into their seats. Darryl had been the glue that held together all of the differing factions working on the antimatter trap. Tom shook his head, wondering what to do next. It was the end of the workday. At least he could stay with Keith and finish his pizza and beer, but after that, he'd better get to work. Just when he thought it was impossible for things to get worse, life had just gotten a whole lot more complicated.

Ray eyed the plain white envelope on his desk. He wasn't sure how it got there. It hadn't been there when he left late the night before, and his admin had not yet arrived this morning. He picked up the envelope and rotated it, looking for any identifying marks, but there weren't any. Putting it back down, he sighed and grabbed his coffee cup. He had a feeling he better have some more caffeine before dealing with its contents. He walked over to the office Keurig machine and made his favorite Dark Magic Extra Bold coffee, tossing the pod into the recycle bin.

Ray walked back to his office and sat down behind his desk. He exhaled and picking up his letter opener, deftly pushed it under the seal and cut through it. He opened the edges and pulled out a piece of paper. The letter had been done on a word processor to further dispel any attempts to identify the writer. Ray read the single sentence:

Stop the government effort with the Cygnans or someone else will. Your way would be better for all concerned.

He stared at the cryptic note for several minutes. *The sabotaged aileron was aimed to stop the government effort and the explosion at CERN was no accident.* He dropped the note onto his desk. Picking up his cell phone, he dialed Joe Ricinski.

"Hello Ray, good to hear from you. How are things at your end?"

"Not so good, Joe. I just got an anonymous note. My guess is another sabotage attempt, if I don't comply."

"You're right, that doesn't sound good. Come on in and bring the note. We'll figure it out."

"On my way." *The gas and oil lobbyists have lost their minds. It has to be them. They'd better stop using me for their messages.* He picked up the note and his eyes fell on the last words of the first sentence:

Or someone else will.

Anger made his eyes blur. *Bring it on, you jerk. You're messing with the wrong guy.*

32

Tom was bent over the battered wooden desk in Darryl's tempo-rary office at CERN, trying to make sense of the records Darryl had left behind. The man was a meticulous project manager. He'd left behind spreadsheets and Gantt charts detailing exactly where their project stood, the milestones they needed to reach and by when, and the all-important budgeting. Tom had always consid-ered project management a waste of time, but he might have to rethink that opinion. A knock on the door interrupted his thoughts.

"Come in," he called, as he continued to pore over one of the Gantt charts. If they wanted to stay on schedule, they had to get that cooling system up and running. Maybe tonight's conference call would provide a solution to the problem.

Brett came over to the worktable and surveyed the myriad of documents Tom had spread out.

"What's up?" Tom asked as he continued to study the chart, looking for a way to shift the workload without changing the timeline.

"Bad news, I'm afraid. Rachel took me to see Feraganjo this morning. He's in the dorm with Keraganjo, and he's pretty sick, sweaty, and achy. Keraganjo trained in basic first aid, but obviously he's not a doctor. He's trying to keep him comfortable and hydrated, but he's not sure what else to do."

Tom pounded the table with his fist in frustration. What else could possibly go wrong? He'd pushed his concern for Lanjo to the back of his mind, knowing he was unable to help him. He had to trust in Lanjo's doctors for his care. But Feraganjo was here and his responsibility. "Thanks for letting me know. I'll see what I can do. In the meantime, ask Keraganjo to stay with him and keep him comfortable."

As soon as Brett left his office, Tom called Joe Ricinski. He needed to get medical help for Feraganjo. Maybe Joe could talk to the doctors treating Lanjo. They would know more about Cygnan health.

"Hello," Joe's voice sounded muted.

Oops, he'd forgotten about the 6-hour time difference. "Sorry to wake you, Joe, but we're having a problem here. Our lead Cygnan scientist, Feraganjo, has come down sick. He's sweating a lot and feels very achy. The other Cygnan, Keraganjo, doesn't know what's wrong. I could really use some Cygnan medical advice."

Joe yawned. "You're in luck. A doctor arrived from Lanzeron and is at the hospital with Lanjo. We can arrange for him to call and speak to the other Cygnan on your team and determine how to proceed from there."

Tom almost dropped the phone. "A Cygnan doctor? How did he get there?"

"We needed medical expertise quickly to help Lanjo. A doctor volunteered to travel from Lanzeron through the wormhole Paranganjo has been using to communicate with Jonathan Howe's team. But keep all that under your hat."

Tom stood stunned, as he absorbed this information. Regaining his composure, he swallowed and asked, "So how is Lanjo?"

"I'm sorry. The doctor just saw him today. His prognosis is not good. We'll know more in a few days. Stephanie is still with him."

Tom swallowed again. "Okay. Please keep me posted and tell Stephanie she can stay as long as it's okay with her mom. She loves Lanjo."

"I know. I'm really sorry. Let's see what we can do to help Feraganjo. I'll get on the horn and arrange a call with the Cygnan doctor and get back to you."

"Okay, thanks." Tom hung up, sank into a chair, and buried his face in his hands.

After delivering Tom's message to Keraganjo, Brett returned to the main lab area where their team was working on constructing the power source. Alan had spent the last several days reviewing the schematics from Project Daedalus and modifying them to fit their current design. He looked up and frowned as Brett approached.

"Your arrival is fortuitous, Brett. Come look at this." He pointed at a section of the design they'd been wrestling with. "When we initiate the fusion reaction via the antimatter, the intense light flash from the thermonuclear explosion will wreak havoc on the system optics. We need to find a way to shield the optics, or the design won't work."

Brett rubbed his cheek absently as he studied the design. How could they properly shield the optical system? The optics were necessary to the ignition design for triggering the release of anti-matter. The problem was that same release would destroy the optics. They were going to need help with this one.

"Good catch. I think I'll see if we can get some help from NASA engineers. They have optical shielding systems on some of their spacecraft. Maybe Theresa or Keith could call in a favor and get one of their buddies to come out and take a look."

"Sounds like a good call. Are you going to tell Tom, or shall I?"

Brett sighed. Tom had enough on his already full plate. He hated to add to it, but as the interim project manager, he needed to know. "I'll tell Tom."

"Tell me what?" Tom came through the lab door and strode to Alan's workspace.

"A bit of bad news, I'm afraid." Alan looked sideways at Brett. "We have a shielding problem. As soon as we initiate the fusion reaction, the intense heat that results will damage the optical system that was incorporated into the design. Our laser energy source would have had less gain, so we didn't need to take that into consideration when we first proposed the inertial confinement design. With the change in power source, it's now a problem."

Tom stood for a long moment, processing Alan's words, and finally asked, "How big of a problem?"

Brett cleared his throat. "At the moment, a pretty big one. But we have a plan to call in NASA engineering to help. Hopefully, we can leverage their expertise in heat shielding to come up with a work-able solution." Brett had tried his best to inject confidence into his words, but he could tell Tom saw through him. He tried again.

"It's not insurmountable, but it could hurt our timetable . . . uhhh . . . pretty badly. It'll depend on the time they take to design something, the modifications we'll need to incorporate into the design, and the cost and availability of the material."

Tom gritted his teeth and closed his eyes. When he opened them, he said, "Just do the best you can."

"We will," Brett replied.

"Yes," Alan added. "We'd better get cracking. We'll figure it out."

"Thanks," Tom said. "I hope so. A lot depends on it." He walked away, shaking his head. *What else could go wrong?*

⚛

The GBC television studio hummed with activity. The director raised three fingers and counted them down to a fist, causing the large light on the camera to switch from red to green. "We have a very special guest on the *Great Day in the USA* show, world famous astrophysicist from Edinburgh, Timothy Cantrell. Dr. Cantrell, it's an honor to have you on our show." *Great Day* hostess Candice Sutton wore a stunning blue dress that complemented her bright blue eyes. She smiled warmly at the famous scientist. His sandy hair was somewhat tousled, and he was wearing a rumpled jacket with elbow patches. "I loved the movie about your life, *To Follow the Stars*. I'm so glad you were able to find a spot in your busy schedule to spend some time with us."

Dr. Cantrell smiled broadly in return. "Thank you, Candice, the pleasure is mine. Please call me Timothy."

"Thank you, Timothy. I know we only have a few minutes with you, so I want to get right to it. You expressed concern about an alien presence long before the Cygnans showed up on Earth. You articulated your fears by referring to Dr. Stephen Hawking, your colleague from Cambridge, who has pointed out that the challenge isn't whether or not aliens exist, but rather, what they would be like. Dr. Hawking also compared a First Contact scenario with Columbus discovering America and the outcome that event had on the Indians."

Candice swiveled her shoulders forward towards the astrophysicist, clasping her hands tightly. "Dr. Can—," she paused, "Timothy. Now that the Cygnans have been on Earth for a while and we've gotten to know Lanjo from press conferences, do you still feel the same way?"

The smile left the astrophysicist's face, and an expression of concern took its place. "Yes, I do, Candice. We really don't know anything about the Cygnans, except what they tell us. Dr. Hawking also said something about the ability to adapt to change is a mark of intelligence. The Cygnans have certainly brought change, but intelligence is also making an *informed* adaptation to that change. We simply don't have enough information to make valid assumptions. Are the Cygnans wolves in sheep's clothing? For me, the verdict is still out."

"That's an interesting perspective on the Cygnans." Candice smiled uncertainly. "Coming from one of the most brilliant minds in the world, I must admit that makes me a bit nervous."

"It should make you nervous, Candice. That's the only intelligent response," Timothy replied, his smile returning. "Let's hope my negative suppositions prove to be in error. As good-looking as I am, I don't have such a large ego that I must be proven correct. It would be better for all of us if I'm wrong."

Timothy's self-deprecating sense of humor did not steer Candice from the gravity of his words. "So, what do you suggest, Timothy?" she asked. "What would be an intelligent response?"

"To gather more data before throwing in our lot with the Cygnans. We're in an untenable position at the moment. Since we already know they are technologically superior, we must rely on their good will, yet we have no true understanding of the Cygnan moral compass. Lanjo is a likeable fellow, a nice guy if you will, but is he truly representative of the Cygnan government and their intentions, or are we being duped?"

Candice nodded. "You make some great observations, Timothy. Thank you for coming on the show today to share them with us." She leaned over and offered her hand for a brief handshake. "It's been an honor to have you on our show. Unfortunately, we're out of time." She smiled into the camera. "Now, I'm turning it over to Megan Whorley, who has some representatives of CAET with her in the studio."

"Thanks, Candice, and thanks, Timothy, for coming onto our special show exploring how America feels about the Cygnan presence." Megan's brown hair was a sharp contrast to Candice's blonde, and her dark pants suit accentuated her white blouse. "Next up, we have a representative of the organization CAET: Citizens Against Extraterrestrials, a grassroots organization that questions the wisdom of the Cygnan-human effort and challenges the U.S. government to listen to the voice of the people. Renowned astrophysicist Dr. Michael Arrington is their spokesman."

Megan gestured to her guest, dressed in a business suit and impeccably groomed, his black hair perfectly in place. "Dr. Arrington," Megan smiled. "It's great to have you on the show. I've always loved astronomy, and I'm an avid stargazer. So, tell me, why did you decide to become involved with CAET? Shouldn't we be excited about making a First Contact and finding so many similarities between our species? Especially since they're willing to share their technology?"

Dr. Arrington shook his head. "Actually, I find the whole Cygnan-human effort puzzling, as do many of my fellow Americans. We don't need their technology to solve our energy problems. We have proven to do quite well with good old-fashioned American innovation. A few years ago, when SETI desired to send a message from Earth to any extraterrestrial intelligence that may be listening, I thought that was foolish. We don't give our address to strangers, because we don't know if they pose a threat or not. To intentionally give out our location to aliens we know nothing about was not a good idea. Unfortunately, the Cygnans found us, and First Contact has been made, so we can't go backwards. However, we must be wise in going forward. Survival of the fittest is a belief held by many. What if the Cygnans subscribe to that theory and believe *they* are the fittest? Why would we expect aliens to be altruistic towards species other than their own? I'm concerned about their true motives."

Joe's jaw clenched as he picked up the remote on his desk and clicked off the television. He'd seen enough. The wave of popular opinion in response to the *Great Day* show could hurt their efforts. He would need to institute some damage control. With Lanjo out of commission, he needed someone to become the face of the Cygnans, rather than let the public's imagination run wild. He also needed some famous scientists to applaud the Cygnan collaboration. He would have to pull a couple of the team members from CERN to do some public relations repair and fast. They couldn't afford for the public to respond to the *Great Day* show with xenophobic hysteria. He picked up his landline and called Tom.

"Yeah, Joe." Tom sounded tired. "Have you gotten hold of the doctor for Feraganjo?"

"Yes. He'll be giving you a call in a couple of hours. But I'm calling about something else."

"What is it?"

"Did you see the *Great Day in the USA* television show?"

"The *Great Day* show? Why would I be watching that?"

"Well . . . Timothy Cantrell and Michael Arrington just weighed in on the Cygnan presence on Earth, and it wasn't pretty. I'm going to have to pull a Cygnan and a human from your team to fly back to the states to try to counteract the damage."

"We're behind schedule and have multiple obstacles that need to be overcome, before we can make real progress." Tom's voice sounded strained. "Losing any member of our team will hamstring us."

"We've gotta do it, Tom. If we don't keep the public in favor of the Cygnan-human effort, we can kiss the whole project goodbye."

"Feraganjo is incapacitated. If I send you Keraganjo, we won't have any Cygnans on the team until Feraganjo recovers."

"I'm sorry, Tom. We don't have any choice."

Tom blew out a long breath. "Okay, Joe. Who else do you want?"

"Theresa. The public already knows her and loves her from her Moon missions."

Tom was silent for a long moment. "Okay. I'll get them both on a plane." His voice cracked. "Can you give me a couple of days? I would like to know what this Cygnan doctor has to say about Feragango before Keraganjo leaves. At the very least, we need to have a little time to go over some Cygnan schematics, since we won't have a Cygnan scientist available when he's gone, until Feraganjo recovers." He paused. "And I have something I would like to finish with Theresa."

"Sure, but no more than that. I appreciate what you're doing. You should hear from the Cygnan doctor soon."

"Okay, thanks."

Joe hung up and rested his chin on his palm, intentionally taking slow, calming breaths. *Too bad Darryl's not around to handle things. Hopefully Tom won't crack under the strain.*

"Dang it, Dan, what part of no do you not understand?" Jonathan glared impatiently at his subordinate, tossing the papers in his hand onto his desk for emphasis.

"Whoa, there boss, I didn't mean to step on your toes," Dan replied. "I really believe this is a great opportunity and I don't want us to miss it."

"Great opportunity for us, or for Paranganjo? I don't trust his agenda. I agreed to partner with him to mine helium-3 on the Moon, but his tactics stink. Trying to steal NASA astronauts from under the government's nose was a bad idea and not exactly ethical. What else will he ask us to try in order to make a profit?"

"Paranganjo is eager to beat the competition. He's just ready to move forward. He needs to know you are, too. Geoffrey Clarke's announcement made him very nervous, and he doesn't want to be left behind. We don't want him looking elsewhere for a more willing partner, do we?"

Jonathan remembered Joe's instructions—keep an eye on Dan, and report any new developments. He took a breath and mentally calmed himself. He couldn't let Dan see his reluctance to deal with aliens. It could squash the deal, and Paranganjo would seek a different business partner not as protective of U.S. interests. "Of course not, Dan. But you already made me look foolish with your attempted end run to gain access to the Antiproton Decelerator ahead of Lanjo's team. I don't want another fiasco like that one. It not only failed, it got the government breathing down our necks."

"All the more reason to move forward with Paranganjo's plan. If we're going to beat the government effort, we need to commit. It's not unethical—it's good old-fashioned capitalist competition."

Jonathan looked at his assistant thoughtfully. "Okay, let me think about it. Tell Paranganjo I'll get back to him."

"Okay, boss. But I wouldn't wait too long, if I were you."

"Understood. Just stall him a bit. I need a little time to think this through."

"I'll try, but I don't know if he'll be willing to wait."

Jonathan's face reddened. "The government effort has been plagued with problems, and just because Geoffrey has a working fusion reactor doesn't mean it's ready for energy production—not by a long shot. I don't think Paranganjo has anything to worry about. If the Cygnans have such superior technology, he'll be able to figure out an energy source without CERN. If he wants an effective partner for helium-3 mining and clean energy production on the Moon, he'll just have to wait a few days. I don't take kindly to being pressured."

Dan paled, his frame tensing. Jonathan looked at him curiously. "Neither does he," Dan muttered under his breath. Then, more audibly, "Okay, boss. I'll see what I can do."

Jonathan decided not to pursue Dan's odd response. He needed to keep the charade going. "Thanks. Just keep me in the loop."

"Will do."

Jonathan watched Dan exit, then walked over and closed his office door. He'd better update Joe on Paranganjo's push to move forward.

"We got the report back from the FBI." Joe sat in his customary chair in the Oval Office. He usually enjoyed the opportunity to admire the Resolute desk but was too preoccupied with the results of the FBI investigation to even glance at it. "Their criminal informant was able to get some intel linking the gunman in the cockpit to gas and oil lobbyists—specifically the NPC. It's not strong enough for a conviction, but it does point the finger their way."

"Yeah, that's what I was afraid of." President Ferris leaned forward on his desk and steepled his fingers. "So, what do you think we should do? This has the potential to blow up in our faces politically, but the consequences are much more far-reaching. We can't let a lobbyist group force U.S. policy. And we certainly can't let them get away with their attempted sabotage. Is the gunman talking?"

"No, not yet. And there's more." Joe scratched his head. "We think the cut aileron cable was perpetrated by a separate entity, not working in partnership with the gunman. Evidence suggests that a rogue element of IPEF is involved. However, we don't have specific proof to confront them. I think our best bet for now is to go through unofficial channels and let all of the players know we are aware of their activities. I hate giving up the element of surprise, but if they know we're watching, they'll probably back off. With the current climate regarding the Cygnan presence, we don't need anything else to stir up a public outcry."

Joe's eyes narrowed and he crossed his arms over his chest. His voice took on an edge. "I'm not suggesting we forget what happened. We'll find everyone involved and bring them to justice. We just need to delay temporarily, while we get a handle on the current situation. One of the Cygnan scientists and Theresa McDonnough will be in transit back to the U.S. in a couple of days to help dispel fears and reinstate public confidence in the Cygnan-human partnership. The *Great Day* show shook up a lot of people."

The president exhaled. "I was afraid that would happen. It's the price we pay for living in a democracy. It's a great privilege, but sometimes it's also an onerous task. But I wouldn't have it any other way."

Joe nodded. "Me neither, sir. How would you like to proceed?"

The president rubbed his neck, then placed his hand on his cheek, thinking. He dropped his hand. "Go ahead and move through back channels. At least we can try to prevent any more attempts at sabotage. As for the rest, we'll live to fight another day."

"Yes, sir, I'll keep you posted. Which brings up another topic. Additional intel suggests Jonathan Howe has a connection to CAET. He's not making his position public, but we've had eyes on them for a while, and Jonathan's one of their top contributors. To make matters worse, our criminal informant also heard some chatter that CAET was approached by NPC. No details yet. And we've found out that Sheila Palazzo is one of the architects behind CAET. She's been doing a good job keeping a low profile since we threatened to arrest her if she pulled any more antics like her unscheduled television interview, but it seems she just can't help herself."

The president loosened his collar, his face reddening. He hadn't appreciated having to make an impromptu televised address because of that woman's poor judgment. To find out she was involved with CAET was the last straw. "Okay. We need Jonathan to continue to cooperate with us and monitor Dan's activities, so we have an inside understanding of where Paranganjo is going. Just put a bug in Jonathan's ear that you aren't happy to find out he's contributing to CAET, but don't give him too much grief and scare him away from our team."

"Should be easy enough," Joe replied. "He's been fairly cooperative, so far."

"I still can't figure him out. On one hand, he claims he doesn't like extraterrestrials and is contributing to CAET, on the other hand he was willing to partner with an unscrupulous Cygnan businessman. Where does Jonathan's true loyalties lie?"

"People are pretty complex, sir. I'm not sure either, but I can say one thing about Jonathan Howe. I don't think he would intentionally compromise national security interests. We just need to make sure he doesn't do something unintentionally—or that he inadvertently lets Dan do something with Paranganjo that could destroy the Cygnan-human alliance we've been working so hard to establish."

The president nodded. "Agreed. Anything else?"

"I think that's more than enough for now, sir."

"Thanks, Joe—keep me in the loop, will you?"

"Yes, sir!" Joe turned to leave.

"Oh and Joe," the president called out. "Have you heard anything else about Lanjo? We've been praying for his recovery."

Joe turned back and shook his head sadly. "I'm sorry, sir. It's not looking good. He's still in a coma and the Cygnan doctor is not hopeful."

"That's too bad," the president's chin trembled. "I was hoping he'd recover."

"Yes, sir. We all were, but there just doesn't seem to be much hope. Tom's daughter Stephanie is with him and refuses to leave. They don't know if he can hear her voice or not, but she reads to him from Mark Twain and sings to him, from what I understand."

"Mark Twain, huh?" He smiled. "He'd like that."

⚛

"Thank you for insisting on coming in person and on such short notice, Doctor." Tom held out his hand. The Cygnan grasped it and grimaced. His expression was polite and professional, lacking Lanjo's easy warmth. But then, Lanjo had an exuberance about him that was hard to match. "How was your flight?"

The doctor's grimace grew slightly larger. "Much longer than my trip through the wormhole, but with better amenities." It seemed he shared some of Lanjo's sense of humor after all. "On my return trip to Lanzeron, I'll have to bring along some airplane snacks." He looked around the lab curiously. "Where is my patient and what is his current condition?"

Tom bit back several questions about Lanjo. "Feraganjo's back in the dorm," Tom replied. "We're so glad you're here—he's not responding to our doctor's treatment. He has an elevated temperature and flu-like symptoms that are getting worse. Right this way."

Tom led the doctor down the hall to the dorm area and they entered Feraganjo's room. Brett dozed restlessly in a chair next to Feraganjo's bed. The doctor placed what must be his medicine bag on a table in the corner. Brett woke and stood as Keraganjo entered from the bathroom with a dampened wash cloth. Keraganjo spoke to the doctor in Cygnan, seemingly oblivious to everyone else in the room. The doctor responded by gesturing to where Feraganjo lay sleeping.

Keraganjo sponged Feraganjo's forehead with the washcloth, then gently squeezed his arm. Feraganjo's eyes opened. He took in everyone's presence, then focused on the doctor and struggled to sit up. Brett grabbed some pillows and propped him up in the bed.

The doctor squeezed past everyone and went to Feraganjo's bedside. He asked Feraganjo questions in Cygnan. Feraganjo struggled to answer, fatigue overcoming him. The doctor eased the sheet down and inspected Feraganjo's torso, then each arm, palpating each elbow.

When he finished his examination, the doctor addressed Brett, while Feraganjo dozed off. "It seems Feraganjo has some sort of infection. The supratrochlear lymph nodes are enlarged." He picked up Feraganjo's right hand and peered between each finger. He stopped at the space between his fifth and sixth fingers and peered into the crevasse between the two digits. He gently rotated it and lifted it, revealing two barely detectable puncture marks. "Feraganjo has been the unfortunate recipient of a spider bite. Cygnans do not react well to Earth arachnid bites."

"How could our doctors have missed that?" Brett asked, agitated.

"The supratrochlear lymph node enlarges in infections of the hand and forearm. In a human, an enlarged supratrochlear lymph node would be clearly visible. However, Cygnan elbows are larger, and the node enlargement is much more subtle to the human eye. Your doctors should not feel bad for not finding this. It would have taken specialized training in Cygnan biology to—"

"So what's Feraganjo's prognosis?" Brett interrupted anxiously. "What can we do to help him recover?"

The Cygnan doctor's face broke into the biggest grimace Tom had yet seen. He opened his bag and selected a vial containing a purplish fluid. He held it up to the light, the bottom of the tube resting on his extra finger. "This will take care of it. It's a generalized antidote to Earth arachnids we prepared as soon as the decision was made to have a joint Cygnan-human team work on Earth. It was an oversight not to have a Cygnan medical kit go with you. With this antidote, we can expect a full recovery for Feraganjo in a matter of days."

"Woo-hoo! Time for a Snoopy happy dance!" Brett jumped up and down in the small space.

Feraganjo's eyes popped open and focused on Brett. For the first time in days, Ferganjo managed a weak grimace. "Don't worry, Brett. I wasn't going to let you have all the fun."

Brett stopped jumping and leaned over his friend, his eyes moist. "I know you weren't, buddy. It's good to hear you'll be back soon." He turned to the doctor. "When can Feraganjo have the antidote?"

"How about right now?" the Cygnan doctor grimaced, his eyebrows quivering slightly. He poured the contents of the vial into a cup and handed it to Feraganjo.

Tom recalled the first time he saw Lanjo drink a glass of water and smiled wistfully. "As Lanjo would say, 'Tastes great, less filling!'" He turned to Keraganjo. "Are you about ready? Theresa is waiting for you in the foyer."

Keraganjo looked at Feraganjo and grimaced. "Yes, now that I know my superior will be okay." He turned to Brett. "Do you have any other questions about the schematics to control the circuitry for initiating the fusion reaction?"

Brett smiled. "If I have any more questions, I'll email you." He slapped the younger Cygnan on the back. "You did a great job."

"Thanks," Keraganjo replied, the skin on his forehead lightening at the compliment, the Cygnan blushing response. "It has been a pleasure working with you."

Tom stepped back and smiled to himself. Even though he'd been excited about the First Contact, he had also been nervous. It was wonderful to see Cygnans and humans working together. They weren't much different after all. His smile turned into a frown. He was losing his only healthy Cygnan scientist and the woman he loved, to a public relations blitz.

Marco stifled a yawn and poured himself another cup of coffee. It had been a busy night. While SETI was concerned with the radio spectrum, no astronomy buff could resist the lure of watching a meteor shower unfold around them. Last night the Perseid meteor shower peaked. He'd taken time out from monitoring his equipment to stretch out on a lawn chair and enjoy the show.

Bringing his coffee mug to his lips for another sustaining swallow, he heard banging and almost dropped it. He always kept the doors locked until public hours began in case some misguided zealot decided it was SETI's fault Earth was being invaded by aliens. Putting his mug down, Marco walked to the door, and peered through the glass. Dan Ross glowered back at him, face red and shining with sweat. *What was he doing here?* He hurriedly unlocked the door, and Dan burst through it.

"When do we expect our next communication with Paranganjo?" Dan demanded.

"Whoa, Dan. Calm down." Marco automatically made his voice soothing, as his brain scrambled to understand Dan's sudden change of demeanor. He was usually so calm and collected. "We aren't due to talk for a couple of hours. What's wrong?"

At Marco's words, Dan slumped into one of the chairs at a nearby workstation. "I'm sorry, it's just that we're so close, and now it looks like Jonathan may back out. This is my life's dream. I can't let it slip away."

His life's dream? When had Dan Ross, stable, practical businessman with an interest in astronomy, become that obsessed with their project? He took a breath and then slowly measured his words. "Dan, what are you not telling me?"

Dan stared back at Marco, panting. He started taking longer breaths and began to calm down. "There's a lot at stake right now. Jonathan's getting cold feet. I need to figure out a way to stall Paranganjo before we lose this business deal."

Marco didn't buy it; something else was bothering Jonathan's assistant. A muscle in Dan's jaw kept twitching and his eyes darted around the room. Jonathan's reluctance to move forward with Paranganjo would affect SETI's efforts, too. "Okay, Dan, what are you proposing?"

"We need to get Paranganjo to agree to wait on Jonathan. I need more time to convince Jonathan that partnering with Paranganjo is in his best interest."

"And why would Jonathan be dragging his feet? I thought a deal between Paranganjo and Jonathan would benefit both our species. Do you think Jonathan thinks Paranganjo has an ulterior motive?" He paused, staring at Dan's twitching jaw. "Is there something about Paranganjo you're not telling me?"

Dan studied the tips of his Oxfords. "We just need to talk to him, that's all."

Marco picked up his coffee mug and took a sip. The pleasant feelings of tranquility from watching the meteor shower had evaporated. He turned back to Dan. "Not until you tell me what this is all about."

"I can't. I just need to communicate with Paranganjo, so I can settle this thing."

Marco eyed Dan thoughtfully. Paranganjo was scheduled to call in two hours. If Dan went crazy on him, he could always pull the plug on the connection. Dan still needed him to provide the technical knowledge required to connect the call through the wormhole. "Okay, I'll set up the call when the time comes. But you better not be doing anything unethical, or I'll cut you off."

"I'm here to help the situation. The best way to do that is to talk to Paranganjo."

"All right. I have some work to do. You might as well grab yourself a cup of joe while you're waiting."

"Thanks, Marco."

It wasn't exactly what Tom had been planning, but since Theresa had to be on a plane in an hour, it would have to do. He asked her to meet him at the entrance to the site of ATLAS where they'd shared a kiss on the catwalk when they first arrived. Some part of him hoped he could recreate the experience. It seemed like months ago. Could it have been only three weeks? Watching Theresa striding purposely towards him, her wavy brown hair curling at the bottom the way he loved, Keith's words came back to him. *If you're a career astronaut, being in a relationship can be a distraction. When a relationship starts getting serious, a person has to decide if they're willing to devote time and energy to that distraction. The other person also has to be under-*

standing of what the job takes. Both parties have to be willing to sacrifice to make it work.

How could he show Theresa he would support her career, even when it kept them apart? He opened his mouth to speak but stopped as she came nearer. There was no trace of the sweet softness he'd felt that day on the catwalk. She already had her mission commander persona firmly in place.

"Sorry, Tom, I don't have much time. Joe Ricinski wants to brief me, and I have to take his call in fifteen minutes. What did you need?"

Tom's heart froze in his chest. "Uhh, nothing really, I just wanted to tell you . . ." Whatever he was going to tell her—he wasn't sure what—died on his lips. For once he let his heart overrule his head. *Here goes nothing.* Without another word, he took her face in his hands and kissed her. The instant his lips touched hers, her body went rigid. Her jaws clenched under his hands, and her lips didn't move. They didn't even twitch.

His own lips froze, along with his hopes.

And then her lips softened. They still didn't move, but they softened, and two warm hands cupped his shoulders. Like a spaceship launching into the sky, he could feel the passion igniting between them. He kissed her more deeply, gratified at her response. They stopped to breathe, their heads pulled apart slightly, and gazed into each other's eyes. Theresa's relaxed expression and slight smile gave him courage to try again.

"Just promise me one thing." She went rigid again, and Tom spoke the rest of the words in a rush. "I'm not asking for a commitment. I understand your dedication to NASA. I'm just asking for you to give me a chance. I want to be a help in your life, not a hindrance."

Theresa dropped her arms and stepped back. "I hear you, Tom. I'm really sorry, but I have to go."

Her words fell between them, colder than the -455 degrees Fahrenheit of outer space. His shoulders already felt naked without her touch and the hollow feeling in his belly threatened to overcome his entire body. "Will you think about it?" Tom couldn't keep the note of pleading out of his voice.

Theresa's eyebrows knit and her facial muscles tensed into a frown. "That's part of the problem. I do think about it—a lot. I don't need any distractions right now."

Tom reached out to take her hand, hesitated, and let his own hand fall back to his side.

"I understand. Go do what you have to do. Our country needs you." He reached out again and not letting himself stop this time, he placed his palm tenderly against her cheek. His voice softened, with just a hint of desperation. "But I need you, too."

Theresa's frown relaxed slightly into a more neutral position. "I really have to go."

Tom gave a half-hearted smile. "I know. Go."

She turned and headed across the parking lot towards where her ride to the airport was waiting and Tom entered the ATLAS Point 1 facility alone. He needed to lose himself for a while. What better place than in a cavern 100 meters below ground?

Theresa reached the Suburban, opened the passenger door, and stopped. She turned to face the building, just in time to catch a glimpse of Tom's back before the door closed behind him. Gazing at the building, she ran her fingers through the bottom curls of her hair. She suddenly felt cold and hugged herself. She blew out a long breath and climbed into the car.

"I'm sorry, Jonathan needs a few more days." Dan sat in the office chair and leaned over the mic on the table. He did his best to keep his voice level, using SETI's communications equipment to communicate through the wormhole. Paranganjo was at the other end, somewhere on the Cygnan home planet of Lanzeron.

"We can no longer wait on Mr. Howe. If he doesn't wish to move forward, we will assume he is no longer interested and we'll have to go to an alternative plan."

"I'm sure Jonathan will agree to a deal that is equitable to both sides. He just needs to clear his proposal through some additional channels. We have to make sure we're adhering to government regulations, or they can shut us down. We're in new territory here: a trade agreement with an extraterrestrial requires additional vetting. Jonathan is just, as we like to say, 'dotting the i's and crossing the t's.'"

"I'm not a fool, Dan." The edge to Paranganjo's voice sharpened. "Jonathan has had plenty of time to dot his i's and cross his t's. He's wasting my time."

"But Paranganjo, I—"

"I've heard enough. I am a businessman. The success of this venture depends on the financial backing I have managed to obtain through my reputation, which Jonathan is putting in jeopardy by dragging his feet. We agreed I would supply the technology to build nuclear fusion reactors on the Moon and he would supply labor and materials. If he doesn't come through with his end of the bargain, it will be clear to me that humans are not dependable and therefore not needed. Rather than compete with you over helium-3, we will destroy you."

"Wait, what do you mean?" Dan gasped, the hair lifting on the back of his neck and his hands turning clammy. The stories his grandfather had regaled him with had never shown this side of the Cygnans, and his brain froze, unable to comprehend Paranganjo would even consider such words.

Marco's coffee mug fell to the ground and shattered, the dark liquid splashing unnoticed onto his tennis shoes.

Paranganjo's cold voice came across 500 light years instantaneously through the wormhole and sounded like he was in the room. "If Jonathan can't commit to a suitable agreement in three days, your planet will be the recipient of a device through the wormhole that will make you wish he had. It will wreak havoc on your atmosphere and cause your own sun to go supernova."

Dan's voice became shrill. "But, but why?" *He should never have convinced Jonathan to go after a deal with Paranganjo.* "Why would you do that when you have the opportunity to make a very lucrative business deal instead?"

"Strictly business, Dan. I don't have patience for those who don't have the resolve to get things done. I want to be the main supplier of helium-3 as an energy source for our new planet. I need to partner with someone who won't slow me down and allow the competition to get ahead. Don't think I'm unaware of Geoffrey Clarke's company Fusion Origins and the progress they've already made. If I don't mine helium-3 on the Moon, I can find it elsewhere. A human business arrangement would have been convenient, but it isn't essential. I have other resources."

"But why blow up the Earth over a failed business deal? Isn't that rather extreme?" Marco asked.

"I'm not about to leave resources in place for my competition. What kind of businessman would that make me? Not a very smart one."

"How do we know you can really do what you say?" Dan asked, beads of sweat dribbling down his forehead and stinging his eyes, as he frantically tried to stall. "It's hard to believe you can make our sun explode."

"Ask Feraganjo," Paranganjo responded. "I've had enough. Contact me with an agreement in the next three days, or spend the next three days saying goodbye to each other. At this point, I personally don't care which one you choose."

Paranganjo broke the connection with a deafening click, followed by silence. Taking in Marco's rapid blinking and the frown etched on his face, Dan's eyes glazed. He began to tremble. *What just happened?* Marco looked at the large analog clock hanging in the lab, and Dan's eyes followed his. They had seventy-two hours to avert the destruction of Earth. Marco's eyes bulged as he reached for his phone.

"Who are you calling?" Dan asked, tilting his head.

"Your boss. We gotta let him know what's going on. He can call the president or something. This is too big for us to handle."

Dan slammed his fist against the table. "It wasn't supposed to go this way."

Marco's eyebrows went up and he gave Dan a hard stare. "You've always been the Cygnans' biggest fan. Are you sure?"

Dan went rigid and glared back. "What do you mean, 'Are you sure?' Of course, I'm sure!"

Marco shrugged, wrinkling his nose. "Okay, but I can't help but wonder. You were awfully cozy with Paranganjo before this phone call." He dialed Jonathan's number on his cell phone and walked away. Dan knocked the mic over and gripped the edge of the table, his knuckles turning white. He could hear snatches of Marco's conversation with Jonathan, " . . . Paranganjo said you're wasting his time . . . Yes, threatened to destroy the world . . . I don't know why Dan didn't convince him . . ." and decided he'd better get back to the office. If Marco was going to accuse him of collaborating with Paranganjo against the United States, he wanted to make sure Jonathan heard his side of the story. And if Paranganjo was serious about his threat, they needed to figure out their options, and fast.

35

Jonathan paused and glanced about the Oval Office. Like countless people before him, he was unable to walk through those doors without feeling an elevated sense of awe.

The president's secretary interrupted his visual exploration. "Have a seat anywhere you like, Mr. Howe. The president and Mr. Ricinski will be in momentarily. Can I get you some coffee?"

Jonathan nodded, his heart pounding in response to the meeting he was about to have. "That would be nice, thank you."

"Cream and sugar?"

"Just black, thanks." Jonathan swiveled his head around, trying to decide which chair to sit in.

Before he could make a choice, the doors swung open again and President Ferris appeared, accompanied by Joe. "Jonathan, good to see you. Thanks for coming on such short notice, I really appreciate it." The president strode over to where Jonathan was standing, touched his shoulder and held out his hand. "We could really use your help with this whole Cygnan thing. Come, sit down." He turned and waved Joe further into the room, then sat behind his desk and smiled. "You too, Joe. Take a seat. Let's get to work."

Jonathan and Joe took the chairs nearest the president's desk. Jonathan started to speak, but paused as the secretary came in and placed a tray with a coffee pot and cups on a small round table. She poured the coffee and handed a cup to each of the men, then left, closing the doors behind her.

Jonathan picked up his cup and took a sip, gathering his thoughts. Deciding not to speak first after all, he waited while the president added sugar and cream to his coffee and stirred it. Cradling his cup between his hands, Joe assumed a position of watchful waiting.

"Well." The president finished his task and looked intently at Jonathan. His light-hearted attitude evaporated. "It seems your assistant has caused quite a stir. An apocalyptic stir, in fact. So tell me, what's going on?"

Jonathan squirmed in his chair like an errant schoolboy summoned to the principal's office. He swallowed and returned the president's gaze. "First of all, Mr. President, I want to assure you that I had no idea Paranganjo had the potential to make such a threat or the capacity to carry it out. I never meant for this to—"

"I already know that. Joe has assured me, you are not a traitor. I'm not nearly as interested in finger pointing right now as I am in finding a solution. My question for you is, how do you think we should respond?"

Jonathan glanced at Joe and breathed a sigh of relief. "Well, sir, I've been thinking. There's no way out of this except compliance with Paranganjo's demands." He tried to frame his thoughts in a way that wouldn't look like he was taking advantage of the situation. "If I agree to partner with Paranganjo, that'll buy us some time. The logistics of what we're attempting to do are enormous and will take months to actually implement. Geoffrey Clarke's announcement of a working fusion reactor may have been what prompted Paranganjo to act."

The president and Joe exchanged a quick look. Joe's brow furrowed. "That just might work." He hesitated, giving a sideways glance at the president. "I don't really see any other options, considering the alternative." He gazed piercingly at Jonathan and his voice took on an edge. "We're aware of your connection with CAET. You're not the best candidate to interface with Paranganjo. Can you trust Dan to continue in his present role as your liaison?"

Jonathan shuffled his feet. One thing he did have control of was how his company's resources were allocated. He didn't under-stand Dan's fascination with space and aliens, but Dan had been his assistant for several years now, well before the First Contact on the Moon. "Yes, I believe so. Dan has always had an extraordinary fascination with all things space, but he was a different man when he returned to the office and told me what happened. He was scared. I really don't think he was expecting Paranganjo's response."

The president leaned forward. "Okay, then. We have a plan. Jonathan, ask Dan to inform Paranganjo you accept his deal. You'll have to announce it so it looks real to the Cygnans—write up a press release and have Joe take a look at it, before you give it to the press." He paused and his eyes narrowed. "I'm sure I don't need to say that everything we have discussed, including Paranganjo's threat, is not to go any further?"

"No sir, of course not. I've already instructed Dan not to discuss what happened with anyone else. I'll arrange to have him speak to Paranganjo during their usual communications window tomorrow morning."

"Good. Keep me posted on any new developments." The president got up and walked around his desk, and Jonathan stood. The president shook his hand again. "Thank you, Jonathan. We really appreciate you putting your country's interests above your own."

"Of course, sir," Jonathan stuttered. "I could never do otherwise. It really isn't all about the money, you know."

The president smiled. "I know."

Joe and the president watched Jonathan leave, and after the doors were shut behind him, the president turned to Joe. "Do you think it'll work?"

Joe shook his head grimly. "Maybe for a few days, but Paranganjo is no fool. He knows the first thing we'd try to do is stall. He may very well see Jonathan's agreement as a delaying tactic, but I didn't want to scare Jonathan. He's already very disturbed over what's happened, and you can't blame him. All the guy wanted to do was make a business deal, not be party to the destruction of Earth."

The president inclined his head sympathetically. He liked Jonathan. "I know. I've got nothing against guys making business deals. Entrepreneurs are the backbone of American industry."

"Should we've told him Clarke doesn't really have a working fusion reactor?"

"I don't really see what that would help, sir. It may or may not have been the impetuous for Paranganjo's demands, but it's a moot point now. The fewer people that know, the better."

"You're right. Which reminds me, I have a phone call to make." The president walked over to his desk phone and pushed a button. "Mrs. Crippen, could you please get Marco Esposito at the SETI facility on the phone?" Moments later, one of the phone lines began to blink, and he picked it up. "Hello Marco, it's the President of the United States. I wanted to personally thank you for being so prompt in reporting the communication between Dan and the Cygnans this morning. You understand this is a matter of national security, and I need to ask you not to speak about this to anyone else." The president paused, listening.

He gave Joe a thumbs up. "You haven't? Very good, Marco. I'm personally asking you to continue to facilitate contact between Dan and Paranganjo and to monitor their conversations…Yes, yes. Jonathan will be giving Dan instructions on how to proceed, and they will need you to facilitate their communications in the morning as usual…Yes, very good. Thank you. Joe Ricinski will be in touch tomorrow after Dan speaks with Paranganjo…Yes, okay. You are doing a great service for your country."

The president hung up and looked at Joe. "One day at a time, my friend. Let's see what happens tomorrow after Paranganjo and Dan talk."

"Yes, sir. One day at a time to save the world."

Stephanie brushed her hair out of her eyes with one hand while holding onto the iPad with the other. The guards had taken up a collection and surprised her with it. It helped her pass the time while she waited for Lanjo to wake up. She knew what it felt like to be alone after her parents divorced, and no way was she going to leave Lanjo. She might not be related to Lanjo, but to her, he was family. If only her dad was here. Dad loved Lanjo, too.

She rose from the chair that had become her "spot" over the last couple of weeks. It was almost time for her daily phone call with her mom. Her mom was handling her refusal to leave Lanjo better than she thought she would. Maybe her mom was tired of trying to fill her summer with activities. Maybe she realized Stephanie would just run away again, if she made her return home. Whatever the reason, Stephanie was glad it was so.

She walked the five steps to Lanjo's bedside, leaned over the railing, and gently stroked his cheek. She waited a breathless moment, but his eyes didn't open. His chest rose and fell evenly. His features, nearly as familiar as her own, didn't change. She let her hand drop. It dragged along the cold metal bed rail as she turned away.

36

Tom sat at the same table he had begun to frequent at CERN Restaurant 1 and sipped his beer. His notepad lay in front of him, and he began to scribble on it as thoughts popped into his head. The current timeline for the project was outdated. The repairs were not yet complete from the sabotage that had damaged the cooling system during the antimatter trap test. The call to the original engineering team on the stochastic cooling system had been very helpful. They had to take a two-pronged approach: optimize the depth and periodicity of the notch filters and efficiently suppress the common mode response in the transverse cooling systems.

They also had their latest obstacle to deal with: Brett and Alan were still waiting on a NASA engineer to help them overcome the shielding challenge. If they couldn't solve that problem, their design would be dead in the water. Tom sighed, rubbing the back of his neck. He needed to utilize their resources as effectively as possible. He wished Darryl were here. At least, with the exception of the shielding issue, Brett and Alan were making good progress on the inertial confinement design.

Tom doodled on the edges of his notepad, thinking. Brett and Alan were supposed to assist with the antimatter trap and then head back to George Washington University to begin building the nuclear fusion prototype, but he decided to divert all of his engineering resources to repairing the cooling system. Without antimatter to fuel it, their design wouldn't work anyway. He glanced at his watch. It was still early. He gathered up his notes, left a tip on the table, and headed for their lab area.

⚛

Brett studied Tom a moment before responding. "You want to divert Alan and me away from the nuclear fusion design in order to solve the cooling problem?" He shook his head. "Are you sure you want to do that, Tom? I've already taken some time on it, and we're way behind our original timeline."

"I know, but I don't see we have much choice. Keraganjo is no longer available, Feraganjo will need a couple more days to recover, Darryl is gone . . . we simply don't have anybody else. We need to be able to leave CERN and finalize our prototype at GWU, but we can't leave without the antimatter, or everything else is for nothing. Fixing the stochastic cooling system has to be our priority."

Alan had stayed quiet, listening to the younger men's discussion. He chose this moment to speak up. "It's a good call. The situation's changed and we have to change with it, if we're going to get the work done. So, what do you propose?"

Tom breathed a sigh of relief. "Thanks, Alan. We just need to reprioritize our tasks and utilize our available resources for peak effectiveness. We never meant to continue the design process at CERN. Our primary goal was to gather the antimatter we needed for our energy source and get back to GWU as quickly as possible. We may have lost personnel, but our objective hasn't changed. I'd like to shift every available engineer and scientist to implementing the solution we received from the original cooling system design team. We only have a week to fix the cooling system if we're going to get back on a competitive timeline."

He grabbed a marker and listed their action items on the lab's whiteboard:

- Troubleshoot and repair stochastic cooling system (Cygnan-human Science Team)
- Inspect Antiproton Decelerator and run tests to verify correct operation (CERN Scientists)
- Verify antimatter trap functionality (Feraganjo)
- Collect Antimatter (Cygnan-human Science Team)
- Return to GWU

He put the marker down and turned to face Brett and Alan. "I have the solution for the stochastic cooling system repair. We just need to implement it. My estimation is it'll take us three days. Items 2 and 3 can be done concurrently, assuming Feraganjo needs one day to check over the antimatter trap. As soon as we collect—" Tom's phone went off, the ringer playing "Danger Zone." He looked down to see who it was. Darryl. Glancing apologetically at the others, he pressed the button and put the phone to his ear.

"Hello Darryl, is everything all right?"

"Yes. I just called to let you know they did the transfusion, and Sandra is responding well. They think it was a temporary issue with her immune system that may have been triggered by one of her medications. Since they changed her meds, her blood count is going in the right direction."

"That's great news! Glad to hear she's doing better." Tom gave a thumbs up to Brett and Alan as they waited for him to finish.

"Thanks. Sorry I had to leave you with a mess."

"Don't worry, we have it under control. We have a fix for the cooling system that we're just about to implement."

"Good to hear. I was a bit worried about the project because I saw Theresa and Keraganjo on the *Great Day* show this morning. You're running very shorthanded."

"Yeah, well, it wasn't my choice. Another dog and pony show to garner support. The government is trying to counteract the media damage from *Great Day*'s previous guests. Nice to hear they're offering equal time."

Darryl sighed. "Yeah, at least they left you with one Cygnan. How's Feraganjo doing?"

"That's another story. I didn't tell you because you needed to focus on your family, but after you left, he got pretty sick. We didn't know what was wrong at first, but we found out it was a spider bite. It was pretty rough on him for a few days, but we got the antidote, and he'll be fully recovered in a day or two."

"Glad to hear he's on the road to recovery." Darryl paused. "I have some news about our Cygnan friends, too. I just wish mine was as good as yours."

Tom got that awful squeezing in the back of his throat that travelled down to the pit of his stomach and settled like a rock when he was anticipating bad news. He cleared his throat. "What is it?"

"I went to see Lanjo yesterday. Stephanie's doing fine. She's determined as ever to stay by his side. She wouldn't even go out to lunch with me, so we compromised on the hospital cafeteria." Darryl paused and his voice grew strained. "But nothing's changed with Lanjo. His Cygnan metabolism has kept his body in a steady state while he remains comatose, but that will begin to degrade if something doesn't happen soon. I'm sorry, Tom. The doctors think he may only have a couple more weeks."

Tom swallowed hard, moisture gathering in his eyes and threatening to overflow. "Thanks for letting me know." He glanced at Brett and Alan, who were trying not to seem too obvious about their eavesdropping. "Thanks for checking on Stephanie. I'm not surprised she's held out this long, but we need to think about what to do with her. School will be starting up soon and she'll need to go." Left unspoken was the most likely solution to Stephanie's dilemma.

Tom abruptly changed the subject. "Great news, about Sandra." Brett and Alan vigorously nodded their heads, all pretenses of not listening gone at the happier subject. "We're all relieved."

The smile entered Darryl's voice again. "We're very grateful our little girl is doing so well. We're hopeful she can go home in the next few days."

"We hope so too. Keep us posted on her progress, and I'll let you know when we get our antimatter and are on our way back to GWU."

"Will do. I know I left everything in good hands."

"That may or may not be true." Tom laughed. "But thanks for the vote of confidence." Tom hung up and turned his attention back to the science team.

"Darryl said Sandra is doing much better and that Lanjo remains the same." His voice faltered. "But that may change if something doesn't happen for him in the next couple of weeks."

"Wonderful news about Sandra, Tom. So sorry to hear Lanjo hasn't improved." Alan squeezed Tom's shoulder.

Brett stirred from where he had been listening to the exchange. "Lanjo's not only a nice guy, he sacrificed himself to save all of us." He shook his head and looked at Tom and Alan. "I guess the best thing we can do for Lanjo is help save his planet. Let's get to work."

Tom strode to his office and grabbed a couple of printouts from what the original design team had emailed him. Returning to the lab, he spread out a schematic of the cooling system on one of the work tables and the three men began to study it. "I already talked to Dr. Auer. His team will take their inspection of the Antiproton Decelerator as far as they can without the cooling system. It's up to us to get it working so they can complete their tests, and we can move on to the collection phase."

Tom indicated places he'd already marked with red Xs on the schematic. "These are the notch filters. We can access them here." He pointed to a rectangle at the bottom. "According to the original design team, they are probably the biggest contributor to our inability to get the system operating correctly. We need to optimize them to the proper periodicity and depth."

He picked up the second printout where he'd left it on the table. "Here's the procedure. Brett, can you grab a couple of o'scopes? We might as well get going on . . ." he hesitated. Looking at the clock on the wall, he realized it was well past five o'clock.

Alan grinned. "Let's get cracking."

Tom fidgeted as he sat in front of a computer monitor in Patch Barracks, home of the US European Command in Stuttgart. He had hoped to sightsee around Europe, but this unexpected excursion at Joe Ricinski's request was not exactly what he'd had in mind.

The comm officer assigned to him nodded briskly. "We're securely connected, sir. The meeting is scheduled to begin in just a few minutes."

Securely connected to the White House. For a meeting with the president. "Thank you, uh . . ." Tom glanced at the young man's name badge. "Thank you, Lieutenant Nguyen."

"You're welcome, sir. I'll be right outside if you need me."

After the young man left, Tom breathed a sigh of relief. He felt extremely awkward with the lieutenant shadowing him through the complex. These service men and women reminded him of Theresa when she was on duty and became "all business." He felt a brief stab of loneliness, but forced his thoughts to the matter at hand. He shouldn't be worrying about his love life when national security was at stake.

As he waited in the office he'd been assigned, he doodled. The notepad and pen were all he'd been allowed to bring in with him. His thoughts drifted to Lanjo, and his gut clenched. *The doctors think that he may only have a couple more weeks. His Cygnan metabolism has kept his body in a steady state while he remains comatose, but that will begin to degrade if something doesn't happen soon.*

The desktop computer monitor in front of him bleeped and displayed a video feed. Tom watched as men and women in dark suits and military uniforms gathered around a large conference table. Banks of monitors were attached to the walls. One huge monitor hung on the wall at one end of the conference table, and the Presidential seal was on the opposite wall.

Tom had never been in the situation room in the White House, but it looked just like it did in the movies. Joe Ricinski sat beside Dr. Sorrel from NASA. Tom could also see the National Security Advisor, the Chairman of the Joint Chiefs, the Secretary of Homeland Security, and the president's Chief of Staff, along with several other men and women he didn't recognize. He heard a low buzz as the participants chatted among themselves. The door opened at one end of the room, and the chatting immediately stopped. Everyone in the room got to their feet as the President of the United States made his way into the room, and Tom instinctively joined them.

The president surveyed the participants. "Please everyone, be seated. Thank you for making time in your schedules today. Let's get to work." He slid into his customary place at the head of the table. With no further pleasantries, he turned to Joe. "Joe, fill everyone in on the current state of affairs regarding Paranganjo and the Cygnan threat."

"Yes sir, Mr. President." Joe addressed the attendees. "As you may already be aware, Paranganjo is a Cygnan businessman on Lanzeron who has made contact with Jonathan Howe, the CEO of HoweTek Communications. Jonathan has made no secret of his desire to mine helium-3 on the Moon as an alternative clean energy source. Working with SETI's equipment, Jonathan has been able to establish reliable communications with Paranganjo by utilizing a wormhole made stable by Cygnan technology. We knew of Jonathan's efforts, but did not deem them a national security risk. Until now." Joe paused before dropping the bombshell. "We're now at ThreatCon Charlie. All agencies are being informed as we speak."

The room exploded into conversation. Tom googled ThreatCon Charlie. His stomach dropped somewhere below the seat of his chair. *ThreatCon Charlie indicates some form of terrorist action against personnel and facilities is imminent.*

"Are you saying Jonathan Howe is in league with the Cygnans against the United States?" The voice of the National Security Advisor pulled Tom's attention back to the monitor.

"No, I am not," Joe said. "Let me make myself clear. Jonathan Howe is not the reason for the ThreatCon Charlie, but the communications he's received from Paranganjo indicate an active, imminent threat not only to the United States, but to our entire planet." Joe glanced down at his notes. "Their business proposal is for Paranganjo to supply the technology to build nuclear fusion reactors on the Moon and Jonathan to supply labor and materials. Jonathan was concerned about a possible security risk and notified us. We advised him to proceed with caution and to keep us informed. When Paranganjo asked him to move forward with his proposal, Jonathan decided to stall while he evaluated the situation. Paranganjo perceived Jonathan's foot-dragging as a betrayal of their relationship."

"What's the nature of the threat?" asked the Chairman of the Joint Chiefs.

"In Paranganjo's words, if Jonathan doesn't come through with his end of the bargain, it will be clear to him that humans are not dependable and therefore not needed. He told Jonathan that, rather than compete with us over helium-3, he will destroy us." He tugged at his tie and made eye contact with each person around the table. "If Jonathan doesn't come up with an agreement that Paranganjo finds acceptable in three days, we will be the recipients of a device through the wormhole that will cause the Earth's Sun to go supernova."

Tom's vision blurred; the computer screen shimmered. He clenched his fists, the nails digging into his palms. He could feel sweat dripping down his forehead and his stomach tightened even more. What about Stephanie . . . and Theresa. How could he keep them safe? He exhaled and relaxed his fists, watching the screen stabilize. *Why was he observing this meeting? He'd seen enough—he needed to warn the others and go get Stephanie.* He looked around for the lieutenant that had guided him so he could get back to the lab. Reaching for his notepad and pen, he glanced back at the video feed. His mouth dropped open and his hand froze in place. Tom could see his image come up on one of the big screens that filled the walls of the room.

"We have Tom Whitaker on standby," Joe's voice said. "He's the head of our team working with the Cygnan scientists to build a working fusion reactor. Tom, thank you for joining us today." Joe smiled at him reassuringly.

Tom's eyes bulged as he stared back and nodded nervously. "Thanks, Joe. I'm not sure why I'm here . . ."

"Sorry to have kept you in the dark. Since you've been the closest human to Lanjo, we need your perspective on the Cygnan threat. Lanjo previously informed us Paranganjo is known to be untrustworthy and self-serving. Has he told you anything else about him? We've already questioned Feraganjo, and he verified the technology to cause a sun to go supernova does exist. What we need to understand is Paranganjo's moral compass. Would he destroy an entire world to eliminate his competition? We're asking you, as our liaison to the Cygnans, to share any insights you can think of. The more information we can gather, the more effectively we can determine an appropriate response."

Tom balled his hands back into fists to stop them from trembling. *They were discussing the fate of the planet—over Skype.* He cleared his throat. *Focus, Tom. They want insights on Paranganjo. What had Lanjo said about him?* "Lanjo did mention Paranganjo to me. He referred to him as an unscrupulous businessman."

"And you agree with that assessment?"

"Yes, I trust Lanjo's judgment. He had no reason to lie about Paranganjo's motives. He did warn us about him. I believe Lanjo had—" *Has. Lanjo has. He wasn't dead yet.* "I believe Lanjo *has* an intense dislike . . ."

He started his sentence again, fighting to maintain his composure. "I believe Lanjo has an intense dislike for Paranganjo, which is a very strong indication that Paranganjo is capable of causing harm to humans."

"Our intel agrees, which brings us to a critical question. What can you tell us about wormholes?"

"Wormholes?" Tom jerked back. "I'm not an astrophysicist. I don't know much about wormholes."

"But you're the only scientist we can ask, considering the circumstances. You're aware of the Cygnan doctor who traveled through the wormhole in order to attempt to treat Lanjo. We know they can send objects to us—what we need to know is, can we send objects through the wormhole to them?"

Tom paused to consider Joe's question. *He had a minor in astronomy. That was it. A minor. Six courses, and he was their expert? With the fate of the planet hanging in the balance?*

He sucked in a breath, forcing his thoughts to focus. Wormholes. What did he know about wormholes? The fact that the top officials of the United States government were waiting did not help the process. An image flashed in his mind. Dr. Irvin, junior year, Intro to Astrophysics. Energetic professor that hosted star parties on the roof of the parking garage and played a fiddle. He could hear Dr. Irvin lecturing in his head. He gazed into the monitor.

"Wormholes are basically a passage through space-time that links two separate points, essentially shortcuts across the universe that can be predicted by the theory of general relativity. They hold many dangers including the possibility of sudden collapse, high radiation, and exposure to exotic matter. What makes both communication and travel through one possible is Cygnan technology. They've found a way to stabilize the wormhole and prevent it from collapsing, so that radio waves and even life forms can pass through it. The radio waves have been traveling in both directions—that's how Jonathan and Paranganjo have been able to communicate."

Tom paused, rubbing his chin. "We can't be one hundred percent certain that a life form or an object can do the same, but we have a high degree of certainty. The Cygnan doctor has not yet attempted to return home through the wormhole, but that is probably his intention. Since Jonathan has been utilizing equipment at SETI for his transmissions, we should be able to get the necessary coordinates from them."

He hesitated. "There is a caveat. The properties of the wormhole are not fully understood, but we do know that Cygnan technology only provides windows of opportunity for using the space-time tunnel characteristic, which is why Paranganjo's communications must be scheduled. He has to wait for an available window in order to use the wormhole."

Joe bobbed his head. "Thanks, Tom. Please stay with us, we may need your expertise again." Tom leaned back in the chair and exhaled noisily, then hastily muted his mic. Hands still shaking, he picked up the notepad and pen and resumed doodling, this time sketching an imaginary wormhole. Joe turned his attention back to the government officials around the conference table.

"Given the data, it's reasonable to assume Paranganjo's threat is not empty. The reason the President asked all of you here is to get your input on how we should respond. The stakes couldn't be higher, so it's critical we determine a course of action that will, in effect, save humanity."

38

The room burst into conversation again as reaction settled in. The president let it go for a couple of minutes, before calling the meeting back into order.

"Okay, everyone. Let's settle down. We need to determine how to proceed and we don't have a lot of time. I've overheard several solutions being offered, so let's just go around the table." He nodded at the National Security Advisor, a man in his late forties wearing an army dress uniform, the ribbons on his left breast displaying a vast array of decorations. "What do you think, General Santiago? How should we address this threat?"

The general sat with both hands flat on the conference table. "I think the best solution is to stop Paranganjo's threat before it starts." Leaning forward, he looked with a steely gaze directly at the camera giving Tom the live stream, like a lion about to spring for his prey. "Tom, you said the wormhole is only available at certain times, is that correct?"

Tom swallowed and nodded. "Yes, sir. The properties of the wormhole indicate cyclic windows of certainty followed by low periods when we can't be certain what is being sent through will actually arrive."

"Do you have that schedule with you?"

"No, sir," Tom shook his head. He was about to follow that with a statement absolving himself of blame by saying no one had told him it would be needed, but realized no one in the room would care. They were men and women of action and wouldn't be interested in excuses, just results. "But I can get that for you, sir."

"No need, Tom," Joe interjected. "We can get it from SETI fairly quickly, but thanks." He motioned to one of the people at the table Tom didn't recognize. "Call and find out the schedule for the wormhole over the next three days." The young man nodded and slipped off.

Tom breathed a sigh of relief at no longer being the focus of attention.

General Santiago steepled his fingers, his gaze searching the room. "So we can predict with certainty the windows of opportunity Paranganjo has for sending his doomsday device through the wormhole, and he has given a three day ultimatum, but how can we be sure he'll wait the three days?"

The attendees broke into chatter once again until the president stood up, regaining everyone's attention. "Can anyone address General Santiago's concern?"

Tom hesitated. He just wanted all of this to go away so he could focus on solving the problem of fusion. He forced himself to wave his hand, catching the National Security Advisor's eye. The general turned towards the camera again. "Yes, Tom?" The president sat back in his chair and the room quieted down to hear Tom's words.

"Well sir, if we were dealing with Lanjo, from my experience we could have a high degree of certainty. But Lanjo's opinion of Paranganjo indicates Lanjo didn't trust him either." Tom caught himself using past tense again and clenched his fists. "Lanjo has studied the English language and has an excellent command of vocabulary. By referring to Paranganjo as unscrupulous, he was pointing out that Paranganjo has no moral compass to guide his actions. I think the determining factor of when Paranganjo might carry out his threat is not the three-day deadline, but the wormhole window."

General Santiago nodded. "A reasonable assessment and one we should heed." Heads were bobbing in agreement all around the table. Tom was relieved when the general turned to listen as Joe signaled with his hand for attention. "Tom is right on the mark. We'll know how much time we have when we get the wormhole schedule. Unfortunately, that doesn't leave us with much time to respond either way."

The general spoke up again, "No, it doesn't. I propose we destroy the wormhole before Paranganjo can launch a device through it."

"How would we do that?" asked the Secretary of Homeland Security.

"Ideally, we could deliver a package remotely and detonate it. We'd need to determine what type of explosive and how much it would take to disrupt the wormhole permanently," the Chairman of the Joint Chiefs responded. He looked at Dr. Sorrel. "What do you think, James?"

The NASA administrator leaned back and narrowed his eyes, running through the possibilities in his mind. "Drones are designed to work with an atmosphere to propel through, and space has no atmosphere. Whatever we come up with to accomplish the delivery would have to have a propulsion system on board. The good news is, it wouldn't take a whole lot to disturb a wormhole and force its collapse. We could even minimize it, so that the collapse would be temporary. The bad news is, while we have some drones in the R&D stage for propelling through space, none would be ready in time. We could possibly do it with a satellite launch. Depending on the coordinates, we may be able to pull a Star Wars missile into duty. An explosion of that caliber would permanently destroy the wormhole, rather than disrupt it temporarily."

"Star Wars?" asked the Chief of Staff. "I thought that when the program was cancelled, all space-based missile programs were recalled."

"Most of them were," commented a man Tom didn't recognize, dressed in an ordinary suit and completely inconspicuous until now. "But we have a few that were left in service."

The Chairman of the Joint Chiefs nodded. "That would be an option. The missiles in question can be brought online within twenty-four hours. We'll need the coordinates of the wormhole."

Joe looked around. "Any other options, folks? We will likely only get one shot at this and if we fail . . . well, you know the consequences."

One of the women sitting at the conference table cleared her throat. The insignia on her uniform indicated she was an Air Force Colonel. "The X-37B Orbital Test Vehicle may be available."

"The what?" Joe directed his gaze at the woman and raised his eyebrows.

"Sorry, sir. Most of its missions are highly classified. The OTV is an experimental unmanned space test platform for the U.S. Air Force."

"What exactly is it, Colonel?"

"The OTV is a spacecraft we're using to test out technologies for future spacecraft. It also carries experiments to and from space. A recent payload included an Air Force experimental propulsion system."

"A propulsion system?" The Chief of Staff jumped on that. "Could we use it to propel a device through the wormhole?"

"Not sure, sir" replied the Air Force colonel. "But it may be an option."

"There is another possibility," interjected the Homeland Security Advisor. "Our job is to consider all threats regardless of their origin, including the likelihood of an asteroid approaching the Earth. We could attempt to redirect an asteroid through the wormhole."

Tom felt bile rising in his throat. *What?! But that would destroy Lanzeron. Asteroids were nicknamed planet-killers in the science world.*

The room became dead still as the implications of such an action sunk in. The president stood up again.

"I did ask for all options to be presented, but no, that option is off the table."

Tom sagged in his chair in relief. Images of Lanjo saving Stephanie's life, Feraganjo and Brett studying a schematic and laughing, and Keraganjo and Rachel dancing in celebration of a successful integration test, flew through his mind. While Paranganjo may be threatening Earth with annihilation and must be stopped, it was unthinkable for humanity to respond in kind.

The president continued. "As far as we know, Paranganjo is not a fair representative of his species, and even if he were, we would never consider genocide as an acceptable option. He may be planning to eliminate humanity, but we would lose our humanity if we planned something likewise in return."

The table broke out into conversation again. Finally, the president called for everyone's attention. "Destroying the wormhole is our best option. We need to determine how we're going to do it, and when. Joe, has Marco responded yet?"

Joe pulled out his cell phone and checked his texts. His aide had managed to reach Marco, and the wormhole's schedule was on his cell phone's screen. He turned and faced the group.

"Parangango gave Jonathan his ultimatum this morning. The wormhole window opens again in 39 hours."

"Okay." The president took command of the meeting. "It would've been nice to have more time, but we have to work within the parameters we're given. I'm willing to consider the satellite launch or the OTV to deliver a device to temporarily close the wormhole, rather than destroy it, but using a Star Wars missile seems to be the only option that will work within the timeframe we have to beat Paranganjo's play." He turned to the Chairman of the Joint Chiefs of Staff. "General, please update me as to when you are ready to fire."

"Yes, sir."

The president took off his glasses and waved them about in one hand. "We still have one more issue to consider. How much information should be released to the public?"

Joe stood up. "Every person here wants to be with their families and loved ones in case of the worst. The question is—doesn't everyone deserve the same opportunity?" He rubbed the back of his neck, his face etched in sadness. "But the reality is, the panic which will most certainly ensue could negatively impact our efforts at resolving Paranganjo's threat peacefully."

The president met the eyes of each of his most senior trusted advisors and allowed them to see a rare moment of personal angst. He dropped his glasses on the table and brushed his hand across his forehead. "It's not my first choice, but if we reveal to the nation the current threat, Joe's right, the public response can hurt our chances for a successful resolution. We're at ThreatCon Charlie, but we also must maintain all information divulged in this room as the highest level of top secret/sensitive compartmented information." He exchanged a long look with Joe. "Make sure your aide knows." Joe nodded.

"How do we respond when we're asked why we're at ThreatCon Charlie?" asked the NASA administrator. The president smiled. "Just tell them it's on a need-to-know basis, and they don't need to know."

"That won't stop wild speculation, sir."

"No, it won't. But under the circumstances, that's all I got."

"Yes, sir."

"Okay everybody, thank you for coming. Let's get to work. Continue to research the satellite and OTV options as contingency plans, but we'll direct our main efforts on prepping the Star Wars package. I'll expect updates every two hours."

"Yes, sir," chorused the men and women around the table as they got up to leave.

The data feed stopped, and Tom sat staring at the blank screen. Someone knocked on the door, causing him to jump. Lieutenant Nguyen entered the office.

"Sir?" the lieutenant inquired gently.

Tom hastily got out of his chair. "Yes, lieutenant?"

"I'm here to escort you—your plane is waiting."

Tom glanced down at his watch to mark the time. He had 39

hours. He had no idea what he was going to do, but an idea was forming inside his head. If he was going to listen to it, he'd better hurry. He strode to the door. "Thank you, lieutenant. I'm ready." Ready for what, he wasn't exactly sure. He hoped the plane ride back to CERN would give him time to clarify his thoughts.

39

It bothered Tom the entire flight back and continued to nag at his brain. If the wormhole was destroyed, so was any chance of Lanjo returning to Lanzeron for the therapy the Cygnan doctor mentioned. He knew it wasn't a guarantee, but it was Lanjo's only chance to survive. The doctors thought it was too great a risk for Lanjo to travel, but if he was going to lose his mental capacity in two weeks anyway, what did it matter? Not only that, if the wormhole was destroyed, none of the other Cygnans would be able to return home.

As soon as Tom reached his office, he went inside and shut the door. He began to pace, considering his options and the possible ramifications of each. A plan began to form in his mind. He tried to reject it as nonsense, but it persistently interrupted his thoughts. He finally sat down and pulled out his cell phone. He stared at it for a full minute, then dialed Theresa's number. *Pick up, pick up, pick up.* Finally, he heard her voice.

"Hello."

"Theresa, it's Tom." Feeling momentarily foolish knowing she must have caller ID, he hurriedly continued. "How are you?"

"I'm fine but a bit busy at the moment. How can I help you?"

Tom's heart sank at her formal tone, but he plunged forward anyway. What he had to say went beyond their personal relationship and he needed to make Theresa see that.

"I know this is going to sound crazy, but it's really important. I need your help."

He could almost hear her sigh and see her eyebrows crinkle as Theresa evaluated her next move. "I'm sorry, but they have us on a very tight schedule. Isn't there someone there that can help with whatever you need?"

Tom closed his eyes. "I wish it was that simple."

"What are you doing here?" Jonathan stood up angrily as Sheila entered his office. "I told you never to come here. The last thing I need right now is to be associated with CAET."

Sheila held out her hand in a soothing gesture. "Calm down, Jonathan. It's not like anyone is following me. NPC contacted me, and I needed to let you know. They view Paranganjo as competition and want to see him gone as much as we do."

Jonathan shook his head in frustration. This was rapidly propelling out of proportion. The NPC were heavy hitters, known to use shady tactics to get what they wanted. Even if they were on CAET's side, they were not people to be messed with. "So what do they want?"

"They want to fund CAET. As a condition, they want you to back off your partnership with Paranganjo." Sheila smiled. "Now you can quit dealing with the Cygnans, and NPC will take over your funding of CAET. It's a win-win."

Jonathan's eyes tightened and he pursed his lips. *They can't possibly know what's at stake.* He gazed at Sheila intently. "Tell them you delivered their message, and I'll think about it."

"But—"

"No buts. This is very complicated, and I won't be pressured by lobbyists, no matter how influential."

Sheila opened her mouth and closed it again. She nodded and turned to leave. She turned back to try another tack and was surprised to see Jonathan sitting down behind his desk, his head in his hands. Something told her to keep her mouth shut, and she continued out the door.

Tom checked his watch for the fifth time in the last half hour. Brett and Alan were still working on the stochastic cooling system. Keith should be arriving any moment. He was already en route with the NASA engineer they'd requested to help with shielding. Tom would need the engineer's expertise when he revealed his plan. He checked his watch one more time, then headed out the door. Keith and the NASA engineer were just pulling into the parking lot.

Keith opened his door, and Tom practically pulled him out of the car.

"Whoa, Tom. What's up? What's the rush?"

"I'll explain inside." Tom propelled Keith towards the entrance. "We don't have much time." He beckoned to the NASA engineer. "What's your name?"

The engineer hesitated. "Phil. Phil Mason."

"Come on, Phil. We need you, too."

The three men entered Tom's already crowded office, the rest of the science team having squeezed in a few minutes earlier. Tom peeked his head out the office door and checked the hallway. It was empty. He closed the door and mentally tallied the presence of everyone on the team. No outsiders besides the newly-arrived NASA engineer.

Now he just had to get them all on board. He wiped the sweat that was trickling down his neck, and tried to calm his respiration rate. The room fell silent as he pushed past Brett, walked over to the whiteboard, and faced the assembly. Expressions ranged from curious to impatient. He took a deep breath. "I need your help."

Tom turned to the whiteboard and erased all of the equations he had painstakingly written over the course of the last several days with a few quick swipes, and heard several gasps. He picked up a dry erase marker and held it poised, ready to write. *He couldn't believe he was doing this.*

He shook his head and forced his thoughts to the task ahead. He began drawing a timeline on the board. He checked his watch yet again and marked 4:37 p.m. Tuesday at one end, made a mental calculation, then marked 3:30 a.m. Thursday at the end point. He then marked the next time the wormhole window would open on the line. He turned back to his audience.

"At approximately 3:30 a.m. this Thursday, the United States government is going to launch a missile in order to cause the wormhole between Earth and Lanzeron to collapse."

Silence filled the room as every person present absorbed Tom's words. The silence didn't last long.

"But why?" Feraganjo cried out. His face darkened and the

anguish was clear on his alien features. Brett pushed to his friend's side, putting his arm around Feraganjo's shoulders. Feraganjo and his fellow Cygnans would be stranded on Earth forever.

Tom took another deep breath. His next words might send him to prison for sharing classified information, or even get him branded a traitor—if the Earth survived.

"I just came from a meeting with the president and his senior advisors over a secure line. Paranganjo has threatened to destroy Earth if Jonathan Howe doesn't agree to his business proposal." He turned to Feraganjo. "Paranganjo said if we didn't believe he could do it, we should ask you."

Feraganjo turned as dark a shade as anyone had ever seen on a Cygnan. He closed his eyes as desolation rippled across his face, then opened them and met Tom's gaze. "Yes, we have a device created for scientific purposes that would enable us to cause a star to go supernova. If Paranganjo managed to obtain one or hired scientists to duplicate one, all he would have to do is send it through the wormhole. It could be programmed to strategically enter your sun's orbit at a calculated location and explode, creating a chain reaction that would cause the sun to annihilate itself. Joe Ricinski sent me an email asking if such a device existed, but didn't say why. I assumed it would be for a science experiment similar to our own."

More gasps caused Tom to look about the room. He took in the expressions of horror crossing each person's face. Gripping the dry erase marker so tightly his hand hurt, he returned his gaze to Feraganjo. "Paranganjo has given Jonathan a three-day ultimatum, but everyone is in agreement that he can't be trusted."

Feraganjo nodded. "That's true. He can't. Lanjo briefed us about him when Paranganjo first made contact. He was upset Paranganjo had been granted access to the wormhole. It has been our main transportation hub for this sector for many years." Feraganjo gazed into the distance. "He said the Cygnan government must have caved to private sector pressure. Once it was determined we had only a limited amount of time to save our planet, we needed to get every available resource working towards our safe evacuation, and that was the price Paranganjo demanded in exchange for his help. Access to the wormhole."

Still gripping the marker so hard his knuckles were white, Tom turned to the whiteboard. He pointed at the beginning of the timeline. "This is the time our meeting started. We know the threat is real. We know how our government is responding. But the problem with the government's response is that it closes all of our options. We will no longer be able to contact Lanzeron." He turned back to face his audience. "While many people on Earth might think that is a good thing and an acceptable trade-off, everyone in this room has a personal stake in keeping the wormhole open for future use."

Tom paused to let his words sink in—and to steel himself to utter his next words. "I have another idea." He paused again, knowing he was about to cross an uncrossable line. "I'm going to steal a spaceship from NASA's hangar and go through the wormhole during its next window." He pointed to the mark on the timeline. "I'll attempt to talk Paranganjo out of destroying Earth. I will also be kidnapping Lanjo from his hospital bed and taking him to Lanzeron with me, so he can receive some experimental therapy not available here, which might save his life."

He straightened his spine and faced the room. The utterly silent room. He looked from person to person, seeing only blank shock on each face. When he spoke again, it was in a shaky whisper. "I can't do it alone. I need each of you to help. But what I'm asking of you may be construed as treason."

Rather than wait for their response, he turned back to the whiteboard and began writing down the names of everyone in the room, along with their assignment. He wrote Theresa's name first, then Keith's. They each had one of the harder, more complicated roles. Theresa had already agreed. He hoped if Keith followed suit, the others would join in.

Next to Theresa's name, he printed: *help steal and prep lunar ship.* Gasps and muttering came from somewhere behind him, but he continued writing. Next to Keith's name: *Transport team to U.S. destinations/prep lunar ship.* Next to Brett and Feraganjo: *Get Lanjo from hospital room and bring to lunar ship.* Alan and Rachel: *Distract guards to assist Brett and Feraganjo.* He glanced at the man Keith had brought with him and added: *NASA engineer—assist in lunar ship prep for journey through wormhole.* He stopped and gave everyone a moment to read their assignments, then began writing again, this time on the timeline.

He made a mark at 8:30 p.m. Tuesday and labeled it *Leave CERN.* He made more marks at 4:30 a.m. and 6:30 a.m. Wednesday and labeled them *Arrive in Boston* and *Steal Lanjo.*

He made another mark at 8:30 a.m. and wrote *Fly to NASA Houston* and at 1:00 p.m., *Modify lunar ship*, and finally at 3:30 p.m., *Launch to wormhole.*

He tapped the end of the marker sharply against the whiteboard, then turned back to look at everyone in the room. "That gives us 12 hours until the government launches their missile. I have to be in the wormhole and traveling to Lanzeron before they launch, and someone has to convince the president to wait. I will send a radio signal back through the wormhole, verifying Paranganjo is not going to destroy the Earth, in time to halt the missile launch before it starts. The Cygnan doctor took eight hours to arrive on Earth once he emerged from the wormhole." He tapped the end of the timeline with his marker. "That gives us a four-hour pad to work with, in case we need it. Obviously, we need to begin implementing the plan immediately, if we have any hope of it working. Any questions?"

Brett spoke first. "Can we even do it? I mean, is the lunar ship capable of making the trip and can you launch from Houston without being stopped?"

Tom turned to Keith for a response.

"We made extra trips to the Moon and back transporting the Cygnans, so we got plenty of practice. Yeah, we can do it." He looked at the NASA engineer. "But we never took it through a wormhole. We have the Cygnan ship docked in Houston. You'll have to take a look at its exterior and see if our ship needs any additional shielding."

Phil nodded. "Fortunately, I have clearance to do that." He glanced at Tom. "I'm in."

Tom breathed a sigh of relief; for the outsider to buy in immediately made his job easier.

Alan turned to Phil with a puzzled look. "But why would you do that? You just got here, you don't know any of us, yet you just agreed to risk your career for a cause with an uncertain outcome."

Phil's expression turned thoughtful. "There really is no choice. The alternative is to allow the wormhole to be closed. You have to admire the Cygnans. They've known of us for a long time, and if they wished us ill, they could have done it long ago, even without our knowledge. We can't let one rogue element destroy our future with them. That would be like letting a terrorist dictate our country's policies. Achieving something great never comes without cost."

Alan bobbed his head and winked at Tom. "Well said. Welcome to the team." Tom looked around and saw everyone, human and Cygnan, nodding their agreement.

"Okay. We can talk more about your specific tasks on the flight. We need to be in the air at"—he glanced at the timeline—"8:30 p.m.. Get together what you want to take and be at the plane by 8:00. Act normally and minimize what you're taking, so no one suspects you're leaving. Either we'll all be coming back to finish what we started here, or it won't matter anyway."

Tom's statement hung in the air for a moment before Keith interjected, "Wait a minute, what about the coordinates for the wormhole? Do we have those?"

Tom shook his head. "Not yet. But we know who does. I'm working on it."

Tom watched the crowd leave his office, a mixture of pride and dread battling for precedence as he considered what he'd gotten them all into. At least he'd finally get to see Stephanie and Lanjo. He glanced at his watch yet again and headed to the restaurant for dinner. He wasn't very hungry, but he had a feeling it would be his last normal meal for quite a while.

40

Stephanie's eyes opened to dim lighting and the sound of voices outside the door. She recognized the guard's voice, but the other man was unfamiliar. Having spent the last two weeks here, she had gotten to know everyone who had reason to visit Lanjo's room. A feeling of anxiety washed over her, and after glancing at Lanjo to reassure herself he was still there, she crept to the door to listen.

"But Doctor, I was not informed." The guard's voice had taken on a note of uncertainty.

Another voice responded, one she did recognize. "We're nearing the point of no return. I'm going to attempt a procedure. It's his only hope."

Stephanie almost choked in surprise. She'd know Feraganjo's voice anywhere, and she was fairly certain that he wasn't a doctor. Her mind raced, and she ran back to her bed and hid under the covers, just as the door to the room opened.

Stephanie peeked out from under her blanket and saw an older man with gray hair and a younger woman accompanying Feraganjo. All three were dressed in lab coats and wore I.D. badges. They moved into the room and stood by Lanjo's bed.

"I don't know why you weren't informed, young man." The older man spoke in a warm British accent that carried natural authority. He showed the guard his clipboard. "Here's our orders. We're to transport him to the surgical suite so he can be prepped. It's a four-hour procedure." He looked at the guard with compassion. "I can see you care deeply about Lanjo. We promise we'll do our best to save him."

The guard nodded, wiping the back of his hand across his eyes. "Yes, Doctor. Thank you." The British doctor and Feraganjo rearranged Lanjo's bed for transport and carefully removed his IV, then the British doctor turned to the guard. "No worries, young man. Cygnan metabolism is very slow when in a comatose state. He'll be fine without the IV. Could you please hold the door?"

The guard held the door open. The woman stood off to the side next to Stephanie's couch. Checking first to make sure the guard was distracted, she turned to Stephanie, put her finger to her lips, and winked. The woman reached into her pocket and dropped a folded piece of paper onto Stephanie's blanket, then turned back to observe Feraganjo and the doctor as they pushed Lanjo's bed through the door. The woman picked up the clipboard the doctor had set on the patient tray and followed them out.

Stephanie slid her hand across the blanket and grabbed the piece of paper. She stuffed it into her pocket, then threw the blanket off and stood up, drawing the attention of the guard. "What's happening, Carlos? Where are they taking Lanjo?" Stephanie let her eyes get big. "Is he going to be okay?"

"They're prepping him for surgery. They're doing their best, Stephanie. We'll just have to wait and see. There's nothing you can do right now. Why don't you go get some breakfast while you're waiting?"

Stephanie nodded. "Yeah, I guess I'm hungry."

Carlos yawned and glanced at his watch. "Try to eat something, Steph. They'll be gone at least four hours, so you might as well. I'm heading home. I'll see you tonight."

Stephanie gave him her best smile. "Sure, see you tonight." She headed down the hallway to the elevators, forcing herself not to break into a run. She pushed the button and got on, and as soon as the doors closed, she pulled out the piece of paper and opened it. The writing was her dad's. It read, *Stephanie, go to the basement floor as quickly as possible and make sure you are alone. Love, Dad.*

Brett, in an EMT uniform, waited behind the wheel of the "borrowed" ambulance. As soon as Alan, Feraganjo, and Rachel exited the elevators with Lanjo, he pulled it alongside the curb so they could maneuver Lanjo into it. It was eerily quiet in the underground parking garage, but it wouldn't be for long. They had only 20 minutes until the morning shift change.

They loaded Lanjo and secured him in the ambulance. Just as they were about to shut the door, the elevator opened again, and Stephanie raced out. Brett waved her into the back of the ambulance. She leaped in and squatted next to Lanjo's stretcher, next to Rachel sitting in the jump seat. Brett slammed the door and ran around to the driver's seat. Alan was already in place in the passenger side. He'd shed his lab coat and sat in his newly acquired EMT uniform. He turned to Brett and grinned. "I never dreamed I would be part of an ambulance heist. I should've put it on my bucket list."

Brett grinned back and checked his watch. Right on schedule, and the airport hangar was just fifteen minutes away.

He pulled out of the parking garage, exited the hospital campus, and flipped on the lights and sirens. Other drivers cleared a path, and he barreled through traffic lights and stop signs. They reached the hangar twelve minutes later.

Tom and Phil stood just outside the open hangar doors. As the ambulance skidded to a stop, Tom turned away from Phil. He took a few steps towards the ambulance, then broke into a sprint. Brett slammed the shifter to park and cut the engine as Tom threw the back doors open.

Stephanie catapulted herself into her dad's arms. He swung her around and brought her in for a tight hug. Peering over her shoulder, his gaze fell on Lanjo, and his smile froze, then disintegrated. Lanjo was lying motionless on a gurney, face dark and mouth slack. He tore his gaze away and forced a smile. He lifted Stephanie up so he could see her face. He kissed her cheek and pulled her in for another hug.

"It's okay, Dad," came Stephanie's muffled voice against his shoulder. "I can't breathe," she giggled.

Tom let her go and she stepped back, smiling. "I missed you, Dad. I missed you so much."

He ruffled her hair. "I missed you, too, kiddo. I'm very proud of you."

"I'm proud of you, too, Dad!" She tugged at his shirt like she used to when she was little. "So what's next? Why did we steal Lanjo?"

Tom reached out and stroked her hair. "We don't have much time, honey. I'm trying to save the world, and Lanjo along with it. We're going to Lanzeron."

"We are? Awesome! When are we leaving?"

"Whoa, we is me and Lanjo, kiddo."

Stephanie put her hands on her hips and stared up at her dad for a moment, then dropped her arms back to her sides and looked down. "I get it. You think I'd be in the way."

Tom put his fingers under Stephanie's chin and tilted her head up, so their eyes met. "No way, Steph. You'd be great. But it's too dangerous." Stephanie gazed back and finally exhaled noisily, nodding her reluctant acquiescence. "Okay, Dad. I understand."

Tom looked at his daughter sympathetically and realized the best thing he could do for her was to give her a job to do. "Good. I still need your help. Can you take care of Lanjo for me? We're all going to fly to Houston in just a few minutes, including you. I need someone to stay with him while I finish preparing for the trip to Lanzeron."

"Why are we going to Houston?" Stephanie asked.

"That's where my spaceship is," Tom replied with a twinkle in his eye.

"Oh, okay, Dad. This is real, isn't it?" She looked up at him eagerly.

"Yes, Steph. It's real. I just hope we can pull it off."

Alan had been hanging back to let Tom talk to his daughter, but they needed to get going. Thanks to Keith's badge and forged paperwork, the NASA jet was already refueled for the final leg of their journey. "Tom, we have Lanjo settled in the plane. We need to go," he gently interrupted. "We're a few minutes behind schedule, but Keith said we should be able to make up the time in the air."

Tom turned to Alan. "Thanks." He grabbed Stephanie's hand and winked. "Shall we?" Eyes bright, Stephanie nodded vigorously. They ran to the stairs and boarded the plane together, Alan following at a slightly slower pace.

"Commander McDonnough, we weren't expecting you." The lead NASA technician in charge of the lunar ship expressed his surprise at Theresa's appearance in the hangar.

Theresa smiled reassuringly. "It's okay, Jed. I have a mission, but it's not on the books, just like the last ones when Commander Sanders and I brought in the Cygnans. Top Secret—you know the drill."

Jed's eyes widened. "Does this have to do with why we're at ThreatCon Charlie?"

Theresa hid her surprise behind a bland smile. Tom had warned her, but it was still unsettling to hear they were under the elevated threat level. "Yes, but keep it under your hat."

"Yes, ma'am. We'll start getting her prepped for flight. When do you need her?"

Theresa glanced at her watch. Tom should be leaving Massachusetts any time. "Four hours. Do you know Phil Mason?"

"Yes ma'am, we worked together to install shielding on the shuttles."

"Good. When you're done with your prep, he should be arriving to augment the shielding on this girl." Catching Jed's puzzled look, she added, "It looks like we may have some extra dense meteor showers for this mission, and NASA wants to be prepared, just in case." She gave a little laugh. "And I certainly appreciate the additional safety margin."

"Sounds good, ma'am. I'll be happy to assist Phil any way I can."

Theresa smiled. "Thanks Jed—you're the best."

The technician turned and strode towards the ship where two other technicians were lounging by its cargo bay. Theresa could hear him issuing instructions in a brisk voice and sighed with relief. She headed to the coffee pot that was kept in the far side of the hangar rather than venturing into NASA offices. People would be curious about her presence here instead of on the media circuit where she was supposed to be. Keranganjo was covering for her, but her absence would be questioned eventually. Fortunately, by then Tom would be long gone.

Sipping his coffee, Joe watched President Ferris pacing laps around the Oval Office, its design lending itself well to his activity. Joe expected the carpet to start showing bare thread to mark the president's path. The Star Wars package would need two hours to reach the wormhole coordinates, so the president had less than ten hours to order the wormhole to be destroyed—if the other options didn't come through in time. The phone rang and both men jumped. The president answered the phone on the Resolute Desk.

"Yes. Uh huh. Yes. That's unfortunate. Okay. I understand. Yes, go ahead. Make sure and wait for my approval . . . Yes . . . Thank you." The president hung up, and slumped into his chair. He pressed his lips together and shook his head. The two men were quiet for a long moment.

"I didn't think one of the other options would work, but I was hoping there might be another way," the president mused. "I feel like we're closing the door on something momentous."

"I understand how you feel, Mr. President, but look at it this way. We're closing the door on a threat, to prevent our annihilation."

The president gave Joe a weak grin. "Well, I guess when you put it that way, it doesn't sound so bad." He glanced at his watch. "Ten hours to save the world. Most movies do it in two."

Joe smiled. "So we have eight extra hours to work with."

The president sighed. "I just hope it's enough."

41

Tom leaned onto Lanjo's hospital bed in the Gulfstream while Keith taxied to the runway for takeoff. Tom studied his friend's face. The alien yet familiar features were relaxed as though Lanjo were only sleeping. *If only* . . .

He looked up and saw Stephanie watching him. He managed a smile. "What is it, honey?"

"Is there anything we can do for him, Dad?"

"I hope so, Steph. The Cygnan doctor said if he were back on Lanzeron, there were some experimental therapies he could try. It's Lanjo's only hope, and I'm going to do my best to get him there." He touched the friendship bracelet encircling Lanjo's wrist and whispered to himself, "Greater love has no one than this: to lay down one's life for one's friends."

Stephanie wiped tears from her eyes. "I do love him, Dad."

Tom pulled his daughter close, and their tears fell on Lanjo's blanket. "I know, sweetheart. He loves you, too."

Keith landed the plane four-and-a-half hours later and taxied it to his usual hangar at Cape Canaveral. The lunar spaceship was in a spaceport also used by commercial crews, so it wouldn't be too hard for them to blend in. As soon as the plane rolled to a halt and the stairs were lowered, Phil strode down them and headed for the employee parking lot where he'd left his truck. Keith ran through the plan in his mind one more time. Phil had offered his truck to transport Lanjo to where the lunar spaceship was housed. Rachel, Stephanie, and Feraganjo would stay with Lanjo in the plane and wait for Phil to return, while Keith led the others to the spaceport, which fortunately was on the same side of the center's 144,000 acres.

Keith led Tom, Brett, and Alan through the myriad of spacecraft to the hangar that housed two lunar mission spaceships. As they approached the one being prepped, Keith scanned the area. His eyes were drawn to where Theresa sat, her hands circled around a mug of coffee. He glanced at Tom, who was staring at her, and then signaled to the others. "Tom, why don't you go touch base with Theresa? I'll show Brett and Alan around the ship."

Tom nodded, never taking his eyes off Theresa as he continued to walk towards her. Brett, Alan, and Keith exchanged knowing glances and headed to where Jed was running a pressure check on the tires. Keith stuck out his hand. "Hello, Jed. Glad to know our top man is prepping our girl."

"Yes, sir, Commander Sanders. She's coming along just fine." He looked around. "I thought Phil was going to be with you."

"He'll be here soon. He had to take care of something first. I brought a couple of engineers to help. Brett and Alan will be assisting Phil in the shielding enhancements."

Jed glanced at their NASA I.D.s hanging from the lanyards around their necks and nodded. "Sure thing, Keith. Let me know if you need anything."

"Will do, Jed, thanks."

Keith watched Jed finish up and move off, then grinned at Brett and Alan. "Okay, gentlemen, so far so good. I was worried about the heightened security under Threatcon Charlie, but having worked here for the last five years puts us at an advantage. Who would like to see the inside of a lunar spaceship?"

Alan and Brett's eager smiles provided his answer. Keith turned and looked back at Tom and Theresa. They were sitting together at the table, and Tom also had a cup of coffee. He silently wished Tom luck and turned to the task at hand. Lanjo needed a place to safely ride through the acceleration required to exit the Earth's atmosphere. He also needed to figure out how to get Lanjo on board with no one the wiser. He sighed. It was a lot easier to fly a highly complex spaceship than to engage in clandestine activities. He glanced at the familiar loudspeakers, and an idea began to form.

"But what about his IV?" Stephanie's high-pitched voice was filled with anxiety. She didn't know much, but she knew Lanjo had been on an IV during his entire hospital stay. He'd now been without it for several hours.

"Shush, don't worry, Steph." Rachel patted her shoulder. "The Cygnan doctor told your dad Lanjo can go without the IV for up to twenty-four hours. By then, he'll be safe on Lanzeron receiving the best medical care they have to offer."

"Okay sorry. It's just been a very strange day."

"You're worried about your dad and Lanjo going into space —aren't you?"

"Yeah." Stephanie dropped her eyes. "I don't want to lose both of them."

Rachel grabbed her hand. "Look at me, sweetheart."

Stephanie lifted her eyes back up and met Rachel's gaze.

"Your dad is very brave, and he knows what needs to be done. He's doing a wonderful thing." She wanted to add, *It's going to be okay*, but she couldn't quite form the words, so instead she pulled Stephanie in for a long hug.

Phil pulled up to the plane in his pickup truck a moment later, and Rachel gently released her. He rolled his window down. "Let's figure out how to get Lanjo transported to the hangar, okay?"

Stephanie bobbed her head in agreement as Phil got out of his truck. "It's a good thing we don't have far to go." He pointed towards the plane. "Let's use the mattress from the hospital bed and lay Lanjo down in the back. Feraganjo, you and Stephanie will have to ride back there with him. I have a tarp I can throw over all of you. Rachel, you'll sit up front with me. I can pass you off as my intern."

He glanced at his watch. "We'd better get going. We can't get off schedule or we'll be in big trouble." The human engineer and Cygnan scientist climbed up the steps and into the plane. Rachel gave them a thumbs up, and they carried Lanjo down the stairs and slid him into the bed of the pickup. Feraganjo and Stephanie crouched on either side of him, holding the tarp over their heads. Rachel jumped into the passenger seat, while Phil got behind the wheel, and they headed for the spaceport.

Brett stood in the cockpit, staring at the wall of instrumentation, switches, and levers. He turned to Alan. "How is Tom going to manage? He doesn't even have a pilot's license."

Keith grinned. "That's the beautiful thing about working for NASA. It's a pain in the neck sometimes, but there is a procedure for everything and the system is designed for fully automated piloting. Of course, we don't like to advertise that fact, since it somewhat tarnishes our superman image, but in a straightforward flight to a specific set of coordinates, we can upload a program so that Tom will in essence be going along for the ride. There are a couple of things he'll need to do manually, but he'll be able to keep her on auto pilot for the most part." He rubbed his chin. "Which reminds me. We need those coordinates."

Alan pulled out his cell phone and sent Tom a text. No one wanted to interrupt his meeting with Theresa, especially when he'd soon be departing on a mission that did not guarantee his return. "We better get to work on Lanjo's seat. Phil should be here pretty quick."

Keith pointed at a seat towards the back. "This is where the mission specialist contractor sits. Remember Sheila Palazzo? That's where she sat for our Moon missions. We can rig it better for Lanjo, since it isn't an active part of the flight crew accommodations. Here, help me adjust it for him. We just need to extend it. I have a space suit that should fit him, too. We'll need to get that on him."

The three were busy working on adjusting the four-point harness to fit a Cygnan skeletal structure, when Phil poked his head in the door. "Lanjo's downstairs in my truck. He's under a tarp. We need to get him in here without being seen, as quickly as possible. Stephanie and Feraganjo are hiding under it, too."

"Where's Rachel?" Brett asked.

"She's with Theresa. Tom is on the phone trying to get the coordinates for the wormhole. He called the Cygnan doctor, but the doctor said he didn't know. The coordinates were preprogrammed into his ship, and he didn't know how to extract them. Tom called Marco at SETI, but Marco started asking too many questions. Tom's afraid Marco will guess we're up to something and warn President Ferris. The only person left that knows the coordinates is Dan Ross, Jonathan Howe's assistant. Tom is talking to Jonathan now, but apparently he's reluctant to help. He's worried about the president's response to our plan."

Keith dropped the harness strap and pulled out his phone. He called his future father-in-law. "Jonathan, it's Keith. I'm here at the spaceport with Tom. I know you have him on the other line. You can trust Tom. Please do what he asks. It's really important."

Jonathan closed his eyes. Long moments passed. His gut told him he could trust Keith. After all, he was already trusting him with his daughter. He opened his eyes back up. "Okay. I'll put Dan on the line with Tom."

"Thanks, Jonathan. It's the right decision, I promise."

"I hope so, son."

42

Tom climbed the stairs into the lunar spaceship and stood off to one side, observing the focused activity. Alan and Brett were reinstalling a harness on one of the crew seats, and Keith was going through a checklist, verifying the settings on some complex-looking instrumentation. Tom cleared his throat and Keith practically leapt towards Tom.

"Did you get the coordinates?"

Tom grinned. "Yup. You'll never believe who gave them to me. It turns out that Dan Ross is the grandson of Daniel Graham. His role in facilitating contact with SETI was more than coincidental. Long story short, Dan welcomed the chance to help save the world from Paranganjo's threat. He feels somewhat responsible since he'd been pushing Jonathan to make a deal with Paranganjo and he tried to beat us to the Antiproton Decelerator. Paranganjo was using him to get what he wanted."

Tom's voice rose an octave. "We've been dealing with a second contact, not a first one—Dan's grandfather met the Cygnans on his walk on the Moon back in 1974! The stories he shared with his grandson were of a friendly species, not a threatening one. Paranganjo has caught everyone off guard. Dan wanted us to know he never meant any harm."

"I've met Dan a couple of times," Keith said. "He always came across as hardworking and smart—a good guy to have on your team. I was really surprised when it looked like he had some complicity with Paranganjo." He sighed with relief. "I'm glad he provided the coordinates—I'll get them programmed in."

Tom nodded. "Phil's waiting in his truck with Lanjo while we figure out a way to get him in here unseen. He's finished checking the specs on the ship. He can't be one hundred percent sure because we haven't done it before, but he thinks the shielding already in place should hold up for the mission. Any other options couldn't be done in time anyway. He gives an 83.7% chance of a successful entry and travel through the wormhole. The Cygnan spaceship the doctor arrived in has approximately 15% more shielding, but Phil thinks that could be a maximum for warp speed, which we don't have, plus an engineering tolerance. For our purposes, our shielding should be sufficient."

"That's good news. I was wondering how we'd be able to implement additional shielding under these conditions and in the timeframe we're working with. It's not like we can get an adhesive-backed heat shield from AutoZone to throw on her. 83.7% is pretty good odds, but I'm not the one taking the risk." Keith flashed a glance at Tom.

Tom shrugged. "I wouldn't say that. It's a risk you and the rest of the world are also taking. My failure or success is Earth's failure or success."

Keith let out a long breath. "I didn't think of it that way, but you're right. At this point, we don't have much choice." He glanced at his watch. "You need to be launched in the next 45 minutes."

"Yeah, but we have another problem. How can we clear the spaceport so we can get Lanjo out of the truck and on board? Theresa and Rachel are keeping Jed distracted, but we won't be able to sneak Lanjo past him, especially with a ThreatCon Charlie."

"I've been thinking about that, and I have an idea. It'll be credible if Theresa implements it." Keith pulled out his phone again, this time to call Theresa. "If we do it right, we can finish up here and get you and Lanjo launched before anyone's the wiser."

"This is not a drill. I repeat, this is not a drill." Theresa's familiar voice came over the loudspeaker. "Code 34 Black. I repeat, Code 34 Black."

Jed froze as Theresa's words sunk in, then he glanced around, searching for the other technicians. "Come on," he yelled. "We need to go prep the launch pad—NOW." He checked his watch. According to Code 34 Black, they had eleven minutes to execute flight prep. He started to wonder what was going on, but he forced his thoughts to return to the task of getting the spaceship launched. He'd have time later to wonder about the whys—at least he hoped he would.

Keith waved urgently to Phil, who threw the tarp off the back of the pickup. Stephanie jumped down and Feraganjo moved to the back of the bed, picking up the end of the hospital mattress. Phil dropped the gate and began gently pulling the mattress as Feraganjo duck-walked his end. Brett and Alan appeared and grasped each side of the mattress. They walked Lanjo up the stairs, into the spaceship.

The alien space suit was stored right where Keith said it would be, along with Theresa and Keith's space suits. They worked Lanjo's arms and legs into his, then placed the helmet over his head and locked it in place. Next, they gently maneuvered him into the seat they had prepared, and Keith buckled him in.

"Whew, that went pretty well." Keith pointed. "Tom, go ahead and get into the captain's chair and let's get you strapped in." Theresa appeared in the entrance to the cockpit, and Keith smiled. "Theresa can finish up and give you your instructions. I'll finish uploading the coordinates."

On one level, Tom found it very interesting to watch the disciplined concentration that the NASA personnel exhibited as they went about their tasks during an alert situation. On another level he found himself wishing Theresa could step out of her commander persona at least for a minute or two. This might be the last time he saw her, but he understood the need for brevity— she had to make sure he understood what he needed to do to successfully fly the ship. Even with radio contact and autopilot, their success was far from guaranteed.

"Okay, Tom, this is what you need to focus on." She leaned over him and flipped a switch, causing the screen to come to life. A bar graph was illuminated on the left side and a bank of numbers scrolled on the right. "The graph tells you levels of acceleration, fuel, and oxygen." Tom breathed in the clean smell of her wavy brown hair and forced himself to concentrate. "The numbers scrolling by are data measurements that may become relevant if one of the bars goes out of range."

Tom nodded that he understood.

"This spaceship is equipped with an advanced control system that allows for remote operation in autopilot mode. We'll be able to control the ship through the launch and get you to the wormhole coordinates. After you enter the wormhole, we'll no longer have any communication with you. That's your time to shine."

Tom gulped. "So what do I do?"

"When the ship enters the wormhole, you'll have to take control. The wormhole will cause the ship's autopilot to reset to manual. Once you're through it, you'll have to restore autopilot so the ship can land at their spaceport. You should be able to establish communication with the Cygnans within seconds of emerging from the wormhole. You'll have to hand control over to them. Feraganjo confirmed that they'll be able to take over the ship's operation remotely. At that point they can navigate for you, but here's the catch." She hesitated. "They have to be willing to do so."

She paused a moment to allow Tom to process what she'd just said, then pointed to a large round button switch. "Manual shows green. Depress it and hold it for 3 seconds, and it will activate autopilot. Autopilot will be red. Once autopilot is restored, the Cygnans will be able to access the ship's computers and you'll be home free."

"And if they're not willing?"

His words hung in the air between them. All of their plans were based on the assumption that the Cygnans would cooperate.

She leaned back so she could look directly into his eyes. "There's no way you'll be able to do the necessary navigation required to return to Earth."

Tom met her gaze evenly. "That's what I thought. Anything else I need to know?"

"Just this." She leaned in and kissed him on the lips.

They broke apart and the warmth that flared the moment their lips touched coursed through Tom's body. At that point, he felt like he could accomplish anything. He reached out and brushed her cheek gently with the palm of his hand, then moved a wayward curl back into place. "I'm coming back, and when I do, I would like to resume just where we left off."

Theresa smiled. "I'll be waiting."

Tom gave her a jaunty grin. "Well, I'd best get going. Gotta save the world ya know."

"I know."

Keith came up behind her, and she turned to him. "He's ready. Is Lanjo secure?"

"Yes, ma'am. Tom's food and water is stocked, and he's good to go."

"Good, I'll radio Jed." She glanced at her watch. "The pad should be ready in three minutes."

"So how were you able to convince the technicians to get the pad prepped?" Tom asked.

"ThreatCon Charlie has some emergency protocols, including launching the spaceship immediately to keep it from falling into terrorist hands. Jed is our lead technician and fully understands Code 34 Black. I hate deceiving him, but being at ThreatCon Charlie actually made stealing the spaceship easier. I may have just lost all my credentials for future missions, but. . ."

"Thanks, Theresa." He paused, wanting to say more, but realized he hadn't seen Stephanie since the flight to NASA. He wanted to see her before he left. "Where's Stephanie?" Tom called out anxiously, so everyone could hear him.

"I don't know," Rachel said, "but I do know she was very worried about you and Lanjo. She may have found it too scary to come say goodbye."

Too scared. His brave, feisty daughter?

Keith appeared at his shoulder. "It's time."

Oh, no! How could he leave without telling Stephanie goodbye?! But he didn't have a choice. He was out of time. Tom touched Rachel's arm. "Tell her I love her, Rachel. Tell her I'm very proud of her, and I'll see her when I get back."

"I promise," Rachel said, and made her way to the ship's exit.

"Theresa will taxi you to the launch pad," Keith said. "Then she'll leave, and it'll be just you and Lanjo. Once you're on the pad, it's fairly automated, so you'll be able to handle it with no problem." He pointed at the stick, then to the screen. "Just keep her centered if she starts veering off that line. She will auto-lock into the boosters once she's aligned properly, and then we'll launch."

Tom nodded, then held out his hand, and the two men shook. "Thanks. Don't forget to contact the president."

"I won't. You just focus on getting to the wormhole, and we'll take care of things at this end. Godspeed." Tom looked past him at Brett and Alan, who stood behind Keith in the cramped space. Alan mouthed, "You've got this" and winked. Brett reached over and punched him on the shoulder. "It's an honor working with you."

Tom's eyes moistened unexpectedly. "Same."

Feraganjo ran up behind Brett and waved his hands, his eyebrows quivering rapidly. "Tom, I forgot to tell you, make sure when you make radio contact with the authorities to refer to yourself as Tilapatao Lanjo. That should help."

"Help how?" Tom asked, puzzled and a little annoyed to have one more thing he would have to remember.

"No time to explain," Keith interrupted. "If you're going, you have to go now."

Tom nodded. "Okay. Let's do it."

Everyone left the ship except for Theresa, who slid into the co-pilot's seat. She was all business, and Tom knew their personal lives were officially on hold. They had a mission to accomplish.

43

Theresa made a quick exit after getting the spaceship to the pad, and Tom was on his own. He made some minor corrections with the control stick, and the ship locked into the boosters.

Keith's voice crackled in his headphones. "Clear to launch."

Seconds later, Tom was slammed back against the pilot's chair, grateful for his space suit as 3gs pressed him into the seat. The ship shook him to his core. He focused on the bar graph on the screen in front of him, then glanced over his shoulder at Lanjo, still secured and unmoving.

He returned his attention to the bar graph. The acceleration bar was up at 2.8. He could tolerate up to 9gs, but a mere 5.6 would damage a Cygnan body. They were okay. So far.

Suddenly, the ship jerked, the booster rockets dropped away, and the shaking stopped. Tom peered out the window to see a field of lights. Space really did look like a black sky blanketed in stars. His awe was interrupted by a crackle in his headset. He switched it to speaker.

"Bluebird, come in, Bluebird."

Tom smiled. He picked his code name from the day Lanjo had healed the Eastern Bluebird's wing, at the GWU lab in Ashburn. Could it have been just a few short weeks ago?

"I'm here, safe and sound." He could hear Theresa sigh with relief, even though he was well past the Karman line.

"That's a copy, Bluebird. Good to hear. How's your passenger?"

Tom glanced over his shoulder again. "He seems to be fine. Is it safe for me to get out of my seat and check?"

"That's affirmative, Bluebird. You have about seven hours before entering the wormhole. The ship is equipped with enough shielding to eliminate the need for you to dodge small stuff, and we have you on autopilot which will automatically dodge the bigger stuff. Check on Lanjo, make yourself at home, grab a cup of joe, and put your feet up if you want."

"Sounds good. Has Stephanie showed up yet?"

"Not yet. She was pretty exhausted from getting up so early. I'm guessing she's taking a nap somewhere in the spaceport. Rachel is looking for her right now."

His brave, determined daughter was taking a nap during a space launch? That didn't seem—

He froze. She couldn't have . . .

He unbuckled his harness and looked around the cabin for . . . there it was. He strode to the door of the equipment closet and flung it open.

His daughter gazed up at him innocently. "Hi Dad. I guess I must have fallen asleep. Sorry." She tried her best to look contrite. And failed.

"Tom, can you hear us...Tom?"

Tom found his voice. "Yes, I can hear you, Theresa, and so can Stephanie."

He directed his attention to his daughter. "How could you do such a thing? You don't even have a space suit on. You could've been killed."

"No, Daddy. I didn't need to have a space suit. I asked Keith, and he told me that they didn't need space suits for 3g and he also said we wouldn't be going over 3g because we needed to protect Lanjo. His body couldn't handle much more than that."

Tom spoke into his mic. "What were you thinking, Keith? How could you tell Stephanie that?"

"But she's always asking questions. I didn't think anything of it."

That was true, Stephanie was always asking questions.

"Okay, Keith. I get it. Work on getting the president to stop the Star Wars missile from destroying the wormhole. Steph and I will check on Lanjo. Please keep me posted on what the president says."

"Will do. Sorry about that."

Tom glared at his daughter. "Not your fault, Keith. It'll be okay. Bluebird out."

"Oh my," Alan turned and looked at Theresa and Keith. "Quite the rascal, isn't she?"

"She takes after her dad," Theresa muttered. She cleared her throat. "Tom can handle his daughter. Theoretically she shouldn't be in any danger since she won't need to leave the ship, at least until it reaches Lanzeron." She turned to Keith. "We need to get Joe Ricinski on the horn. They know we launched—there's no way to keep that a secret from the NSA."

Keith nodded just as Theresa's cell phone vibrated. She checked the caller I.D. "Looks like Joe's beaten us to the punch." She answered the phone and put it on speaker.

"Hello, Joe, I was just about to call you."

"So you're aware of the launch?" Without waiting for her to answer he continued. "Is Keith flying her?"

"No, sir," Keith said. "I'm here with Theresa."

There was a long pause on the other end while Joe digested Keith's response.

"If you aren't flying her, and Keith isn't flying her, I am not aware of anyone else checked out on the D-467 Lunar Spaceship, or any other lunar spacecraft for that matter."

"You are correct, sir," Theresa responded crisply.

"I was afraid of that. When do you expect Tom to arrive at the wormhole?"

"How did he know it was Tom?" Alan stage whispered.

"That's easy," Joe replied, unrattled. "We chose Tom to be the liaison between humans and Cygnans because of his qualifications. His psych profile indicates he is a very loyal person. He and Lanjo are friends. He was present at our meeting in the situation room. Who else would risk his life to facilitate contact between our species? I'm assuming he filled you in on the topics discussed?"

"Yes, sir," Keith responded. "We believe Tom has an excellent chance at reasoning with the Cygnans. Bringing Lanjo back for treatment was secondary, but will surely help his cause."

"That's your story and you're sticking to it?"

"Yes, sir."

"And you believe Tom is capable of navigating the ship?"

"Autopilot is a wonderful thing, sir."

"And what is it you think Tom will be able to accomplish?"

"Tom plans on talking to Paranganjo and the leaders of Lanzeron to dissuade Paranganjo from following through with his intention to destroy the Earth. Tom is also hoping to get medical attention for Lanjo. Apparently there are some experimental therapies on Lanzeron they can try. We're requesting that the president halt the Star Wars launch, so Tom can enter the wormhole once he arrives at the coordinates."

"Speaking of coordinates, how did you obtain them?"

"I know someone who knows someone, sir."

"Yes," Joe mused, "I believe you do. Okay. I'll tell the president what you've told me, but no guarantees. Tom may have made a very big mistake launching that lunar ship. Is there anything else?"

"Uh, yes, sir," Keith hesitated and looked at Theresa. She nodded.

Keith cleared his throat. "There is an additional passenger besides Lanjo on board."

A brief silence then a long-suffering sigh. "Who might the additional passenger be?"

"Stephanie Whitaker."

"As in Tom Whitaker's twelve-year-old daughter?"

"Yes, sir."

"And why is she on board?"

"She stowed away, sir. We only just now discovered her. She hid in the equipment locker."

"Is she okay?"

"She's fine, sir."

Joe sighed. "I'll let the president know. Stand by for further instructions."

"Yes, sir," Theresa and Keith responded in unison. Joe hung up and Theresa pocketed her phone. She glanced at her watch. The wormhole would open in five hours.

Several news outlets had leaked the elevated threat level, but no one knew who or what was behind it. Ray left the Hill wondering if ThreatCon Charlie had anything to do with his report to Joe about NPC's activities. He recalled the kid that forced him off the road and his threat to do things "the hard way." Sheila had mentioned she was having a CAET meeting at her place. He got into his car and headed to Sheila's apartment.

"Ray." Sheila had cracked the door in response to his knock. "I wasn't expecting you to stop by. You said you wanted nothing to do with CAET."

"I changed my mind. Now let me in." He needed to get in there—now.

Sheila stepped back, and he pushed through into the living room, where a small crowd had gathered. Jessup was nowhere in sight, probably hiding under Sheila's bed. *Smart cat*, thought Ray as he glanced around the room. He spotted the young punk that had forced him off the road and froze. The kid was talking to Frank Custer, a member of the Joint Committee on Energy and Alien Relations. He strode over to them.

"Frank, what are you doing here?" Ray interrupted, ignoring the kid.

Frank looked up calmly. "Hello, Ray. I'm here for the same reason you are, to get rid of the Cygnans. Someone has to step up, and your office certainly hasn't."

The young man smirked. "I told you we'd do it the hard way if necessary. The explosion at CERN was just the beginning. Looks like you couldn't get it done, so we'll have to."

Ray clenched his fists and started counting to ten in his head, barely holding onto his temper. So NPC was behind the sabotage of the Antiproton Decelerator, and a committee member knew about it. "And what about the aileron? Are your people responsible for that, too?"

Frank shook his head. "That is a bit of a puzzle. We don't know who did it, but it was a brilliant attempt that could have gotten rid of all of the aliens in one—"

Ray's fist struck Frank in the nose before he could finish his sentence. Blood spurted all over the kid. His smirk disappeared and he reached for his waistband. Ray grabbed his arm and twisted it away from the gun. He picked him up, spun him around, and pulled his coat back so everyone could see the kid was carrying. The low buzz of conversation came to a complete halt as everyone turned to see what the ruckus was about.

"Sheila, is this really the scum you want to associate with?" Ray looked at each person in the room. "Do you realize you are committing treason? We live in a democracy. You don't get to undermine the majority. CAET is an ethnocentric, bigoted minority acting either out of irrational fear or greed. This stops now."

He released the young man and shoved him back into his chair. "Tell your boss he's finished. If he makes any more moves against the Cygnans, he will be prosecuted to the full extent of the law. And Frank"—Ray turned to face the Senator, who was pressing his blood-soaked handkerchief against his nostrils. "You're finished too. I suggest you start thinking of an excuse to resign from the Senate."

Frank stood and sneered. "You can't prove anything I said this evening."

Ray met Sheila's eyes, then turned back to Frank. "Oh, yes, I can." He scanned the room. "We're done here, folks. I suggest you go on home and make up your minds to act like citizens of the United States, instead of her enemies."

The room emptied, with neither Frank nor the young man meeting Ray's eyes as they shuffled out the door.

Ray closed the door behind them and turned to Sheila, letting his anger fuel his words. "You can't do this anymore. You're going to ruin your life. CAET is undermining our government. Can't you see that?"

"But I don't like the Cygnans. They scare me," Sheila snuffled. Jessup came out from the bedroom and rubbed against Sheila's legs. She picked him up and held him close. "I've been afraid of the Cygnans ever since I met Lanjo on the Moon."

Ray took her by the shoulders and gazed piercingly into her eyes. "Sheila, you have a phobia. Quit trying to destroy the object of it and get help instead. This CAET business is going to land you in prison. You have to respect our government and its decisions, even when you don't agree with them. Trust the process."

Sheila looked down, her shoulders drooping dejectedly as she stroked Jessup's fur. "I'm sorry."

"You can still make this right. Just back off CAET and work on yourself. We all need a little help sometimes. Isn't that why you became a psychologist in the first place—to help people?" Ray patted her shoulder awkwardly. "How about coming to dinner Sunday? The kids would love to see their Aunt Sheila."

Sheila looked back up and smiled hesitantly. "Sure, Ray. I'd like that." Jessup purred his agreement and they both laughed.

Ray left Sheila's apartment and headed back to his office. He still didn't know if the NPC had anything to do with ThreatCon Charlie, but he had a feeling Joe Ricinski would want to know what had just transpired.

44

Tom rested in the pilot chair, trying to relax, twirling around the water bottle Keith had left for him in the pilot's cupholder. Keith was still waiting for President Ferris to postpone the Star Wars launch and allow their mission to proceed. Tom glanced at his watch. They were already eating into their four-hour pad. He checked the bar graphs. Everything was in normal ranges. "Stephanie, come get in the co-pilot's chair. We'll be entering the wormhole soon and I want you strapped in."

"But what about Lanjo? Don't you think I should stay next to him in case he needs me?"

"Lanjo will be fine, honey. Keith made sure he's strapped in securely. I need your help up here."

"Sure, Dad." She walked over to the co-pilot's seat and climbed onto it, her feet dangling. "What do you want me to do?"

Tom got up, adjusted the straps to their shortest length, and began to strap his daughter in. His study of wormholes told him it was probably not necessary, but he needed to do all he could to protect his daughter. He wasn't afraid for himself, but having Stephanie along changed everything.

He pointed at the autopilot control switch on the ship's dash, glowing red. "Once we enter the wormhole, that switch will turn green, and the ship will be reset to manual control. We'll need to reactivate autopilot once we're through the wormhole." *If the Cygnans cooperate.*

"How do we do that?" Stephanie asked with excitement in her voice.

"Simple. I'll tell you when, and you'll push the button until it turns red. You'll have to hold it down for at least three seconds."

"Okay, Dad. Got it."

Tom checked the bar graph. Acceleration, oxygen, and fuel. All good. He closed his eyes and breathed a little easier.

When he opened his eyes, Stephanie was staring at him. "Are you scared, Daddy?"

She hadn't called him Daddy in a long time. "Well, maybe just a little bit."

"Is that why you were praying?"

"Yes, sweetie. But it'll be okay. And it's okay to be scared."

"I'm just scared for Lanjo. I want him to get better."

"Me, too, Steph. Me, too."

"Come in Bluebird, come in." Theresa's voice came over the intercom.

"Bluebird here." Tom stared out at the spherical distortion rapidly filling the view screen.

"Good news, Bluebird. POTUS has agreed to delay the Star Wars launch. But he's giving you only two hours to send a signal that the Cygnans are able to stop Paranganjo and desire peaceful relations. He'll only have another hour after that before the window closes again. He wants to have time to launch if necessary. Marco is standing by at SETI to receive your signal.

"Also, when you reinitiate contact, you'll need to come up with a way to authenticate your signal, so we know you aren't under duress. Bluebird, you are three minutes away from entering the wormhole. At that point, we will lose radio contact."

Tom's foot jittered against the floor and his stomach fluttered. "Acknowledged, Commander." *Three minutes to the wormhole. Two hours to reach an agreement with the Cygnans. Need to come up with an authentication method . . .*

"Tom?"

"Yes, I'm still here."

"I'll be right here waiting for you."

"That's good, because I'm going to need to give you control when I'm back through the wormhole. I'll depress the button for 3 seconds—"

"I mean, I'll be right here waiting for you."

"Ohhhh." Would he ever understand women? He decided to take a chance, since he might never get another one.

"I love you, babe."

Dead silence on the line for several seconds.

"I love you, too." Cheers erupted through the speaker. Tom's cheeks warmed. The whole team had heard them.

Keith's voice came on the line. "Bluebird, see you on the flip flop."

Tom smiled at the CB lingo.

"Radio silence in six, five, four, three, Godspeed my friend."

Tom reached over and grasped Stephanie's hand in his. They both stared out the view screen, mesmerized by the swirling, rapidly-approaching abyss. A multi-colored cumulus cloud filled the screen, and the ship plunged forward into the vortex. Tom and Stephanie were shoved into the backs of their seats. A rushing wind filled their ears. The ship began to vibrate. Tom looked at the acceleration bar. It registered normal, though they were traveling faster than humanly possible.

Tom continued to grip Stephanie's hand. He wanted to tell her to hang on, that it would be okay, but he wasn't able to form the words. His throat had tightened and his vocal cords refused to cooperate. Stephanie gave him a tight smile, as though he'd beamed his thoughts into her head. He turned back to the viewscreen, where nebulae and star systems flashed by, warped into twisting spirals by the wormhole space-time continuum.

He glanced over his shoulder to check on Lanjo, who remained secure in his seat harness, still unconscious. The ship began to shimmy, and the vibration grew stronger. The galaxies passed by faster. Then the vibration stopped as though someone had flipped a switch, and the ship slid out of the vortex and into a star field much different from the one they had left at the other side of the wormhole.

Tom tore his eyes away from the screen and checked the bar graph. Acceleration: normal. Oxygen: in range. Fuel: 3/4 full. The heat shield had held. He looked down at the navigation button. It was green. The ship was in manual control.

He looked at Stephanie, her mouth wide open and her eyes bugging, the same expression she had after a monster roller coaster ride. He felt the same way. He squeezed her hand reassuringly and released it. He pressed the radio transmit button and spoke into his headset.

"This is the Earth space vessel, Triumphant, requesting assistance from Lanzeron. Please respond."

No response. Nothing but static. He tried again. "This is the Earth space vessel, Triumphant, requesting assistance from Lanzeron. Please respond."

He looked down at the green button and remembered Theresa's instructions. If he didn't switch to autopilot soon he would have to manually control the ship, and he had no idea how to do that. His arms felt shaky and he felt slightly dizzy.

He depressed the radio transmit button and tried again, his voice pitched higher. "This is the Earth space vessel, Triumphant, requesting assistance from Lanzeron. Please respond."

Still no answer.

Nausea twisted its way up from the pit of his stomach. He picked up the water bottle and swallowed a sip, trying to remain calm. Sweat beaded across his forehead, even though the temperature gauge read a comfortable 72 degrees.

"This is the Earth space vessel, Triumphant, requesting assistance from Lanzeron. Please respond." *Please respond. Please, please, please respond.*

Still nothing.

Time was running out.

45

"Dad?"

Tom glanced quickly at Stephanie, then back at the instrument panel. "Don't interrupt sweetheart. I have to figure this out, and we don't have much time."

"But, Dad—"

"What?" Tom tried to keep the irritation out of his voice.

"Feraganjo told you to say you were *Tilapatao Lanjo*, remember? I heard him when I was hiding in the equipment locker."

"You're right. Good thinking!" *Anything was worth a try at this point.*

He depressed the transmit button yet again. "This is the Earth space vessel, Triumphant." He paused, then said more firmly, "I am Tilapatao Lanjo, requesting assistance from Lanzeron. Please respond."

It seemed like minutes passed, but in reality it was only about 30 seconds before a voice responded. "Acknowledged Tilapatao Lanjo. Welcome to Lanzeron. How may we assist you?"

Tom let his head fall back and looked heavenward. *Thank God.* "Requesting auto-navigation to your spaceport."

"Request granted. Initiate."

Tom motioned towards the glowing green button. Stephanie pressed it, and together father and daughter counted: "1-Mississippi, 2-Mississippi, 3-Mississippi." The color changed to red, and Stephanie removed her hand.

"Auto-nav initiated, Tilapatao Lanjo. You can sit back and enjoy the ride. ETA approximately seven minutes. Control out."

⚛

The tractor beam gently pulled their ship into the spaceport orbiting Lanzeron. Tom found Theresa's spare space suit and, despite Stephanie's objections, helped her to suit up. It hung loosely on her small frame, but would keep her safe if they lost atmosphere. The Cygnans assured him the airlock between the Earth ship and the spaceport would work, but they weren't designed to match up perfectly, and he wasn't taking any chances. Tom carefully latched his own helmet in place and gazed at Lanjo. "I hope this works, ol' buddy."

He took Stephanie by the hand, and together they walked to the ship's doors. They paused, waiting for the safety sensor over the doors to light up, indicating stable air pressure and breathable atmosphere on the other side. Thank goodness the Cygnans shared similar oxygen requirements. He looked down at Stephanie. "Are you okay, kiddo?"

"More than okay, Dad. This is awesome!"

Tom smiled. He should have known this would be right up Stephanie's alley. Before he could say anything else, the doors opened, and two Cygnans stood before them. They looked similar to the ones Tom had already met, although they were dressed differently. Lanjo and the other Cygnans on the science team had adopted Earth-type dress to help reduce their alien appearance. These Cygnans wore baggy suits made of some sort of metallic looking material, resembling a cross between a jumpsuit and a robe. The taller of the two held out his hand and grimaced. Tom shook it. The Cygnan spoke in a rapid-fire, high-pitched frequency of syllables for a few seconds, then paused.

The smaller of the two grimaced also. "Hello, Tom of Earth, and welcome to Lanzeron. My name is Belarango, and this is Therasanjo, the administrator of our spaceport. I will be your translator. If it is acceptable, we would like to escort you to our planet."

Tom's eyebrows shot up. *How did they know his name? No time to worry about that now.* "It would be an honor, but what about Lanjo?" He turned and pointed towards the crewmember seat where Lanjo was still secured. "We brought him with us to receive medical help."

The smaller one nodded. "Yes, we've been expecting you. We have a medical team on standby and will be transporting him on another ship directly to our medical facilities."

Who told them?! Before Tom could ask, Stephanie interrupted. "You mean, I can't go with him?" Tears welled up in her eyes.

The Cygnans gazed at her curiously and the taller one spoke briefly in the Cygnan language to the other. The smaller one turned to Tom and translated, "Your daughter is leaking. Is she okay?"

Tom put his arm around Stephanie's shoulders. "She's fine. Those are called tears. She cares for Lanjo very much. Stephanie regards him as her uncle. Humans leak tears when they are having very strong emotions."

The smaller one translated Tom's words, and both Cygnans stared at him for a long moment. Finally, the smaller one asked, "Uncle ... Does that make him your brother?"

Lanjo was not only his brother, he was his best friend. "Yes," he nodded. "Yes, I think it does."

The two conferred in the Cygnan language for a moment, then Belarango spoke. "Sorry, Lanjo's niece Stephanie, but you must accompany us. We will see that Lanjo receives the best possible care."

"But ..."

Tom squeezed her shoulders. "No buts, Steph. You need to stay with me. I'm sure Lanjo will be in quite capable hands. You would just be a distraction to the medical team. I know you wouldn't want that."

Stephanie dried her eyes with the back of her hand. "No, Dad, I wouldn't." She looked at the Cygnans directly. "Can you make him better?"

Belarango returned her gaze solemnly. "We'll try our very best."

Stephanie breathed out a sigh. "Okay." Pulling away from her dad, she walked over and stared down at the alien who had saved her life and her dad's life. She touched his helmeted cheek tenderly, then turned to her dad. "I'll go with you," she said in a resigned voice. She ran to the equipment locker and pulled out her copy of *The Adventures of Huckleberry Finn* and handed it to Belarango. He regarded it curiously. "Lanjo loves Mark Twain," she explained. "Please read it to him."

The alien nodded. She took her dad's hand again, and looked up at him. "I'm ready."

The two Cygnans showed Tom and Stephanie to a small, sleek ship, oddly circular in shape with two wings jutting out the sides. Tom glanced at his watch. "Belarango, it's of vital importance that I meet with Paranganjo immediately."

Belarango nodded and grimaced. "Don't worry, Tom. We're taking you to see him now."

Tom exhaled in relief, then furrowed his eyebrows. *How did they know that?* But he had no time to wonder—he needed to rehearse what he was going to say. He'd point out the advantages of a Cygnan-human partnership. Maybe the presence of a human child would soften Paranganjo towards humans, and he would cancel his plans to launch the destructive device through the wormhole.

A small part of him considered what he should do if Paranganjo turned out to be completely unreasonable. He really didn't have any good options. He needed to know he could get Stephanie safely home. A hostage swap maybe? Feraganjo and Keraganjo for him and Stephanie? Would there even be a world for her to go home to? He quickly turned his thoughts away from that line of thinking.

He also needed to devise a signal the president would trust. And all of that had to be accomplished in the next hour and a half.

Tom and Stephanie were led to two seats on the ship, and another Cygnan helped them strap in. Belarango and Therasanjo sat further up towards the pilot's cabin and conversed in low voices.

Stephanie looked at her dad. "I'm kinda scared, Dad. I wish Lanjo was here to help us."

Tom patted her knee. "It'll be okay, Steph. Just stay close."

Stephanie rested her head on his shoulder. Tom leaned back and closed his eyes, trying to convince himself that it would be okay.

So much was at stake. He almost wished they'd never made contact with the Cygnans. Life had been so much simpler then. He opened his eyes and peered sideways at his daughter. She was so brave. They had grown closer since the Cygnans came. He just hoped he could keep her safe. The only way to do that was to keep humanity safe. *But what were the Cygnans' true intentions?*

46

Tom and Stephanie disembarked with their Cygnan hosts, who had remained silent during the fifteen-minute trip to the planet's surface. They found themselves being escorted into another vehicle, similar to a small spaceship and seemed to serve the same purpose as cars on Earth. Its darkly tinted windows prevented them from seeing out and viewing life on this strange new world.

As exciting as it was to be on another planet, all Tom could think of was what could go wrong. His hosts still weren't talking, and he was beginning to get worried. Maybe they weren't on their way to meet with Paranganjo. Maybe they were being taken to be examined by Cygnan medical researchers. All of Earth's crazy ideas about aliens ran through his mind. CAET's claim that they were infiltrating Earth to take it over. Stories of alien abductions. Their hosts hadn't spoken a word to him since they had left the spaceport. Were they really being taken to a meeting with Parangango? Or were they going somewhere else? A laboratory, maybe, where they'd be locked away for scientific research.

Focus. He had to focus. The mission. Paranganjo. His fate, Stephanie's fate, the fate of their entire planet hinged on this mission. Hinged on one conversation. Tom tried to swallow down his rising panic, but he wasn't very successful. His mouth was as dry as a desert and his heart pounded in his chest.

The ship finally slowed to a halt and the window tint faded until it was transparent. Tom was able to see the front of a majestic white building, giving him something else to think about. It was reminiscent of the national museum of Qatar that Tom had visited when he was a grad student. Like the museum, the exterior architecture was made up of hundreds of large discs and what must be thousands of cladding elements subtly interwoven into the surface. Windows were interspersed between the discs in an amazing symmetry of natural patterns. An absence of outside activity made Tom briefly wonder about the rhythms of the Cygnan work day. Or was the absence of activity a security response to their presence?

A Cygnan in uniform appeared at the door of the ship, interrupting his thoughts. The Cygnan opened the door, motioning for them to get out. Belarango and Therasanjo disembarked first, then Tom and Stephanie followed. *Why doesn't anyone speak?* Tom cleared his throat, but the Cygnans ignored him and they continued to walk in silence towards the door of the building. The Cygnan who had opened the ship's door followed a few paces behind.

They entered the building and were led down a long hallway. Like the museum in Qatar Tom had visited, the interior twisted and turned and the ceiling rose and dipped. Tom's eyes widened and he sucked in a quick breath, dragging his feet as he viewed the pictures on the walls. Stephanie held his hand tightly as her head swiveled back and forth. Most of the life forms on display were humanoid in shape and in some type of uniform dress. A yellow and red furry being with four eyes, a round green being with exceptionally large ears and no discernible mouth, and a being that resembled the platypus on Earth were all represented. The humans and Cygnans turned right and came to a disc-shaped doorway.

Stephanie squeezed Tom's hand. He gave her a wink and a nod, attempting to convey reassurance he didn't really feel. *Please, Lord, help me keep Stephanie safe!* They followed their hosts into the darkened room. Dim lights running the periphery of the floor provided barely enough illumination to navigate. Although it was evident people were seated all around the room's perimeter, they were in shadow, and Tom could not make out their features or any of the room's details. *What is going on?!*

They came to a stop and Belarango and Therasanjo, their expressions blank, abruptly turned around and swept past them, leaving without a word. Tom felt a cold stab of fear. Another Cygnan, his expression serious and dressed in a uniform with multiple oddly shaped insignias woven into the fabric, came striding purposely towards them.

Tom's legs became weak and he felt slightly dizzy. *He couldn't let the Cygnan see his fear.* Tom forced himself to remain calm and hold his ground. The alien stopped two feet in front of him. Tom gasped, blinking at his strong resemblance to Lanjo. This Cygnan did not hold out his hand, nor did he grimace. He gazed piercingly at Tom. "Hello, Tom. I am Paranganjo." His tone was devoid of any emotion.

He turned and pointed at two empty chairs against the wall with his sixth finger. "Please, have a seat." Paranganjo moved to the side and took an empty seat a few feet from the chairs that awaited them, keeping his gaze forward.

Tom looked down at Stephanie, her eyes wide and her top teeth digging into her bottom lip. "It's okay sweetheart, let's just do what he said. I'm sure everything will be okay." He turned and led

Stephanie to the chairs and they sat, flinching at the unexpectedly warm surface. The floor beneath them started to vibrate under their feet, creating an odd sensation, and Stephanie squeezed Tom's hand harder. The periphery lights dimmed even further, and their attention was drawn to three screens set in a huge triangle dropping from the ceiling, configured for 360-degree viewing.

Tom and Stephanie jerked their heads back as a bright light emanated from the center of the triangle and high-definition images started to play on the screen in their view. They gasped as they recognized Keith in his space suit on the Moon, an alien hand extended towards him that could only be Lanjo. The picture moved like Go Pro videos back on Earth, coming from Lanjo's perspective.

The film cut to another scene, The President of the United States extending his arm and clasping a Cygnan hand. Tom's heart squeezed as he heard Lanjo's voice. "A friend in need is a friend indeed."

The scenes were moving about thirty seconds apart, each one from Lanjo's point of view. The next one switched to Stephanie, walking by the Potomac River, her dog running ahead of her. Another smash cut, this time to Tom, hand extended, friendship bracelet hanging from his fingers. Next, Lanjo's six fingers of each hand curled around the handlebars of a bicycle, an asphalt parking lot rolling underneath the front tire.

Tom's red polo shirt jittered on the screen, the camera jumping as he carried Lanjo down the stairs of the Gulfstream, bellowing for help. The scene switched to Stephanie sitting next to Lanjo's hospital bed, reading from the book she had given Belarango. Another smash cut showed her crying, then nodding off and falling asleep curled up on the hospital room couch. The scene switched again to the Cygnan-human science team sneaking

Lanjo out of the hospital, then fast-forwarded to the scientists securing him in the flight seat of the spaceship. Smash cut after smash cut . . .

Finally, Stephanie, her finger gently tracing what must be Lanjo's cheek, tears flooding her eyes.

Tom hunched forward in his chair gaping, one hand on his chest, the other gripping Stephanie's hand. The screen went black. Tom could hear the silence punctuated by his own rapid breath.

Tom turned to Paranganjo. "How did—"

"You probably noticed," Paranganjo replied, "Cygnans are not nearly as fastidious about electronic device implants and personal privacy. Lanjo's translator chip is also a GPS tracker and a camera. We accessed the chip as soon as Lanjo was brought out of the ship. It's not difficult and only takes a moment."

"How is he?"

"That's what we like about you, Tom. You have no idea what will happen next, yet you still manage to put your friend's interest above your own. Rather than ask what we're going to do with you, you inquire about your friend's health. Admirable."

Paranganjo stood and waved, his six fingers signaling to someone unseen. The lights came up, revealing a cast of alien characters that would have been at home in the *Star Wars* cantina scene. The hairs on the back of Tom's neck stood up and his palms started sweating, as he took in the audience. Stephanie stifled a half-whimper and squeezed his hand harder, her grip slippery with sweat. A few chairs away sat a tiny blue-green creature, his egg-shaped, spotted bald head at level with Tom's chest. Across the room sat what could only be described as a bright orange and lime-green octopus, its tentacles wrapped around the arms of its chair. On the other side of Paranganjo was a platypus-like creature resembling the picture in the hallway. On closer observation, it had antennas dancing in the air. Tom's mouth gaped open. *What on Earth?! No—not Earth . . .*

Paranganjo approached Tom and Stephanie and they both stood up. Paranganjo extended his elbow, moving it up and down. "Welcome to the Extra Stellar League. As the leader of the planet Lanzeron, I welcome you."

Tom gazed at his elbow in puzzlement and Paranganjo dropped it. *Why did he do that? Was that a Cygnan greeting?* Tom's head jerked around, eyes wide, looking around the room. *What's happening?* "I don't understand," he stuttered, sweat beading on his forehead. "You're a businessman."

"I was a businessman—until I was elected to lead our planet. Which, by the way, is in no danger of a supernova. Our sun is perfectly stable, and we anticipate it will remain that way for the next several millennia."

Tom opened his mouth to speak, when a thought flashed through his mind. "So, you have no intention of destroying the Earth?"

"No." Paranganjo grimaced for the first time. "We never did. Let me explain."

"Wait." Tom glanced at his watch. "I have to get a message back to Earth. We only have eighteen minutes or—"

"Or what?"

"Or the president will take action to close the wormhole permanently. The Cygnan scientists will be unable to return home." He omitted the obvious, that he and Stephanie would be stuck on Lanzeron.

Paranganjo grimaced again. "We can always stabilize another

wormhole, but it is a great deal of trouble, and we would rather preserve the one we have. What do you want transmitted?"

Tom raised his eyebrows. He had not had time to think of how to authenticate his signal. *What would convince President Ferris? It needed to be something the president would trust.* "Do you have a pen and something to write on?" Stephanie tugged at his hand, and handed him a small notepad and pencil she had pulled from her jacket pocket. Tom tore off a page and hurriedly scribbled something down, then handed it to Paranganjo. "Please transmit this . . ."

Paranganjo read what was on the paper, looked at Tom curiously, then nodded. He pulled out a communication device and spoke in rapid Cygnan. "Not to worry. Your message is being transmitted right now."

Tom smiled. "Thanks." He gave Stephanie back her pad and pencil and turned his gaze back to Paranganjo. "Now, could you please tell me what this is all about?"

Before Paranganjo could respond, Stephanie jumped up and down and interrupted, "And when will we be able to see Lanjo?"

Marco looked up from his notepad with a puzzled look on his face. "Mr. President, I'm not sure what this means. The message transmitted from Lanzeron says—" He paused, still shaking his head. "A friend in need is a friend indeed."

The president froze for a moment, then threw back his head and laughed. "Joe, please get on the horn. Operation Star Wars is cancelled. The threat has been nullified. I repeat. Operation Star Wars is cancelled."

47

Sitting in the Cygnan hospital waiting room, Stephanie fidgeted as they awaited the results of Lanjo's medical procedure. Paranganjo had brought them there himself and stayed with them. The room looked similar to any hospital waiting room on Earth, with the exception of the architecture. Discs seemed to be favored on Lanzeron, and the room they were in was a large circular space with chairs scattered throughout. The chairs were an odd combination of upholstered comfort with a deceptively utilitarian look. Large vases were spaced periodically, containing what looked like carved sticks. Tom's stomach fluttered and he forced himself to take a series of deep breaths.

"How much longer? He's been in there a long time." Stephanie shuffled her feet. In the next breath, she turned to Paranganjo. "Do you have an iPad I can play with?"

Paranganjo shrugged, very much like a human would. "To answer your first question, I don't know. The surgery is complex and experiential. I was told it could take up to six hours. And about your request. The embedded microchip that most Cygnans use out of convenience also provides entertainment directly to the brain, without the need of any external apparatus. I am sorry I have nothing to offer you in that regard.

"There's a fairly new experimental therapy for rousing coma patients," Paranganjo continued as they waited. "It's an ultrasonic device that targets the thalamus."

"Do you know what the thalamus is?" Tom asked Stephanie.

"Yeah, we had it in biology class last year. It's the part of the brain involved with sensory and motor signal relay and regulation of consciousness and sleep."

"That's correct," Paranganjo waggled his fingers. "I'm impressed. We're trying to focus ultrasonic waves on the thalamus in an effort to get that part of the brain working again. If we're successful, Lanjo will regain consciousness. However," Paranganjo picked up a stick from one of the vases and started running his fingers up and down its ornamental grooves. "Even if this therapy works, Lanjo will have a long road ahead recovering from the traumatic effects caused by overloading his brain. It may take months for his brain to return to normal operation." He put the stick back and awkwardly patted Stephanie on her shoulder. "But it would be a great first step and an essential one, if he is ever to recover."

Tears began to well up in Stephanie's eyes. Her chin trembling, she sniffed, then nodded. "I understand."

Tom hated to see Stephanie cry. *He'd better change the subject.* "So Paranganjo, I can't help but notice you and Lanjo seem to have a family resemblance."

"That's easy," Paranganjo grimaced widely. "Lanjo is my nephew. Not only that, Lanjo isn't simply a scientist whose field of study is Earth, he is also the Planetary Secretary of Lanzeron and one of my top advisors. His penchant for human history is a hobby he's had ever since he was a young boy. That made him a likely candidate when the mission to evaluate Earth was announced. Lanjo's education and enthusiasm won him the position. His passion for Earth history and his desire to reach out to humanity is very real, even if the reason he was there was a fabrication."

"Lanjo is a high government official, yet he risked everything for us?"

"Don't sell yourself short. You were willing to give up everything for your planet. You had no idea what would happen once you got through the wormhole, yet you were willing to come anyway."

Tom's chest tightened at Paranganjo's praise and he started studying his hands. The door to the waiting room opened, and all three of them turned towards it. A tall female Cygnan in a white lab coat entered. Apparently medical garb was similar on both planets. The Cygnan doctor grimaced. "I have good news for you. Lanjo has emerged from his coma."

Stephanie shrieked, "He's awake! Lanjo's awake!" Tom grabbed Stephanie's hands and swung her around and they danced around the room chanting, "Lanjo's awake, Lanjo's awake," until they noticed the Cygnans staring at them, both with huge grimaces. Tom stopped and set Stephanie down while the Cygnans waited for them to regain their composure.

"When can I see him?" Stephanie demanded.

"You can see him now, but only for a moment. He's very weak and needs to regain his strength. Follow me, please."

They walked along a curved passageway. Medical equipment was scattered about and Cygnan medical personnel were coming in and out of rooms or staring at the equipment, fiddling with knobs and taking notes. They finally stopped at a room at the end of the hall, and the doctor put her finger to her lips. She opened the door slowly, but Stephanie slipped past her and rushed into the room.

She hurried to Lanjo's side and rested her hand on his, her thumb brushing the friendship bracelet that still encircled his wrist.

Lanjo's eyes opened, blank and unseeing at first. He blinked, and his eyes dropped to their linked hands resting on the white hospital sheet. He blinked again, and his lips turned down in a hint of a grimace.

"Stephanie." His voice was a shaky croak, but to Tom, it was the most beautiful sound he'd heard since Theresa told him she loved him. *Was that just this morning?!*

Stephanie bent forward and rested her cheek on the back of Lanjo's hand. "Welcome back, Uncle Lanjo. I missed you."

The president sat at the Resolute desk and cleared his throat. The presidential address was being watched around the world with eager anticipation. He looked down and shuffled papers while the news reporter's voice rolled through the introduction. "We are here tonight to bring you a special message that was delivered to the President of the United States by the Cygnan government. And now, the President of the United States."

President Ferris gazed confidently into the camera. "Good evening fellow Americans and citizens of Earth. This has been an extraordinary year for our planet as we have sought to respond to the alien contact that was initiated during our return to the Moon. As you are aware, the Cygnans came to live among us in a joint effort to help them save their race. Their sun is rapidly becoming unstable and will eventually go supernova, destroying their planet, Kepler 186f, along with it. After developing fusion to power our spaceships, we would provide assistance in transporting their population to another planet. In exchange, the Cygnan scientists have been working with our scientists to develop viable nuclear fusion which would provide clean energy and assure that Earth's future energy needs would be met."

He paused, tapping his pen on his desk for a moment before continuing. "While both of these would be admirable goals, it turns out that neither one is true. The Cygnans have been carrying out a massive subterfuge. However," he paused again, but this time smiled warmly. "It was in order to open a new era for humanity. An era that truly heralds humans as citizens of the universe. It is my pleasure to share with you the following." The president picked up one of the sheets of paper on his desk and began reading:

Citizens of Earth, Greetings from the Citizens of Lanzeron, whom you refer to as Cygnans. We are thankful for the efforts of your people over the last several weeks to work together in order to achieve fusion for our mutual benefit. It is time to reveal that it was never about transportation; it was an experiment between our two species, deliberately fabricated to see to what extent you would be capable of altruism towards a species not your own. Both the human scientist Tom Whitaker and the Cygnan diplomat Lanjo have shown themselves to be examples of beings willing to lay down their lives in the ultimate sacrifice for someone else very different from themselves. My name is Paranganjo, the leader of the planet Lanzeron whose sun is happily stable and in no danger of a nearby star disrupting it. We are members of the Extra Stellar League, a union whose members are comprised of alien races across the universe. We Cygnans were assigned as mentors for the human race.

After years of study, we determined that there was a high probability Earth was ready to enter the League. It was all a test. The test had three components: developed morality, technical aptitude, and altruism and empathy for others different from yourselves. From a distance it was difficult to tell if humanity had indeed developed sufficiently in these areas, but after deliberate interaction and evidence presented by Cygnans on the ground, it has been determined that humanity has reached the appropriate stage of development for acceptance into our ranks. Along with membership in the alien federation comes responsibilities and privileges that include sharing of technology, such as the fusion you seek in order to supply your energy needs. In return, you will be asked to embrace our primary objective, to help one another in times of need. It is a reciprocal relationship of friendship, which has already been modeled by Tom and Lanjo. The universe is vast, and it is made a little less lonely by having friends willing to help one another. You have an Earth proverb that encompasses this idea: "A friend in need is a friend indeed."

The president looked up. "There's more, which we will make available through the White House press secretary, but that's the gist of it. I called this presidential address to inform the American public and the world that the Cygnan-human effort will continue as an exchange in diplomatic relations. I am pleased to announce that I will be bringing before the United Nations a resolution that defines the Earth's membership in the Extra Stellar League, asks for a vote for all nations to join, and in anticipation of the resolution passing, opens the floor to designate the first official diplomat to Lanzeron and the first representative to the Extra Stellar League. Thank you."

"So Dan, you knew the entire time?" Jonathan stared at his subordinate in awe.

Dan smiled sheepishly. "Yes, boss. I'm sorry for the deception, but Paranganjo asked me to go along with his fabrication. All I wanted to do was help realize my grandfather's dream. When

NASA didn't believe my Grandpa Danny about the Cygnans, he was disappointed. When the Cygnans asked for his help, he put Paranganjo in contact with me. I was excited to be a part of it, and working for you made it all doable.

"Me and the Cygnans on the science team knew all along what Paranganjo was trying to do, but if I told you, it would have skewed the test. You would've reacted differently, and so would everyone else. Although I must admit, at one point we were all pretty worried. He didn't tell Feraganjo or me he was going to pretend to threaten Earth. Feraganjo and Keraganjo were pretty upset, and I thought I might have made a huge mistake when that happened."

Jonathan nodded. "Just glad to know we're on the same side."

Dan smiled. "Me too, boss. Hey, did you hear? Marco has applied to be a member of the diplomatic team to Lanzeron. He has a good shot at it."

"That's great. If he needs a reference, let me know."

Dan cleared his throat. "Uh, and boss?"

Jonathan looked at his assistant. "Yes, Dan?"

"I applied for the representative to the Extra Stellar League position."

Jonathan nodded slowly. "I'm not surprised. That would be an appropriate use of your talents. I'll give you an excellent reference, but you always have a place here if you change your mind."

Dan briefly closed his eyes and let out a huge breath. "Thanks, boss. Grandpa Danny always said space was our future. I wish he could've lived to see all this." He grinned. "When I was little he told all of us grandkids about his walk on the moon, but he only told me about the Cygnans. He'd take me out in the field behind his house, and we would look at the Cygnus constellation through his telescope. He'd say, 'Someday, Dan, someday we'll pass the test.' I think he's looking down from the heavens he came so close to visiting as an astronaut and he knows we finally have."

Jonathan smiled. "Considering recent events, that doesn't sound far-fetched at all."

EPILOGUE

It was good to be home. It was a different world now that Earth had been inducted into the Extra Stellar League. The president's task force determined it was rogue members of IPEF that sabotaged the Gulfstream. In response, the United States instituted a boycott of IPEF petroleum imports until the wrongdoers were extradited to the U.S. and brought to trial. The sergeant who attempted to take over the Gulfstream was identified by Sheila Palazzo as a fanatical member of CAET. Further probing revealed he also had ties to the NPC. Investigative proceedings by the FBI were ongoing into the NPC's involvement, and CAET membership was rapidly disintegrating.

Senator Frank Custer unexpectedly resigned his seat in the Senate, citing family issues. Thanks to Cygnan technology, clean energy would soon be available, and the president put Ray Donaldson in charge of its distribution. Ray leveraged Bahram Mirzaie's experience, and he was able to determine that U.S. petroleum was sufficient to supply U.S. needs in the interim.

Stephanie was back with her mother and started school only a few days late. Patricia decided to drop her litigation, and Tom was able to resume his visitation schedule with Stephanie without a lengthy court battle. Darryl's daughter Sandra had completely recovered, and Darryl resumed his position as project manager.

Tom and Brett and Feraganjo and the rest of the team returned to GWU where they continued Cygnan-human scientific collaboration to benefit both species. Alan Bond was invited to continue with them. He moved to Virginia and was placed in charge of integrating Cygnan and human technologies to solve existing problems. Keith returned home to spend time with Brittany and prepare for their wedding. The rest of the lunar mission team enjoyed some time off before starting their assignment with Jonathan's newly renamed company, Extra Stellar Communications, and the Cygnan delegation that would be arriving soon to help set up helium-3 mining operations on the Moon.

News from Lanzeron regarding Lanjo's health was hopeful. It would take several months, but his doctors were optimistic that he would fully recover. Paranganjo assured Tom that Lanjo would be able to visit once he was feeling better. The wormhole would continue to serve as the major hub for transportation and communication between Earth and Lanzeron.

Tom wasn't sure what all would happen as a result of Earth's new status in the Extra Stellar League, but he decided to leave that to the diplomats. He would continue to work with his Cygnan colleagues, no, *friends*, on perfecting fusion in the context of Earth's resources. Cygnan science advisors had studied the schematics of their original design and verified he was on the right track. He was relieved he could focus on research again and was looking forward to spending time on their fusion reactor prototype at GWU. But for now, he wouldn't want to be anywhere else, as he and Theresa sat on the patio of their favorite pizza hangout.

Sipping a beer, Tom opened his wallet to tip the waitress when

Joe's business card fell out and onto the table. He picked it up and read the words printed on it out loud.

A citizen is a political and moral agent who in fact has a shared sense of hope and responsibility to others and not just to him or herself.

–Henry Giroux

He turned to Theresa, "Do you think . . .?"

"I don't know…"

They looked around. "Just how many human agents for the Cygnans are on Earth?" Tom mused out loud. They clinked their beer mugs. "I guess it doesn't really matter." They kissed. Nope. It didn't matter at all.

ACKNOWLEDGMENTS

While writing is a solitary endeavor, the creation of *Alien Neighbors* was not a solitary effort. So many people invested their time in contributing to the process. Beta reader Martin T.D. Burnett read the first draft – was it really four years ago, Marty? Joe Izen gave me a peek into the world of physics and CERN. Jessica Torres read a later draft and provided invaluable insights. Janet Alcorn did an amazing job providing comments that helped me dramatically improve the text. My handsome son, Joshua Golden, also beta read the manuscript and provided great feedback. I am profoundly grateful for their interest in my project.

Writing a book is hard. A friend once asked me when I was sharing the plot of *Alien Neighbors* with someone – aren't you afraid they will steal your work? My response was "No. You try putting 92,000 words down on paper into a cohesive story." My cheerleaders have helped me to keep my momentum and not give up. My sister Lynn Sherman has gone on to her heavenly address – I hope she knows what her excitement about *Alien Neighbors* and her encouragement meant to me. My sister Janet Parker and sister-in-law Jane Vaughan have always been a source of affirmation. I would be remiss not to mention Katherine Deans Evanson – for more reasons than I can count.

Scott Taylor and Tom Smallwood have been rocks – Scott's boundless enthusiasm for the written word and Tom's frequent reminders that directors of writing groups need to be writing, too. Alice and Ed Wooten – for the treasure of their friendship and their dedication to the writing craft. Jennifer Crippen is always ready for a writing adventure and we have had many - I am grateful for her support. Sandy Paty's wit is only exceeded by her level of care. Ross Irvin has been an inspiration from the very beginning, and a good friend. Amy Klingele Garman and Andrea Amosson are wellsprings of strength and merriment. As for the rest of the Carrollton League of Writers – their unending support and their passion for writing are a constant source of blessing. I can't forget to mention dear friends Amber and Jake Royer, who have graciously given of their time to mentor me.

Special Thanks to Henry Giroux for allowing me to use his quote – it made a profound impression on me and I am excited to include it in my story. To Alan Bond whose early work with Project Daedalus stirred my imagination. Thank you for agreeing to be a character in *Alien Neighbors* – the story is richer for it. And to Dena G. Weaver for her legal expertise – freeing me to enjoy the process. Thanks also to Paul Stinson, who helped me conceptualize Lanjo, bringing him to life through graphic art. And to Betty Martinez, who poured herself into designing the book cover and exceeded all possible expectations.

Many other people have touched my life for the better in so many ways, too numerous to mention. I would like to take this opportunity to name a few and offer heartfelt thanks for their friendship: Pastors Chad and Jennifer Burton, Bahram and Rosanna Mirzaie, Sabitha Radhakrishnan, Norbert Dushimirimana, Darlene Dentry, and my beautiful daughter-in-law, Naomi Golden.

ABOUT THE AUTHOR

Nancy Golden wears lots of different hats – She is a wife and mom, engineer, IT QA professional, professor, and small business owner. She is also founder and director of a writing group – the Carrollton League of Writers. Nancy lives in a suburb of Dallas and loves to ride bicycles and horses. She has been a Trekkie for as long as she can remember and always wanted to impress a dragon and fight thread.

Nancy's nonfiction works including an Advent Devotional: *Taking Back Advent - Moving From the Mundane to the Miraculous*. Her award-winning flash fiction piece, "How Could I Not," appears in the anthology, *The Roads We Take* by the Carrollton League of Writers. *Alien Neighbors* is her debut science fiction novel.

Best selling author of the Stranje House Novels, Kathleen Baldwin comments on *Alien Neighbors*, "In this promising debut, Nancy Golden weaves together a dynamic plot brimming with science and bubbling with humanity."

Catch up on Nancy's latest writing endeavors and other fun stuff at novelwrites.com

I enjoyed writing *Alien Neighbors* and I am very excited to share it with you. I sincerely hope it was fun to read and it provided a haven from the trials of life - at least for a little while. You can email me directly at nancy@goldencrossranch.com with any comments.

One of the best things you can do for any author is to leave a review - I hope you'll consider doing so.

- ⓕ facebook.com/Lanjo-from-planet-Kepler-186f-Alien-Neighbors-by-Nancy-Golden-103967305384771
- ⓨ twitter.com/ncgolden1
- ⓐ amazon.com/author/nancy-golden